UNMASKING A KILLER

"Steve, I'm surprised at you!" Jayne exclaimed. "That isn't the least bit like you, to nearly solve a crime and then let the police take over."

"Whatever gave you the idea I'm letting W.B. take over? We simply need his help to spring the trap."

I oversaw the rehearsal, while the lieutenant came and oversaw the showgirls. During a five minute break I was able to take him aside and induce him to make certain arrangements. When the rehearsal was finished, I returned upstairs, ready at last to make my move on Wade Hamilton. I telephoned his room, where I seemed to wake him from a deep sleep.

"We need to talk, Wade. I have information linking you to your stepmother's murder, but I wanted to give you a chance to tell your side of the story before going to the police. Come to my suite at eight tonight. Jayne will be out, and we'll have some privacy."

"All right, Mr. Allen. We'll talk."

I hung up the phone and looked at Jayne. The trap was baited and set.

BOOKS BY STEVE ALLEN

BOP FABLES

FOURTEEN FOR TONIGHT

THE FUNNY MEN

WRY ON THE ROCKS

THE GIRLS ON THE TENTH FLOOR

THE QUESTION MAN

MARK IT AND STRIKE IT

NOT ALL OF YOUR LAUGHTER, NOT ALL OF YOUR TEARS

LETTER TO A CONSERVATIVE

THE GROUND IS OUR TABLE

BIGGER THAN A BREADBOX

A FLASH OF SWALLOWS

THE WAKE

PRINCESS SNIP-SNIP AND THE PUPPYKITTENS

CURSES!

WHAT TO SAY WHEN IT RAINS

SCHMOCK!-SCHMOCK!

MEETING OF MINDS

CHOPPED-UP CHINESE

RIPOFF: THE CORRUPTION THAT PLAGUES AMERICA

MEETING OF MINDS (SECOND SERIES)

EXPLAINING CHINA

FUNNY PEOPLE

THE TALK SHOW MURDERS

BELOVED SON: A STORY OF THE JESUS CULTS

MORE FUNNY PEOPLE

HOW TO MAKE A SPEECH

HOW TO BE FUNNY

MURDER ON THE GLITTER BOX

THE PASSIONATE NONSMOKER'S BILL OF RIGHTS (WITH BILL ADLER JR.)

DUMBTH, AND 81 WAYS TO MAKE AMERICANS SMARTER

MEETING OF MINDS, SEASONS I–IV IN FOUR-VOLUME SET

THE PUBLIC HATING: A COLLECTION OF SHORT STORIES

MURDER IN MANHATTAN

STEVE ALLEN ON THE BIBLE, RELIGION & MORALITY

MURDER IN VEGAS

STEVE ALLEN

MURDER
IN VEGAS

ZEBRA BOOKS
KENSINGTON PUBLISHING CORP.

To my dear grandchildren: Dan, Julie, Stephanie, Christopher, Michael, Bobby, Bradley, Andrew and Ryan—in gratitude for their so greatly adding to my happiness.

ZEBRA BOOKS

are published by

Kensington Publishing Corp.
475 Park Avenue South
New York, NY 10016

First Zebra Books paperback edition: August, 1992

Printed in the United States of America

chapter 1

Bora Bora disappeared slowly beneath the waves, sinking into the western horizon until only the perpetual rain clouds above the interior mountains were visible from the vantage point of our deck chairs. I raised my mango juice cocktail to my lips and made a final toast to paradise lost: "Bye-bye, Bora Bora," I said into the breeze.

"Coconuts," said Jayne.

"I beg your pardon?"

"Look over the side, Steve . . . over there, see? There are coconuts floating on the water. I'm surprised to find them so far from land."

I stretched my neck just far enough to see what my wife was talking about, then settled back comfortably into my chair, which was pretty much the most strenuous thing I had done all day.

"Probably the coconuts fell off a tree somewhere and are floating on their happy way to Tahiti, just like us, dear—carried by the trade winds."

"What's a seven-letter word for teeth grinding?" said Jayne, the world's champion subject-changer, who was working on a *Times* crossword puzzle.

"Bruxism," I said.

"Really?"

"Why would I lie at a time like this?"

"But it looks like such a dumb word," she said.

"Actually," I said, "every word in every language of the world looks dumb if you can somehow manage to look at it in the right and of course fresh way. But bruxism is not to be confused with Bronxism."

"What's that?"

"A lower middle-class accent with comic overtones."

Jayne and I were comfortably positioned on adjoining deck chairs not far from the swimming pool and outdoor bar. It was the thirteenth day of our South Pacific cruise on the *S.S. Tahitian Queen*, a gleaming white vessel wending its customary way through the warm waters south of the equator. I felt a sublime and sleepy peace, a sense that the headhunters and cannibals of the world were far away in such distant jungles as Los Angeles and New York. The cruise was a well-earned vacation for both of us after a hard and hectic year. We'd done a two-week run in A.J. Gurney's *Love Letters* at the Theatre on the Square in San Francisco, the Rodgers and Hammerstein musical *Cinderella* during December at the Pantages Theatre in Hollywood, an annual Christmas Parade show for TV station KTLA in Los Angeles, Jayne's lectures on Powerful Women In History, my symphony orchestra concerts and jazz-club dates and—well, we had clearly earned a vacation.

"A game of ping-pong?" I suggested.

"You're too good for me," she replied.

"I'll play left-handed," I offered. "I'll play standing on one foot and blindfolded."

I smiled a trifle smugly. I'm pretty good at table tennis, actually. A long time ago I was even on the Phoenix, Arizona city team, and although the skill isn't particularly useful in ordinary life, it comes in handy on a cruise ship. I had already slaughtered a Wall Street executive, a Beverly Hills psychiatrist, and a little old lady from Oklahoma City.

I greeted an elderly widow from Palm Beach, and inquired after her granddaughter who was confined to their cabin with a case of the flu. After thirteen days on a cruise ship, you're pretty much on a first-name basis with everyone and find that life has taken on a certain gentle rhythm, defined by such major events as breakfast, lunch, dinner, movies, and perhaps a game of bingo in the lounge. Personally, I can do without most of the entertainment—I am able to sit in my deck chair and stare at the endlessly fascinating patterns of water and waves and find myself never bored. There are thoughts to think, memories to ponder, books to read—and write—and plans to be made. After thirteen days of this, I found myself relaxed, happy, lulled into a luscious serenity by the sun upon my face, the motion of the ship, and Jayne by my side.

"Mr. Steve Allen," came a sing-song voice. "Steeeve Allen, please!"

It was a steward, dressed in his whites and his uniform hat, walking from the direction of the swimming pool. I raised my hand so he could find me.

"Mr. Allen, there's a telegram for you just in from the radio room."

I took the sealed envelope with a frown, won-

7

dering who from the tumultuous outside world could want me. I had a momentary impulse to toss the message unread over the side of the boat and let it drift with the coconuts, but naturally I'm too responsible and environmentally aware to dump my garbage into the ocean, and so I opened the thing.

The message was from my agent in Hollywood and it read as follows:

HI-HO STEVERINO:
BOBBY HAMILTON URGENTLY WANTS YOU TO OPEN FOR HIM IN VEGAS OCT. 26 AT THE COLISEUM STOP I REALIZE THIS IS SLIGHTLY SUDDEN BUT BUDDY HACKETT FELL OUT AND BOBBY REMEMBERED THE ROUTINE YOU GUYS WORKED OUT YEARS AGO ON YOUR TV SHOW STOP I'D NEVER PRESUME TO INTERRUPT YOUR SOUTH PACIFIC IDYLL BUT I KNOW HOW MUCH YOU ADMIRE THE GREATEST JAZZ SINGER OF OUR ERA STOP WIRE BACK IF INTERESTED STOP REHEARSALS BEGIN NEXT WEEK
IRVIN

I read the telegram through twice with Jayne peering over my shoulder.

"How marvelous for you!" she cried. "Won't it be lovely to work with Bobby again?"

"Yes, but look at the date. On October 26th we'll be cruising somewhere between Tahiti and Honolulu."

"Yes, but Bobby Hamilton, dear—he's one of your idols. You can't turn down an invitation like this."

Jayne was right. When Irvin described Bobby as "the greatest jazz singer of our era" he was exaggerating, but the man is a legend—has been for an incredible forty years. In terms of sheer musical talent, he is truly deserving of his fame and fortune. There are many gigs I turn down, but a chance to work with Bobby Hamilton doesn't come along everyday. When Irvin mentioned the routine we had worked out years ago, he was referring to the time Bobby appeared on my show in 1963. Besides our usual ad-lib clowning, I had accompanied him on piano through a few numbers, and we ended up doing a little soft-shoe routine. We had so much fun working it all out that we became friends afterwards—not close, since our paths seldom crossed, but when we did meet it was a warm occasion.

Bobby Hamilton, the man with the silver voice, and he wanted me to open for him at The Coliseum!

"Steve, you have a faraway look in your eye."

"No, no. Of course, I'm flattered Bobby thought of me, but there'll be another time."

"Why not now?"

"Jayne, I'm not about to interrupt our vacation just to go to Vegas. And besides, it wouldn't be fair to you."

"But what about you?"

"I'm having the time of my life staring at the waves. You couldn't pry me off the *Tahitian Queen* for a hundred Bobby Hamiltons," I assured her.

"Whatever you say," Jayne said, squeezing my hand. I closed my eyes and lifted my face into the mellow warmth of the sun, but somehow I couldn't find quite the same bliss I had felt just moments before. I kept imagining a crowded room in Vegas with a spotlight in my eyes, the brash sound of laughter and applause, the orchestra beginning to play . . .

Well, it *was* disappointing to miss such an opportunity, but it couldn't be helped. At my age, I've learned not to mourn the impossible. As I've mentioned, Jayne and I had been really busy this year—particularly Jayne—and it wouldn't be at all fair to interrupt her vacation just because the greatest singer of our time happened to want me for what would probably be the biggest show to hit Vegas in months. It was all right, though. At least I wouldn't miss the ship's shuffleboard tournament next week.

When I opened my eyes, I was surprised to find Jayne was not in her chair. A few minutes later I saw her coming my way from inside the ship.

"Have you had too much sun?" I asked.

"Not at all—I was just having a word with the purser about our plane tickets."

I let this sink in a moment, as my fingers play rapid arpeggios on the arm rests of my chair.

"Plane tickets?"

"Of course, dear. From Tahiti to Los Angeles, and straight on to Las Vegas."

"But our cruise . . ."

"Steve, don't try to pretend with me. You know you're dying to work with Bobby Hamilton, and if you don't go to Vegas, you're going to be perfectly miserable company the next two weeks. Besides, this ship will be here next year."

I was about to object, but I looked at Jayne, and she looked at me, and I realized there are times when it's best to simply accept gifts that are lovingly offered.

I took her hand, drew her close and kissed her

lightly on the lips. "You know, you're kinda cute," I mentioned. "A few weeks with you in a Las Vegas suite could have a good effect on a guy."

"You can bet on that," Jayne said.

chapter 2

We reached Tahiti three days later. That afternoon we left the cruise ship and began a series of flights, island-hopping over the Pacific to Honolulu, then east to Los Angeles, and after a change of jets, east again to Las Vegas.

Our plane arrived over Las Vegas at dusk, with an orange glow of sunset still visible over the barren mountains of the Mojave desert, and the city already lit up for the night. From the air, the town sends forth a rainbow explosion of colors into the sky—hot pinks, reds, oranges, blues—a seductive carnival swirl of light to beckon you hither and separate you from your wallet. The real architecture of Las Vegas has little to do with concrete and steel—what you remember from a visit here is the brightest, gaudiest light show on earth.

"I always wonder about the electric bills of some of these hotels," Jayne mused, gazing out the window as our jet made its final approach.

I told her that Las Vegas has some of the cheapest electric power in the nation. Gambling was legalized here in 1931, and the government conveniently provided Nevadans with Hoover Dam in 1935—so why should they conserve energy? The city motto seems to be, "If you've got it, waste it." Or as casino designer Zoli Kovacs once put it, "Anything worth doing is worth overdoing."

As it happens, I'm a fountain of trivia concerning Las Vegas. I could have told Jayne, for instance, that the brightest sign in town belongs to The Stardust, is 18 stories high and has forty thousand light bulbs and 30 miles of wiring. To give you another idea of the proportions of epic waste here, I should mention that the main swimming pool at The Coliseum Hotel is so huge it loses ten thousand gallons a day—*to evaporation*. But people don't come to the town looking for the subtle or the small, or think about such inconsequential subjects as the world's fast-dwindling natural resources.

Our jet floated down into McCarran Airport, which is hardly more than a die's throw from Las Vegas Boulevard, that street of dreams better known as The Strip. The city's efforts to rid you of the inconvenience of loose change begins immediately as you step into the terminal. You will not walk a dozen feet before you find yourself confronted by slot machines of various denominations, dollars to nickels. I watched a young couple who had been sitting near us in the plane make a beeline toward a huge machine that looked like a child's oversized toy bank, in which you could lose five silver dollars at a time, all to spinning lights and rolling wheels that provide a very brief entertainment for your money. Above the giant slot machine was a sign that kept flashing on and off, like a lightning bug sending out a mating call on a long summer evening: ONE MILLION DOL-

LAR JACKPOT! Las Vegas is a city that relies on human optimism.

"Isn't someone meeting us?" I asked Jayne, looking about.

"The Coliseum is supposed to be sending a car."

"I'm hip," I said, "but I don't see anyone."

Jayne and I waited near a row of gleaming dollar-slots that were blinking and throbbing with neon seduction. Exhausted from hours of travel I was beginning to be irritated that there was no one to meet us. I was about to suggest we take a taxi to our hotel, when I caught sight of a strangely familiar figure standing with his back to us at a twenty-five cent slot machine, rhythmically feeding coins into the hungry opening and then pulling down on the handle. Every time he did so, I could hear him mutter a magic spell: "Come on, baby. Give it to me, baby. Cough up some change!"

"Is that who I think it is? It *can't* be," said Jayne.

"It is, indeed," I told her, and we made our way to where this particular ex-cowboy was feeding his one-armed bandit. Just as we came up behind him, a light began flashing on his slot machine, a soft siren began to wail, and a small avalanche of silver came clattering down into the waiting tray.

"Holy Mother! I've done it now!" cried the man, clapping his hands together. I was glad, at least, that he showed some signs of animation. Most of the people who played the machines seemed to win and lose without any apparent change of expression, as though they had taken a bus to Vegas from the land of the living dead, to which they would return once the weekend was over.

"I've won!" the man cried.

14

"Yes, Cass, and now you'd better put that money in your pocket while you're still ahead."

Jimmy Cassidy spun around in surprise. "Steve!" he exclaimed. "Mrs. Allen! You're here already!"

"But what are *you* doing here?" I asked.

"I'm here to meet you, of course. I told the driver from The Coliseum to forget it. Nobody drives the Allens except Jimmy Cassidy!"

I should explain that Cassidy is my part-time chauffeur—in Los Angeles, that is—but I certainly did not expect to find him waiting for us in Las Vegas.

"But how did you get here, Cass?"

"I drove from L.A. How else am I going to get here? Your secretary, Pat, told me you were cutting your South Pacific cruise short and I thought I'd better get here pronto to take care of you guys, so you didn't end up losing too much money," said Cass, simultaneously scooping up the quarters he had won and stuffing them into his pockets. "I guess I lost track of time waiting for your plane to come in," he admitted sheepishly.

"At least you haven't lost your shirt—*yet.*"

"Well, I think this is a wonderful surprise," said Jayne brightly, hoping to make up for my lack of enthusiasm. Cass beamed at her. He must be in his fifties by now, but there is something permanently child-like about his face, especially when he is talking to Jayne, whom he adores.

I should explain that as much as I like Cass, I was not thrilled to find him here; a guy like Jimmy Cassidy can get into trouble in a town like Vegas. He's a former cowhand from Wyoming who came to Hollywood twenty years ago to be a star in the West-

15

erns. Unfortunately, Westerns had gone out of style pretty much at the moment of his arrival—and that is the story of Cass's life. He is simply unlucky. Oh, he has great schemes, but I've never met another human being who can so consistently defeat himself, managing to be at the wrong place at the wrong time. And yet he is never bitter, remains an optimist, and while serving as my driver, he's still dreaming of fame and fortune and a return of the Westerns to box-office glory.

"Cass, I hope you're going to stay away from the tables while you're here," I said sternly as we all walked towards the baggage claim area.

"Steve, you saw how much money I just won. There must have been at least twenty dollars worth of quarters in that little jackpot, and that was just a trial run. Tomorrow I'm on to the dollar-slots and a chance to win me a million."

I sighed. The glitzy hotels of Vegas were fly-traps built especially for dreamers like Jimmy Cassidy. I tried to figure out a way to let him down gently.

"Let's look at this a bit more closely, Cass. You say you won maybe twenty dollars back there. How many quarters did you feed into the machine *before* you hit that jackpot?"

"Well, let's see . . . I bought a ten dollar roll of quarters, and I played with that for maybe twenty minutes. And then I bought a second roll, and I guess I was about halfway through that when you guys showed up."

"In other words, it cost you approximately fifteen dollars to win twenty dollars, so what you actually came away with is a five spot."

"Sure, Steve, if you put it like that it doesn't

sound like a hell of a lot. But my luck was just changing. I felt it in my bones."

"Cass, if Jayne and I had not appeared at that moment to drag you away from that machine, you and your five dollar profit would have quickly parted company. Unfortunately, very few people stop while they're ahead, and if you play long enough, the odds are against you. That's what Las Vegas is all about."

"Okay," he said, "I admit you're probably going to lose money at the airport. I mean, these slot machines can't be too generous, because they figure, hell, people are traveling and just passing through. But if you spend time at the hotel casinos, you can win big."

"And you can lose big."

"Mrs. Allen, can you believe this guy?" said Cass, turning to Jayne for support. "He's a real pessimist, I tell you! Why, outside some of the casinos here they have a sign telling you they guarantee an average 94 percent return on their dollar slots. I mean, they couldn't advertise that if it weren't true, not even in Vegas—could they?"

"That *does* sound pretty good," Jayne said.

This worried me a little. It was bad enough my old friend Cass was eager to take a bath, but Jayne's spending hit closer to home. Unfortunately, there were times when even truth in advertising did not protect a gullible public. In this particular case, the casinos were gleefully telling people they were being robbed blind and some of them thought this was a *good* deal.

"So what do you think this 94 percent return actually means?" I asked.

"Well, it's simple—you have a 94 percent

17

chance to win," Cass told me with a serene smile. "Maybe even win the big million dollar jackpot!"

I tried to explain the truth of the situation, that far from having a 94 percent chance to win, you were guaranteed to lose. The casinos were openly advertising the fact that for every one hundred dollars you fed into their slot machines, you were mathematically almost certain to walk away with a grand total of . . . ninety-four dollars. A good deal? I wonder how well banks would do if they gave you a swell return on your money like that. When I explained this to Cass, however, he gave me a sad look, as if I was being a real kill-joy. It's impossible to successfully argue with a true believer.

"Maybe those are the averages, Steve—but a guy can beat the odds," he told me, with something approaching religious conviction. "All it takes is one throw of the dice, one pull of the handle—and you can be rich."

I smiled but kept my peace. Gambling seems to be an idea whose time has come in America in a very big way. Many of our states, of course, have incredible multi-million dollar lotteries, and in California our increasingly second-rate school system is almost entirely financed by Lotto. One can almost foresee an America entirely financed by alcohol, tobacco and gambling—one great big Las Vegas.

Cass smiled ruefully. He was about to slip his last remaining quarter into his pocket, but seemed overcome by a sudden inspiration and handed the lonely coin to Jayne. "Here, you play it for me, Mrs. Allen. I bet you'll be lucky."

"Now, Jayne, you should set a good example," I cautioned.

"Darling, it's only a quarter," she said. "And

what can you do with a quarter these days except more or less throw it away?"

"How about putting it into the bank?" I suggested stuffily. Both Cass and Jayne flashed me a collective ironic look. "Well, okay," I admitted, "banks are a pretty big gamble these days, too."

And so in this manner we all soon convinced ourselves that we might as well throw away Cass's meaningless quarter into the hungry mouth of the slot machine. Why hang onto it? It is easy to make such rationalizations—and of course, the people who built Las Vegas count on us to think this way. For my part, I was glad to see the damned coin about to disappear—maybe it would teach Jayne and Cass a lesson.

Jayne rubbed the coin between the palms of her hands, muttered a magic spell and put the quarter in the slot. She closed her eyes for good luck, concentrated hard, and finally pulled the handle.

The wheel turned; cherries, bars, oranges and bananas all spun round and round. Jayne opened her eyes—she and Cass waited breathlessly. I stood off to the side with a superior smile on my face.

Bells went off, a siren began to sound, and a light on top of the slot machine began to flash. For a moment I though we were in the midst of an air raid . . . but then an avalanche of silver began to pour down onto the lip of the machine and overflow onto the carpet.

Jayne, usually the most regal of women in public, screamed with excitement. Cass clutched the top of his head and cried, "My God, you've done it!"

I fetched a bucket from an airport attendant so we could carry our haul of silver to the limousine.

Gambling is a terrible thing, all right. Unless you win.

chapter 3

Cass had his burgundy-colored Cadillac stretch limousine waiting at the curb. A number of years ago, I had lent him the money to buy this glitzy though secondhand machine, and he was paying me back a little every year. I would have liked to simply give him the thing, but I knew this would not sit well with his Irish cowboy pride.

When our bags were in the trunk, Jayne and I settled into the back seat, and we pulled out of the airport onto Paradise Drive, then cut westward onto The Strip. On the ground, the lights of Vegas seemed even brighter than what you could make out from the air. We passed The Hacienda where Redd Foxx was playing in one lounge and an ice skating spectacular in the other. CASH YOUR PAYCHECK HERE & WIN MILLIONS! proclaimed a giant electric sign. I tried to ask Cass about the weather so he wouldn't notice the sign; he said it had been very hot during the day but was beginning to cool down at night.

A little further down The Strip we came to The

Excalibur, the newest hotel in town, which is built to resemble a huge fairy tale castle and beckons with promises of a Canterbury Wedding Chapel and an all-you-can-eat Round Table buffet for $4.99, which reminds me of one of my favorite jokes: I see a big sign in front of a restaurant that says ALL YOU CAN EAT—$5. So I go in, get a tray, and start piling up two steaks, three porkchops, a chef's salad, four slabs of pie—and a big guy comes up to me and says, "All right, you. That's all you can eat."

Across the street from The Excalibur is The Tropicana, a high-rise extravaganza with palm trees, burning torches, and huge carved statues that are supposed to make you think of Easter Island. The Tropicana advertises no-smoking blackjack pits, which seems to be an attempt to corner a new type of gambler. After this is The Marina, where you can daily see the MGM lion in a tent in the parking lot.

Believe it or not, to me the lion is a big deal. I have no idea why, but I'm crazy about the faces of lions and tigers. I swear that if such animals could be tamed I would keep one in the backyard and probably even sleep with it on chilly nights. Those big beautiful cats look to me like stuffed toys that are able to walk. I even have a collection of photographs and artists renderings of lions' and tigers' faces, I love them so much.

Then come The Dunes, Aladdin's and Bally's—which is the old MGM Grand, location of the worst hotel fire in Las Vegas history. At last you come to the Flamingo, one of the early hotels, the creation of New York gangster Bugsy Siegel in 1946. The story is, Bugsy wanted to call his hotel the *Flamenco*—"You know, after them pink birds that stand around with one foot up in da air." Apparently someone corrected his mistake, though it isn't clear if he lived to tell his tale, and now the Flamingo is part of the Hilton chain. Jayne and I have played at the hotel—twice—and had a marvelous time.

Across from the Flamingo, surrounded by all this impossible glitter, is The Coliseum Hotel, a throwback to pagan ways which may be one of the most outlandish structures ever built by man. The Coliseum has had some recent competition in the Excess Sweepstakes by such new "theme hotels" as The Mirage, which stands to the north. The Mirage has an astonishing exterior, a series of man-made waterfalls, islands, and palm trees which have been illuminated by Broadway lighting specialist David Hersey, who has designed such shows as *Les Miserables* and *Starlight Express*. The ultimate extravaganza at the Mirage is the volcano, which erupts every fifteen minutes after dark, sending huge plumes of flame up into the night sky and setting the surface of the artificial lake on fire. This may be hard to beat, but for my money, the Coliseum still rules The Strip. Rome may have been fairly gaudy the first time around, but even Nero would have put down his fiddle in disbelief if he had ever seen this.

At night, the thirty-story hotel glows from inside like a giant high-rise illusion of shimmering gold—the walls are solid glass and are said to be glazed with real 18 karat gold, which gives the structure an ethereal, almost hallucinatory appearance. Outside, there is a lake of molten gold and acres of fountains shooting more gold-lighted water into the air. Two pagan barges float upon the lake and once an hour a naval battle ensues, with gladiators storming the gangplanks with short swords, and mostly Japanese tourists on the sidewalks pointing their camcorders or filming like crazy. Cass drove us into the main entrance where a Centurion with a spear and shield opened the door to our limousine.

"*Pax*," I told him.

"Say what?" he said.

We went on inside, past another helmeted Centurion who bowed slightly at our approach. Standing on either side of him were two giant marble statues, at least twenty feet high, of Venus and Dionysus. Both seemed to be emerging from the casino having lost their shirts, pants and underwear, which should warn people of the dangers of gambling, but probably doesn't. The anatomically correct details of Dionysus, god of wine, madness and merriment, has brought a giggle to many a startled tourist from the rural Midwest.

Ah, Las Vegas! You can easily fool yourself that you are in some fabulous land of Oz—but, the moment you walk inside the hotel past the fanciful facade, everything turns into pretty much the same old casino decor: acres of slot machines, crap tables and roulette wheels extending into the lobby. Everywhere you look there are low lights, green felt, and wraith-like men and women pumping the handles of the slot machines with bored expressions on their faces and cigarettes dangling from their lips. Gambling may be an obsession, but from the expressions you see, it is not really fun.

To no one's surprise Las Vegas also specializes in marketing sex, however the word might be interpreted. I wouldn't be surprised that the amount of actual copulatory contact in that community is below, rather than above, the national norm, given that after two or three days in Vegas the average visitor is in a constant state of semi-exhaustion, but

23

the merchandise is nevertheless widely advertised and flaunted. In the casinos, for example, one sees dozens of buxom, long-legged young women, mostly serving as cocktail waitresses. They wear revealing attire and a good deal of makeup so that the first impression they make, at least upon normal healthy American males, is quite pronounced. If you spend a few days in the city, however, a strange transformation takes place. Those very same young women, often coiffed and made up so as to emphasize any vague similarities to Elizabeth Taylor, Sophia Loren or Marilyn Monroe seem, upon closer inspection, several years older than they had at first. Their eyes betray an inner weariness and at those moments when they are not smiling they appear bored rather than stimulated by their surroundings. At first they may seem like prospective young starlets or would-be actresses working their way west to Hollywood. In fact, most of them have rather tragic personal histories. Some, for example, are single mothers whose own mothers, or other relatives, perform baby-sitting duties during the long hours that the young women must spend in the gambling pits. Those who are unattached may, of course, be dated by resident musicians or entertainers passing through town, but the fellows involved are highly unlikely to be looking for a permanent relationship.

"Mr. Allen?" came a voice in my left ear. I turned to see a tall young man who was prematurely bald. He was wearing a very conservative dark suit, and he had worried, deep-set eyes and seemed haggard and pale, not entirely healthy. All in all, this was one of the most middle-aged looking young men I had ever encountered. "I'm Wade Hamilton, Mr. Allen—my father's general assistant."

"Bobby Hamilton's your dad? Nice to meet you! Do you know my wife Jayne?"

We all shook hands, then Wade asked if I would accompany him to the Gladiator Arena where a rehearsal was in progress.

"Are they feeding Christians to the lions?" I wondered. "Or is it just Show Biz as usual?"

"Something like that," murmured the young man. "My father would like to see you."

"Well, lead on, Brutus. *Veni, Vidi, Veci!*" I said, trying to get into the mood. I came, I saw, and hoped I would conquer.

"And *E pluribus unum*," said my wife seductively—if you can say a thing like that seductively, which she somehow can.

"All hail to the Emperor Gluteus Maximus," I muttered, to continue the nonsense. Jayne never laughs at my jokes, by the way. She acknowledges them with a look of mock shock and a whispered "Ope, Steve."

She headed up to our suite with the luggage to unpack. I told her she could instruct the slaves, Nubian or Nubile, to fill my bath with warmed milk of she-goat and that I would be there soon to partake of the cornucopia of delights. Jayne told me to stop kidding. I could tell we were going to have a swell time in Vegas.

chapter 4

A famous country music group, Eddie Courtney And The Texas Arrangers, was currently headlining in the Gladiator Arena and would do so until we opened on Saturday. Normally the incoming production would have an opportunity to rehearse during the day, while the ongoing show would perform at night—but tonight was Tuesday, on which the theater is always dark, and Bobby Hamilton was apparently taking advantage of the available stage time to squeeze in some extra rehearsal time. Bobby has a laid-back performing style, but in his own way is an utter perfectionist.

His son Wade led me to an elevator which took us to the Arena on the second floor.

"So how long have you been in Vegas?" I asked, merely to make conversation.

"Not long," said Wade.

"Having a good time here?"

The young man stared at me briefly as if I were a dunce. "Oh, yeah, Vegas is a *lovely* town," he said sarcastically. "A real mecca of culture."

"Sure," I said. I reminded myself that this was the grown child of one of my friends, and tried to make allowances. "I remember your father telling me you graduated from college recently—Yale, was it?" I asked as we stepped out of the elevator onto the second floor.

"Dartmouth . . . but that was ten years ago."

"Really? Lord, it can't be that long. Well, I suppose you're right."

The young man rolled his eyes; I decided to shut up. It isn't easy growing up in the shadow of fame, talent, money and power, but any way you looked at it this was a rude, unhappy, and therefore unattractive young fellow. Besides being prematurely bald, he had poor posture. His shoulders were bent forward, and his chest seemed almost concave. I wondered if this were due to health reasons or simply low self-esteem. Unfortunately, it is not uncommon for children of famous parents to have a hard time with self-confidence; many have grown up in households where the spotlight was never directed at them.

Wade flashed a backstage pass at a security guard, who unsnapped a red velvet cord to let us pass on through inside the theater. On the enormous stage, a rehearsal was in progress of an extravagant production number of *Satin Doll*, with the full orchestra playing and Bobby encircled by twenty-five chorus girls in leotards and warm-up tights who were doing a dance around him. Bobby, dressed in a comfortable gray jogging suit and aerobic shoes, was singing into a cordless microphone, projecting the song toward the empty tables in the back of the room. After all these years, he still looked great—tall and trim with a head of wavy black hair that had only a few age-revealing salt and pepper traces. I

27

thought his famous face had taken on an almost Mt. Rushmore quality—strong, handsome and apparently etched in stone. There had been rumors of a mini facelift, but so what? One thing an entertainer has to sell is his appearance, so it makes perfect sense to keep the old physical equipment in tip-top shape, by all means possible. I parked myself at one of the empty tables at the rear of the house and listened to Bobby bring alive the old Duke Ellington tune with that relaxed and fluid voice of his that always makes singing seem easy.

The lyric is jazz poetry of a very uptown sort—and why not, with Johnny Mercer the creator—and Bobby is just the kind of man to give it the right delivery. His sound is cool rather than hot, utterly sophisticated—and yet the passion is there too, if you listen closely. The style is very subtle, and even though this was only a rehearsal, I was struck at how he made the words and melody seem brand new. I sat at my table with a smile on my face and a glow in my heart, for this is why I had come to Vegas—not to gamble, certainly, or to admire the architecture—but to be part of a show that featured American music at its best.

By the bridge of the song, the twenty-five dancing girls had stretched out into a traditional chorus line at the back of the stage, their arms about each other's shoulders. The number was going so smoothly, I almost forgot I was watching a rehearsal—but just then a blonde girl in the middle of the line managed to get out of sync, trip and fall. The delicacy of their group balance was such that she brought down the girl on either side of her, and for a moment the entire line swayed as if an earthquake had struck at the epicenter. The orchestra stopped playing, and the rehearsal ground to a halt.

"God damn it! How did you ever get hired in this show?" screamed a little man in a shrill and hysterical voice. This was the choreographer, I presumed, as he came storming up onto the stage. The blonde girl was still on the floor and grimacing in pain.

"You're supposed to kick on two and four, you idiot!" cried the little man. "Do you think you can remember that?"

"Hold your horses, Fritz," Bobby said to the choreographer, calming him down and going over to the girl. "Are you hurt, honey?"

"I'm okay. I just landed a little hard," said the blonde girl. She was out of breath. "I'm so embarrassed, Mr. Hamilton. I sure hate to stop rehearsal like that."

"That's all right, sweetheart. It's my fault anyway—I'm working you guys too hard. Something like this happens, and it reminds me it's only a show. The important thing is that you're not hurt."

"I'm fine, honestly, Mr. Hamilton."

Bobby helped the girl to her feet and suggested that they all take a five-minute break. Fritz looked unhappy, but Bobby put a friendly arm over his shoulder and spoke privately for a moment. I don't know what it was Bobby said, but in a moment Fritz was smiling. Watching this incident reminded me that Hamilton was not only a great musical talent, but also an extremely nice guy who had patience with the people who worked for him. I stood up from my table, and Wade and I walked towards the edge of the stage.

"Steverino!" Bobby cried when he caught sight

29

of me as I stepped up onto the stage. Bobby embraced me like a brother, laughing with the sheer pleasure of seeing an old friend. "God, it's been a while, huh? Listen, man, I'm really sorry I caught you in the middle of the Pacific—but I can't tell you how grateful I am that you've come. You're really helping me out."

"Hey, it's my pleasure," I told him. The man was bursting with energy and it was infectious.

"Man, we're gonna have a ball! I hope Jayne's here." He glanced around the enormous room.

"She went upstairs to unpack."

"I told 'em to give you a real nice penthouse suite, Steve—so let me know if everything's okay. Tomorrow I thought we'd take the day off. I've got this boat on Lake Mead, and I want you and Jayne to come and spend the afternoon on the water with me and Christie and the kids—we can catch up on old times and just decompress a bit. What'ya say?"

"I say Rag Mop," I answered, and he laughed, remembering the old lyric from the '50s.

"As for the show, hell, that'll be easy—a piece of cake," he assured me. "I thought you'd open on your own for twenty or twenty-five minutes, and then introduce me. I'll sing a few numbers and eventually bring you back on. What I'd *really* like is for you to accompany me on the piano at one point, maybe a nice ballad, no orchestra, just bass and brushes on the drums. Something very quiet and *un*Vegas-y. Can you visualize that?"

"What tune would you like to do?" I said.

"That old ballad of yours, 'Impossible.' "

"Really?" I was quite touched. No matter how much success songwriters have they're always pleased that one of their numbers is going to be performed.

"Yeah," he said. "I fell in love with the tune when I heard the original recording of it—by Nat Cole, right? And then later I heard Andy Williams, the Hi-Lo's—and that new record by Diane Schurr."

That was another thing I admired about Hamilton, he didn't just do the same act—the same 10 to 12 songs—year after year as some singers do, but always kept his shows fresh, adding new material when something caught his eye.

"You've actually got a chart on 'Impossible?' " I asked.

"Why wouldn't I have? I'm doing it on my next album. I got the idea of having 12 of the best arrangers do one chart each. Neal Hefti did 'While We're Young' for me. Hank Mancini did a new treatment of 'The Days of Wine And Roses,' Bill Holman did a real swinger on 'Easy To Love,' and—"

"Who did 'Impossible'?"

"John Clayton," he said. "You'll love it."

"I already do," I said. "I'm familiar with Clayton's work."

"And I got another idea. Remember when I was on your old TV show fifteen years ago?"

"That was nearly *thirty* years ago," I corrected gently.

"That long? God, where does it go? Anyway, we worked out that little soft-shoe number to 'Lullaby of Birdland'—remember? I thought we'd do it as an encore."

"Bobby, we did that routine a long time ago. I'm not sure I remember the moves, man."

"Come on, Steve! An old hoofer never forgets. It's in your bones."

31

Bobby had the kind of charm and enthusiasm that made it hard to say no—but I tried. I'm not exactly shy about performing, but dancing is a skill that requires constant practice, and it wouldn't have hurt either of us to be a decade or so younger. I made a pretty good case for leaving the soft-shoe routine back in the memory album, but Bobby wouldn't listen. He said we'd have a *great* time and the audience would love it so much it didn't even matter if we missed a step or two.

"Come on, let's give it a try right now," he said.

"Bobby, I just got off the airplane!"

"Then you need the exercise. You see, I'm doing you a favor. Okay, Chris," he called to the bandleader. "One . . . two . . . one, two, three, and . . ."

You can see what I was up against. How could you even begin to say no to such a person? The rhythm section began to play, and it was entirely too much fun being on stage with Bobby Hamilton to worry about anything so minor as knowing the correct steps. But the funny thing was, I found I remembered our old soft-shoe routine almost as if we had just done it yesterday, and in a moment I was dancing about the stage, my movements in sync with Bobby's, both of us carried away by the magic of the George Shearing melody.

Actually, if we had been doing a really complicated, professional routine I wouldn't have been able to cut it. But the soft-shoe steps are pretty traditional. You've probably seen Bob Hope doing them, on some of his TV specials. Even George Burns used to, when he was a few years younger. A great dancer I'm not, chiefly because during the teenage years, the time when most of us learn to move about on the dance floor, I was pressed up against the stages of those glamorous rooms where the big bands used to play, holding a young woman in my arms, to legitimize my presence on the floor, but actually doing no dancing at all, just staring up in deep admiration at Tommy Dorsey, Bunny Berrigan, Woody Herman, Bob Crosby and the other leaders of those great old orchestras of the 1930s and '40s.

It was pure exhilaration, and when it was over even the chorus girls whistled and applauded. I might be stiff tomorrow but right now I felt as if thirty years had been lifted from my shoulders. I had an absurd desire to go on dancing all night.

"You see?" said Bobby, laughing. "Us old guys still got a trick or two left. We're going to knock 'em dead here, amigo!"

"Sure we will," I said. But there came a time when I was sorry he had put it in quite that way.

chapter 5

When Bobby said he had a boat on Lake Mead, I wasn't expecting to find a rubber dinghy, but I wasn't prepared either for the sleek sixty-five foot cabin cruiser, *Sing For Your Supper*, that had a helicopter pad on the top deck, and looked big enough to cross the Atlantic.

This was only the first surprise. The second was the size of the party. In fact, this turned out to be no simple family outing with the wife and kids as Bobby had promised, but a real show-biz bash.

Jayne and I arrived at the Boulder Beach Marina at about one o'clock in the afternoon, after a forty-five minute drive from Vegas through a parched and arid landscape that seemed as empty as the moon. You don't expect to find water here at the end of your journey, for Lake Mead is entirely man-made, a surreal blue mirage surrounded by the brown earth of the Mojave desert. I might mention that this is a *big* man-made lake, with 550 miles of shoreline, created when Hoover Dam was put up to block the flow of the Colorado River, which runs into

Nevada through another interesting piece of American real estate—the Grand Canyon.

Jayne and I stepped out of Cass's air-conditioned limo into searing desert heat. I was wearing loose white jogging clothes, ready for a casual afternoon with close friends in an informal setting. Jayne had on something silky and salmon-colored and Italian, a pantsuit I suppose you'd call it—flattering, but quite casual. And so we looked in dismay at seeing a pride of other limousines—half a dozen of them—crowding close to the dock, as well as a few paparazzi whose presence signifies a Hollywood A-list event as surely as vultures circling overhead indicate the proximity of death. The photographers immediately turned their attention our way to see if we were someone important. Apparently we were, for shutters began to click, at which I put on my smile-mask.

"The flash bulbs are giving me retinal damage," I said to Jayne out of the right corner of my mouth, since she always stands on that side when our pictures are being taken.

"Be brave, Steve," said Jayne, smiling radiantly at the cameras. She likes parties more than I do.

Not only were there paparazzi, there were even a few mamarazzi, plus a small crowd of gawking fans, lookie-loos, and rubber-neckers, which are terms usually applied to those who slow down to witness accidents on the Los Angeles freeways.

It all added up to something quite different from my idea of a casual day on the water.

To my surprise, I saw Wade Hamilton waiting for us by the foot of the dock. Wade was wearing a well-tailored white linen suit, but there was a sullen expression on his face and the bright sunlight only made his complexion look even more like unbaked pastry dough.

"Good," he said. "You're here. Now I can get out of the damned sun."

"You've been waiting for us?"

"My father thought you might have trouble getting past security and finding the boat," he told us with a shrug. "He thinks everyone's an idiot except himself."

"Who all is here?" I asked, bypassing the negative remark about his father.

"People," said Wade unhappily. Then he mentioned the name of a Very Famous Movie Star who was passing through town, as well as a Fabulous Tycoon who owned approximately half of Manhattan. "And my sister Michelle is here, of course," he added sourly.

"How lovely," said Jayne. "I haven't seen Michelle since she was just a little girl."

Wade flashed us a look which seemed to mean that Michelle was a little girl no longer. A security guard opened a gate onto the dock and Wade led the way through. Cass said he was going to rent some tackle so he could do some fishing while he waited for us. I briefly considered sending Jayne to the party without me and catching some trout with Cass, but it was a coward's fantasy. From fifty yards away, I could already hear party sounds of laughter and music coming from the sleek white yacht at the end of the dock. This had all the earmarks of the kind of party I might not enjoy.

We passed boats with names like *Royal Flush*, *Full House*, and *Lucky Seven*. You'd almost think people liked to gamble in Nevada. *Sing For Your*

Supper must have been the largest craft in the marina, maybe the largest in the whole damned lake, and we found it waiting for us at the end of the dock close to the open water. The engine was idling in neutral, coughing up little clouds of white smoke at the stern.

Bobby, who was standing at the top of the gangplank, helped us aboard. "All right, the gang's all here!" he cried.

Bobby was wearing deck shoes, white pants, a blue-and-white striped French Riviera T-shirt, and a jaunty captain's hat. He also had an amber-colored drink in one hand. Some of the liquid and ice sloshed out onto the deck as he gave Jayne and me enthusiastic bear-hugs.

"You guys look fabulous!" he said, though looking at Jayne. "Look, a few friends dropped by kinda unexpectedly. I think we're gonna have a party!"

Bobby was revved up. I could see a dozen or so people standing around the various decks. Beautiful people. They were dressed for leisure time in the most expensive leisure-wear that money might buy in places like Palm Beach and Rodeo Drive. The Very Famous Movie Star came over, and he and Jayne started talking about some mutual acquaintances. I noticed the Fabulous Tycoon from New York sitting with a pretty redhead half his age. From what I could overhear, the Tycoon was telling everyone what a genius he was and how he had been making incredible deals the last few days in Vegas. The man seemed to have a very high opinion of himself, which I suppose is why he had renamed much of the Eastern seaboard after himself—hotels, office buildings, airlines, even sporting events. Personally I find this a bit tacky. Sometimes, in odd moments, I might try to imagine Steve Allen Airlines, or The Allen Towers Hotel, but it isn't quite me. To tell the truth, I'm not even sure I'd want a salad dressing named after me, unless it was for a *very* good cause.

Though Bobby Hamilton was my friend, I soon concluded this party wasn't my scene at all. The atmosphere was shrill and forced; everyone seemed determined to have a great time, no matter what. Christie Hamilton—Bobby's wife of twenty-five years—came hurrying over. She seemed thrilled to see us, particularly Jayne.

"Honey! Damn, it's been a while, hasn't it? You guys look *great!*" cried Christie. She was a handsome woman in her early forties, with honey blonde hair, deep golden tan and a smoky voice. Her wrists jangled with gold bracelets and there was a giant diamond on her wedding finger. Like Bobby, she had a drink in one hand that seemed to be an extension of her fingers. I remembered her as a very pretty Hollywood starlet who surprised the gossip columnists by marrying fabulously well, a man more than twenty years her senior, becoming Mrs. Bobby Hamilton.

"Let's get you a drink, and I hope you're hungry 'cause we've got a ton of food. Do you water-ski, Steve?"

"Not while I'm eating," I said.

Actually, Jayne and I had gone through our water-skiing period years earlier, back in the mid-1950s when I was approaching *The Tonight Show* phase of my career. We had rented a little house in Amityville, Long Island, chosen simply because it was on the water, after which we made the happy discovery that there was anchored, not very far offshore, a sizable old barge from which a championship skier named Bruce Parker conducted a water-ski instruction business. My sons Steve, Brian, and David were with us that summer, so the five of us paddled out to Mr. Parker's base of operations, introduced ourselves, and became very involved in the sport.

A couple of years later, when we were doing *The Tonight Show* from Miami for a couple of weeks, we got back into it again, in a big way.

I would be doing a disservice to the truth if I tried to describe the party itself in a linear sort of way, one thing after another; in reality, this was the sort of occasion in which everything seemed to be happening at once. In a five-minute period after boarding the yacht, I met four strangers, including the Fabulous Tycoon, requested two glasses of Perrier with lemon from a roving waiter, told Christie Hamilton all about our cruise to the South Pacific, and helped Bobby cast off from the dock. This last bit worried me somewhat. I noticed several waiters in white coats helping to serve drinks and *hors d'oeuvres*, but the crew of the boat itself seemed to be strictly a family operation. Wade climbed up to the wheel on the upper deck, while Bobby untied us from the dock, threw the rope to me, and then jumped nimbly back onto the bow. He backed the huge cabin cruiser carefully out of the dock and edged us out onto open water. The boat was so big and ornate it made me feel as if I was in a luxury condominium— only this particular condo moved. In a few moments we were skimming along the glassy surface of the lake with a wake of foam spurting up behind us.

Jayne and I found a place to sit on the rear deck beneath a royal blue canvas awning. The Tycoon was nearby, and he began asking me questions about costs and grosses of some recent Hollywood films. I sensed the man was secretly plotting to buy Hollywood for himself and give the town his own celebrated name. Tycoonwood, perhaps.

I'm partly kidding, of course, but I have long felt that the acquisition and buy-up mania will someday result in the entire earth being controlled by one corporate entity. It won't be planned that way but will happen by a series of simultaneous sales and purchases. General Motors, for example, will buy Chrysler just at the time that Chrysler is buying MGM, which—by coincidence—will happen at the time that MGM is purchasing what remains of the British Empire, which itself will be, during that same period, assuming financial control of the Catholic Church, which simultaneously will have decided to resolve the present difficulties in Eastern Europe by purchasing Poland, which by a series of intricate financial maneuvers will assume management of the Sony Corporation which, it will then be revealed, will have just acquired management of the Mafia, which, through the acceptance of a tender offer from Hollywood's talent representatives, CAA, will have purchased both the American Tobacco Company and Schering Drug, which will have at the same point taken out a monopoly patent on the cure for cancer, the profits from which will enable it to purchase both IBM and AT & T precisely at the point where those two companies will have assumed the American federal national debt, which they will then use as a tax write-off, thus making possible a re-invigoration of the Star Wars program which, though astronomically costly (no pun intended) will nevertheless enable the same conglomerate ownership to acquire General Dynamics and other major defense corporations.

Toying with the idea that my new friend might

be playing at least a minor role in these international machinations, I suddenly began to feed him misinformation designed to defeat his plans. I told him 3-D was about to make a gigantic comeback, and smart money could really make a killing here. Jayne momentarily jabbed me in the ribs with her elbow— she had been talking with Christie, but my wife has the extraordinary ability to participate in two conversations at once.

"Be nice," she whispered in my ear.

"I was born nice," I assured her.

But this was not my kind of party. I'd rather spend social time with my grandchildren, or have a nice quiet dinner with three or four old friends. With all the forced laughter and the throb of the boat's engine, it was difficult to have an actual conversation consisting of more than three or four sentences, and then something terrible was added. Loud rock music at an ear-destroying volume erupted from somewhere on deck. I certainly don't want to seem *completely* negative about rock and roll—where would Western civilization and culture be without Elvis and the Beatles? But this was not the Beatles. It wasn't even Madonna. It was the kind of rock that sets your teeth on edge and makes you want to listen instead to the soothing sound of pneumatic drills tearing up 47th Street. There was no melody, not even any harmonic chords, nothing but an insanely repetitive rhythmic phrase and a girl's whining adolescent voice singing the same few words again and again: "Let's do it! Yeah. Oh, baby. Uh-huh. Let's do it! Yeah. Oh, baby. Un-huh. Let's do it . ..." Ad infinitum, ad nauseam, ad wolgast.

I am a mild-mannered man. But I wanted to kill the young woman singing this song. I also wanted to

41

find the stereo that was making this horrible sound and pull the plug forever.

Another problem I have with rock is rooted in the fact that relatively few singers in that genre sing in their actual, natural voices. So far as I know this is a development unprecedented in the long world-history of vocal music itself. To refer to only relatively modern examples, one has always been free to evaluate Bing Crosby, Frank Sinatra, Perry Como, Eydie Gormé or whoever, but they did sing with their own voices. The voice and the singer comprised a unity. Most rock singers, by way of contrast, even if they grow up in Milwaukee, Chicago, Boston or London, adopt an American hillbilly twang or rasp that is totally foreign to their style of speaking. And many, of course, wish to sound not only rural but rural-black. They would therefore not dream of singing a lyric that included the phrase *my baby* in the way they would speak it in the street.

Instead it becomes *mah babeh*. If the singer himself is black and from the rural south there is no such problem. It was reasonable that Elvis or Jerry Lee Lewis sang like Southern country boys because that's what they were. Otherwise you've got a phony persona problem. And this young woman, too, was obviously trying to sound as if she had spent her early years in a black ghetto. There's something dumb about that, ladies and germs.

I am, of course, conditioned to such reactions by the beatific blessing of some forty years of exposure to the most glorious popular music any national culture has ever produced—that characterized by the genius of Jerome Kern, Cole Porter, George Gershwin, Irving Berlin, Richard Rodgers, Hoagey Carmichael, Duke Ellington, Harry Warren and the

42

lyricists who served them so well. As an amateur historian I am, of course, aware that nothing remains unchanged and that evolution is inevitable. But such evolution is supposed to lead to improvement. When it heads in the opposite direction one must start complaining and never stop until interrupted by death.

In the midst of the party's auditory madness, Bobby came dancing onto the deck with a girl who was hardly older than a teenager—a very pretty blonde with a stunning figure who was wearing a rumor of a bikini. Bobby seemed to be going through a second childhood. The two gyrated around the deck for a few moments, dancing with abandon until the song came to an end—followed by the blessed relative silence of the engine and the boat rippling its way through the water.

"So what do you think, Steve? Do you like the record?"

"We-ll . . ."

"It's Michelle's! You remember my little girl, don't you?" Bobby put his arm around the blonde bombshell in the bikini, who I presumed must be his "little girl." She flashed me a I-can't-be-bothered-with-people-over-thirty sort of look from beneath a shag of hair which half-covered her china-blue eyes.

"Well, so that's you singing, is it?" I asked.

"Yeah," said the girl.

"She wrote the music and lyric and played most of the instruments too," said proud father, whose own musical taste is impeccable.

"I'm impressed. What sort of, er, instruments did you use?"

The girl shrugged. "Three drum machines, a sequencer and a Korg MX-1."

"Ah." I have a weakness for violins and pianos and saxophones and real drums played by real drummers, not machines. But because this was my old friend's daughter, I cast about for something positive to say.

"It certainly is . . . danceable."

"Isn't it?" said Bobby. "My Michelle's gonna be a big star—and this is only a demo you just heard."

"Daddy, I wanna go get a drink," said Michelle sulkily. I had clearly lost her tender interest.

"Hey, muffin—go right ahead," said her father. We both watched Michelle walk off toward the inside bar.

"Kids!" said Bobby nostalgically, coming to sit down alongside me. He lowered his voice. "Michelle's in Vegas for six weeks to get her divorce, you know. She was married to the lead singer of Manic Depression." At least that was the group's latest name. Previously they had been known as Authorized Personnel.

"My condolences," I murmured.

Bobby smiled ruefully. "They had the number one single for six weeks in a row."

"Pity," I enthused.

"Yeah," he said, not hearing. "Anyway, for Michelle this will be divorce number three. Before Manic Depression, there was a race car driver, and before that a French playboy. These kids . . . well, it takes them a little time to settle down."

"How old is she?"

"Twenty-three."

We were silent a moment, two old-timers contemplating "twenty-three." No matter how you looked at it, three quickie marriages in such a short lifetime did seem a lot. From his silence, I sensed

44

Bobby was trying to bring himself to ask me something.

"Look, Steve, I have this idea . . . and I want you to tell me if you think I'm crazy."

"Sure, Bobby."

"I'm thinking of asking Michelle to sing a number with us in the show. I mean, the audience will dig the fact she's my daughter, and she really has a *lovely* voice—particularly when she's doing material that's a bit more musical than her demo tape. And the main thing, you see—it would give her something to do while she's sitting around waiting for her divorce. I'm hoping maybe it might inspire her with a little direction."

I nodded, torn. My eardrums were only just recovering from three short minutes of Michelle's voice, and on an aesthetic level, the thought of appearing on stage with her made me want either to book an immediate flight to the outback of Australia or get out of show business. However, this was Bobby's daughter, and Bobby was an old friend, and he clearly had a problem.

"It's your show, man," I told him.

"Don't cop-out on me, Steve. I want this to be your show, too. So tell me what you think. Will the audience accept it if I bring her out on stage?"

I had to tell him the truth: "Only if she can sing well enough so it doesn't become an embarrassment."

Bobby sighed. "Maybe we can think of some tune that doesn't have much of a range," he said mournfully.

" 'One Note Samba'?" I suggested with only a touch of sarcasm. He looked at me with a hurt ex-

pression that made me sorry. "We'll find something," I said gently.

"Sure we will," he said.

Just then a trim and dapper gentleman with
silver hair and a charming smile appeared on deck
from inside the cabin and immediately came our
way. "Hi, Steve . . . Jayne! Sorry I've been hiding
out down below. Actually, I've been on the phone to
Tokyo setting up a concert tour this Spring. Thank
God for the Japanese, huh? They really *love* American Jazz."

The dapper silver-haired gentleman was Elliot
Block, one of the most successful agents in Hollywood. At present, however, he had just one client,
Bobby Hamilton—and Elliot and Bobby went back
a long time.

The intimate moment I'd had with Hamilton
was over; he once again put on the face of a host
absolutely determined that everyone should eat,
drink and be merry. Elliot, Bobby and I were soon
discussing a Japanese jazz label that was re-releasing
American classics from the forties and fifties. Jazz is
actually America's only original contribution to
world culture, but it is more appreciated in Europe
and Japan than in the States. Bobby, Elliot and I
commiserated about this fact.

The sun shone down, the water glistened an
impossible blue, and we all proceeded to have a bois-
terous and friendly time. In the way of parties, people grouped, broke apart, and regrouped again. A lot
of alcohol was being consumed, particularly by Michelle, who appeared on deck from time to time looking increasingly fuzzy and unfocused. It was a
curious family. Occasionally, I glanced up to the top
deck to see Wade Hamilton all by himself piloting

our way through the deep blue waters of Lake Mead. The others on the boat seemed to have forgotten his existence. About an hour after we had set out from the marina, I decided to climb up the steps to Wade's perch on the top of the boat and say hello.

"Hey, can I get you a drink, Wade? You seem to be the only one working here."

"No, thanks, Mr. Allen," he said gloomily, staring ahead through the windshield.

"This is quite a boat," I said, looking at the compass and all the buttons, dials and throttles at Wade's command. "So where are you taking us?"

"There's a cove my father likes to go to another mile up the lake, at Black Island. We'll drop anchor there and have lunch."

"How long have you been working for your father?"

"Ever since I graduated from college—ten years ago," he reminded me. I was trying to think if there was any polite way to say what I wanted to say, namely: *Your father's a great guy, kid, but maybe you should get out from under his thumb and start living your own life somewhere*. Wade may have had a glimmer of my thoughts for he turned his head to look at me briefly.

"It's not so bad," he said quietly. "The old man pays me eighty grand a year, room and board, and I get to drive his boat and carry his luggage. I would say I'm the highest paid gopher in the entire history of gopherism."

"I see. And what did you major in at Dartmouth, Wade?"

He turned to look at me again, apparently surprised I had actually remembered the name of his alma mater. "I was pre-med," he told me. "I had a crazy idea I wanted to be a doctor."

"That doesn't sound so crazy."

"Well, it is if your father is Bobby Hamilton. I mean, why should anyone else have a career except him?"

I knew I was on delicate ground, and this was probably none of my business but—

"Look, I really like your father a lot, and he's maybe the greatest singer of our day—but that doesn't mean your career is less important than his."

He treated me to a rare ironic smile, though his lips didn't seem accustomed to an upward tilt. He was about to say something when we heard Christie calling his name from below.

"Wade, honey, would you stop the boat—I want to water ski."

To my surprise, Wade ignored her, continuing to steer straight ahead.

"Wade!" shouted Bobby over the throb of the engines. His voice carried a trace of anger. "Pull up, son! Your mother wants to water-ski."

"She's not *my* damned mother," said Wade softly—so softly I would never have heard him if I hadn't been standing close. Soft as it was, I sensed a bottomless rage to his words. Still, he did exactly as his father told him. His face went blank of all expression, and he pulled back on the throttle until we were floating dead calm on the water.

chapter 6

What Wade said about Christie not being *his* mother reminded me of the old stories—stories I hadn't thought about for years. Generally I go out of my way to avoid Hollywood gossip about my friends' marriages, divorces and affairs, but back in 1966 the alleged details of Bobby Hamilton's love life came screaming at you from the covers of every tabloid. If you ever found yourself waiting in a supermarket line, it was hard to avoid.

Bobby's first wife was Rose Morgan, the singer, who was big back in the forties, starring in her own radio show after having worked with some of the great bands of the era. In fact I remember a joke I did—it must have been 30 years ago—in talking about Rose on television one night.

"I remember when she went on the road with Charlie Barnet," I said.

"Oh," said my announcer, Johnny Jacobs, unintentionally playing great straight, "did she sing with Charlie Barnet?"

"No," I said, "she just went on the road with him."

But the story is that Rose, already famous, discovered Bobby singing in a small club on West 52nd Street in New York and gave him his first important break by inviting him to make an appearance on her show. Rose helped a lot of people in those days; she was a lovely lady in every way except the physical. In fact, not to mince words, a lot of her vocal power came from her massive frame and the fact that she was about fifty pounds overweight. "Big Rose" Morgan was her nickname, and while the public loved her earthy humor and soulful renditions, men generally gave her a wide berth. Maybe that was why she was able to sing such sad songs about love lost.

Rose was ten years older than Bobby and she took charge of his career at just that moment when her own fame and fortune were beginning to wane. No one suspected there was romance between the two so people in the music industry were surprised when Rose and Bobby eloped in 1950 and had a quiet wedding in Niagara Falls. There was natural skepticism concerning a match between a handsome young man and a woman who looked like his mother. Some assumed Bobby was using Rose to get ahead, but I didn't have that impression at all. I remember seeing them together in those years and they seemed always to be having a wonderful time. I think Bobby saw past Rose's outward form to the radiance underneath, particularly that special quality that made her a great singer.

Then, too, we're talking about an emotional oddity for which I have never heard an adequate explanation—those cases in which strikingly handsome men marry remarkably plain and sometimes even unattractive women. Obviously there may be Freudian factors involved. If the man's mother looked like the wife then he would perceive her physical attributes more favorably than others would. But I know of situations in which the fellow's mother was quite beautiful, which only deepened the mystery of his marriage choice.

Lest feminist friends accuse me of one-sidedness, I simply don't think it is nearly as puzzling that a good many women marry the kind of men that Jayne refers to as "baby frighteners." A number of such marriages take place simply because the man is enormously wealthy and therefore powerful. Such women, I suppose, simply don't place a very high value on romantic love, are extraordinarily concerned with financial security and therefore make a choice that, considering their priorities, seems reasonable to them.

It's also a fact that physical appearance is not as important in men as it is in women. There are, apparently, quite a few things that Mother Nature is apparently still tinkering with. But Bobby's and Rose's careers, unfortunately, were heading in different directions: the fifties were extremely kind to Bobby Hamilton, but Rose Morgan found herself suddenly labeled old-fashioned. The very year her radio show was canceled, Bobby was nominated for an Academy Award—for by this time he was a film star as well as a singer and his career had hit the stratosphere. Yet I always had the impression that he did his best to make Rose feel their reversed positions were no great matter.

The son, Wade, was born about 1958, as I recall. The Hollywood community was both surprised and pleased—it seemed reasonable that such a huge star and sex symbol as Bobby Hamilton would devote himself to the joys of family life. Then, around 1962, everything changed. Bobby had a highly publicized affair with the beautiful co-star of his latest film—a lady unfortunately married at the time to the picture's producer—and both their marriages suddenly fell apart. The tabloids hit new highs—or lows—of speculation, and Rose and Bobby were divorced. After all the hullabaloo, the world generally assumed Bobby would now marry his co-star—but it didn't happen, even though she had freed herself from her producer-husband and was reportedly expecting to become the next Mrs. Hamilton. Bobby, it seemed, liked his new freedom, and for the next few years he was a dashing bachelor about town, with his name, not always accurately, linked with some of the most beautiful and celebrated women of the time.

Then in 1966 the world was surprised to read of his wedding to the extremely pretty (and young) Christie Kelly, who had a small but highly visible role on a hit TV series. The tabloids made the usual fuss, and then something happened to make them go wild: two weeks after the wedding, Rose Morgan committed suicide by sticking her head in an oven. There were reports of a suicide note in which she accused Bobby of robbing her of the best years of her life and then leaving her high and dry. "EX-WIFE BLAMES BOBBY AND DIES," screamed a tabloid. "ROSE MORGAN'S FINAL CURSE ON BOBBY AND CHRISTIE," cried another. The rumored note was never found, but this did not bother the tabloids, which sometimes invent whatever they feel will sell papers. Of course, what such publications failed to mention was that nearly five years had passed between the end of Bobby's marriage to Rose and his wedding to Christie. I've never talked with Bobby about any of this—and I don't plan to—but I'm sure he was extremely upset at Rose's suicide. Still, I don't see how he can be blamed for the tragedy.

Anyway, that's the story, as much as I know of it. I hadn't thought about any of it for years until I heard Wade's angry remark about Christie not being *his* mother. I wondered if Wade held his real mother's suicide against his stepmother. It wouldn't be fair, since Christie hadn't stolen away a married man or broken up a family, but sometimes children believe what they want to, and they may wish for their real mother and father to be together against impossible odds.

I must have been quiet for a time as these memories sifted through my mind.

"Heads or tails?" asked Bobby with a grin, lifting the lid of the barbecue at the stern of the boat to reveal an enormous whole salmon—head and all—roasting on the coals.

"Oh, *gross!*" said Michelle. She appeared alongside the barbecue dragging a bottle of white wine by the neck. Her shaggy blonde hair was partially obscuring her eyes, and she was still dressed only in what I considered a vulgarly small bikini. She seemed unmindful of her near nudity; a new breed of careless young savage, this girl. Bobby beamed at her.

"How's my muffin?" he asked.

The muffin took a swig of wine straight from the bottle and stared moodily at the cooking salmon.

I stared moodily at her, without the slightest admixture of carnal interest. I am at least as susceptible to the appeal of sexual attraction as any other normal male, which is not an unmixed blessing, but there seems to be considerable confusion in the minds of a good many people in our society as to just what it is, in a woman, that most interests a man. Part of the confusion, I'm sure, concerns the American difficulty with that factor referred to as *more*. To suffer from the more disease means that one can never be content, even if disinterested observers might consider one's estate highly enviable. The reader might assume that he would be ecstatically pleased to suddenly possess, say, twenty million dollars, but there are those incapable of enjoying such good fortune as long as they know that there is someone else in their social circle who is even more financially secure.

As for young women, some of them seem to feel that since men are titillated by the revelation of a bit of kneecap, breast, shoulder or navel it logically follows that to quickly proceed to a state of either near or total nudity is a wise course. They are quite mistaken in this. Or, to put the matter in simpler terms, one Sophia Loren is worth a thousand Madonnas.

We had dropped anchor off an island in the middle of Lake Mead—Black Island it was called, though from my vantage point it appeared as brown as all the other visible land. Wade, who had come down from the upper deck, was silently holding a dish of olive oil, garlic, lemon juice and herbs while his father basted the fish. Bobby, wearing an apron, seemed to be quite the outdoor cook. He had a beer in one hand, a basting brush in the other, and looked like a man who could have been happily found in any suburban backyard across the country.

Lunch was finally ready close to dinner time, but turned out to be well worth waiting for. The salmon was sublime, and Christie casually let it slip that the fish had been caught fresh off San Francisco that morning and flown on a private jet, packed in ice, to Las Vegas in time for our late lunch. Bobby was very modest about this—he seemed embarrassed for us to know how much money he had spent on our meal, and he tried to indicate that flying fish around the country on chartered jets was no big deal. Still, I found myself eating more slowly, savoring every hundred-dollar bite. This had to be one of the most expensive fishes in the entire history of salmondom.

"Do you still call it lunch?" Jayne asked, "when it's served at 4:30?"

"A perfectly fair question," I said. "The first time we ever worked here it occurred to me that because people tend to stay up very late and remain unconscious during part of the daylight hours, a number of new words were required. *Brunch,* for example, is obviously made by mashing together the words *breakfast* and *lunch*. But around Vegas people may have their first meal of the day quite late, in which case it should be called *brinner*. And if it happens during Christmas week they might called it yule-brinner."

"Maybe *dekfast* would serve just as well," Jayne suggested.

Anyway, whatever this meal should have been called, it was served buffet style, and we all ate in various spots around the rear deck. I sat with Bobby, Elliot, and the Tycoon on my left. There was a heated discussion about whether the Japanese were going to prosper in Hollywood now that they owned two major studios, Columbia and Universal.

"Making movies is *not* like making cars," insisted Bobby. "Man, those guys are going to commit *sepuku* when they see what it's like trying to bring a picture in on budget!"

The Tycoon and Elliot heartily agreed. To my surprise, Wade spoke up on behalf of the Japanese; he said it was about time someone treated the entertainment industry like any other business, and he reminded us that the Japanese were supplying Hollywood with what the town always needed most: great infusions of cash.

"You don't know what the hell you're talking about," Bobby said, surprisingly harshly, to his son. He seemed to realize he had spoken rudely and turned to the rest of us with an apologetic smile. "My kid's real gun-ho these days about the Japanese—he thinks they're the answer to all our problems."

Wade glowered at the comment and retreated into his usual morose silence. Elliot changed the subject to a critique of a new Robin Williams film.

So that was what was happening on my left. On my right, Jayne and Michelle were having a conversation. This seemed such an unlikely event that I couldn't help but listen in from time to time.

"He never even remembered my birthday," pouted the girl. I presumed she was speaking of her recent husband, the illustrious lead singer of Manic Depression. "And he wanted to bring his groupies home; can you beat that?"

"Fortunately, I can't," Jayne said dryly.

"Men!" snorted Michelle. "I'm tired of being a victim all the time!"

"Perhaps you should just live on your own a while," Jayne suggested gently. "Find out the things *you* want to do in life, and then eventually the right man will appear."

"I don't know. The guys I get involved with are

such bigshots. Just like my father. They always want to tell me what to do all the time. Like I've been put on earth for *their* pleasure."

"Those are just the men you're attracted to, Michelle," said Jayne.

The girl was silent for a moment, taking this in. "So you think I can change?" She was trying to be flippant, but I felt there was desperation in her voice.

Jayne took her hand. "You can change by learning to believe in yourself, dear. That's the first step. Everything else follows from there."

"Yeah, believe in yourself," she said bitterly. "Only I can't do nothin'—so what's there to believe in?"

"You sing, don't you? Your father seems to think you're going to have a career."

"Yeah . . . only if my father weren't Bobby Hamilton, I wouldn't get to first base."

It was a crushing admission, and I found myself with a new respect for the girl—she was honest at least. However, Michelle could apparently only take this kind of introspection in short spurts. She stood up and announced loudly that she was going for a swim.

Christie, who had appeared from inside the cabin, anxiously took hold of her husband's hand. "Honey, don't let her dive in," she pleaded. "She's had too much to drink."

"Nonsense," said Bobby. "She swims like a seal. Let her have some fun."

Michelle didn't wait for anyone's permission. She simply climbed over the boat's railing and jumped into the water below, hitting with a big splash and a small scream. I was getting a bad feeling about the moment.

"You know, Bobby, it really isn't a good idea to get into the water after so much to eat and drink," I said.

"Steve, it would probably kill either you or me, but these kids, they're indestructible."

I wasn't so convinced about their indestructibility, after observing Wade and Michelle Hamilton all afternoon. Christie stood nervously by the rail to watch her daughter's progress in the water. Michelle swam a few awkward strokes away from the boat, then abruptly sank beneath the surface.

"Bobby! She's gone under!" cried Christie in a shrill voice.

"Honey, she's just playing games. She's probably swum underwater to the other side of the boat."

I walked to the opposite side of the boat and peered down into the water, but there was no sign of Michelle. "Bobby, she's not over here," I called.

"Oh, God! Bobby, *do* something!" cried the distraught mother.

"Honey, she's going to come back up to the surface in a moment *laughing* at us."

The Famous Movie Star climbed up on the rail, and for a moment looked as if he were going to be a cinematic hero and dive in—but he hesitated, perhaps reluctant to ruin his lovely Dunhill blazer in the water. To my surprise, it was Wade who finally did something. Without a word, he stepped out of his shoes, slipped off his jacket, and dove over the side of the boat in his shirt and pants. I saw him look around once, take a deep breath, and then he too disappeared under the surface.

We all stood by the rail, watching and waiting. Even the Tycoon was momentarily silenced. After what seemed like a very long time, Wade came to the

58

surface with one arm around his half-sister. Michelle coughed, sputtered and took a gasping breath of air.

"Oh, thank God!" said Jayne, who had come up alongside of me and was unconsciously squeezing my arm with her hand. When Michelle showed signs of life, I felt Jayne's hand relax.

Wade brought the girl along to the rear of the boat where there was a chrome ladder for water skiers. He managed to push her toward Christie and me. We reached down to get Michelle under each arm and hauled her aboard.

"I'm okay . . . okay," said Michelle, as she began to climb the ladder on her own power.

"See what I mean? Indestructible!" said Bobby, coming up behind us with a big smile. Parents can be awfully blind, but for the life of me, I couldn't understand how Bobby could refuse to see that his daughter had nearly drowned.

"You know, Steve, sometimes I feel like the luckiest man alive—I got a beautiful wife, two fabulous kids, and the greatest friends in the world! Now who wants another drink?"

Bobby was an old friend, but I found myself incapable of returning his cheery smile. I was beginning to think there was something awfully wrong with this family.

chapter 7

The bedroom shuddered and swayed, rolled and shook. Not violently as if we were at the epicenter of a massive quake but more than enough to shock me up out of a disturbing and vaguely erotic dream, the details of which were immediately scattered by the winds of consciousness.

My eyes popped opened wide, the way sleepers' eyes sometimes do in horror films, and my heart was beating fast, but whether from the nightmare or the sensory intrusions of the moment I could not say. Two seconds later the analytical part of my brain clicked into action, instantly considering and rejecting two possibilities—one, that the drama of the moment *was* the storyline of the disturbing dream and two, that for reasons unknown I had somehow entered the Twilight Zone of general craziness. This wasn't San Francisco, after all, it was Las Vegas, where earthquakes were presumably unknown.

"Are you all right?" Jayne said, having noted my agitated state.

"Boy," I said, "that must have been some dream. I thought we were having an earthquake."

"Look at the chandelier, dear."

The massively gaudy light fixture in the middle of our sumptuous bedroom was swaying like a pendulum. This was no dream. Jayne picked up the phone on her bedside table and dialed the hotel operator.

"Hello, this is Mrs. Allen in the Bacchanalian Suite—did we just have an earthquake? I see . . . Goodness! Are you sure we're safe? . . . This happens all the time? Don't people ever complain? . . . Well, thank you."

Jayne put down the phone and shook her head. "Imagine that!" she said. Jayne sometimes thinks so fast that she neglects to communicate relevant details including the most essential.

"Imagine *what?*"

"It was only a nuclear bomb, dear. Nothing to get upset about."

"Only a nuclear bomb!" I cried. "Who are we at war with?"

"Ourselves, I think."

"Maybe," I suggested, "some natural rival, like Atlantic City, is attacking Las Vegas."

Jayne did not laugh but gave me an "Ope, Steve."

"Or perhaps," I continued, "they've just opened a new hotel called Ground Zero, like those fake-disaster attractions that are part of the Universal Studios Tour."

Jayne ignored that line altogether but proceeded to explain that what we had felt was a nuclear explosion underground at a test site a hundred and ten miles outside of Las Vegas. Apparently this is quite normal. Besides having the gaudiest architecture created by greed, one-upsmanship, gambling, legal brothels, and alcohol served twenty-four hours a day, Nevada has the distinction of being a testing ground for Armageddon. I heard later on the TV news that this particular blast was a hundred times more powerful than the one that destroyed Hiroshima, causing perhaps seventy-five thousand deaths, and it was felt in Las Vegas as a 5.6 tremblor, shaking the taller buildings about town.

It put me in a dark mood. Frankly, the buzz-grate of an alarm clock is bad enough; I don't like to be awakened by a thermonuclear device.

"Don't take it personally, dear," said my wife. "Even Howard Hughes couldn't stop the underground testing when he lived here, and he nearly owned the state."

"Hmpf," I said, staring out the window at the early morning. I tried to remember the dream I had been having when the earth shook. It seemed an important one somehow; something I should know about. But it was gone, all due to the fact that, despite the recent collapse of the Evil Empire, a bunch of weapons specialists seemed interested in exploring the possibility of reducing our planet to radioactive rubble.

"Well, let's call room service and have breakfast at least," I grumped.

"I sent Cass out to the market last night, and we have everything we need in our fridge," said Jayne. "You know I like to avoid unhealthful hotel food as much as possible."

"Except when you're hungry."

"Steve," Jayne said with a patient smile, "most likely, Los Angeles air pollution will get us even quicker than The Bomb, salt and dietary fat—but you might as well be healthy when you go!"

With this bit of optimism, Jayne and I made breakfast of fresh grapefruit juice, bran muffins, piping hot decaf, and half a crenshaw melon each.

I should describe our penthouse on the top floor of The Coliseum, but mere words will never do it justice. We had a sunken living room, a putting green on the terrace, a TV in each of our three bathrooms, a veiled bed large enough for a harem, a mirrored ceiling in the bedroom, and a gleaming, white concert grand piano that also functioned as a bar—to be precise, a piano bar with stools around the perimeter. Liberace could have lived here and been happy. There was gilt on the walls, a statue of Adonis in the foyer, a Roman bath, a sauna, jacuzzi, two bidets and a panoramic view of the city stretched out at our feet. When Las Vegas tries to summon up its fantasy of luxury, it doesn't take a chance on missing anything. If this had been Rome, it would have made me long for the simplicity of classical Greece.

Being literally compulsive about playing pianos I decided to give the massive instrument in our suite a try. Many that look marvelous as furniture and which in fact are distinguished by beautiful lacquerwork are decidedly inferior as musical instruments.

That is the case at present with pianos manufactured in China. The Japanese, by way of contrast, have thoroughly mastered the art of piano manufacture. My theory about this is that whereas China has traditionally considered itself self-sufficient—even if in fact it never was—and therefore was consciously closed to outside influence, the Japanese have wisely welcomed and absorbed foreign instruction so that their manufacturing expertise is now unequaled in the world. Part of this, oddly, grew out of their accidental association with our World War II enemy, Germany. The Germans had long been experts at producing pianos, beer, lenses, cameras and automobiles. Somehow this all seems to have rubbed off on their axis ally with the striking results now universally recognized. The particular piano I was playing was a Yamaha, a brand name that still makes some Americans smile because they associate the company name with the manufacture of motorcycles and automobile engines. Discussing this during a comedy concert I once said, "It's true that their pianos do drip a little oil, but what the hell."

On our walk through the airport the previous day we had passed a young couple just at the moment that the woman was saying, apparently to her gentleman friend or husband, "Well, I want a Jaguar."

"Okay, baby," her big spender responded, and then we were past them and heard no more. But that brief snippet of conversation floated back into my consciousness at this moment, as a result of which the mysterious part of my brain that cranks out an astonishing volume of new melodies clicked into action with the result that I found myself writing a song called "Baby Wants A Jaguar," which, several months later, would become a feature of my Big Band concert shows.

After a few minutes the richness of the piano's tone and the ease of its key-action gave me a feeling of being at home, at which it occurred to me that we could get rid of the statue of Adonis, the mirror over the bed and a few assorted frills—maybe haul the mattress out onto the living room floor and sleep by the piano, and I might actually survive life here in Vegas. That is, if there weren't any more thermonuclear interruptions.

In the middle of my mental redecoration of the Bacchanalian Suite, the phone rang. Jayne picked it up and I could hear her talking from the bedroom. In a moment, she made the long trek toward where I sat in the sunken living room at my own private piano bar.

"It was Christie. She's invited me to work out with her this morning at the VIP spa on the third floor. Supposedly it's a fitness club that's open only for *very* special guests."

"Around here," I said, "that means anybody with big bucks. But if you want to work out why don't you just invite Christie up here and the two of you can jog a few laps around the bed?"

"Don't be such a smarty-pants," Jayne said, sounding morning-nasal like Myrna Loy in an old *Thin Man* film. "Christie sounded upset. I think she wants to talk about her problems with Michelle and Bobby. That was quite an eye-opener on the boat yesterday. I think that marriage is in trouble."

"Come on, Bobby obviously spoils the girl rotten and totally ignores his son, but he and Christie seem in okay shape. Some people just aren't meant to be parents. In fact, that's one of the world's chief problems. Too damned many people, with no qualifications for the role, becoming parents."

"You know, I sort of *like* poor Michelle," Jayne said. "She's adorable somehow, like a puppy you might find at the pound. Someone just needs to take her under their wing."

"Please, not *our* wing!" I said. Jayne has a habit of adopting strays.

"Now don't be selfish, dear . . . Lord, what's the matter, Steve?"

I had gone pale, I suppose. I was staring straight ahead, lost in thought, and then I looked up to see my wife standing above me, her face full of concern.

"What did you say?"

"Are you all right?"

"Oh, yeah . . . I just remembered something, that's all. I'm fine."

I had to get up and walk around a little to show Jayne I hadn't had a heart attack or a bad reaction to radioactive crenshaw melon. I almost convinced her I was all right, but actually I wasn't. I had just remembered the dream I was having when the nuclear device exploded a hundred and ten miles away to disturb my sleep. The memory of dreams is often beyond our conscious control, but this one came all at once, as if a veil had been parted.

In the dream, after having erotic but unfulfilled designs on an unidentified but highly desirable woman, I was suddenly swimming in an ocean at night and there was a great city on the horizon far away, tall buildings lit with many lights. Unfortunately, I knew exactly where I was, and it was a memory my conscious mind would rather have forgotten. Last year I was on a private yacht which sank in New York harbor off Wall Street, and I had been thrown into the sea—an adventure I chronicled in my book, *Murder In Manhattan*. I had almost drowned in that mishap, but was saved by a helicopter just as I was going down for the third time. I suppose being on Bobby's boat yesterday and seeing Michelle nearly drown had brought back the traumatic memory.

66

But there was more in the dream . . . something awful. I had to think very hard for a moment, and then it came back to me.

In the dream, swimming in the cold water, I all of a sudden came to a bloated corpse floating on the waves. The body was horrible, sloshing on its back, staring up to the night sky with sightless eyes. As I swam closer I saw it was a man—Bobby Hamilton—and there was a red bullet hole in his forehead.

I stood up from the piano so I could walk closer to the window and the warm morning sun.

"You're *not* okay," insisted Jayne, following closely on my heels.

"It's only a dream I remembered." I tried to tell her about it. She could see my night-fantasy was gruesome, disturbing, and that it touched upon that frightening incident off Lower Manhattan where I had nearly died—but what Jayne couldn't understand was that it seemed to me not so much to concern the past as the future, perhaps as a portent of things to come.

"You know, dear, I can't help it, but I have the feeling that Bobby's in trouble. It's as if he's dead."

"Steve, I just talked with his wife—remember? Don't you think she would have mentioned a little thing like her husband being killed?"

"Well, these suites are awfully large," I protested weakly. "Maybe he drowned in his Roman bubble bath and won't be discovered until the slave girls pull the plug."

Jayne took a telephone from the nearby coffee table and plonked it down in front of me. "All right, Edgar Cayce—why don't you give him a call then? Set your mind at rest."

I was able to dial directly to Bobby's penthouse,

the Aphrodite Suite, which was on the top floor of the hotel not far from our own. Wade answered and handed the receiver to his father. I felt pretty foolish.

"Er, hi, Bobby . . . I just wanted to thank you for that wonderful day yesterday on the lake. Jayne and I had a marvelous time."

"You did? Great, we'll do it again soon then. Maybe a dinner cruise in the moonlight."

We talked a few more minutes and I hung up the phone saying I'd see him later in the morning at the rehearsal downstairs. Jayne was giving me an I-told-you-so look.

"Well, darling? Perhaps living here in glorious downtown Rome is getting to you. Beware the Ides of March."

"March I dig," I said, characteristically hiding behind a joke, "but what the hell are the Ides?"

For a man with the uneasy feeling that murder was very, very close I suppose I was being too facetious.

chapter 8

I remember everything that happened during the next few hours with particular clarity, because I was forced to go over it again so many times in my own mind, and with the police.

At about 9:30 A.M., Jayne and I took the elevator together down from the top floor of the hotel. She stepped out onto the third level to meet Christie Hamilton in the VIP spa, and I continued down to the Gladiator Arena for my rehearsal with Bobby. It was Thursday; we were opening Saturday night and the theater was full of activity with everyone getting ready for the show. As I walked into the show-room, I saw the twenty-five long-legged chorus girls standing on the apron of the stage under the work lights, dressed in feathers and plumes and skimpy rhinestone-studded swimsuits, showing off their costumes to someone with a clipboard who kept saying things like, "No, no! She's not supposed to look like an *ostrich!* She's a *girl*, damn it!"

Bobby stood up when he saw me. He had been seated at a table near the orchestra in conference with his son Wade, Fritz the choreographer, Chris Carter, the leader of the orchestra, and a man with curly black hair by the name of David Starr who seemed to be the producer or overseer of this spectacular. I was introduced to one and all. Despite the presence of all these highly-paid experts, Bobby was obviously in charge.

"Steverino, I was just going over the rehearsal schedule," he said. "I didn't figure you'd need any time to rehearse your solo comedy routine at the beginning, so I thought we'd get right to where I bring you back on stage. Okay?"

"Let's do it," I said.

The choreographer clapped his hands together and the chorus girls ran from the stage like a flock of colorful birds in flight. Bobby wanted to run through the two songs we'd be doing together, with me accompanying him on the piano. The first was the 1930s classic ballad, "Imagination," a moody and introspective love song. Chris gave me a chart for the tune in B-flat, and I sat down at the grand piano at the edge of the stage.

The work lights dimmed, and an electrician threw a pale blue light upon us both to set the mood. The James Van Heusen ballad, which has a lovely lyric by Johnny Burke, with whom I had written a few numbers myself, has a rare sweetness and beauty.

Hamilton's basic vocal tone, his sound, was probably no better than that of Frank Sinatra in his prime, Perry Como, Andy Williams or any other smooth-voiced, light baritone. What was relatively unique about him was his ability to convey emotion, an aspect of talent that even many of our better singers have never actually possessed. Ella Fitzgerald, I suppose, would be the classic example. For decades she's been one of America's favorites, and deservedly. Her incredible sense of rhythm, the beauty of her tone, the girlish sweetness of her voice, and her true feeling for jazz made her widely appreciated. But somehow she could never make you cry with her ballad singing. Barbra Streisand, Eydie Gormé, Judy Garland, and a few others do have that mysterious extra emotional something. Sinatra, too, had it when he was young and seemed vulnerable on stage, though in later years he became the professional swinger and lost the early tenderness. But Bobby Hamilton had that magic. When he sang a sad love song, such as this one, you had the feeling that he was not just singing to an audience but thinking aloud about a particular woman.

Bobby did the song so well it brought a chill to the back of my neck. Besides being a great singer, he is an actor too, of course—and there was something about his delivery that reminded me of Hamlet standing center stage and expressing his thoughts. The way he handled the lyric turned the tune into a meditation, a moving soliloquy on love.

We went through the song once, I took a 16-bar piano solo, and then Bobby came in once again on the bridge. He stopped singing abruptly, dangling on an F seventh flat-nine chord that was waiting to resolve. I looked up from the piano to see what was the matter. Bobby was staring at two young Japanese men in royal blue suits who had appeared in the empty theater, standing near the stage. They were expensively dressed. One was thin and tall, the other shorter and slightly overweight. Both had jet black hair and pale, indoor complexions. There was something ominous about these figures. They had cold, stony faces and looked to me like well-dressed thugs. The overweight man had what appeared to be a knife scar across his left cheek. Bobby was clearly agitated by their arrival.

"I'm sorry, Steve . . . would you excuse me a minute? There's something I've got to take care of."

With no further explanation, he walked off the stage to meet the two Japanese. Wade joined the group, and they all conferred in low voices for a moment. Then all four walked out a rear exit of the theater into the hotel.

I looked at my watch. It was 10:17. The incident gave me a strange feeling that was linked to my bad dream, but I told my suspicious mind to behave itself. For all I knew they were going out to get an order of *yakatori* and a few bottles of Kirin beer to wash it down. However, David Starr, the executive, seemed as surprised as I was by Bobby's sudden departure.

"He *never* leaves a rehearsal in the middle like that," he said worriedly. "Bobby's a real pro."

"Maybe it's something personal," I suggested. We stood around uncomfortably for perhaps ten minutes making small talk. Then Chris, the band-leader, suggested that we might use the time to run over the soft-shoe number, which made perfect sense since Bobby and I would be doing the same steps and I was sure I was rustier on them than he was. I sat down at the piano while the musicians looked for the arrangement and put the parts up front on their stands. Two days earlier I had casually noticed a magazine ad for Hidden Valley brand salad dressing, a detail which the lyric-writing part of my brain now worked into the song.

Baby wants a Jaguar;
Baby wants a ring,
And a home in Hidden Valley
Where the bluebirds sing,
And if I just live long enough
I swear to get baby all that stuff.
You'll see—
She can count on me.

In case it seems odd that in the middle of a rehearsal—well, the middle of anything, really—I would get back to work creating a song, I should explain that whether it's right or wrong, that's the way my mind works. Every time there's a vacuum in my daily routine, even if the blank time-space runs only a minute or two, the old machine turns itself on, at which point I either reach for my ever-present pocket-sized tape recorder or head for the piano.

"What's that?" Carter said, having rapped his musicians to attention.

"Just a little number I'm working on," I said. "But I'm ready to do the soft-shoe thing." I started, as planned, at the piano and then after eight bars rose and moved, in rhythm, to downstage center, which we refer to as working "in one." We ran over the number once, then repeated it. I thanked Carter for the much-needed run-through, took a moment to enjoy a glass of cold orange juice, then looked at my watch again.

It was 10:42. Fritz, the choreographer, ambled over and suggested he spend the time working with the dancers, and maybe we could get back to my routine with Bobby later in the afternoon. It seemed a better idea than all of us standing around doing nothing. I stood up from behind the piano, and

73

that's when I noticed a disturbance across the room. To my surprise, it was Jayne, who was rushing toward the stage, dressed in a terrycloth robe. Sensing something wrong, I bounded off the stage and moved to her side.

"What's the matter, dear?"

"Murder," she managed. *"That's* what's the matter!" I saw she was very pale.

"Good God, has Bobby been killed?"

"You had the right premonition . . . wrong victims," said my wife. Then she fainted rather delicately into my waiting arms.

chapter 9

Victims, she had said. I noted the use of the plural, and didn't like it.

I learned the general outline of what had happened within the next half hour, and then over the following days and weeks Jayne filled in the details, often at odd times of the day and night as she was about to put on her make-up, bite into a grapefruit, or get ready for bed. The shock of witnessing violent death lingers; it takes time to talk it through and gradually work it out of your system. From Jayne's various accounts, garnered over time, I am able to offer the following account:

When she left me at the elevator, she walked down the hall and was admitted to the VIP spa by a vibrantly healthy young woman and young man dressed in white gym suits which were bordered with gold trim.

"Hi, I'm Debbie," said the pretty young thing with the toothbrush-fresh smile. "I'll be your hostess today."

"And I'm Ken, your host."

Debbie and Ken were blond and cheerful, and looked as if they could be twins. They were so healthy, polite and good looking—smiling at Jayne with such unflagging good humor—that she was momentarily tempted to pinch them to make certain they were real. Since she was already in her gym suit, she allowed Debbie to lead her past an indoor swimming pool toward the exercise room where she was told Christie and Michelle were waiting for her.

The VIP spa was sumptuously appointed in a neo-classic style and had everything conceivable that an exercise salon might possess—except people working out. Jayne found Christie and Michelle by themselves in a huge room with mirrors, faux Greek columns and rows of gleaming Nautilus machines, treadmills and weight-lifting equipment. The women were in a far corner, side by side on two exercise cycles.

"Hi-ya, honey," Christie called to Jayne. "I was able to convince my lazy daughter to join us."

"Honestly, Mom—this is like *totally* boring," Michelle complained.

"Muffs, you'll find as you grow older that a flat stomach is more important than a college degree."

Apparently neither alternative interested her daughter, who remained silent.

Jayne mounted a third cycle and the three women pedaled their merry way toward their mirrored reflections across the room.

"My God, did you feel the world shake this morning?" asked Michelle. "It reminded me of an orgasm I had once at the Grand Hotel in Rome with . . .

"Michelle!" cried her mother.

"Well, honestly Mom—I mean, I've been mar-

76

ried *three* times. Thank God for sex, at least. I mean, without *that*, I'm not sure it's worth the trouble to get involved."

Jayne tried to tell Michelle that there came a time in every woman's life when companionship took on a good deal of importance.

"Gosh, Jayne—you and Steve must have been married a *zillion* years!"

"Not *quite* a zillion," said Jayne. "It only seems that way, on the bad days."

"Well, I've had it with men," Michelle assured her. "From now on I'm just going to drink instead."

"Honey, I've been wanting to talk to you about that," said her mother, but was interrupted by the arrival of Ken, their handsome host.

"Oh, look what we have *here!*" said Michelle under her breath, her vow to forsake the male gender apparently forgotten in the instant.

"I just wanted to check that everything was all right," said Ken with his eager-to-please smile. "Can I get anyone some carrot juice? Or can I whip up a batch of Slim-Fast banana smoothies?"

"I'll have a martini with olive *and* onion," said Michelle.

"No you *won't*, young lady," said her mother.

Michelle stopped pedaling, wincing in pain. "Oh! *Ouch!* I think I pulled something right here in the small of my back."

Later, when Jayne told me this detail I improvised an instant parody on Cole Porter's "In The Still Of The Night" singing "In the small of my back—while I gaze from my window—as I moon in my flight—"

Jayne told me to knock it off, as she had every right to do.

"It hurts right here," said Michelle, putting her hand on her back, just above the bicycle seat. "I think it's my sanctum."

"You mean sacrum," her mother said.

Trying to retain some degree of professional detachment, Ken put his hand on the sore spot which Michelle had indicated, and probed for anything wrong there.

"Well, I can't feel anything particularly, but perhaps some deep massage . . ."

"Yes!" cried Michelle, jumping off her machine and taking poor Ken by the hand. "Mommy, Ken and I are off to the massage room. I'll see you this afternoon. 'Bye, Jayne!"

"Michelle, don't you dare . . . Michelle, come back here!"

But the wayward daughter was off and running, with a giggle. Ken, who seemed constitutionally incapable of saying no, was dragged from the room by the hand, not quite sure what had hit him.

"I can't deal with this anymore!" cried Christie, bursting into tears the moment her daughter was gone. "You can see what it's like! God, my life is just falling apart . . ."

"There, there," said Jayne. "Why don't you tell me all about it?"

chapter 10

"**L**ord, I'm such a failure, Jayne! My life just seems to add up to a great big zilch—as a parent, a wife, a human being—I'm not even a very good hostess at a party," said Christie Hamilton with a sigh. She thought a moment, and while she was at it decided to list her other faults: "And I can't cook, or play a musical instrument, *or* have a serious conversation about a book. And besides that, I never even followed through and became an actress like I wanted. I've let Bobby support me all these years like I was some big helpless dummy."

"Hold on a moment," said Jayne. "Perhaps you should look at this more closely. As a parent, for instance, you're only *half* the equation. There's your husband to consider, and from what I saw yesterday on Lake Mead, I'd say you're the better half in *that* particular department."

"Oh, I don't know. Wade can't stand me, and Michelle may be spoiled, but she sure as hell is daddy's little girl. They all prefer him to me, I can tell you that."

"Stop it, Christie—you're just making yourself feel bad, and I'm sure it isn't true anyway."

Christie had stopped pedaling her exercise machine. She gave a long, sad sigh. "Anyway, I'm about to ask Bobby for a divorce," she said quietly, staring at her fingernails. "I guess that's what I'm trying to tell you."

Jayne had to stop and take this in. Like a lot of people spilling out their problems, Christie had been going from one thing to another in a stream-of-consciousness release.

"Are you sure you've thought this through?"

Before Christie could answer, the dapper Elliot Block appeared in the doorway. The agent was wearing running shoes, shorts, and had a towel over his shoulder.

"Hi-ya, girls! Losing those inches, are you?"

"More or less," replied Jayne without much warmth. She had never particularly liked Elliot Block; the man was altogether too smooth and oily for her taste—and she did not now want to encourage conversation.

He seemed to feel the icy blast. "Well, ladies, I think I'll hit the sauna and then go for some laps in the pool. Gotta keep my boyish figure so the fair sex will find me desirable!"

"What a jerk!" said Jayne, after Elliot had winked and departed towards the men's sauna with a self-satisfied smirk.

"I *hate* him," said Christie with a sudden passion. "Sometimes I think I'd really like to kill that man!"

"Honestly, Christie, this is really none of my business, but maybe you should begin at the beginning. There must be some way to find a happier

80

solution to your problems than murdering your husband's agent."

"You think so?" asked Christie with only a small smile. "Look, why don't we head on into the sauna, Jayne? I'm such a coward, maybe I can tell you about all this better in the dark."

Debbie, the pretty young hostess, helped Jayne and Christie settle into the ladies sauna, on the wooden benches with towels wrapped around their bodies. Jayne saw no sign of poor Ken and wondered if Michelle had eaten him alive.

The sauna was a large pine-paneled vault, dimly lit with a small protected yellow bulb overhead and a tiny window in the thickly insulated door at the far end. The heat was dry and painful, burning to the nostrils. Jayne put on a sleep mask and sat with her feet tucked beneath her body on the slanted wooden bench, feeling herself relax. Christie sat across the sauna on a bench of her own.

"Did you ever see me on *Spy, My Lovely?*" she asked. "I was pretty good in that old show, don't you think?"

"Of course you were!" said Jayne. "And what a lovely figure you had, too!"

Spy, My Lovely was a hit TV series in the Sixties on which Christie had a small part—she was the lovely, in fact, but the two male co-stars carried most of the action. Talking about the old show brought a happy vibrancy into Christie's voice.

"Lord, I was twenty years old, Jayne—how can I have been so young? I know it wasn't really a very *good* show, but we had such fun making it every week, and I felt I had my whole life ahead of me. I planned to be a big star—I was very ambitious. And the offers were beginning to pour in. Did you know

I was considered for the part of Bonnie in *Bonnie and Clyde?*"

"No, I didn't know that, Christie."

"Well, I was. Arthur Penn, the director, had me read for it twice, but then Bobby asked me to marry him, and, of course, that was an offer I couldn't refuse, so there went my acting career. Faye Dunaway got the part in the movie and *she* went on to be an enormous star!"

"Didn't Bobby want you to continue working?"

"Well, he didn't say so in so many words, but he arranged our lives so that it was fairly impossible. I mean, the first thing he did was take us on a three-month trip around the world for our honeymoon. He was awfully sweet to do it, and we did have a wonderful time—but I had to quit my series, of course, and tell Arthur Penn I wouldn't be able to do the screen test for *Bonnie and Clyde*. At the time, you see, I was madly in love and it seemed, well . . . that Bobby had a big enough career for both of us."

"But when you returned from your honeymoon, surely you could have gotten back in the swing of things," suggested Jayne.

"Oh, it's all my own fault, I suppose, like everything else," said Christie. "At first it was so much fun being Mrs. Bobby Hamilton I didn't *want* to do anything else—there were three houses to run, in Beverly Hills and Palm Springs and Malibu, and parties to give, and premieres to attend . . . and, well, there didn't seem to be *time* to call up my agent and go to auditions. A few years went by like that, and pretty soon everyone forgot all about my little role on *Spy, My Lovely* . . . you know how it is, Jayne. I let my magic moment pass me by. In Hollywood, they don't very often let you grab the golden ring a second time."

"Tell me about it," Jayne said. "My God, when I married Steve, I gave up everything. I'd had a Broadway career, worked with Kirk Douglas and Richard Widmark when we were all just kids starting out. Pandro Berman brought me to Hollywood and I had one marvelous part after another—worked with David Niven, Robert Montgomery, Ty Power, Gregory Peck. . . ."

"And Steve stopped all that?"

"Oh, no," Jayne said. "I got involved in a very foolish marriage, to a man almost twice my age, and when that fell apart I walked away from Hollywood and went back to Broadway. I hadn't even met Steve at that time. At first I had marvelous luck. Mark Goodson signed me for what turned out to be a seven-year stretch as a panelist on the *"I've Got A Secret"* show, and I did all the great dramatic series. But then I met Steve, we got married, and it was like what you were just describing. I was so busy being Mrs. Steve Allen, helping him get *The Tonight Show* off the ground, giving parties, doing publicity, raising kids, that—well, we can talk about me some other time. I just wanted you to know that you're not the only woman in the business who has problems of that sort. But Christie, you've got to be realistic; there couldn't possibly have been any guarantee that even if you had stuck with your career it would all have been a bed of roses for you."

"Oh, I know that! And I really feel horrid complaining about my life," cried Christie. "Probably I wasn't even a very *good* actress, and wouldn't have gotten very far at all—but at least I would have known for sure. As it is, I've just been bored. And boredom, you know . . . well, idle hands have a way of getting into trouble."

Jayne waited. She had a feeling she would momentarily hear what this trouble might be. And indeed it came.

"Jayne, did you ever take drugs?"

"No," Jayne said. "Well, wait a minute. There was one time, at a party at Irving Lazar's, where I suddenly realized that almost every other woman in the room was smoking a marijuana cigarette, and suddenly Sue Mengers—you know, the agent—offered me one, just to be polite. I felt devilish at the moment so I accepted it. 'Well, my God,' Sue said. 'I never thought I'd live to see the day that Jayne Meadows would smoke pot. The funny thing was, it didn't affect me at all."

"Really?"

"Not at all," she said, "Oh, I just remembered one other time. Steve and I were in Jamaica for a week, as the guests of our friend, Lyle Stuart—the publisher—and I came down with a terrible cold, or flu, whatever. Lyle's black housekeeper told me that if I just drank some *ganja*, that would clear it up. I guess that's the Jamaican word for marijuana. Anyway she made up this big mess of tea and I drank gallons of it. It did seem to help with the cold but otherwise had literally zero effect on me."

"What a drag," Christie said.

"Oh, no," Jayne said. "To me life itself has always seemed so interesting and stimulating that I've just never seen the point of artificial additives."

"Well, you're lucky. For me, life—especially married life, began to seem very *un*interesting and I gobbled up all the 'additives' I could find. Uppers, downers, pot, booze . . . and recently, cocaine."

"Christie! I had no idea—why, you poor thing! But I'm sure your ability to talk about it now is a good sign. And if you're ready to change your life, there are some very good places you can go for help."

"Oh, I've been so stupid!" she cried. "It isn't only drugs. Looking for something to fill up my life—*anything*, I suppose—I've been, well . . . having affairs. You know how it is—a secret romance can give you the illusion you're still young and having fun."

"Does Bobby know about this?"

"God, no! I can't tell you how guilty I feel. Of course, Bobby has his own problems, particularly with the children, but he really *is* the sweetest husband you can ever imagine. It certainly isn't *his* fault I'm bored. He has an absolutely fascinating career and probably wouldn't even understand what I'm talking about. And that's why I've decided I have to leave him."

"But Christie, have you tried talking to him at least? Perhaps together you can work out some solution."

"Oh, Jayne, he'll talk me out of it if I let him. From his point of view we have a good marriage! But I feel if I don't get away and somehow stand on my own two feet I'm just going to die."

"Well, of course only you can decide that. Would you try to pick up your acting career again?"

"Oh, I don't know. Maybe. I just want a job, *any* job that's useful. You're going to laugh, but I've been thinking of working at a daycare center in East Los Angeles for homeless children."

"Why, I think that's a marvelous idea, Christie, but you don't have to get a divorce to do it."

"I only want to be able to get out of bed in the morning and feel my life is useful to *somebody*. I want to leave my mark somewhere—I don't want to spend the rest of my life being only Mrs. Bobby Hamilton, bored celebrity wife!"

"Darling, I understand exactly what you're going through," said Jayne. "I'm only suggesting that after twenty-five years of marriage, you should talk it over with your husband first."

"You mean, tell him everything? Even about the affairs?"

"I don't know about that, but at this point what do you have to lose, Christie? Maybe Bobby will be more understanding than you think. You could end up running the daycare center in East L.A. and have a better marriage because of it."

"The problem is, he'll be *too* understanding, Jayne. That's what I'm afraid of—he'll talk me into staying, and then I'll be lost forever—don't you see?"

Jayne could see that there was a lot to unravel here, a backlog of years. She was about to suggest that Christie seek professional help, a marriage counselor perhaps, when she thought she heard the door to the sauna open and close.

"Debbie? Is that you?" asked Jayne, thinking it must be the hostess.

There was no reply.

Jayne started speaking rapidly to rid herself of a very spooky feeling. "Anyway, my dear, I think what you are going through is quite understandable, and with some professional help. . . . Christie, are you all right?"

Jayne heard a soft gurgling sound, and she was almost certain she heard the sauna door open and close one more time. She had to fight against a rising panic.

"Christie?" Jayne pulled off her sleep mask to darkness so thick it was nearly a tangible thing, like being underwater. She stood, crossed toward Christie's bench, groping about with her hands. Inch by inch—dreading what she might find—she felt her way along the smooth surface of the wood. When she came across an inert leg, she was so startled she backed away in shock.

"Oh, *there* you are," she said, laughing at her own fear. "Poor dear, I thought you'd fainted from the heat."

This is what Jayne *wanted* to imagine, at least. She reached out once again and felt the leg, a towel-covered thigh, and slowly her hand traced upward over the unconscious form, until coming to a cord wrapped tightly about Christie's neck. It had been pulled with such vigorous force that Christie's neck seemed broken, with her head lying to one side at an impossible angle.

Jayne loosened the cord, though she knew it was too late. Her heart was racing. "Oh, *dear!*" she said. It was impossible to fool herself any longer into thinking this was a faint—Christie Hamilton had been murdered.

Jayne forced herself to take a few deep breaths. She told herself it would do absolutely no good to scream and carry on. *I must remain absolutely calm and find a way out of this nightmare*, she told herself firmly.

She stood up and moved slowly, with her hands held out in front of her body, toward where she thought the door must be. She succeeded in walking into a wall, but very rationally reminded herself that there were four walls here, and though this was a fairly large sauna, if she moved along the wall she must eventually come to the door. After a long minute, Jayne had the doorknob in her hand.

Now came the moment of truth. For the past few minutes she had been fighting the dreadfully claustrophobic notion that perhaps she was locked in this sauna with a corpse, the heat turned up full blast. It seemed to her she had seen a James Bond movie with a scene like this. Hours later, she might be found, cooked like a chicken in a pot.

But Jayne was not to be stewed; the door swung open easily at her push, and she stepped out into the hall.

Standing outside the sauna, she could see that the VIP spa lay in darkness, except for an eerie turquoise light coming from around the corner of the hall, sending a shimmer of moving refractions against the walls. Jayne walked cautiously toward the strange glow, not making a sound—reminding herself that whoever had wrapped the cord around Christie's neck might still be nearby.

When Jayne passed around the corner, she saw that the light was coming from beneath the surface of the indoor swimming pool, which apparently had somehow escaped the power failure. After a few more steps, she stopped abruptly.

Floating face down on the surface of the pool—outlined by the glowing turquoise water—was Debbie, the pretty young hostess, no longer so healthy or full of life. Blood was flowing from the back of her head into the water, streaming the pool with graceful swirls of red.

Jayne had reached her limit; two murders in one morning was rather a lot. She permitted herself a good loud scream.

chapter 11

Back in the Arena, Jayne drank a glass of water while I hovered anxiously above her.

"I think I should call a doctor to look at you," I worried.

"But *you* look at me just fine, darling," insisted my Jayne, scorning yet adoring the fuss I was making over her. She seemed quite pale. "I feel so badly about poor Christie and that nice young girl . . . so young to die, both of them."

The hotel security people had been alerted, and we were waiting for the arrival of the Metropolitan police. The security force of a big Las Vegas hotel is like a small army, and the theater had filled up with muscular men wearing dark green blazers who kept talking rather importantly into walkie-talkies—as if that would help matters any.

"Someone should try to find Bobby Hamilton and his son, Wade," I suggested. "You might try their suite upstairs, or the casino, or even the different bars."

"Which bar was he going to, Mr. Allen?" asked

a hefty gray-haired man who seemed to be the chief Green Blazer.

"I was just using that as an example. He could be anywhere!"

"Then why did you say he went to a bar?"

"I didn't say he went to bar—I said he left here with two Japanese guys more than forty-five minutes ago, and *someone* should try to find him."

"Can you describe these Japanese men, sir?"

"Well, they were in their mid-twenties, and they wore rather expensive-looking blue suits, and they were, well . . . *Japanese*. I saw them for only a moment."

"Were they American-Japanese, or the real McCoy from across the sea?"

"We didn't stop to discuss geography."

This was becoming frustrating. I'm sure hotel security was great when dealing with drunks and card sharks and guarding the gamblers' money lying around in the back rooms, but a murder investigation was quite another matter. Bobby needed to be located fast; I decided to enlist Cass's help.

"Jayne, I'm going to find a telephone. Why don't you let me call a doctor for you at the same time?"

"Steve, stop worrying about me and just find Bobby and Wade. They could be in trouble."

"Yes, somehow I feel they are," I agreed.

I found a phone on a worktable near the apron of the stage and dialed the operator downstairs. "Hello, this is Steve Allen—I'm trying to locate my chauffeur, Jimmy Cassidy. Do you think you could page him in the casino? . . . Yes, I'll hold on."

After waiting more than five minutes, I was beginning to despair that Cass was in the casino after all. But then I heard his voice, and he was just where I suspected all the time: "Steve, you interrupted a mighty serious baccarat game!"

"Cass, this is more important. I don't have time to tell you all the details now, but Christie Hamilton and a spa attendant have been murdered—and Bobby and Wade are missing. What I want you to do is check at the front of the hotel with the bellboys and parking valets and find out if anyone saw Bobby leave the hotel."

"Will do," said Cass, hanging up the phone. He may sometimes appear the flakiest chauffeur east of Beverly Hills, but when things get serious and you really need him, he comes through.

"Well, well, up to your eyeballs in murder again, are you, Mr. Allen?" came a weary voice from behind me.

I turned around and couldn't quite believe my eyes: There in front of me was the familiar short, round and thoroughly rumpled figure of Sergeant W.B. Walker of the Burbank police. The sergeant was gazing at me with the suspicious and unhappy eyes of a cop who had seen too many bad things. He was wearing the same wrinkled brown suit I remembered from years before, a suit that always managed to look as if it had been slept in for a week.

"Good God, it's Sergeant Walker!" I cried, quite stunned—for I had not seen him for at least three years. "What in the world brings you to Vegas?"

"If you don't mind, it's *Lieutenant* Walker these days, Mr. Allen," he replied grumpily. "And if you have to know, I transferred here two years ago to the Metropolitan homicide squad."

"But how could you tear yourself away from Burbank?"

"I was seeking a new life style," he said with a shrug.

I had to laugh. Sergeant Walker . . . excuse me, *Lieutenant* Walker has a gloomy, deadpan attitude which really kills me—if you can say that sort of thing about a homicide inspector. Unfortunately, he did not seem as pleased to see me as I was to see him. I should mention that he had been assigned to a murder case in Burbank some years back, and I—well, I actually beat him to the punch, poor guy, solving the mystery first. I don't think he ever forgave me for that.

"I hope like hell you're not going to start playing amateur detective again," said W.B. "If you do, warn me at least—maybe I'll get myself transferred to a traffic detail somewhere."

"Hey, as a team, I thought we did pretty good on that last case."

"As a team, we stank," said W.B. "Now you'd better tell me about this new corpse of yours."

"Actually, it's Jayne's corpse," I told him modestly. "And it's plural, *corpses*—though I think we can assume the spa hostess was killed so someone could get at Christie."

"*I'll* do all the assuming if you don't mind," said Lieutenant Walker, and then turned to face Jayne. "So, Mrs. Allen, he has *you* finding bodies now too, I see. Is this some sort of family hobby or something?"

"Lieutenant, I can assure you this is not my idea of a good time," Jayne said.

"Well, you'd better tell me about it then," said the policeman, sitting down backwards on a chair, as if he were straddling a horse.

Jayne repeated her story, and this time more of

the details were flushed out in her account. I learned, for instance, that Elliot Block had come into the spa and was last seen headed into the men's sauna—a detail Jayne hadn't mentioned the first time around.

"Maybe he's still there," I suggested. "Someone should check to see if he's all right."

W.B. gave an exasperated sigh. "*Mister* Allen, I think the police have the situation under control." Still, the lieutenant summoned a uniformed cop to his side with an imperious wave of his right hand. "Officer, take another man and see if there's anyone in the men's sauna at the crime site upstairs. If not, put out an A.P.B. on this fellow Elliot Block. Can you give me a description, please, Mrs. Allen."

"You can tell by his laugh that he's not to be trusted."

"Mrs. Allen, please; I'm looking for his physical appearance."

"He's about six foot one with silver hair, in his late fifties," I put in. "He's trim and in good shape for his age—the kind of older man who looks like he plays a lot of tennis."

"You got that, Officer?" asked W.B. to the uniformed cop at his side. "Now, Mrs. Allen, let's get back to the murder. You say you were actually sitting in the sauna next to Mrs. Hamilton when it happened, is that right?"

"I was sitting *across* from her, Lieutenant—on the bench facing her."

"And how close was she to you?"

"Three, or four feet," said Jayne.

"And you were closest to the sauna door?"

"No, Christie was closer to the door. Didn't I tell you that?"

Lieutenant Walker shook his head. "This is

crazy, Mrs. Allen. You were three, or four feet away—surely you must have seen the killer."

"But I didn't," said Jayne. "It was quite dark in there. And I had a sleep mask on. I was just relaxing."

"It was dark you say? Then how did the killer find the victim? You see my problem? This doesn't make a whole lot of sense, if you'll pardon my saying so."

"Look, Lieutenant, my wife has been through a terrible experience. And if you don't mind—"

"Mr. Allen, *please,* let me do my job. Now, Mrs. Allen, I want you to answer a simple question. How could someone find Christie Hamilton in the dark and murder her? The killer might have gotten *you* instead."

"Jayne, do you want to lie down for a while? You can answer these questions later."

"No, I'm all right, dear. And I've been thinking about this, of course. Here's a possibility—the killer came into the VIP spa and looked through the window of the sauna when the lights were still on, and he got our positions fixed in his mind. It would be easy—once he knew Christie was on one side and me on the other, it wouldn't be at all hard to find her in the dark. Then this—this vile person somehow turned off the power, took care of Debbie the hostess, and then returned to the sauna to kill Christie. If . . . well, I suppose I shouldn't say that."

"Say what, Mrs. Allen?"

"This may be speaking out of turn, but *if* Elliot Block were the killer, it would have been quite simple for him to arrange everything."

"Murder is rarely simple," said Lieutenant Walker with a gloomy smile. "But Mr. Block will

94

certainly have some explaining to do when we find him. Now—"

"There's a phone call for Mr. Allen," said one of the hotel security people, coming over.

I excused myself and took the call at the work-table where I had talked before. It was Cass.

"Steve, I talked with one of the doormen outside the hotel—he's one of those guys all dressed up like a Roman soldier, in a miniskirt and everything."

"A tunic," I corrected.

"Whatever," said Cass. "Anyway, the guy said he saw Bobby and Wade Hamilton get into a white Lincoln Continental limousine with two Japanese dudes, and they all drove off together going north on The Strip."

I told Cass he had done a good job and returned to where Lieutenant Walker was making Jayne go over her story a third time. There must have been something about my expression that made W.B. turn from Jayne to me.

"Well?" he asked. "Anything interesting?"

"It's peculiar, at least," I said. I told him about Bobby, Wade, and the two Japanese leaving the hotel in a Lincoln Continental. "I have a bad feeling about this, W.B. For the life of me, I can't imagine Bobby walking out of a rehearsal like that and just driving away without telling anybody—unless he was under some kind of pressure. What if he's been kidnapped? I think we should—"

"*We* should do nothing!" warned W.B. "Leave this matter to the police, Mr. Allen, okay?"

I was about to say something sarcastic, but changed my mind. I was depressed about the two murders, but Walker was right. This was not my battle.

"Believe me, W.B., I came to Vegas to entertain, not get myself involved in a murder investigation," I told him. "Just make sure Bobby and Wade are okay, and you'll get nothing but cooperation from me."

"Yeah, sure," Walker said, giving me a skeptical look. I couldn't imagine why he didn't believe me.

chapter 12

Jayne, Cass and I sat on a pink sofa in the sunken living room of our penthouse suite watching the first reports of Christie Hamilton's death on television.

"She was too young . . . too young," said Cass, with a sad shake of his head. "Damn, this rattles me, man. It really offends my sense of justice."

Offended or not, Cass was lounging with his feet up on the coffee table, demolishing a turkey sandwich on a plate that was balanced on his stomach. I too, was becoming more depressed now that the reality of Christie's death was sinking in, driven home by the attractive young newswoman on the TV screen who was talking self-importantly about the murder, somehow managing to disguise the fact that the police knew almost nothing, and she knew even less. In order to fill airtime in this vacuum of hard fact, the station showed a film clip of Christie from her old series *Spy, My Lovely*, in which she was wearing a miniskirt and looking so pretty it was enough to break your heart.

"Steve, I'm counting on you to help catch the monster who did this," said Jayne, who had been unaccustomedly silent.

"Me?" I cried. "You heard what W.B. said—we're supposed to keep out of this."

"It just seems so unfair," said Jayne. "Christie had her problems, but she was about to make a fresh start. *That's* what makes me so angry—her life wasn't ready to end. She was just beginning! And, of course, that's doubly true for that poor young girl, Debbie."

"Don't you worry—we'll find the guy who did this, Mrs. Allen," said Cass. "Ole' W.B. Walker don't know nothin' if he thinks Steve is gonna keep out of this investigation!"

"Now hold on, Cass," I said. "I meant exactly what I told W.B.—I've come to Vegas to do a show, if we still *have* a show, and that's exactly what I'm planning to do. As for a murder investigation, I'm leaving that to the police."

"But, darling," Jayne said, "Aren't you curious—"

"Of course I'm curious," I told her.

The doorbell to the suite rang. Cass rose from the sofa to see who it was, taking his sandwich along. Lieutenant W.B. Walker walked in, giving Cass's turkey sandwich a brief though lustful scan.

"Some spread," he said, tearing his eyes away from the food long enough to take in our penthouse. "Mind if I look around a little?"

"Go ahead," I said.

W.B. wasn't the kind of man to smile. He cast us only a brief mournful glance, then made a quick but thorough survey of our living quarters, poking his head into various closets and bathrooms. He even got on his hands and knees and peered underneath our emperor-sized bed, God knows why. I guess cops always expect the worst. At last Lieutenant W.B. Walker, in his wrinkled brown suit, strolled back into the living room and settled himself on a dainty pink love seat opposite our sofa.

"So tell me, Mrs. Allen," he said with a heavy sigh, "what did you have against Christie Hamilton?"

"Nothing at all, Lieutenant—what do you mean?"

W.B. leaned forward on the love seat; I was afraid the little chair might break beneath his weight. "You think maybe she was getting too chummy with your hubby, was that it?" he asked with a conspiratorial nod.

"I hope you're kidding," I said, angrily.

"Sure I am," he said. "But Mrs. Allen, you were right there when the murder happened, so make it easy on yourself and tell me the whole truth."

"She *is* telling you the truth," I said.

"Fine, then let's go over her story one more time. Okay?"

There was nothing to do but to tell it again. Jayne repeated the story she had told downstairs, recounting once again every detail. W.B. listened carefully, folding his arms across his vast stomach. I couldn't help but notice, however, that his attention shifted briefly as Cass devoured the last bite of his sandwich, licking his fingers to clean off any excess mayonnaise. W.B. was visibly moved.

"Are you hungry, Lieutenant?" I asked. "I could call room service and order you a snack."

"No thanks," he said curtly. And then added: "I'm on a God damn diet."

"Why, that's wonderful!" said Jayne.

"What's wonderful about it?" said the lieutenant. "Now where the hell were we?"

I knew we were in trouble—a grouchy cop on a diet was not a fun figure to do business with. Jayne continued the retelling of her experiences in the sauna. W.B. didn't seem pleased.

"What about Elliot Block?" I interrupted at last, unable to hold back any longer. "You're going on and on about Jayne, but where was *he* when this was going on? And where was Michelle, for that matter?"

W.B. gave me a heavy-lidded look. "The girl's still missing, but at least we've located the agent," he said. "It seems Block only spent a few minutes in the men's sauna when he remembered some important business he had to take care of upstairs—a phone call coming in from Tokyo at 10:30 concerning a tour of Japan that he's arranging for Mr. Hamilton for next Spring. Block's story is he forgot all about the call until he was actually in the sauna—then something about bathing reminded him of Japan, and he had to make a fast dash up to his room on the twenty-third floor to find his notes before the call came."

"And you checked with the hotel operator about this alleged call, I presume?"

"Naturally. The alleged call, as you put it, was placed person-to-person from Tokyo, and the phone company has it logged from 10:31 to 11:05. That gives Elliot an alibi for the time of the murder."

"Wait a minute," I objected. "This seems like a pretty shaky alibi to me. For example, what if the caller from Tokyo spoke to someone who only *pretended* to be Elliot Block? A stranger from Japan wouldn't recognize his voice."

"Sorry," said the lieutenant, "But the hotel operator recognized Elliot's voice. You see, Mr. Block has been keeping the operators busy with these calls to Japan for the past week now—sometimes there are four or five of them a day—so the operators know him."

"I still find that a little hard to believe, W.B.— this hotel has nearly two thousand rooms, and with all the calls coming in and out, surely an operator isn't going to recognize one particular voice."

"You don't think so? Well, I didn't say Mr. Block has a *perfect* alibi, but it's an alibi nonetheless. Meanwhile, we're cross-checking with the person he claims to have been talking with in Tokyo."

"Good. Suppose for a moment we accept this overseas phone call as an alibi," I said. "Elliot might have killed Christie earlier, say at 10:20, and *still* had time to make it to the twenty-third floor by 10:31."

"But the murder didn't happen at 10:20—it happened at 10:30—at just the time Elliot has himself covered for."

"How the hell do you know the murder was committed at 10:30?" I asked heatedly, for I didn't like the neatness of Elliot's alibi. "Jayne certainly wasn't wearing a metal watch in that hot sauna, and I doubt if even the medical examiner can give you the time of death within ten minutes."

"That's true, sir. But an electric clock on the wall was stopped at 10:27. That's the time the power went off in the VIP spa. Say three minutes went by before Christie was murdered—10:30 seems a good estimate of the time of death."

"But look, W.B., the killer could have changed the hands of the clock after the power was out to deliberately mislead us. I think I saw something like that in a movie once. And by the way, what *about* the power? How did somebody turn off everything in that area except the swimming pool light?"

"Simple—the spa has its own circuit breaker near the entrance. Anyone with any familiarity with the place would have known where it was and how to turn it off. As for the pool light—that's on a separate power grid, along with the pool heater and pump."

I scowled, deep in thought. "You know, this doesn't sound so simple to me. In fact, the whole thing seems very professional and well-planned—the careful timing, the way the power was turned off. . . . I wouldn't be surprised if this turns out to be a mob hit."

"You've been seeing too many movies, Mr. Allen. *If* Mrs. Allen didn't do it, my bet is it's going to turn out to be the husband—just like ninety percent of these homicides do."

Both Jayne and I both exploded at this unfair accusation. It was ridiculous enough to imagine Jayne as a suspect—but Bobby Hamilton! We vouched for Bobby's great love for his wife and his basic decency as a human being—and besides that, Bobby was last seen leaving the hotel in a white Lincoln Continental and still hadn't been found.

"You know, W.B.—this *could* be a mob hit," I told him again. "But not just any mob. We may be dealing with Japanese criminals here—after all, Bobby was seen leaving the hotel with two Japanese thugs, and Elliot's alibi for the time of the killing is he's on the phone to Tokyo. Add all that up and maybe we have some secret Ninja sect trying to get a foothold in Vegas. The Mafia has lost a lot of its old monopolies, you know."

I finally succeeded in getting a brief, sad smile

out of Lieutenant Walker. "I guess you're trying to be funny," was all he said.

The phone rang and I picked it up. "It's for you," I told him, passing the receiver.

"Walker here . . . yeah, I see," he said into the receiver. "Did anyone get hurt? . . . So where the hell is she now?" The lieutenant sighed. "All right, keep your pants on—I'll get there right away."

"What is it?"

"Rich people!" he growled, slamming down the phone. "This time it's the daughter, Michelle. God, what a family, these Hamilton's—she just tried to gun down one of the biggest hoods in Vegas."

"My goodness, who?"

"Well, uh, actually it was a Japanese hood . . . a guy by the name of Johnny Nakamura."

"Ah-ha!" I said, with only a hint of triumph.

The lieutenant muttered something under his breath. He stood up from the pink love seat and was about to dive out the door, but at the last minute he turned toward us.

"Well, what the hell—why don't you two come along? You might find this interesting."

Jayne and I didn't need a second invitation.

chapter 13

Cass drove Lieutenant Walker, Jayne and me northward on The Strip towards downtown Vegas in the burgundy-colored limo, while the lieutenant's driver followed in their unmarked police car.

It was midafternoon, and in the bright sunlight the city seemed somewhat shabby and devoid of glamor. I was reminded of a theater with the work lights turned on above the stage, revealing things too obviously as they were. By daylight, the Las Vegas Strip seemed absurd and derelict, with wide stretches of barren earth separating the hotels, the ground strewn with broken glass, papers and garbage. Outside the car window, I saw groups of grim-faced gamblers shuffling from one casino to another, clutching plastic cups full of change for the slots and wearing dark glasses and sun visors to protect them from the glare of daylight. These pale pedestrians seemed anxious to return quickly into the permanent night of the gambling halls.

W.B. directed Cass up Fremont Street to the Lucky Horseshoe casino, which was standing between an adult bookstore advertising a 25-cent Peeporama, and the Blue Belle Wedding Chapel, which featured 24-hour "credit weddings." I found myself briefly wondering what kind of people get married at three o'clock in the morning in Las Vegas, and pay for it later with interest—maybe for the rest of their lives. The thought was depressing.

The Lucky Horseshoe was a low two-story building trying to look like an old-fashioned Western saloon. There was a covered wooden sidewalk and a painted wooden Indian standing by the main door. On the outside facade, a high neon blaze of lights announced this was "the best li'l' old casino in Nevada," and a big sign below that showed a grizzly old prospector driving a team of horses that were pulling a wagon full of gold. The prospector was grinning like crazy, pleased that he had won big bucks at the Lucky Horseshoe. A brightly lit marquee facing Fremont Street told people they were welcome to cash their social security checks inside, free of charge, and that there was a $3.99 N.Y. Steak-Snow Crab Chuck Wagon Special served every evening between two and 6 A.M. in the Jackpot Coffee Shoppe. I reminded myself that this authentic piece of the Old West was now apparently owned by the Japanese.

"So who's Johnny Nakamura?" I asked. "Is he the proprietor of this honky-tonk?"

"He's the grandson of the owner, but the old patriarch mostly stays home in Yokohama and lets the kids run the day-to-day business," said W.B. "The Nakamuras have been buying up some of the older casinos downtown and refurbishing them— they're not really big time players yet on the Vegas scene, but they're ambitious. The Japanese have been flirting with this town for a while."

"You said Johnny Nakamura was a hood," I reminded him.

"Yeah, but there's nothing we can prove. We think the real estate is bought with laundered money from the Asian heroin trade, but that's even harder to prove with foreign gangsters than with home-grown scum. There's been talk Johnny's skimming the profits off the slot machines to avoid American taxes, but we can't nail him down. A few people mysteriously disappeared who might have testified against him. To tell the truth, it's a pity the Hamilton girl missed."

"W.B.!" said Jayne disapprovingly.

"Sorry, Mrs. Allen, but being a cop can make a guy a little cynical. Anyway, wait 'til you meet this guy—he looks like he's seen too many American gangster movies."

We left Cass at the curb and walked into the nether world of the casino. I noticed the blackjack dealers were older here than those you'd find in other hotels and some of the cocktail waitresses could have been grandmothers—but beyond that, there was the same green felt and flashing lights that made you feel it was always Saturday night.

We walked through an aisle of crap tables to the Cactus Hole Bar where the shooting had happened. Michelle was seated at a table with a sullen pout on her pretty face, staring off into some distant space that seemed far, far away. The girl wore a lacy white shift with black tights underneath; her shaggy blonde hair was partially obscuring her eyes and looked as if she had just gotten out of bed. There were two uniformed cops on either side of her and various members of the casino's security force. Across the table from Michelle was a handsome young Japanese man in a white linen suit who was eating a plate of raw *sashimi* with chopsticks. The young man had jet black hair slicked back from his forehead, reminding me somewhat of an oriental version of Robert Taylor. A *sushi* chef was standing at attention by his side, ready to do his master's bidding.

One of the uniformed cops hurried over to Lieutenant Walker and handed him a snub-nosed revolver. "This is what the girl used—a .38. She took two shots at Johnny, but she's not exactly the marksman of the year—one of the bullets shattered that mirror over there, and the second one whacked into a slot machine."

"Has the girl said why she did it?"

"Not a word," said the uniformed cop. "She's just been sitting there like she's catatonic or something."

W.B. led the way towards the table, with Jayne and me close behind. The young Japanese man who reminded me of Robert Taylor rose to meet us, but Michelle only continued to stare straight ahead.

"Lieutenant Walker-*san*, you do me a great honor to visit my casino. Would you care for some raw tuna?"

"Can it," said W.B. gruffly. "Now what the hell's going on here, Johnny? Why did this young lady try to gun you down?"

"Golly, I can't imagine," said Johnny Nakamura, sitting down again and casually crossing his legs. He smiled sarcastically. "Maybe she's in love with me."

Johnny snapped the fingers of his right hand,

and an extremely large Japanese man appeared instantly at his side—a guy almost as big as a Sumo wrestler—and offered a cigarette from a gold case. Nakamura was clearly a man used to the more arrogant trappings of wealth and power; he took the cigarette with a soft, well-manicured hand and put it to his lips. The wrestler produced a gold lighter and held the flame until the cigarette was lit. Johnny inhaled smoke, blew a cloud toward Lieutenant Walker, and the enormous Japanese man bowed and disappeared into the shadows. As I studied Nakamura, I saw his cold eyes turn my way, and he returned my stare with interest, as if he could not decide what to make of me, or why I had made an appearance in his world. He seemed about to say something to me, but then Michelle screamed and all our concentration turned to her.

"No!" she shrieked, apparently answering some question W.B. had put to her. "I don't remember! I don't want to talk about it!"

"Is this your gun? We'll soon find out, of course," said Lieutenant Walker, but Michelle pressed her lips together and would not answer. "Talk to me, Michelle—where did you go when you left the VIP spa? I'm waiting for your answer, young lady!"

After her single outburst, Michelle retreated into herself and refused to say a word. Her lips were pressed so tightly together they were pale and bloodless, but as I watched, a single tear squeezed out of the corner of her left eye and rolled down her cheek. This was too much for Jayne, who rushed forward and took Michelle in her arms.

"You poor thing!" Jayne said.

With such encouragement, Michelle burst into

tears. The two women spent some time making feminine noises.

W.B. turned to me. "Jeez, it's not exactly like Michelle's some blushing schoolgirl," he complained. "The chick just tried to murder someone."

"Perhaps she had good reasons," I suggested.

"Yeah? Well, that's exactly what I'm trying to find out. Look here, young lady," he said again sternly, turning his attentions back to Michelle. "You can tell me about this here, the easy way, or I can take you to the police station and sweat it out of you. Now what's it going to be?"

Michelle turned mutely to Jayne for support. "There, there," said Jayne. "I don't want to worry you, but your father and brother are still missing, and anything you can tell us will be a great help."

The girl wiped the tears from her cheeks with the back of her hand and peered reluctantly at Lieutenant Walker.

"Well," she began in a small voice. "I was at the spa with my mother and Jayne, you know. And then I met this fantastic guy—I mean, he had these very kind, sensitive eyes I felt I could really relate to."

"Look, kid—you can skip the part about Romeo's eyes," said the lieutenant.

"Well, I wouldn't want you to think I invite just any guy up to my room—but this time I thought it was something special. So Richard and I . . . I *think* his name was Richard . . ."

"Ken," said Jayne softly. "His name was Ken, dear."

"That's right! Anyway, Ken and I went up to my room, and well, I'm not the kind of girl to go into details—"

"Thank God for that," Walker said. "Just tell

109

me how long you were up in your room with this bozo."

"How long? I don't know."

"Gimme a ball park estimate," said an increasingly irritated lieutenant.

"Well, one hour, maybe. Or it could have been fifteen minutes. How the hell should I know?"

"Kid, I definitely hope we never have to put you on a witness stand," sighed W.B. "Anyway, what happened next?"

"Well, Ken was afraid he'd get fired if I kept him any longer, so he left, and I took a shower, and then I got dressed. . . . And then I got this like totally wonderful idea."

"Yeah?" said W.B. with encouragement. He seemed to feel he was about to hit paydirt. "What was your wonderful idea, Michelle?"

"Well, I thought I'd go back to the spa and find Ken, and maybe suggest he take the day off, and maybe we could do something special like go to the zoo and look at the penguins—that is, if they *have* any goddamn penguins in this town, which I seriously doubt. But then I got off the elevator at the third floor, and I heard these two maids talking about . . . about what had happened."

"About your mother being killed?"

Michelle nodded, but her eyes took on a semi-catatonic look again, and I was afraid we were losing her.

"Go on," said the lieutenant gently. "What did you do then?"

"I . . . I don't remember."

"What do you mean you don't remember? You *gotta* remember. Somehow you got hold of a gun, Michelle. Try to think."

110

She shook her head violently. "I don't *like* guns," she said. "Jayne, tell him to stop asking me all these questions."

"Can't this wait until later, W.B.?" asked my wife.

"Mrs. Allen, I gotta ask these questions now when everything's still fresh. I mean, if she doesn't remember now, she *really* won't remember later."

I was trying to sort out the logic of this statement as W.B. turned toward Michelle and tried to smile at her as if he was her favorite uncle. She didn't appear to be fooled.

"Now Michelle, sweetheart . . . somehow you got hold of a gun, and then you came down here to the Lucky Horseshoe. Why did you take two shots at Johnny Nakamura? Did you think he was involved in your mother's death in some way?"

Michelle looked about wildly, saw Nakamura, and burst into a torrent of tears. The girl was making a scene, enough to cause a few old women playing the dollar slots nearby to peer at her over their machines as they continued to rhythmically pull down the handles. Jayne held the girl while she sobbed. It was clear that W.B. wasn't going to get any more from her.

"You're going to have to wait, Lieutenant," said my wife. "Can't you see how upset she is? Her mother's dead, and her father and brother have disappeared—why don't you let me take her back to the hotel? Perhaps she'll be able to talk to you later."

"Yes, let her go, Walker-*san*," said Johnny Nakamura with an imperious wave of his hand. "Frankly, I don't wish to press charges, and she is beginning to disturb my customers."

111

"They're right," I told Lieutenant Walker, adding to the general chorus. "Michelle's in no shape to give you any more information."

"So you and Jayne will look after her, I suppose?" asked W.B. suspiciously, giving me a hard look.

"Well, we'll take her back to the hotel, of course."

"Yeah, and if the girl starts talking, I want to know—understand? You give me a call, night or day."

"Absolutely," I assured him. "I wouldn't think of withholding information from you."

"Yeah? Well, here's my card—night or day! You got that?"

Jayne and I more or less propped Michelle up between us, and we walked her out of the casino into the blinding sunshine. On the sidewalk, I saw a homeless family sitting on a blanket near where Cass was waiting in the limousine. It was a pathetic sight—a dirty young man, a ragged young woman and a beautiful blond, blue-eyed baby held in his father's arms. The child was just an infant, and the father was holding him with such a sad, dejected look on his unshaven face that I couldn't walk by without giving them something. I reached into my pocket and pulled out all the loose change I could find—it could not have added up to much more than two dollars—and put it into the waiting cup on the sidewalk.

"God bless you, mister," said the young man. He roughly handed the baby to the woman, scooped up the change and dashed inside the casino.

"Remember, do the *progressive* slots!" called the woman after him. "And don't come back unless

112

you've won something, you bastard!" The baby began to cry.

I felt foolish, but as if this weren't bad enough, Michelle squeezed my arm and Jayne's, and spontaneously kissed my cheek.

"Wow, I think you two are like the most fantastic people I've ever met," she said enthusiastically, "I'd like to come live with you forever and ever!"

I cannot claim the distinction of being Jewish, but a whispered *oy* escaped my lips at that moment.

chapter 14

Our little sitcom, *Life with Michelle,* began immediately. Since the girl couldn't stand the idea of returning to her own suite, Jayne invited her to ours.

Left to my own devices, I might have tried something simple, like just asking Michelle why she had taken those shots at Johnny Nakamura—a question I was rather curious about, despite my resolve not to embroil myself in this case. But Jayne insisted we avoid speaking of anything related to the murders, so we had a more-or-less normal evening playing Scrabble, having dinner sent up from room service, and watching old movies on TV. Michelle was rather sweet the entire evening, and seemed to regress in our care into a lovable blonde puppy dog, who flopped comfortably over the sofas and never strayed far from Jayne's side.

"Isn't she adorable?" asked Jayne, as we met in the olympic-sized bathroom. "And have you noticed—she hasn't touched a drop of alcohol all evening?"

"Yeah, she's going to give Mother Theresa a run for her money, no doubt about it," I agreed. "And you know, dear, how I've always wanted to adopt my very own Las Vegas divorcee."

"Steve! She's helpless. She needs us right now."

"All right. I'll have Cass walk her down to her room when it's time to go to bed, and if you like we can have breakfast with her tomorrow."

"Darling, she's got to stay right here."

"*Here?*"

"She's just a girl, Steve—an orphan, practically."

I was about to protest that this particular orphan was twenty-three years old, a maneater of the first degree, had been married three times, and would eventually be worth more money than Jayne and I would see in a lifetime—but I could see by my wife's expression that because her maternal instincts had been roused, further argument would be useless. Fortunately, our hotel suite was so enormous it may have had two zip-codes, so I took my pajamas and robe and headed toward a guest bedroom—since poor helpless Michelle was going to take my place at Jayne's side in the master bedroom.

"Just for this one night," Jayne promised. "I'm sure she'll feel stronger tomorrow. You're an absolute saint, Steve."

"Bless you, my child," I said.

I made myself a cup of hot lemonade and headed toward the guest bedroom with a copy of Isaiah Berlin's *Against The Current*, determined to turn in early. So far Las Vegas had not exactly proved barrels of fun, and I was beginning to regret not having stayed on the cruise ship.

As I climbed into the cool bed with its freshly

pressed sheets and luxuriously large pillows, my mind flashed back to a summer Jayne, Steve Jr., Brian, David and I had spent at Mamaronrack, New York, in a lovely old house on the water. Through some connection with *The Tonight Show*, which I was hosting at the time, we had been given the use of a little boat with an outboard motor. One day as we were happily putt-putting around the bay, moving past assorted ocean-going yachts, I said, "You know, I'm very grateful that I wasn't born rich," by which I meant that if I had been I couldn't possibly have appreciated that little boat and the carefree fun it afforded us as much as I did. I will go to my grave being grateful for the comfortable beds that my station in life now makes available, simply because in my childhood it was not always so. I had run away from home in Chicago at the age of 16 and bummed around the country for a few weeks, living the sort of existence now associated with those we call the homeless. All you really need, I think, to make you forever appreciate a warm, soft, clean bed is one cold, fog-bound night in Houston, Texas, sleeping on the concrete ledge of a warehouse loading dock.

Comforted at the moment by my hot drink and Professor Berlin's fascinating study of European thinkers who had opposed the dominant intellectual currents of their time, I relaxed completely. When I suddenly realized I had read a particular paragraph on page 19 three times with minimum comprehension, I put the book down and yawned like a relaxed lion. Instead of the arms of Morpheus, however, I was confronted with worries about Bobby and Wade. Had they been found yet?

I tried to put the thought out of mind, but it

would not go away. Eventually, I gave in to an urge to phone Lieutenant Walker for an update.

"Sorry to disturb you at home, W.B."

"No problem. What's up?"

"I was wondering if Bobby and his son had turned up anywhere?"

"I'm afraid not," said W.B. "You'd think someone that famous would have a hard time getting lost, but it's like the earth just swallowed them up."

"What about the white Lincoln Continental limo they were seen driving away in? Surely that's not such a common car, even in Vegas."

"We've been on that angle from the start. The car could have come from anywhere, but we *do* have six white Lincoln Continental limos registered in Clark County. Five of them belong to various Wedding Chapels, but number six, as it happens, is owned by the Lucky Horseshoe. It's used to ferry high-rollers back and forth from the airport."

"Well, that's it then!" I said. "I told you there were two Japanese guys who took Bobby and Wade off with them. They had to be sent by Johnny Nakamura."

"Yeah, that's all very nice and circumstantial, but as it turns out, Nakamura's Lincoln has been in the shop the past two days having its air-conditioning overhauled."

"Oh. You sure about that?"

"Yeah. Now what about this loony-tune Michelle? Has she said anything about her shooting spree?"

"Sorry, W.B.—Jayne's been trying to avoid the subject, at least for tonight. We just sat around playing Scrabble and watching movies on one of those cable channels."

"Swell. I thought you celebrities spent your evenings in more interesting ways."

I said goodnight, hung up the phone, turned off the light, and again attempted to sleep. But it was no use. My mind was wide awake, thinking back over the events of the day and trying to make some sense out of what had happened. Tomorrow, I decided, I'd bypass Jayne and get Michelle to talk about Johnny Nakamura; I wanted to figure out the Japanese angle to all this, and I had a feeling he was the key.

I did fall asleep eventually, of course. I was dreaming Jayne and I were working as singing waiters in a *sushi* bar when the phone rang on my bedside table. I reached out into the darkness and pulled the receiver to my ear.

"Yes? What time is it?"

"Steve, thank God I got you. It's Bobby."

"Bobby!" I cried, instantly awake. "Are you all right? Where the hell are you?"

"Wade and I are both okay, but . . . look, it's a long story, man, and I'll tell you all about it as soon as you come pick us up. We're stranded at a phone booth somewhere. . . . I think we're in North Las Vegas, but that's just a guess."

"You don't *know* where you are?"

"I told you, it's a story. . . . Hold on a minute, Wade's looking at a street sign. . . . Okay, we're on Cheyenne Avenue, and I can see a freeway from where I'm calling—I think it's Interstate 15. We're at a phone booth outside a Shell station. You think you can find that?"

"Yeah, I'll get a map. But Bobby, if you're in trouble, I think you should call the police."

"No, Steve—no police. Not yet, anyway. You

118

gotta trust me on this, pal. I'll explain when I see you."

When I stood up I saw it was just past two-thirty in the morning. I hoped Bobby Hamilton had a *very* interesting story to tell to justify getting me out of bed at this time of night.

chapter 15

I dialed Cass's room on the twelfth floor and let the phone ring for nearly four minutes before he answered. He wasn't pleased to hear my voice at such an hour, but I convinced him to meet me downstairs in five minutes time. Fortunately Cass was in a good mood—he had won over $600 at Baccarat and was eager to rub the sleep out of his eyes and let me know of his success.

"You see the way it is, Steve. I guess I got the golden touch," he grinned.

"Sure you do, Cass. Now I hope you're smart enough to quit while you're ahead."

He just kept grinning and making little chortling sounds. It worried me, but I had other things on my mind. We drove to a 24-hour gas station next to the Excalibur Hotel to pick up a Clark County map, and I found Cheyenne Avenue by searching through the street index on the back. The road seemed to be a major artery going east-west in the town of North Las Vegas, and I was glad to see it intersected two freeways—I-15 and I-95. Since Bobby thought he

120

was within sight of I-15 when he called me, it seemed reasonable to start there.

Cass drove onto the freeway at Sahara Avenue, and I guided him northward about twenty miles, through the downtown maze to the exit for Cheyenne Avenue. We came off I-15 onto a wide boulevard lined with gas stations, fast food restaurants, and a rambling shopping center. Unlike The Strip, where everything was open day and night, the suburban landscape here was largely deserted of cars and people, with empty parking lots stretched out beneath harsh white lights. Since there wasn't a casino in sight, I presumed we were some place where the real people of Las Vegas lived. I saw a Shell station near a Jack-in-the-Box restaurant and told Cass to pull over. The station was closed, and for a moment I saw nothing but deserted pumps standing in the glow of the service islands. Then Bobby and Wade came out from behind the office and jogged quickly over to the car. I got out to greet them.

"Thank God you're both all right," I said.

Bobby gave me a brief bear hug. "I knew you'd find us, Steve. Thanks. We were hiding behind the office in case those bastards came back."

"Any particular bastards?" I asked pointedly.

"Let's get the hell out of here," said Bobby evasively. The three of us slipped into the rear of the limo, and I told Cass to head back towards The Strip. In the bright lights of the gas station, I had noticed that both Bobby and Wade appeared exhausted and disheveled. Wade's shirt was torn and spotted with grease and dirt. Bobby had a slight cut across his cheek. They settled back into the passenger's seat of the car with a few groans and sighs, while I faced them from the fold-out jump seat, my back to Cass.

121

"Do either of you need a doctor? You look like hell," I said.

"No, we're okay," Bobby said. "We were lucky. Nothing a hot bath won't fix."

"But what happened?" I asked, exploding with curiosity. "We've been worried about both of you."

"Hey, to tell the truth, I was a little worried myself," said Bobby with a boyish grin. "Remember those Japanese guys who came to the rehearsal this morning? Well, we hadn't driven two blocks with them up The Strip when they turned down a side street, pulled out guns and blindfolded us. They drove us somewhere and left us tied up in a house, not far from where you picked us up."

"You were kidnapped? But why?"

"They didn't explain, man. In fact, they didn't say much of anything, except we'd better keep quiet and do exactly as they told us. They tied us to different chairs so tight my arms and legs went numb, and then we heard them leave the house and drive away. When they didn't come back, Wade and I started trying to work our way out of the ropes. Unfortunately, those guys must have been the Jap equivalent of Eagle Scouts when they were kids, because we weren't getting anywhere fast."

Bobby turned on the rear light for a moment and showed me his wrists, which were raw. "This is what I got from rubbing against those ropes for a couple of hours or so. If it weren't for Wade, I think we'd both still be back there."

"What did you do, Wade?" I asked.

The young man glanced briefly in my direction, but it was his father who continued the tale.

"We were still blindfolded, you dig—but Wade inched his chair around the room feeling about for

122

something sharp to cut through the ropes. Finally, he found a glass coffee table, and backed himself against the thing so he was able to rub against the edge. Even then, it took, what—another two or three hours to cut through?"

"It was a long time," Wade agreed.

"Anyway, the long and short of it is Wade eventually got free and then he untied me. The house was locked from the outside, but we were able to crawl out a second-story window, climb down a tree, and find our way to that gas station where we called you. And that's all there is to it, Steve. Lucky our kidnappers didn't come back, or I guess we wouldn't be sitting here now."

A diesel truck coming from the opposite direction cast a fleeting light on Bobby's weary but handsome face. None of his story made much sense to me.

"But why?" I asked. "Why did you go with them in the first place? Why did they kidnap you? And why did you call *me* instead of the police?"

"Hey, I'm sorry to get you out of bed this time of night, but . . ."

"That's not the problem. Bobby, you and your son were abducted at gunpoint, blindfolded, tied-up—when you finally managed to escape, I just can't understand why you'd telephone—you know, a comedian instead of the cops! The police should be out looking for those two sons of bitches right now—maybe they should be hauling Nakamura out of bed and asking *him* a few questions."

I had thrown this name out experimentally, and was pleased to see Bobby look up at me sharply at the mention of the owner of the Lucky Horseshoe.

"I guess I owe you an explanation."

"You don't owe me anything, Bobby—but I'd like to help you if I can."

Hamilton seemed to be weighing matters in his mind. "Look, Steve, about why I called you instead of the cops—you gotta appreciate my position. If I go to the cops with this story, it's going to be a big headline all across the country in tomorrow's papers. BOBBY HAMILTON KIDNAPPED! Can you imagine the hype? By tomorrow night I wouldn't be able to go to the bathroom without a bunch of cameras and microphones stuck in my face. So I thought I could keep this so low key that—"

"Wrong," I said. "So Lo Key was the prime minister of Cambodia before the coup of '62."

Hamilton laughed heartily, which was one reason comics enjoyed working with him; he was a pushover.

"You see?" he said. "Now *that's* why I called a comic instead of a cop. But seriously, I figured that if I could reach you I could do a little checking around myself. You know, maybe find out what the whole deal is about before making a big public fuss. Besides, Wade and I are okay—I mean, except for a few scratches climbing out the window and down that damned tree, there was no real harm done."

"No harm done?" I said, outraged.

"Look, man, I'll go to the cops tomorrow if you think I should, but I'd rather just be a hell of a lot more careful whose car I get into in the future. Hell, maybe it was my own fault going off with those schmucks in the first place."

"I'm glad you mentioned that," I said dryly. "Now who the hell *were* those guys, and why did you leave the rehearsal with them?"

Bobby looked uncomfortable. "Steve, I wish I

could tell you about this, but I—I just can't. I know I'm being a pain in the ass, getting you out here in the middle of the night and leaving you in the dark about what's going on. But the whole thing is . . . well, it's extremely personal."

"Is it about Michelle?" I asked, like a gambler putting a coin in a slot machine, I suppose, and hoping for the jackpot.

"No, it's not," he said. "Why do you ask?"

"Because she tried to gun down Johnny Nakamura this afternoon," I told him.

Bobby's grabbed my wrist hard. "*What?* For God's sake, is she okay?"

"She's fine—and so is Nakamura, as a matter of fact. Now are you sure you don't want to tell me about this?"

But Bobby just shook his head wearily, sighing all the more unhappily. Wade stared out the window, apparently uninterested in the entire conversation.

"Steve, I know I got you involved in this, and I feel like a real louse. I tell you what," he said. "Let me talk all this over with Christie tomorrow, and I'll get back to you. If she says I should tell you, I will."

It was my turn to sigh. Ever since I had picked up Bobby and his son at the gas station, I had been hoping that they knew about Christie's death, and that I would not have to be the messenger of such terrible tidings. I told myself they could have heard the news in a dozen different ways—on a passing car radio, for instance, or from the headline of the afternoon papers on a rack on the street . . . but it was clear they did not know, and now I struggled for a way to put the tragedy into words.

My mind drifted back to the one other time I

had to tell someone about the death of a loved one. Jayne and I were having a little Christmas dinner party for the members of my office staff. Eight or nine of us were gathered around the dining room table when suddenly, through the large picture window opposite my chair, I saw a strange car race into the driveway and heard incessant honking of an automobile horn. Unable to make sense of the intrusion I hurried to the front door and opened it just in time to see the car continue to hurry around our large oval driveway.

Why the driver did not get out and communicate a coherent message I don't know, except that he was probably in a state of shock. All I could hear as he lowered his window were some shouted words that sounded like, "Somebody—police! You'd better check," and with that he was gone. Two young men who worked at my office had followed me to the front porch.

"What did he say?" one, named Dennis, asked.

"I don't know," I said, "I couldn't make it out."

At that I ran back to the kitchen to get a flashlight, then the three of us walked out into the darkness. Whatever the stranger had seen was obviously out on the street. As we started down the driveway we encountered a numbing sight. A body lay at the bottom of the slanted driveway and two young police dogs, on leashes, were frantically barking, whining and trying to disentangle themselves from a strap attached to both their collars.

As the three of us approached we saw that the body was that of a middle-aged man wearing a cool-weather jogging suit. The poor fellow, it turned out,

126

had suffered a fatal heart attack while out walking his dogs.

"Go call the police," I said to one of the men with me. To Dennis I said, "God, how do we find out who he is, or where he lives? He's obviously a neighbor."

In the left-hand pocket of the man's jacket we found a small plastic cylinder that contained prescription pills, as well as the names of the doctor and the man who had just died. With only this as a clue, I hurried back into the house, got on a second phone line, called information and got a nearby number for someone with the same last name.

After writing down the number, my hands suddenly started to shake. Discovering a body on your doorstep is terrible enough, but suddenly the thought that I would have to call the man's house, speak to his family and share this dreadful news with them made me awfully uneasy. I have never dreaded anything more than having to make that call. The woman who answered was, as it happened, the poor man's wife.

"Ma'am," I said, "I'm terribly sorry to have to tell you this, but a man who was out walking his dogs just happened to—"

At that moment the woman screamed.

"Who is this?" she said.

"I'm Mr. Allen," I explained. "We live near you and, as I started to say, there's a man who has collapsed in our driveway."

The poor soul next uttered a long, terrible, "No-ohh." I started to repeat our address, but she said, "I know where you live; I'll be right there."

By the time she arrived, just a few minutes

later, a police car was in the street, its light illuminating her husband's body.

For what I suppose are understandable reasons, that horrifying drama played itself out in my mind now.

"What's the matter?" Bobby asked, seeing my discomfort.

"Bobby—there something I have to tell you . . . it's about Christie, I'm afraid."

"What about her?"

"Something terrible has happened. She's dead," I said. The words seemed to hang suspended in the sudden silence of the limousine. "She's dead, and I'd do anything not to be the one to tell you this. Christie was murdered this morning—just about the time you were kidnapped."

"Hey, is this some crazy joke?" he cried angrily. "I don't believe this."

"I wish I didn't believe it either," I said. And I went on to tell him the details of what had happened in the sauna. It's not easy to accept news of the death of a mate of twenty-five years. I watched Bobby Hamilton go through several stages of denial, disbelief, shock—and then at last he buried his head in his hands and wept great heaving sobs which racked his entire body. He cried so hard for a while I was afraid he couldn't breathe.

I kept one hand on Bobby's shoulder as he cried. I felt helpless to say anything wise or redeeming, but I wanted him to know I was still there. I felt desperately sorry for him.

Wade had not said a word. He was so silent I nearly forgot about his presence in the car. I'm not sure what made me look over his way while his father

128

was still sobbing. Wade was sitting bolt upright by the side window, his face in the shadows.

"This is a hell of a thing, Wade," I said soothingly. "You're going to have to help your father through this."

"Sure," said Wade. We passed under a harsh blue-white light above the freeway and for a fleeting moment the young man's face was revealed in the passing glare: He was staring at his father with a cruel and inappropriate smile playing across his lips.

The Cadillac plunged back into the shadows, and Wade's face was lost to me in the darkness of night. It all happened so fast, I tried to tell myself I must have been mistaken. Wade Hamilton could not *really* be happy his stepmother was dead.

Or could he?

chapter 16

I saw dawn break from a window in the police station at City Hall. The eastern sky turned a faint orange, then vivid red, and soon an angry ball of fire rose above the desert to dispel the night. For a few brief moments, Las Vegas seemed clean and fresh and new.

I was sitting half-awake in a plastic bucket seat in a large squad room which contained rows of desks, computer terminals and sleepy-looking cops. I was waiting for Lieutenant W.B. Walker to finish questioning my friend Bobby Hamilton in a private interrogation cubicle down the hall. Wade had already been questioned, and was now in the plastic bucket seat next me, his head slumped forward, actually sleeping peacefully. I envied him, but I doubt if I would have been able to sleep myself even if the chair was remotely comfortable—which it was not.

We were at the station because I had insisted this was a matter for the police, and after Bobby had learned of his wife's death, he had no more heart to resist my suggestions. Lieutenant Walker had told us to meet him at the station—he talked with us all together for nearly half an hour, and then he separated us, questioning first Wade, then Bobby. I suppose his strategy was divide and conquer. Personally, I think I'd have confessed to any crime at all, if only to be allowed to return to my hotel to sleep.

I watched a procession of petty criminals brought into the room by various uniformed police: I saw a man with blood on his shirt who had been in a fight, a married couple from Utah who had tried to rob a liquor store, and of course, a few ladies of the night. You can learn a lot about life in a police station at dawn. I had always thought, for instance, that prostitution was legal all over Nevada, but I now learned it is allowed only in certain counties outside the city limits, so that good Christian families might not be discouraged from coming to Vegas with wallets full of cash. Perception is everything in this town, and Las Vegas has worked hard to present itself as offering good clean wholesome fun for the entire family. For this reason, the word *gambling* is almost never used; rather one hears constantly the more harmless *gaming*—an ambiguous term designed by PR consultants in an attempt to make poker seem almost like Parcheesi. Meanwhile, the money keeps pouring in.

My mind was swirling around the edges of all sorts of early morning thoughts, when Lieutenant Walker finally appeared out of the cubicle with Bobby at his side, looking terrible. All his jauntiness and youthful appearance seemed to have departed in a single night, and from his desperate look, I sensed he was on the verge of emotional collapse. I tapped

Wade on the shoulder and stood up to stretch my legs.

"Hang in there, Bob," I said with as much cheer as I could muster. "When you get a few hours sleep, you'll be able to deal with this a whole lot better."

"Hell, I don't know," said Bobby bleakly, with a dazed look. "Just yesterday, I felt like the luckiest guy in the world. And now—Oh God, Steve, I just don't know about anything anymore."

A cop, as well as two flashily dressed prostitutes, asked Bobby for his autograph. I was outraged, but like an automaton Bobby signed the pieces of paper that were thrust in front of him. At this particular moment, being a superstar seemed about the loneliest job I could imagine.

"Come on, I'm getting you out of here," I said, taking him by the arm.

"Wait a minute, Mr. Allen," said W.B. "Mr. Hamilton and his son are free to leave, but I'd like to have a word with you, if I may."

I was not pleased, but W.B. can be very stubborn when he sets his mind on something. I sent word to Cass, who was waiting downstairs, to drive Bobby and Wade back to the hotel and then come back for me. Then I followed the lieutenant back to the small office cubicle and sat opposite him across a desk. I noticed he was wearing what appeared to be the same wrinkled brown suit I had seen him in the day before.

"Would you like a cup of coffee?" he offered. "I could send out for breakfast."

"No thanks. Besides, I feel so bad for Bobby I can't imagine being hungry—it's such a tragedy for him about Christie."

"Is it?" asked the lieutenant.

"What do you mean?"

"What I mean is, maybe Bobby Hamilton got exactly what he wanted—his wife's death."

"Jesus, do you know what you're saying?" I asked him angrily. "You can't seriously imagine he had anything to do with Christie's murder!"

"I'm saying it's a possibility, that's all."

"I don't believe this!" I cried. "First of all, I've known Bobby Hamilton for a long time. The guy is truly a sweetheart—did you see the way he signed those autographs back there? I mean, this is somebody who's been up all night, his wife has been murdered, and he still can't stand to disappoint anyone."

"Yeah, he *appears* that way," said W.B., "But how well do you really know him? Over the many years you say you've been friends with this man, how often have you seen him? Say, once a week?"

"Well, no—of course not."

"Once a month, maybe?"

"Sometimes years went by where I didn't run into Bobby, but you're wrong about him. Not only is he one of the kindest, most humble human beings who ever became a superstar, but he absolutely adored Christie, and they've had a wonderful marriage for twenty-five years."

"I suppose that's why Christie told your wife she was about to file for a divorce."

"Now wait a God damn minute!" I objected. "You heard what Jayne said—Christie wasn't blaming Bobby a bit. In fact, she insisted it was entirely her own fault. The problem was simply the circumstances, the fact that Bobby had such an exciting career and she had none. She was bored being Mrs. Hamilton and wanted to do something meaningful with her life, and she was afraid Bobby was such a strong personality she'd never stand on her own feet unless she left him. I think she was wrong, but there it is."

"So you don't think maybe he was smothering her? Making her life unbearable?" asked W.B.

"Not intentionally. Look, Bobby comes from a generation where he's a bit of a male chauvinist without even knowing it—probably it never occurred to him that Christie might be bored or want a career of her own. From his point of view, he gave her houses, boats, cars, status, security—everything he believed a woman might need. So, I'm sorry, but you're totally out in left field here. A guy like that's incapable of murder."

"Relax, Mr. Allen. I know he's your friend, but you've got to look at this from my angle. As I told you earlier, there's generally no mystery at all about homicide. Ninety percent of the time you'll find it's the husband or the wife, or the boyfriend or the mistress. I'm not saying I've come up with a motive yet why Bobby Hamilton should want to off his wife, but I expect we will. I see these things happen all the time."

"Well, that may be ninety percent of the time, but not *this* time, Lieutenant. And you can't send a man to the gas chamber just so you can have a convenient statistic. Besides, aren't you forgetting someone?"

"Who's that, Mr. Allen?"

"Johnny Nakamura. If I were you, I'd try to find out why he sent two of his goons to kidnap Bobby and Wade for the day."

"We'll look into that, of course," said Lieutenant Walker without much enthusiasm. "But you seem to be assuming Bobby really *was* kidnapped.

Maybe it was just a set up, a way to give himself an alibi for the time of the murder."

I had to laugh. "This is ridiculous."

"Is it? Then how come Mr. Superstar won't tell me a thing about the two Japanese guys he voluntarily left the rehearsal with? This supposed kidnapping didn't start out in a very convincing manner, if you ask me."

"He didn't explain that to you?" I asked, surprised Bobby was still holding back.

"Hell, no. He said some bullshit about it being too personal—which seems like some heavy evasive action to me. Did he tell you about the Japanese guys, Mr. Allen?"

"Actually, no," I admitted uneasily. "He told me the same thing, that it was personal—and naturally I wouldn't think of pressing him on something like that."

"Yeah, well I would," said W.B.

"Okay, but what about Wade?" I suggested hopefully. "He was there and *he* certainly can corroborate the kidnapping, at least."

"Yeah, I guess so," said W.B., tapping the corner of his desk with a pencil. "So far he seems to support his father's story. But he's lying—I can feel it—and believe me, Mr. Allen, we'll get the truth out of him in the end. Quite honestly, that kid scares me a little."

I was about to open my mouth and protest Wade's innocence as loudly as I had protested Bobby's—but there was something about Wade that did not add up, and I found myself falling silent.

Unfortunately, in this instance I had to agree with Lieutenant Walker: Wade Hamilton scared me, too. He scared me a lot.

chapter 17

I woke in a darkened bedroom, not knowing whether it was day or night, or what day of the week it was, or even what woke me. This is what comes, I suppose, from staying up all night in a town like Las Vegas. Jayne was not by my side, which was momentarily confusing, but then I remembered I had shuffled into the guest bedroom just as Jayne and Michelle were rising for the day. Coming from the Metropolitan Police Station, I had felt like some kind of night shift figure from the underbelly of town.

Somewhere far away a doorbell was ringing.

"Yes, yes . . . coming!" I croaked. I stepped out of the darkened bedroom into the blinding brightness of the living room, with sunlight pouring in the windows. On the music stand of the piano I saw Jayne had left me a note:

MICHELLE AND I HAVE GONE FOR A NICE DRIVE INTO THE DESERT IN SEARCH OF EXOTIC CACTI. HOPE YOU

She always signs her notes *me*.

I couldn't imagine anything exotic growing in this particular stretch of the Mojave, not even cacti, but I supposed Jayne and Michelle would discover that on their own. The doorbell buzzed again, sounding like some large mosquito, and I continued on my way towards the front door in a disheveled mood.

To my surprise, it was Wade Hamilton. He looked terrible. His face was gaunt and there were dark circles beneath his troubled eyes.

"Excuse me, Mr. Allen, but I'm looking for my sister, Michelle. Elliot said she was here."

"Well, she and Jayne have gone for a drive. But come in, Wade—I've been wanting to have a chat with you."

"I really don't have time right now, Mr. Allen."

"No, please—just for a moment. It's important."

"All right, just for a moment," he agreed.

Wade was dressed that morning in khaki slacks and a button-down Oxford shirt, which passed for casual in a young man who generally went about in dark business suits. I was still in my hotel-provided, peach-colored terrycloth robe, one-size-fits-all unless one weighs 200 pounds and is 6 feet, three inches tall, as I am.

"Sit down, make yourself comfortable," I said. "Can I get you a cup of coffee? Some juice?"

"Nothing at all, Mr. Allen. I can only stay a minute," he reminded me.

As we settled near each other on the pink sofa in

the sunken living room, I felt I had better get down to business fast before I lost him.

"Wade, I don't know what's the least troublesome way to say this, but the police are a little suspicious about your father's kidnapping story. I was hoping to hear your account of what happened."

"What's there to add? Daddy dearest does everything so much better than me—including tell stories to the police. So I think I should just keep my mouth shut."

I found his attitude unsettling. "Look, partner, this really is vital. For some reason Bobby refuses to tell us a thing about the two Japanese guys who came for him during the rehearsal yesterday. If you can shed any light on those two, and *why* they should kidnap you and your father, it could be a very great help to him."

"You think so?" asked Wade with a thin smile. "You think the truth would help him?"

"Why wouldn't it?"

Wade retreated into his shell, and I was pretty sure I wasn't going to get anything out of him. But then, to my surprise, he began to talk.

"I only know them by their nicknames—Tako and Ahi. *Tako* means *octopus* in Japanese, and *Ahi* is *tuna* in Hawaiian. They're both professional "bodyguards," which I say means gunmen. Johnny Nakamura brought them in from Honolulu."

"I see," I said calmly, hiding my excitement. "You're sure they work for Nakamura?"

"Of course I'm sure. Johnny sent them over because he's been trying to blackmail my father, and he was insisting on seeing him right away."

"Blackmail," I said slowly, trying out the sound

of the word. "Well, well—now what was this blackmail all about?"

"About my *step*mother, of course," said Wade distastefully. "What else could it be about? She was sleeping with Johnny Nakamura, which should give you *some* idea of her general taste."

"Are you serious?" I was actually shocked.

"I'm serious." I saw the thin smile return. "Well, a picture is worth a thousand words, as they say, and Johnny had some pretty steamy stuff on videotape of my dear stepmother and him in the sack. Frankly, I think Christie missed a great opportunity to be a porno star. But that's only half of what the blackmail was about."

"Tell me the other half," I said with a heavy sigh.

"Cocaine. Lady Snow. It all went up my stepmother's nose. Unfortunately, Johnny had a second videotape of her buying ten grams from one of his friends in a hotel room. He was threatening to send copies of both tapes to all the tabloids, and with the anti-drug mood in the country these days, it would have been more than embarrassing—Christie could have gone to jail."

"And Johnny wanted money to destroy the videotapes? Is that it?"

"Not quite that simple, Mr. Allen. Little Johnny is trying to move up in the world—he's making a bid on one of the hotels on The Strip, and if my father will sign a contract guaranteeing to appear on stage a few weeks every year, then there's a bank in town that'll provide the necessary capital for Nakamura to buy the joint. So that's what he wants from my father—just a little entertainment, you see. I've been advising Dad to just say no. After all, if the world learns Christie was a junkie and a nymphomaniac, it would serve her right."

"You're all heart, man," I told him. "So Tako and Ahi—is that their names?—they came to the rehearsal yesterday looking for an answer?"

"They came with a message that Johnny wanted to talk with my father, immediately—he didn't say why. As far as I know, Dad hadn't decided what he was going to do about the situation, but he went along, I guess trying to stall for time."

"And so the two Japanese drove you over to the Lucky Horseshoe?"

"No—they *told* us that's what they were going to do, but as soon as we got into the car, they pulled their guns and blindfolded us, just like my father told you."

"And they drove you to the house in North Vegas and tied you up?"

"You got it."

"But why? If Johnny wanted to see you both, that doesn't make sense."

"Well, they didn't explain themselves, and now I really have to run."

Wade stood up to leave, but I stood up to detain him. "Wade, listen to me—this is very important. You're telling me, then, that your father's story about the kidnapping is true?"

"Hey, pretty sharp, Steverino."

I ignored the sarcasm. "What about the time? Do you have any idea exactly when you got into the Lincoln Continental?"

"Sure. It was 10:25."

"How can you be so precise?"

"Because my dad was worried about leaving the rehearsal, and just as he was stepping into the limou-

140

sine he asked the doorman outside the hotel what time it was."

"And the doorman said it was 10:25?"

"You got it. My father's been having trouble with his old Rolex, and he reset his watch to match the doorman's."

There was something about the detail of asking the doorman for the time that bothered me; it smacked too much of setting up an alibi. Still, I felt myself relaxing. If what Wade was telling me were true, Bobby was definitely in the clear—the time of Christie's death had been established at 10:30, and there was no way he could have driven off at 10:25 and committed the crime. I was looking forward to passing on this tidbit to W.B.

"I can't tell you how important this is," I said to Wade. "Now are you *sure* this is the entire truth?"

"Sure I'm sure," said Wade with a fatalistic shrug. And then, just when I was feeling so optimistic, he had to go and spoil it for me.

"Yeah," he said, "At least that's the way I'm going to tell it, Mr. Allen—unless you can think up a better story to get the old man off the hook."

chapter 18

I couldn't settle down to anything after Wade left. It was frustrating that Bobby *seemed* to have an iron-clad alibi for the time of his wife's murder—but did he really? I wanted to know for sure.

I tried getting Hamilton on the phone, but there was no answer in his suite. Next I tried Elliot, still searching for Bobby, but he was not in—and then I tried to reach Lieutenant Walker, but he wasn't around either. There are days like that when you just don't connect. Finally I took the elevator down to the Gladiator Arena on the second floor, where I ran into Fritz the choreographer. Fritz told me the rehearsal had been canceled for today, but apparently there would be one tomorrow. Incredibly, despite his wife's death, Bobby still planned to open Saturday night. Fritz saw it as quite an act of courage on Bobby's part. I strongly disagreed, but I had a feeling the man was simply desperate and wanted to work himself so hard he wouldn't have time to think about the tragedy that had befallen him. I suppose I was reacting a bit selfishly, too. I mean a singer can actually go on in front of an audience in a situation of that general sort. All he has to do is smile through his tears, and he's a cinch for a standing ovation. But how would you like to try doing comedy in front of a thousand people who can't stop thinking about murder, tragedy, scandal, mystery?

This does happen to comics from time to time, usually in the context of some national tragedy. A public figure gets assassinated, a space shuttle blows up, a devastating earthquake takes place, and then, all over the country, assorted funny men and women have to go out and do a show anyway. It's tough.

But my chief objection was on Hamilton's behalf. I actually thought it would be in the most dreadful taste for him to be seen in public at all immediately after the murder of his wife. I was sure the casino could arrange for some other entertainer to replace him for a few nights.

I wandered back up to my suite, made some business calls to my office, and did about an hour's worth of dictation. About mid-afternoon Jayne and Michelle returned from their drive in the desert with Cass.

"See any swell cactus?" I asked.

"A few marvelous Joshua Trees," Jayne said. "That's a *very* peculiar cactus, darling. It looks like something Dr. Seuss might have dreamed up."

"Yeah, but it's a tree, not a cactus," said Cass.

"No it isn't," said Jayne.

"Is too," said Cass.

Apparently this question had already been discussed at some length. Jayne called a concierge, who shortly thereafter delivered an unabridged Webster's dictionary.

"Ah," Jayne said thoughtfully, quickly turning the pages, "Joshua Tree . . . *yucca brevifolia.*"

"Yes, Mrs. Allen—so you see, it's a yucca, which is like a tree not a cactus."

"But where does it say it's a tree?"

Cass was peering over her shoulder, squinting at the small print of the dictionary. "Look here. 'Joshua Tree . . . a *treelike* plant.' "

"That's still not a tree, Cass. It means *like* a tree. Anyway, I know how we can settle this. Ten dollars says I'm right."

"You're on," said our gambling chauffeur.

This was turning into serious business. Jayne went to the phone to call a friend who works at the Smithsonian in Washington, D.C., and I turned my attention to Michelle, who was being unaccustomedly quiet.

She appeared changed from when I first met her on the cabin cruiser on Lake Mead—an event which now seemed eons ago. Today the girl wore no makeup, but her complexion was so clear and youthful it didn't matter. She wore a simple outfit of jeans and a loose fitting blue shirt. Her hazel-green eyes seemed clear and sober. Perhaps the death of her mother had laid to rest her adolescent rebellion.

"Well," I said, "did you have a nice drive in the desert?"

"Oh, yes—it was nice of Jayne to take me. I just wanted to zone out awhile. Stare at the desert. Think about my mom."

"I'm awfully sorry about your mother," I said.

She shrugged, trying to be brave. "Yeah, well, I'm sorry too, but there it is." Without her make-up, Michelle looked closer to seventeen than twenty-three. It was hard to imagine she had failed at marriage three times. "Can I ask you something, Steve?"

"Sure."

"Well, this might sound strange . . . but do you think, well, it's a *good* idea for my dad to keep on with the show right now? I mean, after my mom's death and all, it might look . . . well, you know what I mean."

"Michelle, I think your father *wants* to work—perhaps he needs to be active with a project—with anything—so he doesn't find himself with a lot of free time to miss your mother."

"Yeah, but what if the murderer is still around, and someone else gets killed?"

I looked at her sharply. "Who else might get killed, Michelle?"

She turned away from me. "I don't know. I didn't mean that *specifically*. It's just . . . well, it's kinda scary. But maybe I'm only nervous because my dad wants me to sing with him on stage—can you believe it?—and that's like *terrifying.*"

"Don't you want to sing with your father?"

"I guess so. Only it's a lot of pressure, and the music I really like to do . . . well, he *hates* rock, you know, and I'm not sure how good a voice I have for ballads or jazz. Hell, anybody can sing rock. I thought maybe with my mom's death he might have forgotten about inviting me to sing with him, but this morning he brought it up again. He said I was all he had left, his little girl, and all that, and maybe we could even go on to record an album together."

"Well, of course he still has his son Wade."

She shrugged, "Yeah, Wade . . . well, you know what Wade's like, for God's sake."

Actually, I did not know what Wade was like,

but Cass and Jayne reappeared in the living room after discovering they *both* had been wrong. A Joshua Tree was neither a tree nor a cactus, but a member of a separate genus. Apparently a yucca was a yucca was a yucca.

Comedian Maury Amsterdam once wrote a song called "Yuka-puk," which always brought to my mind the image of a hockey puck made out of yucca wood.

"I still think it's *more* of a tree than a cactus," muttered Cass.

I managed to take Jayne aside. "Sweetheart, I hate to interrupt the deliberations of the World Botanical Society, but by any chance did you get Michelle to tell you why she took those shots at Johnny Nakamura yesterday?"

"*Steve!* She's had a very harrowing experience—I didn't want to bring it up."

"Right," I said. "After all, it was only attempted murder."

Jayne's eyes narrowed. "But sweetheart," she said, "I thought you weren't taking an interest in this case."

A while later I asked Cass to introduce me to the doorman he'd found yesterday—the one who had witnessed Bobby and Wade drive off in the Lincoln with the two Japanese kidnappers. It wasn't that I was precisely committing myself to the case, but I knew I'd rest more comfortably knowing that Bobby had a solid alibi for the time of the murder.

Cass and I left Jayne and Michelle, who were about to order tea, and we took the elevator down to the ground floor casino. Outside the hotel, two doormen stood with their plumed helmets, tunics and spears. All Roman Centurions look alike to me and I

146

would have had trouble distinguishing one plumed helmet from another. Cass went first to one, then the other.

"That you, Dan? Remember I asked you yesterday about seeing Mr. Hamilton and his son leave here? Well, Mr. Allen would like to ask you about that."

Dan, the Centurion, was quite young, probably not more than nineteen—a freckle-faced kid with red hair spilling out just a little from his Roman helmet.

I tried to put him at ease with some small talk. "So what do you want to be when you grow up? Julius Caesar?"

"I'm a business major at the University of Nevada," said the Centurion. "One day I might manage this hotel, Mr. Allen."

"I bet you will, Dan. Now you actually saw Bobby Hamilton drive off in the limousine, is that right?"

"Yes sir. I couldn't forget seeing a big star like that."

"And you're sure it was him?"

"Absolutely. I caught his show at The Sands a few years ago. I'm a big fan of old-time music."

I let the 'old-time' comment pass.

"Did Bobby speak to you?" I prodded, remembering what Wade had told me about Bobby asking for the time, but not wanting to put words in the young man's mouth.

"Yeah, he asked me what time it was," said the future manager of the hotel. I was liking the kid more and more.

I sprang the big question: "And do you remember what time it was when you looked at your watch?"

147

"It was 10:25."

"Are you sure of that? It seems a pretty small detail to remember."

"Well, gosh, I had never spoken to someone so famous—to tell the truth; I remember everything about the conversation. I bet I could repeat it, word for word. Mr. Hamilton showed me his gold Rolex, and it was almost five minutes slow. We both laughed that such an expensive thing didn't work right, and I told him it had just turned to 10:26 when he actually got around to changing the time."

So there it was. The strange unease I had felt after my conversation with Wade disappeared. It still struck me as perhaps *too* convenient that Bobby had established the exact time he left the hotel, but in the end, what did it matter? If he left the hotel at 10:26, he could not have been the murderer—it was as simple as that. Oh, I knew W.B. could still argue the point—he might say, for instance, that Bobby hired someone to do the actual killing while he gave himself a good alibi. Still, if the kidnapping had been faked for the purpose of providing an alibi, Bobby would have done a lot better to simply remain at the rehearsal under the watchful eye of twenty-five chorus girls, a full orchestra and large crew. As far as I was concerned, W.B.'s idea of a domestic homicide was seeming more and more absurd, particularly with Johnny Nakamura's growing profile in the case.

I gave Dan a five dollar bill to help him on his way to the top, and then Cass and I walked back inside the icy air-conditioning of the hotel lobby.

"Well, I guess you got that time angle nailed down," said Cass.

"With your help, Cass."

"Yep. The old team rides again!"

148

I was feeling pleased we had managed to find information that put Bobby in the clear. Cass and I were walking through an aisle of slot machines towards the elevator bank, when I saw something that made me stop in my tracks. There was a newsstand near the reception desk, and I had just caught sight of the enormous half-page headline on the afternoon paper. After my careful detective work, I could not quite believe what I was reading: SINGER BOBBY HAMILTON ARRESTED IN MURDER OF WIFE.

chapter 19

The Las Vegas City Hall is one of those vague and modern structures whose basic shape defies description: There is a sort of wedge-shaped slice of pie rising ten stories or so above a brick plaza, and, across this space, the public library and Metropolitan Police Station reside in a squat building which looks as if it broke away from the rest of the pie and fell into place at a slightly askew angle.

This afternoon there was a large and restless crowd of media people, men and women, gathered on the brick plaza before the glass doors of the police station. They held cameras and video equipment, lights and microphones—and looked hungry for blood.

When Cass let me out of the Cadillac at the curb on Las Vegas Boulevard, I walked toward the police station with some misgivings, lowering my head so that the gathered reporters might not recognize me. Alas, after 40 years on television, it was a useless gesture.

"It's *someone* famous, someone connected to

this case," I heard a reporter say. "It's those glasses. . . ."

"Just let me through, please," I said with as much dignity as I could muster. Microphones had been thrust in my face, cameras were taping, and I was encircled by men and women who stood three-deep around me, blocking my entrance to the police station. I felt as if I was the main course at a shark-feeding frenzy.

I was hoping they might lose interest and go away, but just then a bony little woman with short blonde hair and a microphone in one hand elbowed her way past her male competition. "Steve Allen!" she announced victoriously, laying claim to me. "Valerie Fox, Channel 6 Eyewitness News. . . . Have you come to see Bobby Hamilton?"

"Yes," I told her, trying to make the best of the situation now that I had been recognized.

"Tell us, Steve—do you think he murdered his wife?"

"Absolutely not. I've known Mr. Hamilton for years—and Christie too—and I can assure you that this is a gentle and kind human being who would not deliberately hurt a soul. Now if you'll excuse me. . . ."

"Is the show at The Coliseum going to be canceled?" called out another newshound.

"I don't know," I said. "Personally, I'm positive we'll have Bobby out of here in a matter of hours, with a big apology from the police."

"Steve, is there any truth to the rumor that Bobby was kidnapped yesterday?"

"I'd rather not comment on that."

"Was his wife having an affair?"

"Please," I said, wincing.

Apparently the media people were getting no information from the police inside. Dozens of voices began asking questions all at once: Had Christie been about to file for a divorce? Was the rumor true that Bobby was about to run off with Kim Basinger? What kind of evidence did the police have against him? Had *I* been an old beau of Christie Hamilton?

Just when I was about to give up hope, a flying wedge of policemen came out from the station and rescued me from the jaws of the six o'clock news, pulling me through the glass doors and depositing me in front of a gray-haired desk sergeant.

"I'm Mr. Allen," I panted. "Here to see Lieutenant Walker."

I was buzzed through the bulletproof security door into the inner sanctum. W.B. met me in the sprawling squad room and didn't seem sure whether to be worried or amused at my predicament.

"Well, well—I heard the news boys nearly tore you limb-from-limb out there."

"Lieutenant, how in hell could you go and arrest Bobby Hamilton?"

He grinned mischievously, looking for a moment like a fat little boy. His tie was askew, he had not shaved in at least a day, his shirt was falling out of his formless brown pants—but the man appeared strangely happy. "You think it's stupid, do you? Well, come on back to my office and we'll talk it over."

"He's innocent, and I can prove it!"

"Yeah? Well, won't that be the cat's meow?" he said vaguely.

W.B.'s office was as untidy as his suit. Official-looking papers were piled high on his desk beneath remnants of take-out lunches, empty coffee cups, and diet soda cans. A bowling trophy stood on a metal file cabinet, serving as a hat rack for a battered straw panama. An airline poster on the wall behind the cluttered desk showed a picture-perfect village in the Swiss Alps, but the poster itself had lost a thumb tack in the bottom righthand corner and was curling up on itself like the toe of an oriental slipper.

"Do you like to travel, W.B.?" I asked, sensing new vistas to the man.

"Naw," he said. "I figure it's a lot cheaper just to look at the pictures."

There wasn't a lot one could say in the face of such worldly sophistication. The lieutenant left me for a moment and came back with a glass of water. I was grateful but wasn't ready to let him off the hook.

"You've really blown it, W.B. You should have come to me first before you arrested Bobby—you'll be lucky if he doesn't sue for false arrest."

"Oh, yeah? What if I told you, sir, that I now have a motive for why Mr. Hamilton should want to off his wife? It has to do with Christie wanting a divorce."

"For God's sake, Jayne told us all about that yesterday! Anyway, I doubt if Christie would have gone through with the divorce once she and Bobby had a chance to talk things over. These two people loved each other. And besides, even if she *had* left him, Bobby would have been upset, sure—but he wouldn't have murdered her, for God's sake!"

"Maybe he would if enough was riding on it."

"Okay, spit it out," I told him. "What do you have?"

"Money," he said. "Lots of money. You see, Christie and Bobby Hamilton were married in California where there are strict community property laws. Unlike some marriages today, she didn't sign a pre-nuptial agreement limiting what she would receive in the case of divorce—and so, theoretically, she could have sued for half of the entire estate, which I've heard estimated at $100 million. And from where I sit, $50 million makes a pretty good motive for murder, even for a guy as rich as Bobby Hamilton."

"Nonsense!" I told him. "First of all, Christie was no gold digger—you heard what Jayne said. She was looking for a way to make it on her own. She wanted to show the world she could support herself, certainly *not* take any more money from Bobby. And besides that, Bobby is a very generous guy and if she *had* left him, I'm sure he'd have been glad to give her whatever she might want to start a new life."

"Well, in this case, she had a lot already," said W.B. "You see, over the last decade, a number of assets had been put into Christie's name as a dodge to save on taxes. Christie legally owned their place in Bel Air, the house in Palm Springs, and nearly $10 million in various stocks and mutual funds. So you see, Mr. Allen—being generous is one thing, but being shorn like a dumb sheep is quite another. If Christie had divorced him, Bobby Hamilton would have found himself minus a very large portion of a fortune he'd spent a lifetime building."

"Perhaps," I admitted. "But he still would have been extremely rich."

"I agree. To the average person, forty or fifty mill might seem not too shabby, even if you were accustomed to having twice that. But what you're not taking into account is human nature. I mean, a guy doesn't *like* to be fleeced by a woman he's loved.

154

Sometimes these irrational ideas take hold, and when the pain and anger get hot enough, it can erupt into something very nasty—like murder."

I smiled at W.B., remembering I had an ace up my sleeve: I knew Bobby was innocent.

"So you're saying Bobby hired someone to kill his wife, rather than risk a few million dollars?"

"No, I'm saying Bobby did it himself, with his own two hands—and it's *not* a few million dollars we're talking about here, but a fortune a king might like to get his hands on. And there's something else too—she was screwing around, and no matter how famous you might be, if your wife puts the horns on you, you're still a cuckold. Some guys react very badly to that, Mr. Allen. Very badly indeed."

"So you think Hamilton strangled her in a fit of jealousy?" I asked mildly, disappointed W.B. had not at least come up with a more interesting premise. I knew now I was on completely solid ground: A case *might* have been made that Bobby hired a professional killer, however unlikely that might seem—but he was certainly incapable of being in two places at once, and thus I knew he could not have committed the crime.

"You're smiling, Mr. Allen. Do you think this is funny?"

"Not at all, Lieutenant. I just know for a fact that you're wrong."

"Do you? Do you think you've out-detected me, is that it?"

"Well," I said modestly, "I know you're an excellent detective, but in this case, you're about to strike out."

"Okay, I'll make you a deal," said Lieutenant Walker. "We'll put our cards on the table. You tell me what you got, and I'll tell you what *I* got—and then I'll let you decide if I'm right or wrong."

"Fair enough," I said, and I happily told him about Dan, the Roman Centurion, whose job it was to open car doors outside The Coliseum Hotel. I enjoyed myself a little—if you have read about the last case I worked on with W.B., which I described in the book *Murder on the Glitter Box,* then you'll know that there is a certain amount of competition going on between us. I wasn't exactly expecting him to give me a medal when I was finished with my story, but I was surprised he was still looking smug.

"So that's it?" he asked with a raised eyebrow.

"Isn't it enough?"

"Mr. Allen, tell me something—how much does a gold Rolex watch cost, do you think?"

"Well, they can run into thousands. I don't particularly know what Bobby's is worth—but they can break down just like an old Timex you buy at your local drugstore, if that's what you're getting at."

"Now a great detective like you, Mr. Allen—it doesn't strike you as *suspicious* that Bobby Hamilton made such a big deal of establishing the correct time just as his wife was about to be murdered?" W.B.'s voice was oozing sarcasm.

"It doesn't matter what I think," I answered, "Or what *you* think either. Watches *do* break down, even expensive ones, and Bobby had every reason to be concerned about the time. But the point is, he was outside the hotel four minutes before his wife was murdered, and he was seen driving away. There's simply no way he could have gotten himself upstairs to the VIP spa on the third floor in time to kill his wife. And *that*, I'm afraid, is that."

W.B. leaned back in his chair with a satisfied sigh. "Yeah, it's a problem of logistics, all right," he admitted. "But sorry, Mr. Allen—Bobby's as guilty as can be."

"How can you say that? Even without Dan the Centurion, there's Wade's story too. I know a son's testimony might not carry a lot of weight in court—but the kid corroborates every detail of the kidnapping."

"Yeah, he did at first," said W.B. Now his smile was becoming quite unbearable.

"What do you mean, *at first?*"

"Because he's changed his story. He decided to tell the truth."

"What?"

"That's right, Wade has confessed to the entire hoax. Are you surprised, Mr. Allen? The boy just couldn't keep silent about his stepmother's murder."

"W.B., he *hated* his stepmother!"

"Sure, he admits that. But he's not willing to go to prison as an accessory to murder. You see, those two Japanese guys who came to the rehearsal didn't work for Johnny Nakamura—they worked for Bobby, who brought them in from Los Angeles to create an alibi. Their job was to haul Bobby out of there and make certain they were all seen leaving the hotel at a certain time, just as you say, so that a gullible amateur detective might later believe it impossible that Bobby could have committed the murder."

"But it *was* impossible," I objected angrily.

"Impossible, you say?" said W.B. "Let's take a trip down the hall. I have something I want to show you."

My mind was racing. How could he be so certain

he was right? W.B. may dress badly and keep a sloppy office, but the man is no fool.

"It's Dan the Centurion, isn't it?" I asked as we walked together down a long corridor. "He was paid off to make up a story about Bobby and Wade leaving the hotel at 10:26?"

Lieutenant Walker chuckled. "No, not at all. Dan *thought* he saw Bobby Hamilton at just the time he said he did. You know, Bobby made quite a few movies at one time, didn't he?"

"Sure," I said, frowning. "But what does that have to do with anything?"

"Well, it's just a thought. I mean, movies are a lot of light and shadow and make believe. It's what got me on the right track. A man like Bobby would be capable of creating, shall we say . . . a few illusions."

"This is ridiculous!" I muttered, but I was no longer at all sure of myself. "Either Bobby Hamilton was in that Lincoln at 10:26, or he wasn't."

We had arrived at the interrogation cubicle that Lieutenant Walker had used this morning at dawn. Without further ado, he swung open the door. I was surprised to see Bobby inside, sitting with his back to me, staring out the window.

"Bobby, thank God! I'm going to get you out of this mess, my friend. . . ."

My words died. Bobby turned slowly away from the window and stood up—and I was stunned to discover that this was not Bobby Hamilton at all, but a man who looked incredibly like him: the same build, unruly hair, handsome craggy face. Only the nose was different, and there was something about his chin that wasn't quite right either.

"Steve, I'd like you to meet Mike Corvino," said

W.B. "Mike was employed for many years as Bobby Hamilton's movie double."

My mind rebelled. I was about to remind the lieutenant that Dan the Centurion was *positive* he had recognized the real Bobby Hamilton—after all, he had caught a show several years ago at The Sands and had seen the singer in person. But then I recalled what that event would have been like—the boy and his date had probably had a table towards the rear of the house, and they had seen Bobby under colored lights and in make-up. In fact, anyone who had not actually met Bobby Hamilton in real life might very well mistake Mike Corvino as the real thing. In fact, I've met over a hundred men in the last forty-five years who have told me they'd been taken for me.

"That's right," said W.B., as if reading my thoughts. "This is the guy your doorman friend saw get into the Lincoln and drive away, hired for the role. Just like the two Japanese guys."

"And Bobby? . . ."

"Bobby meanwhile was upstairs getting ready to murder his wife. Don't take it so hard, pardner. You were just played for a sucker, that's all. Happens all the time in this town."

chapter 20

Lieutenant Walker arranged for me to be able to see Bobby Hamilton. We took an elevator upstairs to the city jail, where I had to sign a log book and allow myself to be searched for a hidden weapon.

It was certainly depressing to meet my old friend in such grim circumstances. A duty officer led me through a double metal door and down a long, bleak corridor whose walls were painted institutional green. Finally I was taken into a room that was divided in half by a glass wall. I sat down at a desk, and in a moment Bobby was brought in on the other side of the glass. He was wearing an orange jumpsuit, courtesy of the Las Vegas City Jail, and he looked ten years older than when I had seen him last, his face a sickly ashen-gray. He sat down at the desk on the other side of the glass, and we talked through telephones. I tried not to let him see how shocked I was at his appearance.

"Hey, kid! I hope you're keeping the faith in

there," I told him briskly. "I'm doing my damndest to get you out."

His eyes seemed bewildered and vague. I was reminded of a prize fighter who was having trouble getting up off the mat while the referee continued to count to ten.

"Do you hear me, Bobby? Don't give up now—I understand you have three lawyers coming in from Los Angeles, so you're going to have to get out of there and make some money so you can pay their damned bill!"

He didn't smile. "Steve," he said gloomily, "Can you imagine what it would be like for you if Jayne were killed, how bad that would be? And then later, on top of that, you find yourself in jail accused of her murder?" Bobby shook his head, as though he still could not comprehend where the all punches were coming from. "And then Wade telling those stories about me—you know, it's funny, but maybe that's the worst part of all. Why's he doing it, Steve? Why is my own son turning against me?"

"Let's take this one part at a time," I suggested. "But first you have to tell me one thing—are you innocent, Bobby? Did you do it?"

"You have to *ask* that?" For a moment, Bobby seemed animated with anger, and I felt it was a good sign. But then he simply seemed to deflate, his eyes dropping towards his folded hands. "Well, hell, I guess I don't blame you. Everybody else thinks I'm guilty—so why not you?"

"Look, I'm not saying I think you're guilty. But I have to ask you, just this once, and then we'll put it behind us. I need you to look me in the eye and tell me the absolute truth: Did you kill her, Bobby?"

161

He looked up at me with his defeated eyes. "So what would you do if I said 'yes—I'm guilty?' "

"I would feel very, very sorry for you. I would pray for you, I guess, and probably spend a lot of time trying to figure out who you really were and what went wrong. And then I'd hope they'd lock you up and throw away the key."

Bobby smiled, about the saddest smile I've ever seen. But he looked me right in the eye. "Naw," he said. "I didn't do it, Steve. I know it looks bad, but I'm innocent."

I nodded. "Okay, for what it's worth, *I* believe you. But if I'm going to be able to help, you got to tell me everything you know, starting with your relationship with Johnny Nakamura."

"That creep? Well, I didn't want to tell you about Johnny before, because then you would have found out about Christie . . . her bad habits, and all."

"You knew she was having an affair with him?"

"Sure. I guessed about it even before the guy showed me his videotape collection. I didn't like it, but I'm no prude, and I'm old enough to have been around the block some and know how these things can happen. I mean, the terrible thing is that she slept with the son of a bitch. The fact that a video camera caught it certainly wasn't her fault."

"But it made the blackmail possible," I said.

"Yeah," he said, "but to tell you the truth I was more worried about Christie losing her way in life, getting into cocaine and all that. I mean, I failed her. I was busy with my career, and I guess I couldn't give her what she wanted. So she went to people like Johnny Nakamura to fill the empty spaces."

"When did Johnny first contact you?"

"About a week ago. I had met him a few times

at parties in Palm Springs, and I could tell just by the way Christie was acting around him that something was going on. Well, I tried to ignore it, I suppose hoping it would blow over, like Christie's other affairs, but then a week ago Johnny came over to my suite at the Coliseum, and he showed me the two videotapes he had made—one was about dope, the other sex. I knew it was blackmail from the moment he walked in my door."

"And what did he want?"

"Not money. He wanted me to appear at some hotel he was trying to buy."

Bobby went on to relate the same story Wade had told me earlier—how Nakamura was trying to get financing to buy up a hotel on The Strip by using Bobby's famous name as collateral. Although I had heard the story before, I didn't interrupt Bobby's account. I wanted to make sure it agreed with everything Wade had told me, and it did.

"And what was your answer?"

"I told him I'd need time to think it over. Christ, Steve, Johnny isn't the first hood who's ever tried to put the squeeze on me, but I've always prided myself on steering a clean course—which ain't easy when you've been playing gigs in Vegas as long as I have." He suddenly looked at me more directly. "You've worked the town," he said. "Didn't they ever try to get to you?"

"Yes," I said, "they did. It was back in the '50s when I was doing my prime-time comedy series for NBC. One of my agents at the time told me of an offer from one of the clubs—I can't remember which one it was—but the thing I've never forgotten is his telling me that I could take maybe ten or fifteen thousand dollars of the money under the table."

"Yeah," he said, "that's one way they do it. Or they may offer you broads, dope, unlimited credit if you're a gambling junky. Once you say yes, they've got you—for life. Anyway I was trying to think of some way out of Nakamura's deal, some way I could protect Christie and still not get hung up in Nakamura's plans."

"You know, it seems to me that Johnny's blackmail scheme rested on a simple premise—that you loved your wife too much to let her suffer in the press. Isn't that true?" I asked.

"Sure," he said. "But what of it?"

"Well, it's a point in your favor, don't you see? If we can prove any of this, Nakamura becomes a kind of unwilling character witness on your behalf— because if you loved your wife enough to protect her, you certainly wouldn't kill her. The prosecution can't have it both ways."

Bobby visibly brightened. "Yeah, I see what you mean. That's not bad, Steve."

"All right, then—when's the next time you heard from him?"

"Johnny telephoned me the night you and Jayne arrived. He said he was getting impatient and that he'd only give me two more days to agree to sign a contract for the new hotel, or else copies of the tapes would be mailed out to magazines, newspapers and TV stations. I kept trying to stall him, you see, hoping some miracle would come along. And then those guys, Tako and Ahi—his hired muscle—they came for me during the rehearsal. You know the rest."

"Had you ever seen Tako and Ahi before?" I watched him carefully.

"Yeah. They came to the first meeting at my

164

hotel—they brought along a VCR, in case I didn't have one in my suite."

"And you went with them downstairs and got into the Lincoln?"

"Just the way I told you, Steve—I swear to God. They pulled guns on us, blindfolded us, and tied us up in that house—and Wade got loose, just like I told you, and we phoned you from that gas station."

"All right, Bobby—now we get to the difficult part. Why has Wade changed his story? Why is he telling the cops now that the whole kidnapping was a fake?"

For a moment, Bobby had seemed almost his old self again, ready to do battle to prove his innocence—but at the mention of his son, I watched his posture crumple back to its former attitude of defeat.

"Wade!" he mourned softly. "God, I've been such a lousy father, Steve. I think maybe he's getting even with me for all the years of neglect. I mean, basically that kid saw a hell of a lot more of the housekeeper than he ever saw of me when he was growing up. I was on the road all the time, making movies, doing gigs—doing a dozen things that all seemed terribly important at the time, but now don't seem so important at all. It's funny, isn't it? I'd do it all so differently if I had a second chance, but now it's too late."

"It's never entirely too late. After all, when he was an adult you gave him a job as your assistant."

"Christ, that was the worst thing I could have done! Sure, I felt bad about him, and I was trying to find some way we might have some time together and get close, but making him my all-purpose flunky. . . . It would have been kinder to cut his balls off with a knife!"

165

"Bobby, you're judging yourself too harshly."

"You think so? Look, if that kid ever had a chance to stand on his own two feet, I robbed him of the opportunity. I turned him into a kind of spineless wimp who'd never have to do any real work to give him a feeling of self-respect. I don't even blame him for turning against me. It scares me a little, the hatred he must feel toward me right now. But maybe if he destroys me, he'll have a chance to stand on his own. And if that's true, well, frig it, I hope he succeeds."

"I hope he finds himself too, Bob, but not at your expense. Does Wade have any money of his own?"

"No. He only has what I pay him. Why?"

"I'm trying to figure this out. Even if what you say about Wade is true, this attack on you seems too well coordinated to be some simple father-son quarrel. There's your movie double, for instance—Mike Corvino—who claims he was in the Lincoln Continental fooling the doorman downstairs while you were upstairs at the spa."

Bobby sighed and shook his head. "Damn! There's another guy I thought was my friend. We used to play Chinese checkers on the set and joke around a lot. I gave his kid a pony for his tenth birthday!"

"Have you seen him recently?"

"No, not for seven or eight years—not since my last movie died quietly at the box office, and I figured it was time to get back to what I loved best: music."

"And you can't think why Corvino should be telling this story about you?"

Again Bobby sighed and shook his head. "Maybe somebody made him an offer he couldn't refuse. God, this is such a nightmare. It's like my whole world has been turned upside down. And Christie. . . . I loved that woman with all my heart and soul. How can they say I killed her, Steve? How can they say it?"

A policeman appeared at my side to inform us our time was up. Bobby shot me a desperate look through the glass, as though I were his last link with humanity and with my departure he would be returning to the world of the damned.

"Help me, Steve. Help me get out of this nightmare, please."

"I'll do that."

"You promise?"

"You have my word on it."

chapter 21

By the time I left the police station, darkness had settled over the town, and the lights of the casinos visible from City Hall were busy sending out their nightly call. There was a chill in the air. This time of year, the desert can be burning hot in the day and cool at night, as if the air were too thin and insubstantial to hold any heat.

I left the station by a side entrance to avoid TV cameras. Cass was supposed to be waiting in the back parking lot, and I walked slowly in that direction, past the strange and modern buildings which contained the city offices. My thoughts were going back and forth over my conversation with Bobby Hamilton. I was determined to help him, but how and where should I begin? One thing I knew for certain: I could not leave this to Lieutenant Walker. I could understand how W.B. might have jumped to the wrong conclusion based on the evidence at hand, but there was something he was not taking into account—the matter of a person's character. W.B. simply did not know Bobby Hamilton as I did, and it was my job somehow to turn my intuition into proven fact.

I walked down a flight of brick steps and came to a parking lot brightly lit with cold blue-white lights. The burgundy-colored Cadillac limousine was parked by itself off to one side, near a stand of cypress trees. I didn't see Cass anywhere, but as I drew closer I noticed a sleeping shape stretched out beneath a blanket on the back seat. Cass sometimes does that—he'll climb into the rear of the car while he's waiting for me, begin to read a newspaper or watch TV, and quickly fall asleep.

I was about to open the back door and wake him when a car's headlights hit me from across the mostly-empty parking lot. I was nearly blinded by the dazzling light.

"Mr. Allen," I heard a voice say. There was something about this situation I didn't like. I shielded my eyes against the lights and peered across the lot, but I liked even less what I saw there: Two young Japanese men wearing suits and ties were standing in front of a gleaming white Lincoln Continental stretch limousine. I perceived them as the two who had come for Bobby during the rehearsal: Tako and Ahi.

"Mr. Allen, would you come here, please— someone would like to have a word with you. There's nothing to be afraid of."

Then why was my heart beating so fast? I hoped the sound of voices would wake Cass in the back seat, and that he would do something clever like use the cellular phone in the limousine to call the police station less than a hundred yards away. I tried to steady myself with this comforting thought; it was difficult to imagine even the most gung-ho gangster committing violence so close to City Hall.

"Mr. Allen, please," said the voice. "If we wanted to harm you, you would be already dead."

This seemed reasonable, I supposed. So why should I worry? I was still alive. I walked as nonchalantly as I could towards the bright lights of the Lincoln. In the harsh shadows of the parking lot, I wasn't quite certain if these two young men were the old friends, Tako and Ahi, of whom I had heard so much recently—but then I had only seen them for a brief moment in the Gladiator Arena. Still, I had no doubt who was waiting for me in the back seat of the Lincoln.

"Please," said one of the young men, opening a rear door for me to enter. Japanese gangsters might be deadly as any others, but they were considerably more polite. Inside the limousine, seated in a corner upon white leather, I found a surprise. My parking lot visitor was *not* Johnny Nakamura, as I had supposed.

"Good evening, Mr. Allen. Won't you join me in a cup of tea?"

I was looking at an extremely old Japanese woman who was very small, shrunken with age. She could not have been much more than four feet tall. In fact, this ancient crone was so very wrinkled and small I had a sudden absurd fantasy; she reminded me of Yoda, the little creature in *Star Wars*, and I nearly expected her to have pointed ears. The old woman was wearing an obviously expensive black silk dress with a strand of pearls around her thin neck, and she was holding a small cigar in one wrinkled hand.

I heard the car door close behind me, and in a

moment the limousine took off from the parking lot, gathering speed on Las Vegas Boulevard.

I made an effort to find my voice. "No offense, ma'am, but your cigar smoke is making me sick," I told her. "I'm an asthmatic."

The old woman smiled cruelly.

"Do you know how old I am, Mr. Allen?"

"Thirty-nine?" I offered, hoping to make her laugh with the old Jack Benny routine.

"*Eighty*-nine," she told me. "And I've been smoking these little cigars since I was fifteen. As you can see, it hasn't hurt me a bit. I may even outlive you, sir," she purred dangerously.

It occurred to me that smoking cigars might well have stunted her growth, but I felt it wise to hold my tongue. The two young goons were in the front of the limousine with the window closed between us, but I had not forgotten about them. As we came to a stoplight, I wondered briefly if I could make a threatening gesture and escape out the back door before the young men in front could stop me— but that didn't seem like a very chivalrous thing to do, particularly with an eighty-nine-year-old woman who was hardly more than four feet tall. Jayne would never forgive me.

The woman was watching me with keen eyes. Despite her great age, she seemed not at all harmless. She took one last puff, and then opened her power window long enough to toss her cigar out onto the street.

"Is that better?" she asked.

"Littering isn't nice, either," I told her.

"Are American men always so disrespectful to their elders?"

171

"Only when they haven't been properly introduced."

"You may call me Mrs. Nakamura," the woman said. "I am little Johnny's grandmother."

"Mrs. Nakamura," I said, "Little Johnny shouldn't be sending his grandmother around to do his dirty work. And someone should tell him that blackmail will get him into a great deal of trouble."

The old woman frowned as she spent a moment pouring us each a cup of tea from a pot on a small table by her side. "Sugar?" asked little Johnny Nakamura's grandmother.

"No, thank you."

She handed me the tea in a delicate little cup that had a silhouette of a Japanese temple on the outside.

"Yes," she said, "I told Johnny he is acting very foolishly. He has seen too many American movies. I tell him time and time again—don't kill people, don't beat them up, don't burn down their shops and houses. But does he listen?"

"He should. You sound very wise."

"I tell him—this is a small world, and we should all try to get along."

"That's good advice, Mrs. Nakamura," I told her. "But what does this have to do with me?"

"You are a friend of the famous Bobby Hamilton, Mr. Allen. You can help us help him . . . and at the same time help yourself. Isn't that nice?"

"Unless it's against the law," I said, wagging a playfully stern finger at the woman. She laughed flirtatiously.

"Mr. Allen, do *I* look like a criminal? All we want is for Mr. Hamilton to appear at our new hotel, for perhaps two weeks out of each year, and for this we are prepared to offer him an enormous amount of money. Is that such a bad thing? If my stupid grandson had not tried his blackmail scheme, I imagine Mr. Hamilton would already have said yes, without a moment's hesitation."

"I wouldn't know about that," I said. "And of course, it's a little late now. At the moment, Mr. Hamilton has an unbreakable engagement at City Hall."

"Ye-es," said the old woman thoughtfully. "And that is the reason for our chat. As long as Mr. Hamilton is in jail, he can not help my grandson buy his nice hotel—is that not true?"

"Sounds true," I told her.

"So Mr. Allen, you must clear your friend of this terrible accusation," she told me. "You see, I know how you like to play detective, so this is a perfect opportunity for you. You must free Mr. Hamilton and also convince him it is in his best interest to perform at Johnny's hotel—and by doing this you will earn the undying gratitude of the Nakamura family. Your enemies will be our enemies. Do I make myself clear?"

"Deadly clear. But I'm not certain I can get Mr. Hamilton out of this mess. Perhaps he's guilty," I suggested, fishing the waters a bit.

"I don't think so. You shouldn't be concerned about that."

"Well, if it's not Bobby, I'll have to offer the police some new suspect, Mrs. Nakamura. So why don't you tell me—who should we give them in Bobby's place?"

"How about the young woman?" she suggested, sipping her tea. "As I understand it, the girl was not far away when her mother was killed. And you know, of course, that she was having an affair with my grandson at the same time her mother was. A thing like that could lead to very bad feelings between a mother and daughter."

I stored away this information about Michelle's love life. "Yes, but murder, Mrs. Nakamura? Michelle doesn't seem the type."

"You will find the girl inherits a large amount of money from her mother's death, sir, so she has a motive. And, of course, what is she really but a drunken little slut? You will even find she has a drug conviction in New York in 1988—the police will like that."

"So you think I should throw them Michelle," I said with a forced smile. I found myself angry on the girl's behalf; Jayne was right, there was something endearing about her, even though she was trouble in a big way, mostly for herself.

"Why don't you give me someone else, Mrs. Nakamura, in case they don't buy Michelle."

"Well, there is the son, Wade. A very strange young man, Mr. Allen. Perhaps he is the person you're looking for. Neurotic, repressed. He might even be a psychopath."

"Maybe. But I've got an interesting theory myself, Mrs. Nakamura. Why don't I give 'em your Johnny, instead? The police already suspect him of laundering heroin money into Vegas, and skimming profits off the slot machines. My guess is they'd love to stick a murder rap on him."

"I would forget that possibility, Mr. Allen," the old woman said. Despite her age and small size, her voice suddenly carried a threatening note. "Anyway, the poor boy is innocent. After all, he needs Bobby Hamilton out of jail to conclude his hotel takeover,

174

so why should he do anything to jeopardize business?"

"Oh, I don't know . . . Johnny might have had some pressing reason to get rid of Christie Hamilton. I can think of a number of possibilities."

"Forget this line of inquiry!" said the old woman, her eyes as hard and cold as a snake's. "Do yourself a favor, Mr. Allen—Michelle or Wade, take your pick. You will find either of them will do quite well."

"Say, maybe they planned it together." I said sarcastically. "A brother and sister murder pact."

"That is not bad," said the old woman, with a small, evil smile. "It will sound good in the newspapers."

I noticed the Lincoln had driven in a largely circular pattern, so that we were now back at the parking lot behind City Hall.

"You've certainly given me food for thought, Mrs. Nakamura. Of course, Lieutenant Walker may have some ideas of his own."

"Lieutenant Walker," she said, "earns precisely $39,000 a year, which is not a great deal in this time of inflation and economic uncertainty. Am I making myself clear, Mr. Allen?"

"You think you can bribe him to let Bobby off the hook?"

"I never use that word. Let us say that a modest gift of—oh, $25,000—would help him focus his attention in a more productive direction."

"I see," I said. "And what would I get for *my* trouble, if I might ask?"

"When Mr. Hamilton is out of jail and when he signs a contract to appear two weeks a year at my grandson's hotel, for five years, you will receive

175

$200,000, Mr. Allen. But much more importantly, you will be allowed to live. If you are lucky, you may one day be as old as I am."

As the Lincoln came to a stop near Cass's Cadillac, one of the young men from up front came around to open the door for me. I stepped out onto the pavement, and watched the old woman reach into her handbag for one of her foul cigarillos.

"So, are we absolutely clear on this?" she asked me.

"Oh, we're clear enough," I said. "But I don't want your money, Mrs. Nakamura. And besides, I think Johnny's the one we're after."

The old woman used a gold lighter to fire up her cigar, and for a moment I saw her ancient hooded eyes glare at me coldly as death in the sudden flare of light. Then she closed the lighter, and her face retreated into the shadows.

"As you wish, sir. I have tried to warn you. Incidentally, you will find a present in your car."

The young man closed the door, returned to the front seat, and the Lincoln Continental sped out of the parking lot. I turned toward Cass's Cadillac with a disturbing fear rising inside of me.

"Cass!" I shouted. "Are you all right?"

I looked into the rear window as I ran toward the limousine. The sleeping, covered shape on the back seat was still there, but as I looked at it more closely, I could see there was something not at all right about it.

"Oh, Lord, no!"

"Steve!" came a muffled voice. "Get me out of here, God damn it!"

It was Cass, but his voice was not coming from the back seat.

"Where are you?"

"I'm in the trunk, for chrissake. Get me out!"

I was relieved to hear his voice, but when I tried the trunk I discovered it was locked.

"I keep a hide-a-key in one of those little magnetic boxes by the front left tire," he called. "Hurry up, for cryin' out loud!"

Cass was in a bad mood, understandably. I found the hidden key and opened the trunk. He came up with his fists clenched before him.

"Where *are* those bastards?" he said belligerently, looking around for opponents.

"Relax," I told him. "The fight's over now, and I'm afraid we lost this round."

"They came at me from behind, or those sneaky sons-a-bitches wouldn't have had a chance!"

I opened a rear door, curious about the shape on the back seat. An ugly smell told me what I was about to find. I pulled back the car blanket and found a very large fish laid out neatly on its side across the leather upholstery. A dead glassy eye stared up toward fish heaven.

"Holy mackerel!" said Cass.

"I'll handle the jokes," I said.

"But that fish must weigh a good thirty pounds."

"Not mackerel, Cass, yellow-fin tuna, the kind they use to make *sushi.*"

Cass rubbed the back of his head, deep in thought. "Jeez!" he said. "Hey, you think maybe someone's trying to send us a message?"

chapter 22

"**M**r. Allen . . . there's a phone call," said the pretty slave girl in a pale lavender mini-toga. She was coming over to our table with a small white telephone in hand—a phone that had a short antenna protruding from the top. It was Friday morning, a few minutes past eight, and Jayne and I were breakfasting on fresh fruit and granola in the Aphrodite Tower, a revolving restaurant high atop The Coliseum Hotel. We had come here to escape the constantly ringing telephone in our suite and see the city of Las Vegas spin slowly at our feet.

I took the call.

"Steve! Can you *believe* what's happening?" cried a voice in my ear. It was Elliot Block, Bobby's agent. "First Christie gets killed, now Bobby's in jail—and the people at the hotel—it's like they're having a friggin' heart attack over this! Everyone wants to know if we're going to be able to open Saturday night."

"What are you telling them?"

"What do you think I'm telling 'em? 'Yeah, yeah, yeah—of *course* we're going to open!' Christ, if we don't open we gotta give back a hundred thousand dollar advance *plus* the rest—what a mess!" he cried.

Elliot went on for a while, barking in my ear about how much money it was going to cost him if the police continued to be so insensitive as to hold his sole client for a trifle like murder when a show was supposed to go on! Couldn't the cops get their priorities straight? How could they do this to him?

"Elliot, calm down. There will be other shows. I personally think he should not perform right now. What's important is getting Bobby out of jail."

"Yeah," he said intensely. "That's the answer—gotta get Bobby out. But, listen, Steve . . . if worse comes to worst—and I'm a guy who likes to think ahead—I've already spoken to the people here about you taking over the show. There'd be a big bonus in it for you, of course. *Mucho dinero*. Maybe you could ask Steve and Eydie to work it with you."

"Elliot, there's no way I'm going to take over for Bobby. I wouldn't have the heart. And for that you'd need a superstar anyway. I'm just a lousy *star*."

But Elliot argued with me, dredging up my loyalty to what he called "the Bobby Hamilton legend" to help out in such a time of tribulation. Finally, I agreed at least to take over the rehearsals while Bobby was in jail, with the hope that he would be free by Saturday night.

"But if he *doesn't* get out of jail in time, Steve . . ."

"Well, why don't you put Michelle on?" I suggested, with only a hint of sarcasm. "She can sing."

179

"You trying to give me ulcers, or what?"

"Bye, Elliot," I told him firmly, disconnecting our conversation.

"What a horrible man," said Jayne, slicing a piece of honeydew melon.

I returned to my breakfast, but moments later was interrupted with yet another of this world's necessary evils—a phone call from the Beverly Hills law firm of Seidman, McMurphy, and Taylor, who were to represent Hamilton in the upcoming murder trial. A secretary from the office informed me that all three of these gentlemen—Seidman, McMurphy, and Taylor, that is—were about to leave Los Angeles International Airport in their private jet, and would I be so kind as to meet them at McCarran Airport in Las Vegas in half an hour's time.

"Well, all right," I said, hoping Cass had found time to rid the Cadillac of the smell of fish. Yesterday at the jail, I had already met two representatives from the firm who had hurried east from Beverly Hills to try to get their client out on bail. The bail motion had been denied, however, since this was a first degree murder case—involving a sensational double murder, at that—and the arraignment judge seemed to think a man as rich as Bobby Hamilton might find some way to flee the country if given a chance. Now the senior partners were coming to town to handle the case personally, and Bobby had told them that they were to cooperate with me in every way.

I left my breakfast half-eaten and called Cass to meet me downstairs in front of the hotel. As I stepped outside the lobby into the bright morning, I found the burgundy-colored limo waiting with the windows open wide to let in the fresh air.

"Fish!" said Cass grumpily. "All my life I've hated that smell! Now tell me the truth, Steve—if you were a blind man, would you think this was a limousine or a tuna boat?"

I sniffed the back seat cautiously. Cass had obviously used great quantities of air freshener and disinfectant, which made everything smell like a lemon fresh pine forest. Clouds of floral bouquet hovered above the fortunately faint stench of fish.

"You might attract a few neighborhood cats if you're not careful," I told him. "By the way, what did you do with the offending tuna?"

"I gave the damned thing to some church that feeds the homeless. Someone might as well enjoy it."

I left the windows open as we drove to the airport. The secretary I had talked with on the phone had given me instructions to drive in a side gate at the airport, to a place where we would be able to meet the plane on the tarmac. We passed through a security point where a guard checked my name off a list. Then we drove toward the end of a runway where the private planes came in. Cass kept peering out the open window, gazing enviously at the small planes taking off and landing.

"Boy, I bet it's great to chauffeur one of those babies around! Maybe when I win the big jackpot. . . ."

"Cass, don't even think it. You cause enough trouble on the ground."

We watched a sleek two-engine Lear jet come down the runway and pull to a stop near our car. With a hydraulic hiss, a door towards the front of the plane opened and a flight of steps extended down onto the tarmac. A smartly dressed young woman

181

came down the steps from the jet and walked towards our car.

"Mr. Allen," said the young woman. "Mr. Seidman, Mr. McMurphy, and Mr. Taylor would like you to join them in the conference room aboard the plane."

"Hey, you think I could take a peek at the cockpit?" asked Cass. "I'm thinking of trading in the old Cadillac one of these days."

"Certainly, Mr. Cassidy," said the young woman. Cass seemed tickled she knew his name, and he whispered in my ear that this was his idea of a class act. We followed the young lady up the steps into the jet. Cass stepped off to the left to meet the pilot, and I went to the right, into what appeared to be a small but posh Beverly Hills conference room that just happened to have wings extending outside the windows.

Messrs. Seidman, McMurphy and Taylor, who were seated around an oblong wooden table, rose to greet me. All three were dressed in thousand-dollar suits and custom-made shirts, and they had similarly expensive suntans, and bodies well-toned by exercise salons. Leo Seidman and Jonathan McMurphy were on the elderly side of fifty, each with silver hair, but Bill Taylor could hardly have been much more than forty. We exchanged a few pleasantries, and within moments of our introductions I would have been at a loss to say who was Seidman, who was McMurphy and who was Taylor.

"Thank you for coming to the airport," said one.

"We're on a rather busy schedule," said another.

"And we wanted to have a talk with you as soon as possible," said a third.

We smiled at one another.

"Look, let's be candid," said one of the lawyers. "We'd rather hire a team of private investigators to look into this matter, but frankly—"

"Against our advice," interrupted his partner.

". . . Mr. Hamilton has insisted that you be allowed to investigate the murder. For some reason, Bobby believes you can prove his innocence . . ."

". . . and discover who *really* killed his wife, naturally."

"Nothing personal against you, Mr. Allen, but of course you're not a detective."

"Well, gentlemen, I've had some luck in the past unraveling a few mysteries, but you're absolutely right—I'm a total amateur at this. My feeling is your office should just go ahead and do things your way and forget all about me. Meanwhile, I'll look around a bit in my own amateur manner, and if I find anything . . ."

"You can bring it to our attention," said one of the lawyers more happily.

"So, Mr. Allen, I think we're all in complete accord," said the first again. "Let me give you our card. You can reach us night or day, on land or in the air. And meanwhile, if you need anything . . ."

"Don't hesitate . . ."

". . . we're completely at your disposal."

I realized the three had finished with me, and that I was expected to rise and depart. Actually, these men did not take me at all seriously. As far as they were concerned, their wealthy client had made an eccentric request which they were bound to honor—now that they had done their duty, they

183

could carry on in their best Beverly Hills manner, on land and in the air. This was fine with me, but I wasn't quite ready to leave.

"Please tell me about Christie's drug problems," I asked.

There was a stunned silence, and a few worried looks were exchanged around the table.

"What exactly do you mean?" said Mr. Seidman.

"I understand your firm has represented Bobby Hamilton for nearly twenty years, so I imagine you know quite a few things. Now there's a videotape of Christie Hamilton buying cocaine from a source in Vegas. I want to know how long she was into drugs, and if she was a light user or heavy user, and if she always went to gangsters to get her supply."

The three gentlemen were not happy. I had to remind them that Bobby had instructed them to help me in every way and that if I was to be of any use, I had to know all the painful details. They consulted each other in whispers, bringing their elegant heads close together, and then sat up and turned my way.

The three lawyers told me—constantly interrupting one another—that Christie Hamilton had been a social drug user from the start of the marriage, smoking marijuana when that was fashionable, switching to cocaine when that came into vogue among the Hollywood fast set. For years, Bobby didn't pay too much attention to Christie's drug use—as a musician, he was tolerant of it. His own drug of choice was scotch and water.

By the mid-Eighties, Christie Hamilton's social usage had turned into a full-time problem. She checked into a detox center in Santa Barbara for two

184

months, but quickly reverted to bad habits as soon as she returned to her old crowd. Bobby and Christie began to have separate social lives—he gravitated toward an older, established show biz crowd, people who had been successful for twenty or thirty years and had big houses in Bel Air and Palm Springs; she hung out with an international assortment of rock musicians and younger movie people and writers, who tended to use drugs and live in odd but expensive houses in the Hollywood Hills or at the beach. As far as Seidman, McMurphy, and Taylor knew, Christie got her drugs from personal friends, and never had any dealings with a professional criminal element. None of them had any knowledge of when Christie had met Johnny Nakamura, nor why she would expose herself to the dangers of buying cocaine from a presumed stranger in a Las Vegas hotel room.

So there it was—as much as the three lawyers could tell me. Alas, Hollywood is full of people like Christie Hamilton—nice enough, but lost in the fast lane. She had too much time and money on her hands, and not much to do except flit about in the brain-numbing celebrity social scene. I kept thinking what a shame it was that Christie had not had the time to create her shelter for homeless children in East L.A.—she might have saved herself, along with the children.

"How about Wade?" I asked. "Is he another casualty of fame and fortune?"

The three lawyers once again had a whispered conversation. It seemed one thing to tell me about a dead woman, but Wade Hamilton was their employer's son and was still very much alive.

"Please, anything you can tell me about him is

important," I insisted. "We have to know why he's changed his story about the kidnapping."

In the same patchwork style as before—as if the lawyers were a strange three-headed monster with one body and three mouths—I learned more about Wade Hamilton. I was not surprised to discover the boy had had a troubled childhood. At the age of ten, he'd complained of bad dreams and was sent to a child psychiatrist in Beverly Hills. The dreams disappeared, but Wade never succeeded in fitting in anywhere—he had few friends at school and avoided sports and the kinds of activities that would have brought him into contact with other children. At the age of seventeen, he tried to set fire to his New England boarding school; five years after that, he nearly died in a suicide attempt.

"What about women?" I asked. "Have there been any girlfriends?"

The three lawyers glanced at each other and were silent.

"Please answer my question. Is he gay, perhaps?"

"No, not that. This is *very* confidential, Mr. Allen."

"Do I look like a blabbermouth?"

"No, but you see . . ."

". . . unfortunately, Wade has a certain problem. He goes to prostitutes . . ."

"He mistreats them a little, I'm afraid. It sometimes gets out of hand."

". . . There was one girl we had to pay off, ten thousand dollars, as well as her hospital bills. . . ."

"Another time, the police were involved. The girl nearly died. . . ."

". . . There was almost a scandal. It's hell to keep stuff like this out of the papers."

"Mr. Hamilton blames himself, you understand. He feels perhaps he was a bad father. And he doesn't want *anyone* to know about this."

I shook my head wearily. The Hamilton family was proving not much fun to get to know; they had appeared more glamorous from a distance. "Well," I said, "sad as this may be for Wade, I think it's good news for Bobby. Obviously the kid's deeply disturbed—which means it should be easy to discredit his revised kidnapping story in front of a jury."

All three lawyers vehemently shook their heads. "No, no! Don't you understand what we're telling you? We can't use this!"

"But you've got to—it could put Bobby in the clear. Otherwise, Wade's story about the kidnapping might get him convicted of first degree murder."

"I'm sorry," Seidman said, "but we have to find another way. Mr. Hamilton would rather go to prison than expose his son. He has given specific instructions on this point. We discussed this on the phone yesterday at some length. . . ."

"But the boy needs help!" I objected. "And a cover-up isn't going to help Bobby *or* Wade."

"Sorry, but our hands are tied."

"Well, *mine* aren't," I told them, standing up to leave.

"Mr. Allen, you promised to be a team player!"

"Did I? Happy landings, gentlemen—I think this is where I parachute out."

I left three unhappy lawyers and found Cass in

the cockpit of the airplane, where he seemed to be piloting us through some imaginary clouds. I brought him back to earth, and we drove away in our aromatic limousine.

chapter 23

While I was hovering fifteen feet above the Las Vegas airport with the three-headed monster of Beverly Hills law, Jayne was taking a drive in Michelle's red Ferrari.

Michelle had found Jayne after breakfast and was quite mysterious as to their destination. "Just come with me . . . *please*, Jayne? I really need you right now."

In general, Jayne is not one to dash off on unknown adventures in red Ferraris—not even in Las Vegas—but she took one look at Michelle's earnest expression and said, "Well, dear, we'd better get on our way, I suppose, to wherever it is we're going."

Michelle drove them northward on Las Vegas Boulevard. She wore a black shift with pink pedal-pushers underneath, sunglasses with pink frames, and a multicolored silk scarf about her head. With her blonde hair, pretty face, and her red Ferrari, Michelle Hamilton caused quite a stir among the male population of Las Vegas as she sped up the street—boys in convertibles gunned their cars to get alongside to have a better look, and they waved, shouted and whistled to get her attention.

"Men are such children!" said Michelle, leaving a Ford Mustang full of disappointed young men in the wake of her exhaust.

Jayne told me later she was terrified only about ninety percent of the time. Michelle wasn't a bad driver, but she had a way of seldom looking at the road—she stared at Jayne, at the boys who were driving up alongside, at the casinos they passed—everywhere, in fact, but rarely at the traffic in front of them.

"Watch out for the truck . . . the truck, Michelle," said Jayne anxiously, applying imaginary brakes.

The girl passed around the truck in question and accelerated briefly to 70 mph to make a changing yellow light.

"Goodness, this car has quite a lot of get up and go," said Jayne breathlessly.

"The Ferrari? Yeah, I guess so. . . . I used to love fast cars, ya know, but they just aren't *me* anymore," said Michelle moodily, peering through her pink glasses. "Maybe I'm getting old, Jayne. Sometimes I find myself wanting to slow down and drive a Volvo or something."

"Sounds like middle age all right—or maybe just good sense," said Jayne, with only a touch of irony. "What are you? Twenty-three?"

"*Almost* twenty-four. But my life's been pretty fast and wild, to tell the truth. Frankly, I never thought I'd live this long—do you know how many cars I've crashed?"

"Perhaps you shouldn't tell me about this right

now," said Jayne nervously. But Michelle went ahead and told her anyway.

"Watch out for that Mercedes, dear—Michelle!"

The Mercedes in question was pulling out of a parking space into Michelle's ongoing path. The girl apparently didn't believe in using brakes; she floored the accelerator, and the red Ferrari sprinted around the Mercedes into the wrong lane, narrowly missed a taxi, and pulled back onto the right side of the street without a scratch.

"I guess I lead a charmed life," Michelle said with a sigh. "Actually, I always knew my Mom and Dad would be there to pick up the pieces whenever I got into trouble, so why worry? I'd wreck a car, wreck a marriage, and all I'd have to do is get on the phone and cry a little, and they'd kinda sweep me up and pay the bills, and everything was taken care of. It got so I was testing them all the time. It was like I was saying, 'Okay, you guys—this time I'm *really* in a jam! I dare you to get me out of it!' Do you know what I mean, Jayne?"

"I think so. You wanted to see if your parents really loved you."

"Love!" said Michelle, and she was momentarily silent. "It's funny, isn't it? Now my mother's dead, and my father's in jail, and they can't help me any more. And you know, it's the strangest thing, Jayne, I feel real sad about everything that's happened, but at the same time I'm kinda glad. I finally have to take care of myself, and if I do something really stupid, there's not going to be anyone there to clean it up. I can't quite describe it . . . but I feel like I just woke up after a long sleep."

"It's called growing up, Michelle. And I think

your mother would be happy to hear you talking like this way," Jayne said. "You must always remember that Christie saw her own mistakes quite clearly at the end, and she was getting ready to make some important changes in her life."

"I miss her," said Michelle quietly. She made a turn onto a side street and drove into the driveway of a pretentious Tudor-style, red brick building that had newly planted ivy starting to grow up the sides. A sign outside said this was Irving Carlsen and Sons, Funeral Directors. By a strange chance, the funeral home was next door to the Happy Endings Wedding Chapel, where a marriage ceremony seemed about to begin.

"Well, this is it," said Michelle, squinting at the facade of the mortuary. "I found it in the Yellow Pages."

"You're going to make arrangements for your mother?"

"I guess. You don't mind coming with me, do you? You see, my Dad's lawyers said they'd take care of all this, but I thought about it and told them I wanted to do it myself. I mean, the lawyers, they don't really care—they'd just be doing it for the money. So I thought I should get involved."

"Well, I think that's a wonderful idea," said Jayne. "Did your mother leave any instructions about what kind of funeral she wanted?"

Michelle smiled ruefully. "You kidding? You think Mom would ever let herself even *think* about anything depressing like death? And now it's too late, so I have to decide for her."

"Have you talked this over with your father?"

"Yeah. I went to see him in jail yesterday, and he says I should just go ahead and do what I think is best. He's so blown away by everything that's happened, *he* can't make any decisions. It's strange, but suddenly it's like *I'm* the parent."

"Do you mind that?"

Michelle puckered her lips in thought and then faintly smiled. "No, I like it actually. Maybe it's about time."

Michelle and Jayne climbed out of the Ferrari—which for Jayne really *was* a climb. She followed Michelle into the funeral home, where they were shown into the office of Irving Carlsen, a tall man with pale skin and red hair who was dressed in a somber dark-blue suit. The office tried hard to look like a drawing room out of nineteenth century England, and there was faint organ music playing "Because" in the background.

Michelle sat impassively behind her dark glasses as the funeral director explained all the options, from a quiet cremation and a silver urn to the deluxe special of the house, which seemed to include a horse-drawn hearse complete with hired mourners and acres of flowers. Jayne was not at all certain she would entrust Irving Carlsen and Sons with *her* last remains, but she kept quiet; in this case, it seemed important that Michelle be the one to take responsibility of making the hard decisions.

"I see . . . so what does all this cost?" asked Michelle. And she listened while the funeral director went over his price list of services.

"Wow, I really don't know," said Michelle at last. "What do you think, Jayne?"

"I think you should take your time," said Jayne. "Maybe you need another day to think this over."

"Yeah, maybe you're right."

"Of course, this week we have a special on the horse-drawn hearse," said the funeral director in soft tones. "Until tomorrow, it's only $9999, which is a fabulous savings of nearly a thousand dollars from the regular price."

"Yes, of course," said Michelle seriously. "And I do want to be economical."

It was obvious that Michelle had no practical knowledge of day-to-day dealings with money. "I still think you should wait, dear," suggested Jayne gently.

The funeral director was not happy to have such an easy mark as Michelle Hamilton escape his net—his professional smile tightened as Jayne led the girl away. Michelle and Jayne walked out the front door and found a bench in a shaded spot near a patch of bright purple flowers overlooking the wedding chapel next door.

"I guess I'm screwing this up," Michelle said. "Maybe I should let my father's lawyers take care of it after all—probably they'll know what to do."

"No, I think you're doing fine, dear. I also think your mother would appreciate the fact that you're taking care of this yourself."

"Yeah, but I got to do *some*thing about the body, Jayne. The autopsy's been done, and I can't just let Mom lie there in the morgue."

"Well, try to imagine, if it were you, Michelle—what kind of funeral would *you* like to have?"

The girl was quiet, thinking hard. "I guess I'd like a big party with a really good band," she said. "All my friends could come and dance, and then maybe I'd be cremated and have my ashes scattered over the desert, someplace like where we were driving the other day. I think that would be very peaceful. Maybe that's what Mom would want."

"Did your mother like the desert?"

Michelle shook her head. "No, actually she hated it. She didn't even like going to the house in Palm Springs. So I guess that's out."

"What about the ocean? In California, I've heard of people having their ashes scattered over the sea."

"No, I don't think so," said Michelle gloomily. "Not Mom." The girl seemed quite discouraged, but then brightened. "Hey, I got it! I'll hire a plane to scatter her ashes over Rodeo Drive. I mean, that's where she liked to spend all her time. I'll have Mom scattered between Elizabeth Arden, The Daisy and Van Cleef & Arpels!"

"Well, it's a very *original* idea," Jayne said. "But I'm not certain it's legal to dispose of—"

"But how would they know? I mean, they'd think it's just a little extra smog coming down."

chapter 24

"Jayne, do you mind if I tell you about me and Johnny?" said Michelle out of nowhere. The women had been sitting in silence side-by-side on the bench outside of the funeral home, watching a wedding party arrive next door in a white limousine.

"Johnny Nakamura? The gangster?"

"Yeah . . . I mean, maybe you've been wondering why I took those shots at him, and all that."

"Well, naturally I was curious."

"I've been really stupid—to tell you the truth, I was romantically involved with him for a while. Are you shocked? I mean, you're such an absolute *lady*. I feel embarrassed telling you this."

"I may look to you like something from the age of Queen Victoria," said Jayne with a smile, "But I don't shock very easily."

"Well, I thought going out with a gangster might be exciting, but boy, was I wrong. Johnny turned out to be even more boring than my normal boyfriends."

"Were you aware your mother was seeing him as well?"

"Yeah—I mean, that was part of the interest. Forbidden fruit, and all that. I guess it was like those reckless things I was talking about earlier, wrecking cars and marriages. I wanted to see if my mother would get angry at me."

"Did she?"

"No. When I told her, she just got really sad, and she said Johnny was a bastard and he'd hurt me if I let him, just like he was hurting her. When my Mom was killed . . . well, I thought Johnny must have done it, so I decided to go after the creep."

"But why did you think it was Johnny?"

"Well, he was the only person I knew who did things like that—kill people, I mean. And besides, he and my Mom had a big fight about the blackmail thing—you know, trying to get my Dad to sing at his stupid hotel. My Mom was really angry and threatened to tell some things to the police about Johnny's business—how he was skimming from the casino."

"Are you sure, dear? This could be very important—Christie was going to the police?"

"It's what Johnny told me, anyway. He wanted me to talk my Mom out of it, naturally. He said if she went to the cops there'd be a very big scandal, especially since *I* was involved too."

"I see. And *did* you talk with your mother?"

"Sure. But she said she was only trying to scare Johnny into forgetting the blackmail idea, and that she never had any intention of *really* going to the cops. But Johnny didn't know that, of course. That's why I thought when she died, he must have had some part of it."

"You think he was trying to keep her quiet?"

Michelle shrugged. "Well, I did at first. But it all seems so complicated, and now I'm not sure."

"What about your brother?" Jayne asked. "He seems like a rather unhappy young man. It's an awful thought but could *he* have had any part in your mother's death?"

"I don't know. It's true he hated her—she was only his stepmother, and Wade somehow blamed her for his real mother's death. It was unfair, of course—Dad and Wade's mother were divorced nearly five years before he married Christie, but Wade's not the most rational person in the world."

"Why do you think he's telling everybody that the kidnapping was a hoax?"

Michelle seemed perplexed. "Who knows why Wade does anything? I always thought he loved Dad—but maybe he's hated him all these years and this is his big chance for revenge."

"Revenge? For what?"

"For Dad not loving him in return, I guess. Wade idolized Dad, you see, but Dad was always so busy, traveling and all."

"That's sometimes the price of having a career."

"I know. Actually, I used to think my Dad was the greatest Dad in the world. And he *is* a great guy, of course—but I'm beginning to think maybe he wasn't such a hot father. I mean, he just wanted to be pals, and joke around and stuff. It was like I could drown in front of him, and he'd just keep on laughing it up."

"Like the other day on Lake Mead," said Jayne.

"Exactly! You know, I wasn't really quite as drunk as I pretended. I just wanted to see what his reaction would be, and it was pretty damn predictable."

"It was Wade who jumped in and saved you."

"Sure. Wade and I have stuck together—we've had to, to survive. But I think Wade feels pretty bitter about the whole family situation."

"So you think he's getting even?" said Jayne thoughtfully. "Well, it would be the ultimate revenge, I suppose—his story could put your father in prison for a long, long time. Maybe even send him to the gas chamber. Have your father and brother been fighting recently?"

"Not especially. Wade just does whatever Dad tells him and never complains, so they don't exactly have a lot to fight about. Oh, there was that one thing . . ."

"What was that, dear?"

"Well, it was about Wade hanging around with Johnny Nakamura, actually. My Dad didn't like that, and they had a one-way screaming match about a week ago. I'm not sure you could call it a fight exactly—I mean, Dad screamed, and Wade just sat there all weird and repressed, taking it all without a word."

Jayne's antennae were instantly alerted. "I didn't realize Wade was friendly with Mr. Nakamura."

"You think it's important?"

"Michelle, this could have a great deal to do with why Wade changed his story. How did he happen to know Johnny?"

Michelle giggled. "Now this *is* going to shock you, Jayne—it has to do with prostitutes. Wade goes to them—that's his kicks. Pretty perverted, if you ask me."

"But what does that have to do with Johnny Nakamura?"

"Well, he's a gangster. He is into gambling. Prostitution. The works. Anyway, my brother got a little violent with one of his girls, knocked her around a little. Johnny said he could forget all about it if Wade did exactly what he told him."

"Michelle," Jayne said. "This is all beginning to become disgustingly clear! Johnny told Wade to sell his father on the idea of working at Johnny's new hotel—is that it?"

"Yeah. If Wade came through, Johnny would supply him with all the girls he might ever want to rough up. If he didn't, he'd turn him over to the cops. He said Wade would be convicted as a sex offender and would even have to register with the local police whenever he visited a new town. It would be pretty embarrassing—and of course Dad would have a fit!"

"I thought your father just bailed you out of whatever trouble you got into."

"That's only for *me*, Jayne—Dad has a double standard when it comes to us kids. It's like I can never do anything wrong, but Wade can never do anything right."

"I see. So Wade was in a very bad position, caught between Johnny and his father. Did he try to convince your father to appear at Johnny's hotel?"

"He sure did, and Dad was furious. He said he'd never work for a gangster, Japanese or otherwise."

"That makes him pretty unusual in our business," Jayne said.

"Well, he said that if he ever caught Wade hanging out with that low-life, he'd be damned sorry."

Michelle screwed up her pretty face in thought. "You think this has something to do with the murder?"

"Michelle," Jayne said, "it may be the key to the whole horrid thing."

chapter 25

Jayne and Michelle returned to the hotel suite by mid-afternoon. I was slightly miffed at Michelle, since I had spent the past hour fielding phone calls from a young man trying to reach her who did not wish to leave his name. I tried to explain that she was only a casual acquaintance, I was blessedly not her father, she had a room of her own, and he would do better to leave his messages with the hotel operator—but the young fellow was undeterred, perhaps blinded by love or lust, and he kept trying at annoyingly regular intervals every fifteen minutes on the hour.

"This is too much, Michelle—I'm happy for both of you, of course, but please explain to the guy that I'm not your dating service."

"Hmm, a *guy*," said Michelle with a dreamy detachment. "I'm afraid I'm not interested in guys right now, Steve. If he calls again, tell him to try back in a month or so."

When the phone rang I could tell by the clock

that it was him. "Tell him yourself," I suggested, handing her the phone.

"Don't be so grouchy, darling," said my wife.

"*Grouchy?*" I cried. "Jayne, I've been trying to think—I have this case almost figured out, and these phone calls are beginning to drive me batty."

"Steve, you're already batty. And anyway, don't figure out the case quite yet—I have important new information for you."

"You do? What?"

"Ssh!" said Jayne, putting a finger to her lips and indicating Michelle on the phone.

"It's *Ken!*" Michelle whispered excitedly to Jayne, momentarily putting a hand over the receiver. "He wants me to go to a concert of Handel's *Water Music* at the University this evening."

"So go," Jayne said.

Michelle spoke quietly into the phone for a few moments. "Hmm . . . yeah . . . well, I'm *terribly* fond of classical music too, Ken. But I'm not sure this is a good time for me right now . . . well, okay. I'll see you downstairs at seven."

Michelle hung up the phone and screamed. "God! It's *him*, the hunk! You know, I've been invited to night clubs, parties on yachts, dinners in hotel rooms, all sorts of things—but *never* to a concert of classical music! What do you think I should wear?"

"For Handel's *Water Music*, fishing boots might be appropriate," I suggested. Jayne scowled at me. Michelle pranced about our suite for another few minutes, and then floated out the door to begin to prepare psychologically to meet Ken.

"So much for avoiding men," I said. "You

know, Jayne, I'm too old to suddenly find myself proxy-parent to a big problem child."

"She's *not* a problem child. Not anymore, at least. I believe our Michelle is on her way towards great things."

"Good," I grumbled, trusting these great things would at least lead "our Michelle" somewhere other than here. "Now what's the new information?"

Jayne quickly told me everything she had learned from Michelle about her half-brother Wade's association with Johnny Nakamura, and when she was finished I filled her in on my conversation with Messrs. Seidman, McMurphy, and Taylor. There are times on a case when everything seems to converge, and a big arrow begins to point the way to a speedy conclusion. Jayne and I smiled grimly at one another. The whole business was quite tragic, and I felt bad about Wade Hamilton's part in it all, but it was finished, at least—or nearly so—and we would soon have Bobby out of jail and the real killer in his place. Then perhaps we could even get on with the reason we had come here in the first place—the show.

"So what now, darling?"

"I think it's time we consult W.B."

"Steve, I'm surprised at you! That isn't the least bit like you, to nearly solve a crime and then let the police take over."

"Whatever gave you the idea I'm letting W.B. take over? We simply need his help to spring the trap."

I explained what I had in mind, and then telephoned Lieutenant Walker, whom I invited over for a chat—suggesting we meet in the main showroom downstairs where I would be conducting an afternoon rehearsal. W.B. wanted to know if there would

204

be pretty showgirls around in skimpy costumes, and I said he could look at them to his heart's content.

I oversaw the rehearsal, while the lieutenant came and oversaw the showgirls. During a five minute break I was able to take him aside and induce him to make certain arrangements. When the rehearsal was finished, I returned upstairs, ready at last to make my move on Wade Hamilton. I telephoned his room, where I seemed to wake him from a deep sleep. His voice was groggy and strange, but he became alert when I told him what was on my mind.

"We need to talk, Wade. I have information linking you to your stepmother's murder, but I wanted to give you a chance to tell your side of the story before going to the police."

"Why would you do me any favors?" asked the young man, strangely subdued.

"Because I owe it to your father, Wade. Frankly, he's going to be devastated by all this, and I have to be certain all my facts are right. I haven't told anyone my information yet, but when I do, I'm afraid things will really start hitting the fan."

"All right, Mr. Allen. We'll talk."

"Good. Come to my suite at eight tonight. Jayne will be out, and we'll have some privacy."

I hung up the phone and looked at Jayne. The trap was baited and set.

chapter 26

Wade was ten minutes late. I had begun to fear he wasn't coming, but then the doorbell of my suite buzzed and I found him standing in the hall.

He was wearing a neat blue blazer and gray slacks, but looked unfocused and somewhat disoriented. His hair was disheveled and his tie askew as he glanced nervously up and down the hall before stepping into my foyer.

"Would you like a glass of wine, Wade? A beer?" I offered gently. "Maybe something stronger?"

Earlier I had sent Cass out to a liquor store just in case Wade needed something to help him relax, but he shook his head rather wildly at the offer. "No! I don't want a drink—what is this, a cocktail party? If we're going to talk, let's talk."

"Sit down," I said softly, ushering him towards the sofa. But Wade peered about suspiciously, as if the sofa might be rigged with recording devices. I gave him my harmless Uncle Steve smile, but to no avail.

"Outside," he said.

"What?"

"Let's talk outside on your terrace."

"Fine. No problem."

The penthouse terrace was about twenty-five feet long but less than ten feet wide, a narrow strip of real estate overlooking the street far below. Across Las Vegas Boulevard, the casinos glittered extravagantly with their nightly light show. I sat down on a chaise lounge from where I could see the big pink-red neon tulip outside the Flamingo Hilton, and the Mississippi steamboat next door that was aglow in light. Wade straddled the chaise next to me, but did not lean back.

"Relax," I told him. "Enjoy the view."

"Mr. Allen, you say you have evidence connecting me to my stepmother's murder. You're wrong as hell, but I want to know what you think you have."

"What I have, Wade, is the reason you changed your story about the kidnapping."

"Do you?" he asked sarcastically. "I always knew my father's friends wouldn't like it if I told the truth. After all, Dad's such a pal, isn't he? Such a nice guy! So how could a swell guy like that set up a fake kidnapping and murder his wife?"

"Wade," I said patiently, "let's skip the theatrics. I know about your dealings with Johnny Nakamura. I know what he had on you, and exactly why you were doing his bidding."

"Oh, really?" he cried, and his voice had become quite shrill. "Well, if you don't believe me, why don't you ask my father's double, Mike Corvino? *He'll* tell you the kidnapping was a hoax, be-

207

cause he was in that Lincoln Continental with me while Dad was doing the dirty work up on the third floor. So whether you like it or not, that's what happened. My father killed his wife *and* that lady attendant, who just happened to be in the way, and then he disguised himself and slipped out a side door and drove a rented car to an empty house we'd already found in North Las Vegas. Mike was there. He'll tell you if this is a lie or not!"

"Unfortunately, Mike Corvino has disappeared, Wade. Isn't that curious? He came forward yesterday, but he checked out of his motel early this morning and Lieutenant Walker can't find him anywhere."

Wade shrugged. "Well, what the hell's that have to do with me?"

"It could mean you were afraid Mike's story wouldn't hold up under continued questioning so you thought it best to get him out of town while you were still ahead. The Japanese thugs were for real—Tako and Ahi—but Johnny is hiding them. So in the meantime, we have only your word that the kidnapping was a hoax. And *you're* working for Nakamura. Do you know what that makes you? An accessory to murder!"

Wade tried to laugh, but he didn't do a convincing job of it. "Why would Johnny want my stepmother killed?"

"Because she was in his way. As you know, Christie was angry that Johnny was trying to blackmail your father, and if he didn't stop she was threatening to go to the cops and blow the whistle on his little habit of skimming the profits from the slot machines. So you see, your stepmother had to go, and you helped Johnny make it happen. You had to

208

help him, because Johnny Nakamura owned you, body and soul. You helped him plan the murder, and then you framed your father so that Johnny could walk away clear. This was your big moment, Wade—you could revenge yourself against a stepmother you hated and a father who treated you like a servant, and you could even enjoy yourself with Nakamura's stable of girls."

Wade was watching me with a curious lack of emotion. "Well," he said, "I admit I didn't exactly weep when my stepmother died—and you seem to know about my appreciation of, shall we say, paid companionship. I won't bother to deny any of that. But you're forgetting something. You're suggesting Johnny ordered me to frame my father—but if my father goes to prison, Johnny doesn't get the bank loan for his new hotel. Ergo, your premise is illogical. By framing my father, Johnny Nakamura would not get what he wants—and believe me, he's a man who usually does get what he wants."

I must admit, I had already pondered the point and worried about it. It was one of many loose ends I had not quite wrapped up, but I could see at least one possible answer: "Johnny Nakamura was fighting for his life, Wade, and in this instance there was a lot more at stake than a hotel he might want—namely, his skin. So Christie had to be killed to keep her from going to the cops, and a fall guy had to be found for the murder. Cops are always inclined to believe the killer is someone in the immediate family, and so it was easy to frame your father."

"Oh, who cares about that schmuck Nakamura!" Wade cried, apparently fed up with the subject. "Or my father either. I'm sick of hearing about both of them!"

I remained silent and watchful. Wade's manner had suddenly changed. His lower lip was trembling. "I've had it with all these macho personalities who want to push other people around. I mean, who's ever cared about *me?*"

I nodded patiently. Wade seemed bursting at the seams with nervous energy. He stood up quickly, looked down at the pedestrians on Las Vegas Boulevard twenty-eight floors below, then sat down once more on the lounge.

"All right, you want to know what it's like to be me, do you?" he said in a high-pitched voice, though I had not asked him any such thing. "Well, I'll tell you—it's lousy. All my life I've been nothing but Bobby Hamilton's kid. Most people don't even know *my* name. I walk into a room and I hear people say, 'Oh, here's Bobby Hamilton's boy. Well, I wonder how we can use him to get to his father?' And none of them ever take *me* seriously. As far as they're concerned, without my father I might as well be dead."

I nodded as if this were quite sensible. A good detective, like a good psychiatrist, knows when to shut up and become a passive cup waiting to be filled with information.

"So my father tells me, 'Drive the boat, Wade.' 'Fetch your stepmother's suitcase.' 'Carry the music, Wade.' 'Roll over and play dead, Wade.' . . . But I'm not having it anymore. Do you understand?"

He was glaring at me, challenging me to understand. "I understand," I told him sympathetically. "People probably think it's easy having a famous father, but it isn't at all. It's been tough for my own four sons."

"Oh, it's not like anyone thinks *I* might have

210

any ideas of my own!" cried Wade. "Oh, no! Especially my father! You know, I went to him, and I tried to tell him about this new hotel that was going to open up, and how he could make himself a bundle if he'd agree to appear on stage two weeks out of every year. Does that sound so bad to you? Johnny was willing to pay my father half a million dollars a year for two lousy weeks, but *I* got Johnny to sweeten the deal even more—I made him offer my father a two-percent ownership of the hotel, with a permanent suite at our disposal year round, and even the use of a brand new Rolls as a bonus on signing. Now does that sound like a deal, or what?"

"It sounds like you really put quite a package together, Wade."

"You're God damned right I did! But what happens? The old man yells at me and tells me not to get involved in his business. He tells me not to hang out with gangsters—as if *his* life has been so lily-clean! So it's back to, 'Take out the dry cleaning, Wade.' 'Make sure the car has gas.' 'But don't *ever* do anything important, for chrissake, like maybe make a very good deal for a lot of money and all kinds of perks'!"

"I would be very resentful if I were you, Wade."

"You bet your ass you would! And then there was that bitch pretending to be my mother . . . sure I helped Johnny knock her off—she had it coming. But you're wrong about him asking me to frame my father. I bet you can't guess who he *really* wanted me to set up."

"Who?"

"Come on . . . try guessing!"

"Elliot Block?"

"Naw, Michelle," he shouted, almost gleefully.

211

"Michelle?"

"That's right—I was supposed to make it look like my stepsister did it. But *she's* the only one who's ever been nice to me, Mr. Allen. She cares what I think about things—so I'd never do anything to hurt Michelle."

"So you framed your father instead?"

"Sure. I brought Mike Corvino from Los Angeles—I set up the whole thing. And you see how clever I was? I killed two birds with one stone—I got even with my father *and* Johnny Nakamura all in one sweet move. My father goes to prison, and Johnny's ambitions to be a major player on The Strip come to a sudden end."

"Not bad," I told him. "But Johnny must have been awfully angry. Weren't you afraid he'd turn you in for beating up his prostitutes? With a record for violence against women like you have, Wade . . . well, you might have been institutionalized."

"Oh, I was too clever for that, Mr. Allen. You see, Johnny started out thinking he had the goods on me, but by the time it was over, *I* had the goods on him—in a big way. I told him that if anything happened to me, the D.A. and the IRS would receive a very interesting envelope showing how Johnny was behind my stepmother's murder. There was a hit man, of course, who did the actual killing, but I have a tape recording of Johnny telling me how he was going to have it done."

"Clever," I agreed. "I guess everyone will have to take you seriously, Wade, from now on. By the way, where is this tape recording?"

Wade giggled. "Oh, no you don't—that's for me to know," he said, standing up from the lounge and hovering above me. "Besides, it wouldn't really do you any good. You see, you're about to have an unfortunate accident."

"I don't think so, Wade—you wouldn't be that stupid."

"Sorry, but I've indulged myself telling you the truth, and now I can't leave you around to tell the police, can I? I hope you like flying, man—because you're about to take a high dive off this terrace."

Wade was hovering above me in a menacing way, and I was getting more than a little nervous.

"Listen to me carefully, son. I'm wired with a transmitting device, and Lieutenant Walker is listening to our conversation at this very moment from just down the hall."

Wade grinned at me. "You're bluffing, of course," he said, coming closer. I was taller and heavier, but he was many years younger and revved up with adrenalin. I had no doubt that Wade Hamilton was more than able to pick me up and toss me off the penthouse terrace. This is not exactly the kind of splash I intended to make on The Strip, and I knew I'd better lay my cards on the table fast.

"Take a look if I'm bluffing or not," I told him quickly, pulling up my shirt to reveal a small transmitter and microphone which had been taped to my chest. "So you see, it's too late, son—the police know everything you've told me. Right now you're only an accessory to murder—with a good lawyer and maybe a couple of psychiatrists, you might get off pretty lightly. But if you kill me, Wade, they'll put you away for the rest of your life."

Wade was staring in mute horror at the transmitter on my chest. I needed to keep him talking just a few moments longer—long enough for W.B. to arrive with the cavalry.

213

"You'll get help now," I told him gently, "And in a few years all this torment will be like a bad dream. Now let's you and I go inside and say hello to Lieutenant Walker."

"You tricked me, God damn you!" said Wade in a terrible whisper.

"Look, Wade, this isn't going to be so bad for you. If you testify against Johnny Nakamura, you could even come out of this a hero."

"No," he said, shaking his head slowly. "It's too late."

His mouth went slack; his eyes stared at me with a dreadful intensity. Wade moved one step closer, his fists clenched, his chest heaving, like a madman. All the anger in his soul seemed directed at me, and then as I watched him, he seemed to deflate.

"I guess you win after all, Mr. Allen," he told me bitterly. "Tell my father . . . tell him to think about me sometimes."

I saw too late what he was about to do. "For God's sake, *don't!*" I shouted. But Hamilton had turned from me and walked to the very edge of my narrow terrace. Before I could think of any way to stop him, he climbed up onto the railing, and then leaped, screaming, twenty-eight floors down to the pavement below.

chapter 27

A few hours after poor Wade Hamilton died on the pavement outside of the hotel, I again found myself at the Metropolitan Police Station, this time with Elliot Block, Lieutenant Walker and all three partners of Seidman, McMurphy and Taylor. We were gathered in uncomfortable chairs in the main squad room, waiting for an officer to bring Bobby Hamilton down from the jail upstairs.

Our mood was far from jubilant. Bobby was technically a free man, his name had been cleared— but the price to the family had been enormous. Wade and Christie were dead, and the living were emotional wrecks.

Bobby came down in the elevator in his street clothes, wearing slacks and a sports shirt, standing between two uniformed officers. He was smiling, no longer the ashen-gray figure I had visited only yesterday evening in jail.

"Hey, I want you guys to come to the show tomorrow night," he was saying to the two cops. "In fact, I insist on it, so don't be shy. I'll have my manager leave tickets for you and your wives at the box office. You too, Lieutenant Walker. No hard feelings, okay?"

The thought crossed my mind that Hamilton might be on uppers, so inappropriate was his mood, particularly his determination to go ahead with a public performance at a time when his wife and son were lying in the local morgue. Either he was out of his mind from repressed grief or he was the most insensitive human being I had ever met.

"Hey, Elliot, Steve! Holy cow, we got the big legal brains from Beverly Hills here as well! Look what they gave me as a souvenir!"

Bobby held up an orange jumpsuit for us all to see. On the back was written: PROPERTY OF LAS VEGAS CITY JAIL. And then his voice became grave and full of emotion. "You know, I can't express what I'm feeling right now, but I want to thank you all for standing by me during a tremendously difficult time of my life. I'm going to miss Christie, but it's a comfort knowing I have such good and loyal friends."

The rest of us stood uneasily in the glow of Bobby's gratitude. At last he turned to me. "And I want to thank you especially, Steve. No one's told me any of the details yet, but I understand it was you who proved my innocence and got me out of here."

"No one's told you . . ."

"Not a thing." Bobby said cheerfully, putting an affectionate arm around my shoulder. "But hell, we'll have time for all the stories later."

I realized with a shock that he hadn't heard about his son's death. Neither Elliot Block nor Seidman, McMurphy, and Taylor had had the guts to break the terrible news. Even Lieutenant Walker looked a bit awkward and shuffled slightly to the side. The lawyers coughed and lowered their eyes. But our somber expressions were finally getting through to Bobby.

"Hey, what's the matter, gang?"

I was hoping for a miracle, that maybe one of the lawyers would step forward and speak. But they did not. I finally took Bobby by the arm and led him off toward a window overlooking the street.

"Steve, you're beginning to scare me, man. What's the lick?"

"I think I'd better get this out straight, Bob. There's been another terrible tragedy—Wade's dead."

He just stared at me.

"He killed himself, Bobby. He admitted trying to frame you for Christie's murder and I guess he just couldn't live with himself after that."

Hamilton seemed momentarily unable to take this in. He was left with a strongly blank look, the expression of a man totally bewildered.

"He's . . ."

"He's dead, Bobby. But he told us the truth before he died. It was Johnny Nakamura who had Christie killed—and, I'm sorry, but Wade was working with Johnny. I wish I could have spared you this."

"No!" said Bobby in a harsh whisper. And then he screamed it: *"No! . . . No!"*

W.B. hurried over, and we helped Bobby into a chair. There was still a puzzled look on Bobby's face, and he kept shaking his head.

"I don't believe it! You say he . . . killed himself? How?"

217

I wanted to avoid the details, but Bobby grabbed my wrist, hard. *"How,* God damn it!" he demanded.

"He jumped—off the terrace of my hotel suite. I didn't have time to stop him."

"And he said he framed me?"

"His last words were, 'Tell my father to think about me sometimes.'" I hoped this might bring some comfort, but it did not. Bobby let go of my wrist, and his eyes dropped to the floor in an attitude of total defeat. All around me, the squad room was absolutely still: not a cop, not a lawyer dared move or speak.

Out of Bobby's throat came a strange garbled cry that grew in volume until it was a dreadful roar: "Aaaaahhhhh . . ." Without warning, with the eerie cry still building, he leapt from his chair toward the half-open window at the side of the squad room. W.B. and I, as well as the three lawyers and Elliot Block, all ran after him, tackled him, and hung on tightly so he couldn't throw himself out the window to his death. Even with all of us on him, Bobby's will to die was so great that he managed to smash the glass with his elbow in trying to fight us off. One of the officers summoned a paramedic, who ran and gave Hamilton a shot of something that made him relax.

"We've got to get him to a hospital! How the fuck d'ya dial 911 around here?" cried Elliot Block, who looked as if he was ready for a nervous breakdown himself.

"I'm all right now. I just want to go home," said Bobby unexpectedly in a quiet and normal voice.

"Don't worry, we're going to have an ambulance here in a second," Elliot said.

"Will someone get Elliot a drink, for chrissake," said Bobby wearily. His voice was exhausted but sounded sane. The worst was over; acceptance had set in. "And then I want to get the hell out of here. Please," he added.

One of the uniformed men found a bottle of brandy in a desk drawer, kept for such emergencies no doubt. Elliot Block, still overwrought, sat in a chair and took a long gulp.

Lieutenant Walker sat on the edge of a desk peering at the man in disbelief, an expression on his face which clearly said: *Jeez! What a creep.* Then he spoke aloud to the room: "This is all Johnny Nakamura's fault. I'm going to get that son of a bitch and bring down his whole sick little empire!"

We watched W.B. pick up the phone, call the D.A. and request an immediate warrant for Nakamura's arrest.

chapter 28

Jayne and I had a late breakfast in our hotel suite Saturday morning, having agreed that the show must not go on.

"Personally, I think we might as well start packing," she said. "Poor Bobby wouldn't think of going on stage after so much tragedy."

"I hope you're right. It would be a terrible thing."

About eleven o'clock, I had a phone call from Michelle that settled the question. She was no longer our problem child in residence; Michelle had left our care last night to look after her father, and her voice on the phone was surprisingly businesslike. It was hard to believe this was the same scatterbrained young woman we had seen nearly drown in Lake Mead.

"Steve, we've decided to go ahead with the opening after all. My father feels he'd rather be working than sitting around moping in his room."

"What!"

"Well, at least he's not just staring at the walls

like he did last night, but all the bounce is gone out of the man. I hardly recognize him."

"If I took part in the show at all it would be just to play the piano and introduce your father, although I still hope he'll listen to reason."

"Well," she said, "you'd better talk to Chris Carter, the bandleader, if you're going to be making any changes."

"That's a good idea," I said. "I'll do that. Talk to you later."

"How's our Michelle?" asked Jayne when I had hung up the phone.

"Our Michelle is growing up fast," I said. "Isn't it amazing how a bit of responsibility can turn a kid into an adult overnight?"

I dialed Carter's room.

"Chris," I said, "is Bobby *really* planning to go on tonight?

"I'm with you, man," he said. "I tried to talk him out of it, but you know Bobby."

"Well, if there is a show—and I'm part of it—I'm not going to do my usual Question-Cards-From-The-Audience comedy bit."

"Of course not," he said.

"I'll just do music, and maybe only about fifteen minutes of that, instead of the thirty I was planning."

"What will you be playing? I saw you do 'Misty' one night when you were doing a guest-shot with Jay Leno on *The Tonight Show*. We have a nice chart on that."

"What key is it in?"

"The original, E-flat."

"Perfect," I said. "I'll play it up to the bridge and then come in again for the last eight."

"You got it," he said. "On that kind of a tune, just one nice slow chorus is enough, don't you think?"

"Yes," I said. "Particularly tonight."

"Hey, I've got a great idea! Terry Gibbs is in town working with Buddy DeFranco. I caught you guys on a show one night—I forget what it was—doing your vibes duet. It knocks people out."

"No," I said. "I love the number, but it's too peppy, too upbeat for a situation like this."

"I guess you're right," he said.

"Another number I can do—one that always works for me—is a very flowery Liberace-type treatment of Jerome Kern's 'The Song Is You.' I do it out of tempo, so all I need is for your bass player to bow some arco notes for me and the drummer to give me waves-on-the-beach with his cymbals. Then when I finish—the thing is in D-flat—the band should give me a big, soft closing chord."

"No problem," he said.

"Listen," I said, "you must have some guys in the band who play great jazz, right?"

"Yeah, several. Why?"

"I'll introduce your men, let's say whoever is your best trumpet guy, and whatever saxophone player can play very pretty—and we'll bill it as a small-group special feature and do "Body and Soul." How does that sound?"

"Like music to my ears," Chris said, laughing softly at his own joke.

"Okay," I said. "I'll talk to you later, but I still hope that we don't have to do any of this. I still hope Bobby will change his mind."

Later, I swam in the hotel pool and then sat in the sun for a while reading Berlin's *Against The Cur-*

rent. Every few minutes, I found myself thinking about Wade and Christie and the whole tragic drama of the last few days. I wondered how Johnny Nakamura was enjoying the start of his life behind bars. I hoped his old grandmother was choking on her nasty little cigars! This was so satisfying to contemplate that I found myself tempted to phone Lieutenant Walker to find out what was happening—but I reminded myself it really wasn't any of my business. I had done my part to solve the mystery; it was over.

I was half-dozing, the book opened on my stomach, when a large shadow came between me and the sun. I opened my eyes and was surprised to find W.B. Walker. His suit appeared even more shapeless in the bright sunlight. He was wearing a battered panama hat.

"What brings you here, Lieutenant? Have you wrung a confession out of Nakamura yet?"

Lieutenant Walker sat down on an empty deck chair and sighed. He looked out of place by a swimming pool.

"They said I'd find you out here," he told me sadly. "I guess some people just get to loaf around all day."

W.B. watched a redhead in a lime green bathing suit do a perfect jackknife into the water. He spoke without turning to me, watching as the swimmer came up for air: "Actually, we haven't found him yet."

"He's still on the loose?"

"Sometimes guys like that have a sixth sense about when trouble is coming. He left the Lucky Horseshoe about twenty minutes before we got there. Seems to have gone into deep hiding."

"Well, it's *de facto* confession of his guilt, at least. So cheer up—you'll find him. And meanwhile you've put him out of circulation."

"I suppose so," he said. W.B. finally turned away from the girl in the pool and gave me his full attention. "Look, I need to ask you one more time about the old woman who drove you around the block the other night. Would you mind describing her?"

"Again? Johnny's grandmother was one of a kind, W.B. Believe me, you'll recognize her when you see her: about four feet tall, shriveled, eighty-nine years old and, of course, Japanese. You probably don't have too many people in Vegas answering that description."

"Yeah, well, the funny thing is we can't find her, either."

"Maybe she's in hiding with her grandson?"

"Maybe, but here's the weird part—none of the employees at the Lucky Horseshoe have ever heard of her."

"What?"

"No one I spoke with even knew Johnny *had* a grandmother. I was curious enough to call Immigration to see if an elderly Mrs. Nakamura had come into the country recently from Japan, and they didn't have a thing on her. So then I called a cop I know in Tokyo—we worked on a smuggling case together a number of years back. He checked with his sources and called me back, and you know what he told me?"

"What?"

"He said both sets of Nakamura's grandparents died way back in the '60s. Johnny's father, Hideo Nakamura, is the head of the crime family—oh,

224

there are uncles and brothers and nephews and quite a network of unpleasant relatives. But no grandmothers."

I had sat up and closed my book.

"That's the damndest thing. Well, she *said* she was his grandmother, and she certainly was old enough to fill the bill. I wonder who she could be, and why she was lying?"

"Me, too," said the lieutenant. "I hate it when there's an extra piece left over that doesn't fit into a puzzle. Well, hell, I guess it's my problem. I'll let you get back to your suntan now."

"Are you coming to the show tonight?"

"No, I don't think so. To tell the truth, I'm going to be a little busy until I get that bastard Nakamura behind bars."

"Well, good luck. Let me know when you get him."

"Sure thing. Enjoy the easy life," he said, and then walked away from the pool, shaking his head in mild disapproval.

I opened up my book again and tried to read. It was useless.

I didn't like it either when there was an extra piece that didn't fit into a puzzle. If the old woman wasn't Nakamura's grandmother, who the hell was she? Who—if anyone—had sent her to me, and what did she want?

I had an unsettled feeling that this mystery wasn't wrapped up after all.

chapter 29

The house was packed. We had not only the usual kind of people who come to see the big shows in Vegas—conventioneers and tourists—but also show biz celebrities who had flown in for the event from the two coasts. I saw Red and Alicia Buttons, Ernest and Tova Borgnine, Milton Berle with a tall pretty blonde woman, and Phil Hartman of the *Saturday Night Live* show. And there were journalists and reviewers representing TV stations and publications from London to Tokyo. Extra security guards were added in the lobby to control the crowds who wanted to get in but didn't have tickets. This was more than a show—it was a spectacle of the highest order. The public was clamoring to get a look at Bobby Hamilton, fresh from his tragedy.

As Jayne and I sat in my dressing room backstage, Cass darted about importantly, guarding the door and occasionally telling me names of additional celebrities he'd heard were sitting in the audience.

"Five minutes," said the stage manager to Cass, poking his head in the door.

"Five minutes!" Cass repeated loudly in relay, though I was three feet away.

"Relax," I told him.

"Hey, *you* can relax—you only gotta play the piano, but personally I got $300 riding on this show, man. We got a pool going on how many separate times the audience will applaud. I picked twenty-eight, so if you do me a favor and keep track, maybe you can try not to go over or anything . . ."

"Cass! This is incredible—do you have to bet on everything?"

I rose from my chair, gave myself a final inspection in the mirror, and went out to meet my fate in the Gladiator Arena. The halls backstage were bustling with girls in skimpy costumes. I stood behind a plush velvet curtain until I heard the announcer say, "And now . . . here's Ste-eev-erino!"

The band struck up my theme song, but it was the closing number "Impossible," not the peppier "This Could Be The Start Of Something," which I had thought would be inappropriate under the circumstances. The applause was, of course, thunderous, but in case that sounds like conceit I must explain that had a horse wandered on stage at that point, he would have gotten the same ovation. The volume is basically as meaningless as that which greets the hosts of all the talk shows and game shows on television. Anybody who had just arrived from another part of the universe, hearing that kind of acclaim, would assume that a great personage indeed was being applauded. The reason for such hysteria, in the context of television, is that before the show ever starts a fellow goes out and does about a twenty-minute warm-up, during which the audience is actually instructed and rehearsed as regards the kind of welcome they are obligated to give the host, considering that they got their tickets at no cost. That was, of course, not precisely what was involved in this instance. Opening nights are always justifiably big deals. The Broadway opening nights for *Oklahoma*, *My Fair Lady*, or *South Pacific* establish the point. There is a certain magic in the air when an audience senses that something of major importance is about to take place. It doesn't have to be a theatrical musical. It can be a heavyweight boxing title fight, a Super Bowl contest, a deciding game of the World Series—any event of that general sort.

And, obviously, what made this particular evening of such great importance was the human drama, the mob's unappealing appetite to witness another human in trouble, a man confused enough to insist on entertaining despite the death of a wife and son. All afternoon, Cass had told me, the buzz around town was that the show couldn't possibly go on unless the hotel arranged for other entertainers to replace Hamilton and me. Any sensible person would have voted for the same outcome, but there was still some insatiable curiosity, a sort of sick hope that Hamilton would appear on stage after all.

I learned years ago to evaluate the responsiveness of an audience by simply listening, for a few seconds, to the sounds they make before a show ever starts, before the curtain ever opens. Apathetic audiences are strangely quiet. If you were blind you might almost assume the room was empty. But lively audiences are already energized when they come in off the street. They're buzzing, talking, looking around, laughing, humming with a certain anticipatory excitement. That's how it was this night.

When the opening applause and music finally

died down, I said, "Good evening, ladies and gentlemen. For reasons that I'm sure all of you are aware of, this is quite an unusual night, and because of the attendant circumstances, although there is going to be a show, it certainly can't be one of the conventional sort. Ordinarily, as you may know, I open by trying to think of funny answers to questions from the audience, but I certainly wouldn't—"

"Go ahead," a man shouted from a ringside table.

I was momentarily disconcerted. "Anyway, I told the staff not to pass out cards to your tables tonight because I—"

"We got cards," a woman shouted. "Go ahead and answer them."

I was furious because obviously there had been a slip-up. Somebody—perhaps one of the room captains—had ignored the instructions I had conveyed to cancel the distribution of cards for this particular show.

Chris Carter, sensing the awkwardness of the moment, walked toward me.

"Steve," he said, "are these the cards you're talking about?" At that he lifted a stack that had been placed on the music stand I always use, slightly right of center stage.

"Swell," I said, trying to disguise my annoyance. "Folks, with all due respect for those of you who paid good money to be able to join us tonight, I'm sure most of you would agree that it simply wouldn't be appropriate for me to start doing comedy lines when—Well, hell, let's check that out. Would those of you who agree with me about this, please applaud?"

Thank goodness a hearty affirmative roar of applause rippled through the room, so we were past that danger point.

"Thank you," I said, "What I do plan to do is to play the piano."

Another round of applause.

I spent the next fifteen minutes seated at the instrument, doing the numbers I had earlier discussed with the leader. The audience applauded after recognizing the first few bars of "Misty"—it's one of those songs that always seems to get that reaction, no matter who performs it—and the jazz-lovers in the room particularly appreciated our small-group treatment of "Body and Soul," on which both the trumpeter and alto sax player acquitted themselves nobly.

"Thank you, ladies and gentlemen," I said. "And thank you particularly for your understanding. Well, there's no doubt that you're anxious to meet the star of our show, and it's my honor to introduce him right now. Ladies and gentlemen, the one—the only—Bobby Hamilton."

The crowd went wild. When Bobby stepped on stage wearing a white dinner jacket, there were almost five minutes of cheering, shouting, and near hysteria as he stood humbly in the bright circle of the spotlight. He looked subdued, sad but brave, dignified in his grief.

"Thank you," he finally said. "Thank you so much. I can't tell you what this means to me. . . ."

For a moment he seemed to be choking back tears, and the applause, which had begun to die, started again. I stood watching from the wings, wondering if the crowd would ever be quiet and let the man sing. However, the moment the orchestra began to play, the audience fell as silent as if they were in a church.

He began with Cole Porter's "Night and Day," and went on through Gerswhin, Rogers and Hart, Irving Berlin, Jobim, and more. The production was a Las Vegas extravaganza, with constantly changing lights and showgirls gliding about at assorted moments. Personally, I had always felt Bobby's most moving numbers were when he simply stood alone in a softly colored spotlight, with the rest of the stage darkened around him, singing straight to the heart of the crowd.

"God, he's fabulous tonight, isn't he?" Elliot Block whispered in my ear, coming up behind me. "I love that son-of-a-bitch! Seeing him perform like this you can hardly believe all the crap he's gone through the past few days."

I agreed that Bobby was in fine form, but I could see a difference in his performance from shows I had watched him do in past years. Generally, Bobby Hamilton can be quite funny and chatty, telling jokes and stories and talking to the audience at some length between musical numbers. Tonight he did not joke, he spoke hardly at all, but passed with somber dignity from one song to another. The audience erupted into passionate applause at the end of every number. They treated him as if he were a saint, and it did seem an act of bravery to come on stage and sing after all he had been through. Cass was going to lose his bet in the applause-pool, for the number 28 was far too low.

At last it was my time to rejoin Bobby on stage. We did our soft-shoe routine without a hitch, to applause that was almost frightening in its intensity. Then I sat at the piano, we did "Impossible," and ended the show after these two ballads with a hauntingly slow version of the Fats Waller classic, "Ain't Misbehavin'." That was just the main body of the show; there were three encores. The audience was clapping and stamping their feet; Bobby seemed reluctant to leave them. Finally I mentioned that the casino bosses might start to get unhappy if we didn't let the audience return to the gambling tables.

"Well, was it okay?" Bobby asked, after the curtain had closed.

"You know damned well it was a lot more than okay," I told him.

"I didn't want to let them down."

Elliot came over to congratulate his client, obviously ecstatic. Michelle appeared too, giving her father a loving hug, and led him off toward his dressing room. I was reminded of a wounded Oedipus Rex, tears of blood in his eyes, being led through the streets of Thebes by his daughter.

"Let's you and Jayne and me and Michelle have a late dinner somewhere," Bobby called over his shoulder before he disappeared.

"Sure," I said. I felt unaccountably depressed. There was something bittersweet about the man's triumph tonight; the cost had been too great. Even the encores seemed wrong, as if Bobby was afraid to let the show end and reality begin again.

To tell the truth, I partly understood his decision. There was a time in my life, back in 1950, when my first marriage collapsed and I felt as if I had been an utter failure at everything important. It was probably the most painful time of my life; I still recall the misery of each passing day. But there was just one hour each night when I had no problems at all, and that was the time from 11:30 to 12:30 when

I was on the air. Because the audiences night after night knew nothing about my personal predicament, I did the sort of comedy and music they expected. Their applause, their laughter, their cheerful smiles comforted me so that even for a few minutes after I went off the air I was still somehow protected against pain. A few minutes later, of course, generally by the time I reached the parking lot, the darkness would come crashing down again, but that one hour was a blessed relief. So, as I say, I assumed that Hamilton was using his performance in the same way.

As I drifted towards my dressing room with such thoughts on my mind I was not paying much attention to my surroundings, so I was surprised when two large Japanese men stepped out from behind a piece of scenery and blocked my way.

"Would you please come with us, Mr. Allen?" said the larger of the two. "There's someone who would like a word with you."

I came out of dreamland fast. Neither of these gentlemen were Ahi or Tako—they were older, larger and meaner-looking than the two who had come for Bobby at the rehearsal, and for me in the parking lot outside of City Hall. One of the men pulled a small pistol out of his coat pocket and pressed the end of the barrel into the small of my back.

"Please do what I tell you," said the soft-voiced gangster, "Or I'll be forced to fuckin' blow you away."

"Well, since you put it that way—"

I found myself escorted to a side door with one thug in front, and the other in the rear. As we approached Fritz, the choreographer, I was briefly tempted to cry for help. The man in the rear seemed to read my mind; he shoved the pistol more painfully against my spine.

We took an elevator to the ground floor then walked out through the casino towards the parking lot. There were security guards standing about, quite unaware of my predicament—they were guarding against the theft of money, rather than the theft of a mere comedian from their hotel.

Outside there was a long black limousine waiting. It reminded me too much of a hearse. A door was opened and I was gently shoved inside. We drove off through the crowded streets and then onto a freeway ramp. The two Japanese sat on either side of me and refused to answer any questions as to where we were going. Before long, I noticed we were driving through the dark and empty desert. It didn't seem a very hopeful sign.

chapter 30

We drove in silence for about a half-hour. We passed through a small town in the middle of nowhere whose name I didn't see, hurrying on past a diner, a gas station and a small casino. Further on, we came out into the desert again, and I watched a crescent moon rise over a desolate mountain ridge. It was a lonely sight; if I had been a coyote I would have been tempted to howl. Eventually I saw a body of water outside the car window that I judged must be Lake Mead. The surface of the lake was still and black, with a reflection of the moon following alongside the car. I began to see images of my feet stuck in concrete blocks pulling me downward into a watery grave. I was relieved when we drove past the lake.

We pulled into a scenic turnoff just past Hoover Dam, a point overlooking a deep gorge where the Colorado River continues on its interrupted journey to California. It was past midnight but even at this hour there were several cars parked, as well as a few RVs. Near the barrier at the edge of the parking lot

I saw a family of tourists gazing at the impressive concrete backside of the massive dam, which was bathed in spotlights. I was reassured by the sight of people and lights.

One of the silent Japanese giants opened the door of the limousine and indicated with a grunt and a thumb-point that I should step outside.

"Nice time of night for sightseeing," I said. "But I've seen Hoover Dam before."

The Japanese, unamused, took hold of my arm and marched me across the parking lot toward an RV with Texas plates. For a moment I thought this was to be our destination, but we continued onward and now for the first time I noticed a long dark Cadillac limousine in a far corner of the scenic overlook. When we got to the car, the door was opened for me and there in the back seat was Johnny Nakamura. I was not totally surprised to see him. The gangster looked sharp as ever—his black hair slicked back and glossy. He was dressed in a tan suit, blue shirt and tie of the best quality. There was even a jaunty paisley handkerchief blossoming out of the breast pocket of his probably made-in-Hong Kong suit. This was a gangster with every sartorial hair in place—but I could see a world of worry in his soft brown eyes.

"I'm surprised you didn't send your grandmother for me again, Johnny," I said.

"My *what?*"

"Your grandmother. I assumed she did all your dirty work—you must be feeling pretty desperate to show up in person."

"I don't know what the hell you're talking about," he said irately.

When I sat down next to him on the back seat

236

of the limousine, the door was closed behind me. I wasn't feeling nearly as sure of myself as I pretended.

"Your grandmother visited me the other night," I pressed. "A little old lady—about eighty-nine years old, maybe four feet tall, smokes rotten-smelling little cigars?"

Johnny Nakamura gave me a strange look. "Perhaps you take drugs, Mr. Allen—is this the problem? Frankly, you Hollywood people worry me."

"So you don't have a grandmother answering that description?"

"I have no living grandparents at all."

I couldn't imagine why Nakamura would lie about such a thing, and coupled with the information I'd had from W.B. Walker this afternoon, it was obvious that the old woman had told me a few whoppers.

"Describe this woman once again," Johnny said, gazing at me with troubled eyes. "Are you certain she was Japanese?"

I described her again, as well as my conversation with her, and concluded that Nakamura was indeed as puzzled as I was.

"This is all very strange," he sighed. "Frankly, Mr. Allen, I have brought you here hoping you might be able to help me. I have no grandmother and, more importantly, I have committed no crime. Yet suddenly I am accused of murder and some old bitch is running about threatening people in my name. I think someone is trying to frame me, Mr. Allen."

"So you're innocent, are you?" I asked sarcastically.

His face became very grave. "Please, Mr. Allen—I have done some things you may not approve of, but I am primarily a businessman, and to tell the truth my modest company is not so different from your big corporations. However, I am not a savage—I am ruthless only when it serves some business purpose, and I would certainly not be so stupid as to kill the wife of a very famous man like Mr. Hamilton. I want you to help me clear my name, Mr. Allen."

I felt as if I had entered the Twilight Zone. "Listen, Johnny—I was abducted backstage and brought here at gun point. If you really want to clear your name, you're not going about it in a very smart way."

He shrugged. "I was desperate. I'm on the run, Mr. Allen—the police are looking for me—I could think of no other way to convince you to see me. But please believe me, you are completely safe, and as soon as we have finished talking, my people will return you to your hotel."

"I'm glad to hear it. Unfortunately it seems to me you're as guilty as can be, so how can I possibly help you? Christie Hamilton was about to tell the cops about your slot-skimming operation and you had her knocked off—it's as simple as that."

Nakamura shrugged his elegant shoulders. "Believe me, sir, nothing is simple in this particular matter. But Christie—poor, lovely Christie!—the woman was no threat. Oh, she was a bit wild and she was saying all sorts of things, but I never believed she would actually go to the police."

"Why not? She was certainly angry that you were trying to blackmail her husband."

"Yes, but if she went to the police, she would have exposed herself as well—and Michelle, too, for that matter. All the sex and drugs among the rich and famous would have made quite a splash in the tabloids, eh? And Christie was not a strong woman. I knew she did not have the guts to carry through with such a threat. But most of all, if I had wanted her dead, I would have been much more subtle than strangling the woman in a sauna. Frankly, I would have arranged a very convincing accident that no one would even suspect was murder. Perhaps she would have had too much to drink one night and foolishly driven her car off the road. Or maybe she would have slipped in her bathtub. There are so many ways to die—don't you agree?"

As I listened to Johnny coldly describe how he might have murdered Christie Hamilton, had he been inclined, I felt a chill up my spine. I still perceived the man as a monster, but I could see he had a point. With Nakamura, self-interest was everything, and he was extremely cunning.

"Well, this is interesting," I said. "But unfortunately for your story, I had a long talk with Wade Hamilton just before he jumped to his death, and he described exactly how the two of you planned Christie's death, and how you were hoping to frame Michelle for the murder."

"Wade Hamilton!" Johnny exploded. "How could anyone believe that stupid psychopath? Every time you talked to him you would hear a different story!"

"This time he was telling the truth," I insisted. "Wade confessed, and when he discovered the cops were listening in on our conversation he felt forced to commit suicide. You have to admit, it lends a certain credibility to his story."

"Maybe for anybody else it would. But look, Mr. Allen, you don't understand Wade Hamilton. Do you know how I met this terrible young man? He had tied one of my girls to a chair and burned her in sensitive places with the end of a cigarette—that's right, and *this* is the person you and the police believe is telling the gospel truth! He was nuts, I tell you! Sure, I tried to use him to talk his father into signing a deal with me, but I was always bothered by him. I don't like people who hurt my girls, and I certainly wouldn't have trusted my entire fate to so unstable a person by planning a murder together. The very idea is preposterous!"

Again, as much as I disliked Nakamura, I could see merit in his argument. Wade Hamilton wouldn't have been my choice for a partner in crime either. A murder case which just yesterday had seemed so airtight was now leaking around the edges. Johnny seemed to sense my indecision.

"Please, sir—you may not like me, but you must agree I am no fool. Right now I am running for my life, for things I have not done—and you must believe me, that if I had done these things, it would have turned out quite differently for me. Quite frankly, I would have arranged it all much better."

"There are two men who work for you," I said, "Their names are Tako and Ahi."

"Are you kidding? I have no people in my organization with names like that—these are names from a *sushi* bar. Tako is a kind of octopus and Ahi is tuna—it isn't even a Japanese word, but Hawaiian!"

"I know," I said. "So you didn't send these two guys to pick up Bobby Hamilton the other day?"

"I've never even heard of these people—but I will do some checking, and also I will see if I can find the old woman you say claims to be my grandmother. I know most of the Japanese people in this

240

town and perhaps I can find out who these impostors are who are trying to frame me. I'll let you know when I discover something."

I nodded. "All right, Johnny. I think I'd like to go back to my hotel now."

"Whatever you say. But please, Mr. Allen—will you help me clear my name? I can't go to the cops, obviously—you're the only hope I have for justice."

"I'll continue to look for the murderer," I promised. "If it turns out to be you, I'm going to shout it from the roof tops. If it's somebody else, I guess you'll be in the clear."

Johnny smiled, flashing a row of pearly teeth. "That's all I ask, a fair and open mind. Meanwhile, I am completely at your disposal. I will give you a number where someone can always get a message to me. I will ask you in the spirit of *détente* to be so kind as to not give this number to the police."

Johnny Nakamura offered a pale and well-manicured hand to shake. I hesitated briefly, but under the circumstances thought it wise to return the gesture; I wanted to live to see Jayne again.

It seemed I had gained an unlikely ally in my search for truth.

chapter 31

The following morning Jayne accepted an invitation for an intimate brunch with some old friends who were staying at the hotel—an actress we know who had married a wealthy Italian playboy and retired from show biz to jet around the world from house-to-house and party-to-party. They had arrived in Las Vegas from one of their homes in Monte Carlo for a few days of gambling American-style, as well as a chance to catch the show with Bobby.

The intimate brunch, in fact, turned out to be a party for seventy-five in a top-floor suite of the hotel, with a long table of food and drink—lobster and crab, smoked hams, omelettes to order, and much more, served buffet style by a platoon of chefs wearing tall white caps. It was a lot to take first thing in the morning. The crowd seemed a very rich international set—though partly Euro-trash—none of whom apparently needed to work for a living. Personally I enjoy working, so this was not my scene.

Still, I talked about restaurants, art openings, fashionable places, political gossip.

These days "lite" beer is in vogue, as well as "lite" rock on the radio and "lite" cuisine. This chatter definitely was "lite" conversation, from which I found my mind wandering. From the moment I had opened my eyes that morning, I had been waging an internal war with myself about what to do with the phone number I now had in my possession for the most wanted man in Nevada—Johnny Nakamura. To tell or not to tell W.B.—that was the question. I knew I should, and that the lieutenant would be furious if he discovered I was holding out something so important. After all, there was a massive manhunt out for Johnny, and the phone number I had might make the police's work considerably easier. I briefly considered, for instance, setting up a rendezvous with the gangster in which W.B. might be able to nab him.

Yet something restrained me, though I wasn't quite sure what it was. I didn't think Johnny Nakamura was entirely innocent, and I knew the world would be a safer place with one less criminal on the loose. But he had succeeded in planting enough doubt in my mind that I was no longer certain he was responsible for Christie's death. In fact, I wasn't certain about anything much, and if I let the police grab him prematurely, I might never figure out the riddle of what had actually happened, and why.

Suddenly I saw Jayne approaching. "Darling," she said, "I've been looking for you. Look who I just found." And there behind her were our good friends, Jim Lipton and his lovely Eurasian wife, Kedakai, whose face has graced a number of magazine covers. Jim is both Jack and master of numerous creative trades, producer, director, writer, lyricist, and is perhaps best known, at least to those who read, as the author of *An Exaltation of Larks*, a fascinating study of one narrow aspect of language, that which concerns nouns that somewhat mysteriously materialize around various species, as in *a pride of lions, a school of fish, a covey of quail*, etc.

I would have enjoyed nothing more at the moment than just the four of us going off to a quiet corner, preferably in another location, since Jim and Kedakai have special gifts for the art of conversation. But no such luck.

"I'm surprised to see you two here in Schlock City," I said.

"Don't knock schlock," Jim said. "Our culture would collapse without it."

"Listen," I said, "have you ever known me to be a schlock-knocker?"

"Actually," he said, laughing politely, "I'm here to explore the possibility of doing another special with Bob Hope at one of the local hotels, or maybe doing bits and pieces at several of them." Lipton had earlier produced specials for Bob, most notably the one that originated in China, the initial groundwork for which had been laid by a mutual friend, Schuyler Chapin, when he had traveled with Jayne and me to China several years earlier.

"Would you guys like to have a drink with us later?" Kedakai said.

"We certainly would," I said. "But it's impossible." I could hardly tell him I was trying to solve a murder mystery. "We'll be in New York soon, though, and we'll let you know when we're coming in."

"It's a deal," Jim said, and, with a flurry of show-biz cheek-kisses for the ladies, they were off.

I was talking to a young man about the string of polo ponies he owned in Argentina, when I saw Elliot Block come into the room and head my way. He was wearing white slacks, a blue blazer and a multi-colored silk ascot—he looked at home in this crowd, but I had a sense he had crashed the party.

"Steve! I heard you were here," he said, pulling me away from the young man and his ponies. Elliot smiled mysteriously.

"That certainly was one hell of a show last night! Have you read any of the reviews?"

"I haven't had a chance."

"Wait 'til you see the L.A. *Times!* Rave! As a matter of fact, I have a small gift for you, from Bobby—a little token of his gratitude for all your help in this time of trouble."

"Well, that's nice but not necessary," I said. I couldn't see any signs of a package in Elliot's possession, so I imagined the gift was a small one. Actually, it turned out to be smaller than I had assumed. Elliot reached into his pocket and handed me a set of keys.

"What's this?"

"Let's step out onto the terrace for a moment," he said.

I had been avoiding open heights after what had happened with Wade but was curious enough to follow Elliot outside onto our host's terrace. The agent leaned over the rail and pointed downward to the parking lot. "There," he said.

I peered down cautiously, staying a few inches back from the edge, but could see only a crowded parking lot. Then something caught my eye standing off to the side. "Oh, no, Elliot, not the . . ."

"You got it, babe—the powder blue Rolls-Royce convertible."

"But Elliot, I couldn't possibly accept something as expensive as that! Tell Bobby I'm touched, I really am, but I'm not about to accept a—"

Elliot's smile began to waver. "Look, Steve, he's going to be awfully hurt. I know it's an expensive present, but Bobby can afford it. You know how he is. Last year for Christmas he gave me a forty-five foot sailing yacht, and frankly I felt the same as you. I mean, I don't even sail. But I forced myself to accept it, knowing how disappointed he'd be if I turned it down."

"I'm sure that was a very noble gesture, Elliot, but my mind is made up," I told him. "You can tell Bobby I could use a new fountain pen. Or maybe an autographed set of his early albums."

I pressed the keys back in Elliot's hand. The agent kept shaking his head. "I think this is a mistake, Steve. Bobby's going to be really hurt."

"I'm sure he'll get over it. Why don't you sit down, Elliot. Since you're here, I'd like to ask you a few questions."

He smiled helpfully, but I could tell he wasn't happy. We sat facing each other on two wrought-iron chairs around a small glass table.

"So what do you want to know?"

"I'm hoping you can tell me something about Mike Corvino," I said. "Bobby's movie double. The police still haven't found him. Did he have a grudge against Bobby?"

Elliot darkened. "Steve, maybe it's best to let the cops worry about Mike. I mean, you solved the murder thing. What more do you want?"

"I'm just curious about this. It's my experience

that movie doubles become generally pretty good friends with the actors they work for. I'm surprised he'd make up such a damaging story about Bobby and then just disappear."

"Well, you know how some of these guys are—Mike's kind of a cowboy, a drifter. I always liked him, personally, but I can see how he might be tempted to do just about anything for money, particularly since Bobby wasn't planning on making any more films so his days as a double were over."

"When's the last time you saw him?"

"Not for several years, I guess. Bobby sent him a Christmas card every year with a small check in it, for old time's sake, but we never saw him."

"Bobby was giving him money?" I asked with some interest.

"Just a small annual present," said Elliot with a trace of irritation. "A few thousand dollars or something. As you know, Bobby's a very generous man. He likes to take care of his friends."

"Well, *that's* very interesting. I sure hope we find the guy so he can answer some questions. Elliot, you've known Bobby and his family for what? Thirty years?"

"More like forty. Bobby and I go way back."

"Did it surprise you that Wade turned out to be such a bad apple?"

"Hey, the poor kid was sick. Maybe it was in his genes, maybe it was his upbringing—I don't know, but it was like he was from another planet. He was weird."

"Yeah, but helping Johnny murder his stepmother and then trying to frame his father for it—that's more than sick, Elliot—we're talking about a real monster. I can't quite put my finger on it, but I think Wade was more unhappy than evil. The more I think about it, this whole thing doesn't add up."

"Steve!" cried Elliot, clearly losing patience. "What do you want to do? Rehash this whole terrible tragedy? Look, it's over, and nothing's going to be served by you or anybody else digging around anymore. For whatever the reasons, Wade turned out to be a psychopath, but he's paid for whatever he did. You're not going to bring Christie back, whatever you do. Bobby's out of jail, the cops are happy, everyone's satisfied—except you. So do yourself a favor, buddy. Accept Bobby's nice Rolls and just forget about everything else now except doing the show."

Suddenly I had a terrible suspicion that the offered Rolls wasn't so much a gift as a pay-off. Elliot looked at his watch and made a big deal about how late it was. I had the impression he couldn't wait to get as far from me as possible.

"Wow, I gotta be in a meeting like ten minutes ago, Steve. Look, just think about what I've told you, okay? And if you have any more questions about Mike or Wade, come to me before disturbing Bobby. Or the police. I'll answer you as best I can."

Elliot was talking a mile a minute as he stood up from the wrought-iron chair and made his way back inside to the party. I watched him grab a crab claw from an iced platter as he passed the buffet table and continue without pausing at the door of the suite. I sighed heavily; I didn't like the way this was adding up and had a feeling I needed to talk with Bobby. The young man with the polo ponies reappeared at my side and continued chattering as if there had been no interruption. My mind was elsewhere, but I had a vague impression he was inviting Jayne and me to Buenos Aires the following month. He said he'd send his plane for us.

"I'll have to check with my secretary," I demurred, and excused myself to head into a bathroom to find a phone; all bathrooms in expensive hotels these days seem to come equipped with them. When I dialed Bobby's suite, a strange woman answered the phone. She sounded breathy and young, and she handed the phone to Bobby when I gave her my name. Somehow the presence of the girl disturbed me.

"Hey, man, what's up?"

"Bobby, I just wanted to thank you, sincerely, for the gift, but you know I can't accept a Rolls-Royce from you. It's just too much."

"A what?"

"A Rolls . . . the powder blue convertible Elliot just tried to give me the keys to. I'm touched by the thought, Bob, but I hope you understand why I can't accept it."

"Wait a second, Steve—you're saying Elliot tried to give you a God damn Rolls-*Royce?* You're working with Alan Funt here, right? Where are the cameras?"

"You mean—?"

"That stupid fuck! Look, Steve, this is a big mix-up. I told him to go out and find you a nice present—I really wanted you to know how grateful I was, and frankly I was too busy to look for something myself. But I told him it had to be something subtle and maybe a little silly and sentimental, otherwise you wouldn't accept it. I had no idea he was going to offer you a God-damned Rolls!"

Bobby was obviously upset. He was a man who liked to do the right thing by his friends, but Elliot's choice of a gift had turned out to be embarrassing. I told Bobby not to worry about it; there had been no real harm done. I even suggested Elliot return the car to the showroom and that perhaps the money might be given instead to Portals, the organization that provides desperately needed services for people with severe psychological and emotional problems. To raise funds, they run the Corporate Cookie store on Wilshire Boulevard in Los Angeles, get almost none of the glamorous publicity that attends the more famous charities, but are wonderful people doing heroic work. Bobby said he'd do just that.

I put down the phone feeling restless and on edge, exited the bathroom and wandered back towards the buffet. Jayne appeared at my side and introduced me to a French art collector and his wife, with whom we chatted briefly. After a moment, I found myself gazing out the window to the parking lot below. As I looked, I noticed the tiny figure of Elliot Block in his blue blazer and white slacks step up to the powder blue Rolls and slip into the driver's seat.

Elliot started up the car with the keys I had refused and drove away out of the long hotel entrance onto The Strip. I had a feeling I was going to have to find out a good deal more about the dapper Mr. Block.

Was *he* the guilty party in this drama? I had a final glimpse of the powder blue Rolls merging with the traffic on Las Vegas Boulevard. And then I recalled the breathy young girl who had answered Bobby's telephone.

There was an ugly thought forming in my mind, one I hardly dared acknowledge: Maybe the killer, after all, was Bobby Hamilton.

chapter 32

I turned down an invitation to take a balloon ride across the desert with the Italian playboy and his wife and also an opportunity to go on a shopping spree with Jayne and Michelle. Everyone said I was being a real killjoy, but I felt a need to do some serious thinking.

I returned to my hotel suite, found a spiral notebook and wrote down everything I knew about Christie's murder—all the events as they had unfolded and all the people involved. I hoped when I finished that I would have noticed something I had hitherto neglected, but actually I only came up with one small observation: I realized I knew almost nothing about Debbie, the spa hostess who had been killed along with Christie. We all had assumed that Christie was the intended victim, and Debbie simply had been at the wrong place at the wrong time— killed only because she had seen the murder. But what if it were the other way around? It didn't seem at all likely, but I made a note to check it out.

In the early afternoon, I phoned the police station, set up an appointment to meet Lieutenant Walker, and then dialed Cass's room in the hotel, hoping I could lure him away from the gambling tables long enough to drive me downtown. He answered on the third ring.

"Glad I got you, Cass. I've got an appointment with W.B. in half an hour—so why don't you pull the car around to the front of the hotel and I'll meet you down there in ten minutes?"

There was an awkward pause on the other end of the line. I found myself listening to dead space.

"Cass, you still there?"

"Uh, yeah, Steve. Where'd you say you're meeting the lieutenant?"

"At the police station downtown."

"And you want me to drive you? Is that it? In the limo?"

"Well, yes, of course. Are you feeling all right, Cass? If you're sick, I could take a cab."

"I'm not sick," said Cass flatly, but from the sound of his voice there was *something* the matter with him. I was mystified.

"Cass, what's the matter?"

"Nothing's the matter," he snapped irritably. "Everything's just peachy. So I'll see you outside the hotel in ten minutes."

Cass hung up on me and I was left feeling baffled. Had I caught him at a bad time? Had I said something wrong? Cass may work for me, but I think of us as friends. I couldn't recall having ever heard him sound so depressed and surly. I was wondering about this when the door to the suite opened and Jayne and Michelle came in followed by a tall and good-looking man whose face was just visible above an armful of shopping bags and boxes from Neiman

Marcus and Saks. He was using his chin to hold down the uppermost box in his arms, and it was probably a good thing for him that the ladies had stopped shopping when they did. A good thing for me too, I might add.

"Steve, this is Ken," said Jayne.

"Hi, Ken."

"Hello, Mr. Allen. I guess I'll have to owe you a handshake."

I helped unload him, stacking the boxes on the floor. "Did you leave anything for the other shoppers?" I asked Jayne and Michelle.

"Steve, don't be such a misanthrope," said my wife, who knows I have a weakness for women with large, well-developed vocabularies. "Besides, one of these boxes is for you—a darling set of those brightly colored jockey shorts you like."

"Thanks," I said. "By the way, have you seen Cass today? There seems to be something wrong with him."

"Hasn't he told you yet?"

"Told me what?"

"Oops, I promised not to breathe a word. I think I should let Cass explain."

"Jayne!"

"No, really, darling—anyway, you'll find out soon enough."

This was not reassuring, but Jayne would not budge. Meanwhile Ken, having been relieved of his burden, was standing smiling a bit goofily at me while Michelle looked at him in a possessive manner. Ken was a pleasant-looking young man with short blond hair; he had an undefined, still babyish face that would take on more character, for good or ill, as life took him through its adventures. The clear,

253

guileless blue eyes were gazing at me in a friendly way. I could see I was expected to say something polite.

"Well, well," I said, "So you're Ken."

"Yup," he told me. "We talked on the phone yesterday a few times."

"Ah, yes, every fifteen minutes on the hour."

"Ken's getting a degree in political science," said Michelle proudly. "He's not going to be a spa attendant forever."

"Actually I'd like to be a diplomat," said the pleasant young man. "But working in the spa gives me a chance to stay in shape while I hit the books. I've always believed mind and body should be developed at the same time."

"You're quite right," I said.

I smiled a bit stupidly. There are times I can be pretty good at this sort of thing—I would have continued, but Cass was waiting downstairs, and my mind was full of a number of questions about agents and gangsters and blackmail and murder.

"Jayne," I said, "let me know later what you want to do for dinner. I mean after the show."

"Have you ever been to The Carrot and The Schtick, Mr. Allen? They make a fabulous carrot loaf—you'd swear you're eating Grade-A ground beef."

"Sounds divine," Jayne said.

"Yeah, it was Debbie's favorite place," said Ken, with a sad shake of his handsome head. "I still can't believe she's dead."

Mentally, at least, I was halfway out the door, but I stopped and looked at Ken more carefully, realizing he could be a source of information about the dead hostess, of whom I knew so little.

"What kind of girl was she, Ken?"

"Oh, Debbie was swell, Mr. Allen. We weren't boyfriend-girlfriend, or anything like that—but we got to be pretty close in the four months we worked together."

"Did she go to college, too?"

"Not this term. But she was trying to save up enough money so she could be a full-time student next year. She wanted to be a dietician."

"I think I remember from the police report that she lived alone in North Las Vegas."

"That's right. She rented a small house there and had a really nice organic garden in the back."

"Do you know if Debbie had a boyfriend?"

"As a matter of fact, that's one of the things that really upsets me about all this," said Ken gloomily. "She had a tough time for a while—when I first met her, she had just broken up with someone, and she was pretty depressed about dating. But the last couple of weeks, she was flying high—she'd finally met Mr. Right."

"No kidding? Who was he?"

"She wouldn't say. Whenever I asked, she just got a bit mysterious. I finally thought maybe he was married or something, you know. I tried to suggest that she could end up getting hurt again—but she just laughed and said that this time everything was finally going to turn out all right for her."

"But she wouldn't tell you any of the specifics?"

"Well, I gathered the guy was rich—she let it slip out once that he'd rented some fancy house just so they could have a nice quiet place to meet. But that's about it. Debbie said she had to be real careful and couldn't talk about it yet, but that she'd tell me all about him one day."

This was beginning to bother me.

"Did the police ask you about this, Ken?"

"Sure. A little. They didn't seem terribly interested though—I guess they assumed a pretty girl like that who worked in a big hotel would have lots of boyfriends."

"Did you have the impression the man she was dating either worked or lived in the hotel?"

"Actually, I thought he might be a guest, Mr. Allen, which would be another reason Debbie would be reluctant to talk about him. You see, we employees aren't allowed to date the guests," Ken added, giving a slightly guilty look at Michelle.

"Don't worry—your secret's safe with me," Michelle told him, squeezing his hand.

What Ken had told me about Debbie's mysterious gentleman friend bothered me; it was one more loose end in a case that was fast unraveling. I said my goodbyes, kissing Jayne and telling Michelle and Ken that we'd decide later about The Carrot and The Schtick.

The elevator took me down to the lobby, and I passed through the nether world of the dark casino into the blazing sunlight outside. I stood on the curb and looked about for Cass or his burgundy Cadillac stretch limousine but could see no sign of either.

"Here I am," said a voice behind me. I turned and saw Cass. He looked grim; there was no twinkle today in the blue cowboy eyes.

"You know, Cass, you're beginning to scare me to death," I said. "So you'd better tell me what the hell's wrong with you."

He shrugged. "Why don't I tell you about it on the way to the police station?"

"It's a deal . . . so where's the car?"

"Over here," said Cass.

Cass began to cross the driveway towards a VIP waiting zone. I followed after him, but although I saw a Rolls, a black BMW and a silver Mercedes, I still could see no sign of our burgundy Caddy. Cass came to an untimely halt in front of an ancient, dark green VW Bug, and to my surprise opened the door for me on the passenger's side. The door, I should mention, had a peace symbol painted on the side that made it look as if it were a relic of the Vietnam war. All we needed was a sticker on the rear bumper saying MAKE LOVE, NOT WAR.

"Good God, Cass! What the hell happened to the limo?"

"It shrank," he said grumpily. "Look, the old Bug runs, at least—so do you want a ride downtown, or should I call you a cab?"

I decided to get in. I'm six-feet-three, but managed to fit myself into the old Volkswagen. I knew Cass was upset, and I didn't want to make matters worse for him by taking a taxi. I was beginning to get a fair idea of what had happened.

"You lost it gambling, didn't you?" I asked gently.

"Are you going to say, 'I told you so'?"

"No."

"Well, you'd have a right. I thought I was onto a sure thing with a point-spread on the Forty-Niners–Rams game. I was a little short of cash to take to the Sports Book so I raised money against the Caddy with a used car dealer downtown."

Cass couldn't quite look me in the eye. He looked so depressed there didn't seem any point giving him a lecture. "Well," I sighed, "it's only a car. And hey, maybe you can take a tax deduction by contributing this thing to the Old Volks Home." He didn't even smile.

The Volkswagen sputtered into life, and we hurried off down The Strip. Somewhere near The Stardust we hit a small pothole that sent my head crashing against the roof. From then on, I braced myself with my knees against the dashboard and my shoulder against the door. This will be worth it, I thought, if only Cass has learned his lesson.

We were nearly downtown when we came to a casino called The Lady Luck. Cass looked up at a twenty-foot marquee of lights that said one word: BACCARAT! For a moment he seemed like a man who has just had a vision. The gloom departed; a dreamy smile came to his lips. Cass was an irrepressible optimist. So am I, I suppose, but not about gambling.

"Baccarat!" he said slowly. "You know, that makes me think of James Bond movies—beautiful women in low-cut gowns, dangerous guys in dinner jackets, hundreds of thousands of dollars on the table. I wonder . . ."

"Cass," I told him definitely. "Don't even wonder about it. Count yourself lucky you have a Volkswagen to drive."

"Yeah, you're right. It's not for me . . . hell, I've learned *my* lesson," he said wistfully.

I was not reassured. Vegas was no place for a cowboy with champagne tastes who always believed the next card would give him a winning hand. I had a feeling I'd better solve this case fast and get us all safely home.

chapter 33

I hadn't been sitting in Lieutenant Walker's cubicle at City Hall for more than two minutes when the phone on his desk rang.

"Uh-huh . . . yeah . . . uh-huh," he grunted into the mouthpiece, while making a note on a pad. "The Fuji-Ya Sushi Bar on Paradise Road? . . . Yeah, set up a perimeter—I want every available car to seal off the area. Better give SWAT a call. I'll be there right away."

W.B. slammed down the phone and stood up triumphantly "Good news," he said. "An officer spotted Johnny Nakamura going into a sushi bar. I hope that bastard's enjoying himself, 'cause it's going to be the last raw fish he'll be eating for a while."

I was seeing a new and more decisive side to the lieutenant. He pulled out the revolver from his shoulder holster, checked to see he had a full load, and spun the chamber. John Wayne could not have done a better job of looking grim and macho.

"We'll have to reschedule our little chitchat," he said, ramming the gun back into his holster.

"Look, W.B., why don't you let me come along? We can talk on the way."

"Sorry, this is no time for civilians. Why don't you go back to the hotel and sit around your swimming pool. I'll give you a call when this is all over."

"Okay," I agreed. "I have some important information about Nakamura, but hell, I guess it can wait."

W.B. flashed me a very speculative look. He's a big, gruff cop, but there are certain times he can look boyish. "Okay," he said. "You can come along—but you stay in the car when the action gets heavy. I don't want the newspapers accusing me of losing some damn celebrity at the Sushi Bar Massacre!"

I suppose this was about as friendly a comment as W.B. Walker was ever likely to make about me— "some damn celebrity." The lieutenant threw on his brown jacket and charged out of the office with me in pursuit. We took the elevator to the basement garage.

"So what's this you wanna tell me about Nakamura?"

"W.B., you're not going to like this—but I'm beginning to think Johnny's not the one who killed Christie."

"*Not the one!*" he cried, staring at me in amazement. "Good God, you were the one who convinced me he *was* our goddamn killer."

"Yeah, but I'm not so sure anymore."

When the elevator door opened W.B. stepped out into the underground parking lot and began walking swiftly toward a cream-colored unmarked police car.

"You do remember Wade Hamilton's final confession, don't you?" asked W.B. as he unlocked his car door. "That boy made it pretty damn clear who was doing what before he cut out."

"Yes, and I know it was like a deathbed confession, and the courts are inclined to give something like that a lot of credibility—but we still only have Wade's word for what happened."

"But the boy's story makes sense. It fits everything else we know. Besides, he was about to kill you before he realized you had a wire under your shirt—so what would he gain by lying?"

"I don't know," I sighed. "But Wade was a fairly complicated kid. Who can say what his reasons were?"

"He was nuts," said W.B., putting his emergency red light on the roof of his car.

"And that's why I feel uncomfortable basing our entire case on his so-called confession," I said.

"*Our* case?"

"Besides, there's Johnny's imaginary grandmother and a few other loose ends that bother the hell out of me."

We left some rubber and smoke behind as Walker sped out of the parking lot.

"By the way, does fast driving bother you, Mr. Allen? You still have time to get out if you want."

"I'll be fine," I told him.

I felt like I was in a rocket taking off from its pad. The siren screamed, the red light flashed on the roof, and the other cars on the road hurried out of our way. We fish-tailed through the intersection at Paradise Road, drifting in free-fall for a moment before the tires seemed to regain their hold on solid earth. A station wagon with an elderly man at the wheel came into our path from a side street and W.B. slammed on the brakes, cut to the left and managed to miss him. I kept hitting the imaginary brake on my side of the car.

"Anyway, if Nakamura isn't the killer, who the hell is?" asked the lieutenant, speaking as calmly as if we were sitting safe and sound in his office. We raced through a red light with the speedometer needle edging past 70 mph.

"What about Elliot Block?" I suggested.

"What about him?"

"Well, he was in the VIP spa around the time of Christie's death, and I've never been particularly satisfied with his Tokyo phone call alibi. Besides that, what do we really know about him? If I were you, W.B., I'd try to get a very thorough background check on that man—see if he's ever had any trouble with the law or the IRS. For all we know, Elliot was even one of Christie's secret lovers."

"Whoa," said W.B. "You're letting your imagination run away with you."

"Am I? Maybe Elliot had reasons of his own for getting Christie out of the way."

"You just don't like the guy."

"That's true, but there's one more thing . . . "

I didn't have a chance to say what that one more thing was because we had arrived at a line of police cars that were blocking Paradise Road with their red and blue lights revolving on their roofs. About a dozen uniformed cops wearing bulletproof vests were crouched behind their vehicles, some with rifles in their arms. The street had turned into a battle zone.

"This is where you stay in the car," said the lieutenant; I had no wish to argue the point. I watched W.B. take out his revolver and run in a crouch to a position behind one of the squad cars. A little ways down the street, I could see the facade of the Fuji-Ya Sushi Bar. There was a blue banner over the door with Japanese writing on it and a large plate-glass window facing the street.

Lieutenant Walker raised a bullhorn to his mouth. "All right, Johnny—the jig's up. I'm giving you exactly five minutes to come out with your hands in the air!"

The tension on the street was palpable. I found myself slinking lower in the unmarked police car, just in case a stray bullet came my way. There was no answer from the restaurant.

"Three minutes left!" called the lieutenant over the bullhorn. "And then we're going to come in shooting."

I saw a hand reach out of the door of the sushi bar and frantically wave a white linen napkin. "Don't shoot!" cried a terrified voice.

"Come out slowly, with your hands up!"

The first person out was a frail Japanese man whose hands were visibly quaking as he held them in the air. Next came a young blond couple who seemed equally scared, and then a family of Orientals with three young children.

"Keep moving! Keep moving!" W.B. called to these innocent people. "Where are you, Johnny? I want to see your ugly face *now!*"

Just then, a handsome young Japanese man wearing a white linen suit walked out into the open with his hands in the air. He looked a great deal like Johnny Nakamura . . . but he was not.

"What the hell!" I heard W.B. say into the bullhorn. "Where's Nakamura?"

263

The young man spoke a torrent of words in Japanese; I had no idea what he was saying, but he seemed both frightened and angry, and I had a feeling he would not be visiting America again any time soon. As I watched, the police charged into the sushi bar with pistols drawn, pulling the young Japanese man out of harm's way. A few moments later, they appeared with two terrified waitresses dressed in kimonos, and two sushi chefs in their white *ninja*-like outfits. But no Johnny Nakamura.

After a while Lieutenant Walker ambled back to the car with a discouraged expression. "Can you believe that? The whole thing was a mistake—some stupid patrolman got a glimpse of a guy who doesn't speak a word of English and happens to look a little like Nakamura."

"Well, it's an understandable mistake."

"Yeah," said W.B. with a sigh. "This is not going to sit very well with my captain. Tourism's very important to this town, you know, and Vegas tries awfully hard to maintain its image as a crime-free family resort."

I felt sorry for W.B., but Vegas is Sin City, which is why consenting adults come here in the first place, and all efforts to whitewash the fact are absurd.

"So what's this one more thing you were about to tell me?" asked W.B.

"I beg your pardon?"

"Just before the action came down, you were talking about Elliot Block and saying there was one more thing. . . ."

I was impressed at W.B.'s managing to remember exactly where our conversation had left off. For me, the sight of drawn guns had put everything else out of mind.

"It's about the hostess, Debbie," I told him. "She was dating some guy before she was killed."

"So what?" said the lieutenant. "She was an attractive young woman."

"Yes, but according to her co-worker, Ken, there was some mystery about the man she was seeing. Ken thought he might be married, or someone staying in the hotel."

"So?"

"So what if this person happened to be Elliot? The way I see it, whoever planned Christie's death might have needed someone on the inside. Debbie could have told him how to turn off the lights, and tipped him off when Christie was going to be in the spa—probably she was an unwitting partner and had no idea what Elliot had in mind, so he'd have to kill her, too, in order to keep her quiet. He probably would have killed Ken as well, but Michelle saved *his* life by inviting him upstairs to her room."

W.B. treated me to one of his slow grins. "This is total conjecture, my friend. Thank God you're not a *real* policeman. I mean, this is incredible—you don't have even a single fact to back you up!"

"I know. This is all just a theory—so far," I admitted. "But can you say I'm absolutely wrong? Debbie's mysterious boyfriend *could* have been using her to help set up the murder, and this person *could* be Elliot Block. I didn't say he was."

W.B. Walker was shaking his head. "What the hell am I going to do for entertainment when you go back to L.A.?"

I was undeterred. "This is a betting town, Lieutenant, and I'm putting my money on Elliot Block as the killer."

Lieutenant Walker raised an eyebrow and looked at me with new interest. "Just how much are you willing to bet, Mr. Allen?"

"A hundred dollars says I'm right," I said quickly, glad that Cass was not around to see my bad example.

"A deal," said W.B. We shook hands grimly, each of us certain we were about to be a hundred bucks richer. "As a matter of fact, we've been trying to find Debbie's boyfriend ourselves, but so far we haven't had any luck. I don't think his identity will turn out to be too important, but I'd like to know who he is."

"According to Ken, the guy had money—he rented a nice house somewhere just so he and Debbie would have a discreet place to meet."

"Oh, that will make it *real* easy to find him," said W.B. sarcastically. "We only have to check every rented house in Vegas!"

"Maybe I'll manage to get a line on him some other way," I suggested hopefully.

"You? What could *you* do that we can't?"

"That remains to be seen."

"Well, I can't say I wouldn't be interested in anything you find out about Debbie's vanishing boyfriend—but at this point, I can't encourage you to get involved."

"I understand that. I'll keep you up to date."

"*Sure* you will," he said. The poor man was having a bad day. He looked over to the facade of the Japanese restaurant with a discouraged shake of his head. "This sure was the Sushi Bar Massacre, all right!" he said wearily. "Only *we* were the ones who got massacred!"

chapter 34

By late afternoon, I came up with a fiendish idea, one that both lured and alarmed me. I tried to forget about it, with little success.

Probably it was all Jayne's fault. She inadvertently got me thinking along dangerous lines when she mentioned she was going to see the show tonight at a dinner table which would include two friends of ours from Hollywood—Pat and Larry Gelbart—as well as Elliot Block, who knew these people too. Apparently Elliot had put this little dinner party together, and it was the fact that I now knew exactly where Mr. Block would be that night for several hours that provided the seed for my wild plan.

I decided I would search his room.

After all, what better way to discover the naked truth about people than look under their mattress and sift through their wastebaskets and laundry hampers? There were only two problems with my clever plan: One, while Elliot was safely seated at dinner with Jayne and our friends from Hollywood, I would theoretically be on stage entertaining them—that is, for all but twenty-five to thirty minutes, the time after I left the stage following my opening monologue and before Bobby called me back to accompany him on the piano. This twenty-five minute interlude was crucial. I decided it would be time enough to duck out of the Gladiator Arena, take an elevator up to Elliot's floor, and quickly search his room for any incriminating evidence which might prove him a cunning murderer. This brought me to problem number two, however: the door to his suite would be locked.

Somehow I was relieved that a locked door stood in my way. It was a joy to know I wouldn't be able to carry out my dangerous plan after all. But then, alas, I thought of an answer, a way I could get the locked door to open.

I paced the living room of my hotel suite trying to talk myself out of it. How embarrassing it would be if I got caught. Even a delay could be disastrous. What if a maid came in while I was going through the room, and I was forced to hide in a closet for five or ten minutes? I pictured Bobby downstairs standing on stage telling the audience he was now going to bring back his old friend Steve Allen to play the piano—and Steve Allen would be nowhere to be found!

This was absurd. I decided no, I would not do it, I would be reasonable—and then two minutes later I changed my mind again, imagining all sorts of private letters and incriminating knickknacks I might come across concealed in Elliot's luggage or underwear drawer.

I decided to talk it over with Cass, but he was unfindable—he was not in his room nor in the casino when I had him paged there. This worried me a little, for Cass had been silent as he drove me back to the hotel from the police station in his less-than-spacious VW Bug. But I decided he was a big boy, and I didn't have time to worry about him right now.

I resolved to flip a coin. Heads, I would invade Elliot's room; tails, I would not. I tossed a silver dollar in the air, and it came down tails. "Ah, hell," I said, and decided to do the reckless deed anyway. Would Philip Marlowe quail before such a challenge? Would Dan Quayle quail—forget it.

I now, however, needed the help of an unlikely ally. I found the number Johnny Nakamura had given me at Hoover Dam on a slip of paper stuffed in my wallet, and my fingers did the walking to the phone. Deep inside, a warning voice said: *No, no, Steve—Lieutenant Walker will not be amused.* There was still time to change my mind. But I dialed the number and left a message. Within ten minutes Nakamura called me back.

I made my bargain with the devil.

chapter 35

Elliot Block was staying on the twenty-third floor, in room 2304. If my operation were to be successful, timing was everything. A half hour before I was due backstage I made a practice run from the stage door, down the hallway into the Ben Hur Casino on the second floor and up the elevator to room 2304. The trip took just under five minutes one way. I reminded myself that I could be delayed by a slow elevator, and that I would have to pass a security guard going in and out of the backstage area, and so my absence could possibly be noted. I decided not to worry about that; I could always claim I was making a fast trip up to my own penthouse suite for something I had forgotten.

With at least twenty-five minutes at my disposal, and five minutes walking time in each direction, I would be left with fifteen minutes to search Elliot's room. Better make that ten minutes, to give myself a slight safety margin. Even then I was cutting it close, and if Elliot Block had any deep dark secrets up there, I hoped they would not be too difficult to locate.

After my trial run, I settled into my dressing room in front of a mirror that was lit with a perimeter of bare light bulbs and applied a little pancake. I tried to get my mind in gear for the upcoming show, but my heart was pounding in anticipation of the break-in. I kept thinking of new things that could go wrong. I wondered if they arrested people who broke into rooms that were not their own.

To my surprise, Bobby poked his head in my dressing room door a short time before I was supposed to go on. He was already in make-up, not yet in his stage costume, wearing a silky oriental dressing gown. In his arms he carried an enormous basket of tropical fruit—papayas, mangoes, pineapples, bananas, and more—all wrapped in transparent plastic with a big red bow tied on top.

"Just a *little* gift this time," he said modestly. "I thought Jayne might like a reminder of the South Pacific."

"How nice!" I said, and meant it too, since this was the kind of gift I could gladly accept.

"I wanted to apologize again, Steve—that was pretty tacky, Elliot trying to give you that car. I gave him hell about it."

"Well, I certainly appreciate the thought behind it," I mentioned. We smiled at each other, but I found I had become a thoroughly suspicious person—proximity to murder will do that to you, I suppose. Despite my friendship for this man, I couldn't help but wonder if Bobby himself were somehow the guilty party, and the Rolls had been an attempt to keep me from looking any further into the matter.

271

"You're looking awfully thoughtful, man. What's on your mind?"

"There's something I want to ask you about Elliot. Do you have a moment?"

"Shoot," he said.

"Well, I'm curious about Johnny Nakamura's offer for you to perform at that new hotel he was trying to buy—was Elliot in favor of the deal, or against it?"

Bobby's whole manner changed. When he'd walked into my dressing room holding the basket of fruit, I thought he looked almost himself again. But at the mention of Nakamura's name, the memory of all the bad things seemed to come back to him. I saw a weariness cloud his eyes. Even his shoulders seemed to crumple.

"Hell, Steve," he sighed, "I still can't really take this all in. Christie . . . and Wade. I hope that bastard Nakamura rots in hell for what he's done to my family."

"I'm sorry I brought it up."

"No, no—I need to face this. But now I've forgotten your question."

I repeated what I wanted to know—whether Elliot had advised for or against Johnny's blackmail offer. Bobby had to think for a moment. "Yeah, he wanted me to do it. I remember that now. He was in the room when Wade and I had a fight about the whole thing, and after Wade walked out, Elliot said maybe I was making a mistake—Johnny was offering some fairly serious money for very little work, and besides, if I said yes it would take care of some of my family problems. It would get Christie off the hook and Wade off my back."

"It sounds like everyone wanted you to take that offer."

"Yeah," he said sadly. "Everyone but Christie—she knew it wasn't my style to get involved with gangsters, and she pretended not to care if Johnny's dirty pictures of her hit the tabloids. I knew she *did* care, of course, but she was always taking care of me, you see. Elliot just thought about the money, and Wade, I don't know. I guess Wade was trying to prove himself to me. But Christie. . . ."

His voice choked and he could not continue. I put a comforting arm on his shoulder, alarmed that I had managed to disturb him right before a performance, a true crime in show-business.

"Bobby, I'm really sorry. I shouldn't have brought this up now."

He took a deep breath. "I'm okay," he said in a weak voice. "It's just every now and then when I remember, it's like a mule has kicked me in the stomach. Thank God for music. If I didn't have a chance to sing, I think I'd go crazy."

Lucky audience, I thought. Unlucky Bobby Hamilton. The stage manager knocked on my door and called, "Five minutes, Mr. Allen." Bobby winked bravely, gave me a thumbs-up sign, and said he'd see me under the spotlights. I felt depressed after he left—the tragedy of his double loss kept hitting me in waves, then receding. But I was glad to know where Elliot had stood on Johnny's offer—I wasn't sure how it fit in, but it was one more mark against the glib agent. Now I just had to come up with some hard evidence that he was guilty.

With all this on my mind, I wasn't certain how well I'd do tonight on stage. But all the years in show business came to my aid, as well as that last minute surge of adrenalin a performer always gets stepping out to meet a live audience. The crowd was revved up, too, full of high hopes that had been fueled by the reviews we had received. The orchestra played "Impossible," and I walked on stage to hearty applause. I spotted Jayne almost right away, sitting between our friends, the Gelbarts. Pat used to sing on the original *Tonight Show,* and Larry, of course, is one of our country's premier humorists, writer of the movie *Tootsie,* co-creator of the TV series *Mash* etc., etc. Because the table was fairly near the front of the stage, I could see that Elliot was there, too, smiling, looking relaxed and happy.

I forced him out of my mind and got on with the show, working with the same musical material I had used opening night. All in all, the audience and I had some light fun together, and I felt they were remarkably patient waiting for Bobby to come on stage—a man whose recent stature in the media had increased from legendary singer to near saint.

When I brought him on, the place went wild. Men whistled, cheered and stamped their feet; women applauded and wept. I didn't linger backstage but quickly made my departure. There was dangerous work ahead and not a moment to lose.

chapter 36

The first thing I did on coming off stage was to remove my formal dinner jacket and throw it on the couch in my dressing room, picking up a tan windbreaker in its place. From my dressing room closet, I also grabbed a tropical straw hat with a wide brim and a pair of dark glasses: private eye Allen was about to go incognito.

After this brief stop I continued down the hall wearing the tan windbreaker over my ruffled shirt but carrying the hat and dark glasses in hand. I didn't want to appear *too* incognito until after I had passed the security guard by the stage door. The guard was a gray-haired gentleman named Jack. He had a sallow complexion and sunken cheeks and sat at a desk with a telephone and a row of TV monitors in front of him and a pistol on his hip. I had made a deliberate point of chatting with him for a few minutes as I had come in earlier, and in the breezy world of backstage camaraderie I hoped that Jack and I were already buddies.

"Hey, Jack!"

He looked up at me, surprised. "Goodness, you're not leaving us in the middle of the show, are you, Mr. Allen?"

"Naw, just running up to my room for a second. I forgot one of my props."

"If you want, I can send someone up to get it for you."

"No, that's all right, Jack—frankly, I can use the exercise, and I have at least twenty-five minutes before I go on again."

I thought he gave me a strange look, but I was probably being paranoid. Smiling nonchalantly I kept moving out the stage door into the hotel corridor, where I quickly put on the wide-brimmed straw hat and the dark glasses. Perhaps I looked odd in a hotel corridor at that time of night with a vaguely orange suntan from the makeup I wore, a big hat and dark glasses—but I figured people might find me strange enough that they would tune me out and look away.

The corridor led out to the second-floor casino, where I passed a row of video poker machines and a change-girl dressed like a Roman slave, as well as the escalator leading down to the main floor. People in casinos generally don't make a lot of eye contact with one another under the best of circumstances, and in my present attire they gave me a wide berth—except for a security guard whose suspicious gaze followed me across the room.

I felt guilty as could be, as if anyone with eyes could see I was up to no good. I was on too tight a schedule to stop and worry about such things, however, so I walked quickly past a bar and a row of blackjack tables to another corridor, where I came to a bank of elevators. A small Japanese man was waiting for me with a briefcase in his hand. We nodded at each other. I was expecting someone but was surprised that the fellow was so old and frail-looking. His job, of course, required delicate skill rather than brawn.

We had a pass-phrase to exchange.

"Have you tried your hand at roulette tonight?" I asked.

"Yes, thank you," said the man, giving the required response. "But I have a headache now, and I think I will go lie down."

"I trust your headache will be a short one," I said, finishing the routine. I felt that anyone overhearing this stilted exchange between strangers would be absolutely certain we were suspicious characters of the worst kind. I had just pushed the up button for the elevator when I felt a tap on my shoulder. I turned to find the security guard who had watched me cross the casino. My legs turned to jello.

"Excuse me, sir, but are you a guest at the hotel?"

"I beg your pardon?"

"If you want to go to the upper floors, you must be a registered guest. May I see your room key, please?"

My room key, alas, was on my dressing room table. I had not expected to be stopped like this, but then I normally didn't slink around hotel corridors at night wearing a funny hat and dark glasses with guilt written on my face like a neon sign.

"Hey, I'm Steve Allen," I whispered to the guard.

"Excuse me? You'll have to speak louder."

Just then the elevator door opened behind me and several couples stepped out.

"I'm staying on the top floor—in the Bacchanalian Suite," I said hopefully. The guard's look said plainly, "Hell you are!"

"I'm sorry, sir, but I really must see your room key," he insisted more firmly than before.

This was becoming very frustrating. I took off my glasses and raised my hat and fairly shouted at the man: "I'm Steve Allen, damn it! I'm headlining with Bobby Hamilton in the Arena!"

"My God, it's Steverino!" cried one of the women who had stepped off the elevator. "Honey, look—it's actually *him!*"

"I'm sorry, Mr. Allen," said the security guard contritely, probably worrying about his job. "I didn't recognize you."

That was the point! I wanted to scream at him, but I pretended not to mind. This was turning into a fiasco—two middle-aged couples were now asking for my autograph. Any moment I expected to hear a loud voice over the PA system announcing that Steve Allen was trying to sneak incognito up to the twenty-third floor to break into a room.

"Are you coming, sir?" asked the frail Japanese man. He was inside the elevator holding the door open for me.

"Oh, yes! I'm sorry, but I have to go," I told the people asking for autographs. I slipped into the elevator and gave a sigh of relief as the door closed behind me. I looked at my watch. Eight minutes had passed since I left the stage; I was running late.

"What's your name?" I asked the Japanese.

"Kenichi Takideo," answered the man, giving me a small bow. "At your service."

"Well, Kenichi—this isn't turning out too well so far. I hope you have better luck with the door."

"Luck has nothing to do with it, Mr. Allen. Proper tools are of the essence, as well as the right attitude and, of course, an empty mind."

I sighed, thinking that this was all I needed—a Zen burglar!

"Are you from Tokyo?"

"San Francisco," he said.

We stepped out at the twenty-third floor and walked quickly to the locked door at room 2304. Kenichi set down his briefcase and took out a thin metal shim which he slipped inside the lock.

"I learned this from listening to Alan Watts," he said.

"Housebreaking?"

"No, the proper metaphysical attitude. When a person thinks a certain way, doors tend to open."

"Well, let's get on with the tending," I told him. Normally I might have taken some time to discuss Zen and the Art of Burglary, but frankly I was too nervous. I kept looking up and down the hall for signs of other guests. Or a maid. Or a SWAT team.

Kenichi seemed to concentrate, but the door did not open.

"Can't you achieve the right attitude?"

"In this case a good attitude won't help—this is one hell of a good lock."

"Great! Isn't there anything you can do?"

The old Japanese man smiled ironically. "There's *always* something a person can do. If there were more time, I might even find an artistic and elegant solution to our present problem, but since time is running out. . . ."

Kenichi left the sentence dangling, reached into his briefcase and pulled out an automatic pistol with a silencer attached to the end. Before I had time to object, he shot the lock out of the door, the pistol making two angry pops.

"Good God! This was supposed to be a *discreet* operation!" I objected. "Now Elliot will know someone broke into his room."

The Japanese man shrugged. "Sorry. I didn't realize that detail was important."

I was tempted to call off the whole operation and run like hell, but it seemed a shame to give up just when I had reached my goal. Kenichi and I stepped inside the one bedroom suite and closed the door behind us. The suite was decorated much like mine, full of gilt and smoky mirrors, with a statue of Cupid holding up a lamp shade and red velvet curtains surrounding a round bed. If Nero had been reincarnated as a gangster from New Jersey, he might have come up with furniture like this.

"What exactly are you looking for?" asked Kenichi.

"Not decorating ideas certainly. I'm looking for something that will tie Elliot Block to a girl named Debbie. Also address books, bank books—I want to know what this man is up to in his spare time."

Originally I had requested the services of Kenichi from Johnny Nakamura only to open the door, but since we were running late I asked him to look through the living room while I did the bedroom. With the lock on the door destroyed, caution was no longer important. I pulled out drawers and scattered the clothes I found onto the floor, vaguely hoping that Elliot would interpret this as the work of an ordinary hotel thief. I discovered the man had a taste for expensive silk underwear and that he traveled with enough socks to keep him going for months at a time, even if all the laundries of the world went on strike.

From the chest of drawers, I moved to the walk-in closet where I found several expensive suits, shirts from formal to casual, and a few pairs of shoes. A leather briefcase sitting on the floor in the back of the closet caught my eye. I was about to ask Kenichi's help getting it open—maybe he could shoot the lock all to hell just as he had done to the door—but luckily found the case unlocked. Inside the briefcase I discovered a calculator, a letter writing pad, and a nasty little snub-nosed revolver. It was the pistol that concerned me. I couldn't think of a legitimate reason Block might carry one, but some people are funny about guns and like the sense of power they evoke.

I glanced at my watch. To stay on schedule I could remain in Elliot's room for exactly four minutes more. I realized I was definitely an amateur in the break-in department; this wasn't working out at all. To search the room properly, I would need at least an hour. I slipped the gun into my windbreaker pocket and decided I had time to only spot-check some of the more obvious places.

So what were the obvious places? I'm afraid my total knowledge of room-searching comes from cop shows on TV and paperback mysteries. I looked under the bed, reached my hand between the mattress and the box spring, searched at the back of paintings on the walls, and found nothing. And then I pulled open the drawer by the bedside table and struck gold. On a note pad surrounded by several plastic vials of pills, I saw a name and a telephone number which had been hurriedly written in pencil:

281

My heart raced. This break-in had turned from disaster to resounding success. Debbie Dobson was the spa hostess who had been killed; I had no doubt that the telephone number on the pad would turn out to be hers.

"Mr. Allen, I've found something," Kenichi called from the next room. I slipped the pad into my coat pocket next to the gun and walked out into the living room. At first I didn't see where Kenichi was, then I noticed him crouching under a writing desk.

"There's a manila envelope taped to the bottom of the desk," he said. "Yes . . . here we are."

He stood up and handed the envelope to me. I opened the metal clasp and pulled out a series of six 8 X 10 black-and-white photographs, three of which showed Christie Hamilton in a compromising R-rated situation on a bed with Johnny Nakamura. In the photos, Christie was half dressed and I had no doubt that they might be publishable in any of the racier tabloids. The remaining three pictures showed Christie in a hotel room with a mirror on her lap. On the mirror were two neat lines of cocaine, and the sequence showed the poor woman with a rolled bill of unknown denomination bending over the mirror and inhaling the crystals.

The photographs had a peculiar grainy quality, as if they might be stills transferred from video tape. I could only conclude these were from the infamous blackmail video recording I had heard about, and I wondered what they were doing in Elliot's room. They left me deeply depressed. Christie had certainly been foolish, but she had paid the price in full. My watch told me I had remained nearly five minutes too long. The revolver, the note pad and the photographs seemed like a successful haul. I told Kenichi it was time to get out, fast.

I put on my dark glasses and hat and led the way out into the hall with the manila envelope in hand and the revolver weighing down the right side of my jacket. Unfortunately, four beefy men with red faces came striding down the corridor at exactly the moment Kenichi and I emerged. The men had name tags on their suit jackets and acted as if they had drunk a little too much bourbon away from the watchful eyes of their wives. Kenichi and I tried to act nonchalant as we joined them on the trek down the hall to the elevator.

The elevator seemed to take forever to arrive. I looked at my watch, and to my horror discovered that a full twenty-five minutes had elapsed since I had stepped off the stage downstairs in the Arena; at any moment, Bobby might call me back on stage and I would not be there!

The four men seemed to be in town on a convention. They were telling each other off-color stories and laughing like jackasses. At long last the elevator arrived and we all stepped in together. One of the conventioneers stumbled against me, and we danced uncertainly for a moment before he apologized and stepped back. To my horror, the revolver had somehow managed to slip out of my windbreaker pocket. It fell with a clatter onto the elevator floor. Drunk as they were, the four men with name tags fell immediately and painfully silent.

"Whoops," I said, reaching down to pick up the gun. "Guess I need a holster for this damn thing."

The four smiled nervously. Kenichi Takideo

looked away and pretended he didn't know me; I couldn't blame him. In utter silence, the elevator dropped quickly to the second floor where I stepped out. My borrowed Japanese assistant as well as the four conventioneers continued down to the lobby and probably breathed a collective sigh of relief to see me go.

There had been pluses and minuses to this operation. I had to remind myself that I had found some things that Elliot Block might have trouble explaining. I walked as quickly as my legs could move down the corridor, through the Ben Hur Casino and to the stage door. Jack the security guard looked up from his desk at my hasty entrance.

"I was getting a little worried about you, Mr. Allen. Did you find your prop?"

"My what? . . . Oh, yes, yes," I told him vaguely and hurried on my way. Now that I was backstage, I broke into a jog down the corridor to my dressing room, stripped off the golfing jacket and threw it, along with the gun, note pad and manila envelope, into the back of my closet. Then I fled down the hall toward the wings of the stage, slipping into my dinner jacket as I ran.

I couldn't believe my luck. As I arrived in the wings, I could see Bobby standing on stage, his head slightly bowed, basking in applause. Most likely, repeated ovations had delayed the show and given me just the amount of extra time I had needed.

"And now I'm going to invite back on stage my buddy, Steve Allen, who's going to accompany me on the piano. . . . Come on out here, Steve-o." said Bobby, clapping his hands together.

"Hold it!" cried a voice from behind me.

I froze. I could hardly force myself to turn around. I found myself facing the stage manager.

"What?"

"Your bow tie's crooked," he said.

And that's not all that's crooked around here, I wanted to tell him. But I let him straighten my tie, and then did a little dance step out onto the stage, hamming it up a bit. I let the applause wash over me like a warm bath and seated myself at the piano feeling inordinately pleased with myself.

I hit the first chord and glanced over the footlights to Jayne's table. I could see she was smiling up at me, and the sight of her familiar face reassured me. Then my eyes moved around the table, past the Gelbarts, towards the very guilty, Elliot Block. His chair was empty.

chapter 37

The long arm of the law, as represented by the short and stubby figure of Lieutenant W.B. Walker, was awaiting me in my dressing room as I stepped off stage. In any other instance, I might have been impressed by the swift workings of justice.

"Mr. Allen," said W.B. surprisingly sadly, "I never thought it would come to this."

I tried to bluff it out. "What are we talking about, W.B.?"

"Please," he said, as if I had just insulted his intelligence, "take my advice and confine your professional activities to show business. If you get desperate, maybe you can sell encyclopedias door-to-door, or maybe get into politics, like some of your buddies, but under *no* circumstances should you ever take up a life of crime!"

"Okay. You've, er, found me out, have you?"

"Do you realize how many people saw you sneak up to the twenty-third floor wearing that stupid hat and dark glasses? Not only are there a dozen eyewitnesses—that I know of—including a security guard and four terrified vacuum cleaner salesmen from Nebraska, but as it happens, we have the actual break-in recorded on videotape."

My jaw, as they say, dropped. So did my confidence in the likelihood of a continuance of my career in the theatrical arts. Like a drowning man I suddenly saw my professional life passing through my mind.

"Don't look so surprised. The hotel maintains a hidden video surveillance system in all the corridors just to snag wise guys like you."

"Gee, I didn't know that," I said, the most brilliant riposte of which I was at the moment capable.

"There are a lot of things you don't know, but let's get down to cases. Who's the Japanese clown who shot the lock off the door?"

"Oh, just a casual acquaintance," I said. "We met one night in a sushi bar—he asked me the old Zen riddle, 'What is the sound of one hand clapping?' And I told him."

"You're going to have to do better than that, mister. I hope you realize I could take you downtown right now and throw your ass in jail.

"Not a good place for it, it seems to me."

"Now I'm willing to give you the benefit of the doubt that *maybe* you were just following some harebrained scheme, playing detective, and you weren't actually trying to steal jewelry or money—but you'd better come clean. I want some answers, and I want them now."

"Glad to oblige. W.B., look, I *had* to break in— and as a *result* of breaking in I now have almost irrefutable evidence that Elliot is the killer."

"Yeah? Well, why don't you tell me about this

so-called evidence, and I'll judge whether it's irrefutable or not."

I went to my dressing room closet and brought
out my tan windbreaker and the manila envelope,
ready for show-and-tell time.

"I found these in Block's room. You tell me if
this looks like innocence to you."

As my first sampling of guilt, I offered W.B. the
snub-nosed revolver I had found in Elliot's briefcase.
The lieutenant sniffed the barrel and shrugged his
shoulders.

"A lot of unwise people carry guns," he said.

Next I produced the manila envelope. The lieutenant took out the 8 X 10 black-and-white photographs and studied them with interest.

"So?" he asked finally. He seemed determined
to be a killjoy. "Maybe Block gets off looking at dirty
pictures."

"Well, take a look at *this*," I said, handing over
the last of my stolen bounty—the note pad with poor
Debbie's phone number written hurriedly in pencil.

"What is it?"

"Do I need to spell it out for you? It's Debbie's
phone number. Remember I told you she had a secret boyfriend? Well, this proves that Elliot was dating the poor girl probably with the purpose of setting
up his murder plot. And as soon as he strangled
Christie, the girl had to die as well so she wouldn't
talk."

"My, my—all that from a single note pad!" said
W.B. "You don't think perhaps you're jumping to a
few wild conclusions?"

"Well of *course* I'm jumping to conclusions,
W.B. What other exercise am I getting around
here?" He was, as usual, indifferent—no, impervi-

ous—to my humor. "But what other reason would Elliot have Debbie's phone number in his bedside table?"

"First of all, it may not even *be* Debbie's phone number—for all we know, there's another Debbie D. out there who has nothing to do with this case."

"Unlikely."

"But not impossible."

"And even if it *is* the girl's number, so what? Elliot frequently used the VIP health spa and so he had contact with the girl, on a number of occasions. Maybe he suggested they have dinner one night. Maybe he told her he'd make her a big star. Maybe they were even having some kind of a romance—but none of that indicates any motive for foul play."

"But the gun and the photographs!"

"For all we know, the gun may be a perfectly legal registered weapon, and there's certainly no law against possessing a few smutty photographs, or trying to date a pretty young girl. But let's say for a moment you're right—that all these things together add up to some indication of guilt. Now do you have any idea what you've done by *illegally* removing these objects from Block's room?"

I sighed. "I guess I screwed up on that score," I admitted.

"Screwed up?" cried W.B. "You've absolutely destroyed the evidence! No court in the country would now let me introduce these things into a criminal trial!"

"I hadn't thought of that," I said contritely. "But even if it's not permissible evidence, Elliot has some explaining to do. Somehow, we're edging closer to the truth."

W.B. stared at me coldly. "All right, let's get

back to my first question—who's the Japanese munitions expert who likes to open locked doors with a pistol?"

"His name is Kenichi Takideo. Didn't I tell you that?"

"No sir, you didn't tell me that. But here's an even better question. In fact, this is my personal nomination for question-of-the-month. How did you manage to find a guy like this Mr. Takideo who could help you break and enter?"

"You're going to be angry, W.B. Actually, I phoned Johnny Nakamura and asked if he would lend me one of his—er—"

To my surprise the lieutenant, apparently momentarily incapable of the form of human communication called speech, simply growled, while, with trembling fingers he extracted a small brown plastic vial from his pocket and gulped two white pills.

"Jesus," he said, "and I say that as a Christian myself. How in the name of Christ did you know how to telephone Johnny Nakamura?"

"A good question," I conceded.

"You're certainly right about that," he said. "In fact, I would say it is one of the best goddamn questions you'll ever hear in your whole friggin' life. But let's forget the question. Could we possibly hurry along to the answer?"

"Sure," I said.

I went to my small dressing room refrigerator and fetched him a glass of Perrier. He took a drink but still wasn't pleased with me.

W.B. clenched his teeth. "Okay, I'm calmer now. And ever since Daryl Gates got into trouble we're all a little more sensitive to the problem of beating the crap out of people. Just tell me *how* you telephoned Johnny Nakamura—a man who is currently the object of a nationwide manhunt."

"Ah, that . . . well, he gave me a number where I could—er—reach him."

I was almost certainly wrong—I mean I know it's not biologically possible—but I did have the clear impression that I saw wisps of steam, albeit very small, escape from the poor man's ears.

"I see," he said. "The Las Vegas police, the FBI and the organized crime division of the IRS are all scouring the country for this sonofabitch, and what does he decide to do? Get in touch with a goddamn television comedian. Sir, I think we should continue this conversation down at the station house."

"You're kidding!"

"No," he corrected me. "You're the kidder around here. I'm into serious business. Now do you want to go in handcuffs, or will you come along peacefully?"

Just put it this way, the situation left little room for choice. I walked with the lieutenant out of my dressing room and down the hall, where I had the misfortune to run into Jayne and the Gelbarts. When Jayne saw W.B., she tried to invite him along for a late dinner but at once detected that this was not a happy social occasion.

"Sorry, dear," I told my wife. "I—uh—got a little carried away."

"You look like you're being carried away right now," Larry Gelbart said.

I tend to laugh at his every remark, but at this moment the response was not shared by Lt. Walker. Nor, for that matter, by Jayne, who not only ignored Larry's wit but chose to take a somewhat imperious tone with the detective.

"Lieutenant," she said "what's going on here?"

"Mrs. Allen," Walker started to explain, with remarkable control, given the circumstances. "Until now, while I admit I've tried to discourage your husband from butting into police business, I've never actually forbidden him. I'll even admit he's come up with a helpful idea or two. But he has just committed the crime of breaking and entering and—"

Pat Gelbart put her hand to her mouth. Larry still seemed to think the scene he was witnessing was some sort of put-on. "Steve," he said with mock solemnity, "I always figured you for a breaker—but *entering?*"

Jayne, who correctly sensed that Gelbart didn't have the situation in focus, said, "Larry, do you hear anybody laughing?"

"No," Larry said. "But I attribute that to a bad PA system."

"Larry," his wife said, "Jayne is serious."

"Jayne's always serious," I explained.

"Lieutenant," Jayne said, " . . . exactly what did my husband break?"

"He broke the lock on the door of one of the suites in this hotel."

"And what did he enter?" she asked.

"The Twilight Zone?" Gelbart suggested.

"Larry," I said. "I know that there appear to be certain comic elements to our situation at the moment, but Lt. Walker has high blood pressure."

"How high *is* it?" Larry said, still not getting the message.

"Larry," said Pat, in a leash-yanking tone, "the lieutenant is serious."

"Of course," Larry said. "The straightman is always serious."

I was beginning to worry that Larry might drive the lieutenant to such a pitch of distraction that he'd end up down at the police station with me. "Lieutenant," I explained. "Mr. Gelbart is a professional humorist. Perhaps you've seen his hit musical comedy *City of Angels?*"

Walker, apparently having given up hope of extricating himself from so inane a conversation by any purely rational exchange, simply rang down the curtain on the scene. Taking me by the arm, he said, "That's it. Let's go."

"Sorry, sweetheart," I said to Jayne. "I'll explain all this later."

"Well, I hope so," Jayne said, obviously miffed, and my wife is one of those who must have specialized in miff during the years of her formal education. Later, when I wrote to Larry to ask if it would be all right to describe the incident in this book, he not only said, "Yeah, sure," but that the gesture would go a long way to make up for him and Pat having been cut out of *War and Peace*.

I followed W.B. out the hotel to his cream-colored unmarked car and realized I had better start being more cooperative. I told Walker everything about my late night meeting with Johnny Nakamura at Hoover Dam. We reached the station and settled down into his cubby hole office just as I was getting to the end of my account.

"I was only trying to get to the truth," I assured him. "I'm positive there's more to these murders than Nakamura."

W.B. regarded me a long time, apparently not quite certain what to do with me. "You know, when

I get stressed-out, I start thinking about pizza and hamburgers and all kinds of high-cholesterol food," he said. "It's hard to be on a goddamn diet and deal with someone like you at the same time."

I did not contest the point. "Don't tell Jayne," I pleaded. "She'd never forgive me."

The lieutenant sighed. "Wait here a moment," he told me. "I want someone to check out the gun and the phone number you found. Then we'll figure out what to do with you."

Lieutenant Walker left me by myself in his office. A clock on the wall said it was nearly midnight. They advertise Las Vegas as the city that never sleeps, but I had had too many late nights and the call of sleep was irresistible. Perhaps I should explain, in this connection, that for what are probably genetic reasons, my sleep requirements are greatly in excess of the norm. During my teenage years I often slept twelve or thirteen hours a day, and even now, in my sixties, can remain unconscious for a good ten hours and feel sleep deprived if I get only the traditional eight. I spent a few minutes fantasizing about my own warm and cozy bed back in Los Angeles, and I must have dozed off for a while because when I awoke, W.B. was sitting down at his desk, and the clock on the wall told me some forty-five minutes had passed.

"Have a nice snooze?"

"Did I snore?"

"Yeah."

I stretched and yawned. "Sorry. So what did you find out?"

"The gun is registered in California, all nice and legal. Block even has a special permit to carry it concealed on his person if he wants to. Apparently a few years ago, Bobby Hamilton received some undue attention from an aggressive and obnoxious fan, and the gun was supposedly carried to protect Block's client."

"It still seems suspicious to me." I said.

W.B. smiled grimly. "Then there are the photographs. Now you said this Kenichi Takideo fellow found the manila envelope taped beneath a writing desk in the living room. Did you actually see him find the envelope?"

"No, but I don't see . . . ."

"Maybe he planted the photographs himself— on orders from Nakamura, of course, who is trying to get himself off the hook. Can you categorically tell me this is not a possibility?"

"Well, no. But . . . ."

"Now we get to the last of your stolen booty— the note pad with Debbie's number."

"Yeah," I said optimistically. "That's a bit harder to explain away."

"It turns out to be indeed the phone number of the dead girl, Debbie Dobson."

"You see, I was right!"

"But there's one catch. I had California DMV send me a FAX copy of Elliot Block's driver's license and I checked the writing on the note pad against the signature on the licence—and guess what? Block did not write that phone number."

"Are you sure?"

"Absolutely. It's not his handwriting. Not even close."

I frowned, until a possible answer came to mind. "Then it must be the girl's! Don't you see how it could have happened? He asked her for her number and she wrote it down for him on the pad!"

"Good try, but it's not Debbie's writing either. I checked that too."

"So whose is it then?"

W.B. leaned forward and smiled. "One of Nakamura's guys, I bet. Mr. Allen, you've been played for a sap. You phoned Johnny asking for help to break into Elliot's room, so he had one of his guys go into the suite earlier in the evening and plant a few goodies for you to find, just so you wouldn't come away empty-handed. Probably if you'd had more than a few minutes to search, you would have found some even better stuff than what you got."

I had to admit to the possibility that W.B. was right. Breaking into Elliot's hotel suite was not the smartest thing I had ever done. "So what's next? Are you going to put me in the slammer?"

He flexed his upper lip, reminding me of Humphrey Bogart. "You're lucky, Mr. Allen. The hotel doesn't want to press charges against one of their own headliners, and neither does Elliot—for similar reasons. Nevertheless, laws were broken, including the unlawful discharge of a firearm in a public place and I *could* put you in the slammer, as you call it, if I choose. But I will let you off the hook . . . for a certain price."

"Yeah? What?"

"The phone number you have for Mr. Nakamura. You're going to call him and suggest a secret meeting. When he shows up, we're going to be there too. In force."

"But W.B.—even though the guy's a gangster, I gave him my word. This is a matter of betraying a trust."

"Isn't that sad? But look on the bright side—if you duck fast enough when the bullets start to fly, you might not even get killed."

chapter 38

I used the phone in Lieutenant Walker's office, dialed the number I had been given at Hoover Dam, and told the anonymous voice on the other end that Steve Allen was calling to request a meeting with Johnny Nakamura.

There was a pause. I was certain any gangster in his right mind would smell a trap and begin to consider various ways to eliminate one double-crossing, piano-playing TV comic.

"Where are you now?" asked the voice.

"Well, er, at a pay phone," I lied. And then embellished: "Downtown near the public library."

"Return to your hotel. You'll receive a phone call with further instructions."

CLICK went the receiver as the line went dead.

"Good," said W.B. with a nod. He had already discovered the location of the number I had just called through his contacts at the phone company—it was a private line somewhere inside the Lucky Horseshoe Casino.

W.B. drove me back to the hotel, and I slept

fitfully through the remaining hours of the night, expecting to be awakened at any time by a call that in fact did not come. In the morning, Jayne asked me all the questions she had put off the night before, and I told her mostly the truth, that the hotel and Elliot Block and Lieutenant Walker had very kindly decided to forgive my transgressions. For fear of worrying her, however, I withheld the information that I was about to double-cross a deadly criminal whose back was against the wall and was therefore probably even more dangerous than usual. I figured I was frightened enough for both of us.

I had breakfast with Jayne in the suite, still waiting for the phone call.

"Do you still think Elliot's the guilty one?" she asked me over a bowl of sliced peaches.

I shrugged. "I'm not sure I know *what* to think any more. Maybe it's even Bobby, for all I know."

"Steve, that's a terrible thing to say! Besides, Wade admitted trying to frame his father. Bobby was in that Lincoln Continental at the time of the murder—you proved his innocence!"

"Yeah, I guess so," I said. "Unless Bobby figured out a way to outsmart us. Or maybe it's Elliot, or Johnny Nakamura—or even Michelle, for all I know. I sure wish Mike Corvino hadn't disappeared—now that's a guy who could answer some interesting questions. But the cops can't find hide nor hair of him."

"You need a vacation," said my wife.

"Maybe a nice long cruise in the South Pacific," I told her with a wistful smile.

And it was at that moment that the long-awaited phone call finally came. I picked up the receiver and heard the same neutral, anonymous male voice from the night before:

"Mr. Allen, you are to leave now. Go downstairs to the main entrance and take the first taxi in line to the Excalibur Hotel. Play a few shoes of Baccarat at the casino on the ground floor. Someone will contact you."

CLICK went the line, and the phone was dead. I knew W.B. had my phone tapped; I wondered what he thought of the arrangements and how he could move his people into a crowded hotel.

"Well, I'm off," I told Jayne brightly. "I thought I might go over to The Excalibur and play a little Baccarat before lunch. I feel a strange urge to gamble."

Jayne gave me a funny look. "Steve, dear, are you sure everything's all right?"

"Everything's fine," I told her, and gave her a tender kiss, in case I might never see her again. Her eyes looked up at me with a kind of girlish surprise. I turned quickly, snatched a pair of dark glasses from a table by the door, and left the suite.

I walked outside the hotel into yet another bright day—the weather never seemed to change in Nevada. I was about to ask the Roman Centurion by the front door to hail me a chariot when I saw Cass. He jogged across the driveway from his VW Bug parked in the waiting zone.

"Steve, thank God I've found you. I got big news."

"I can't talk now, Cass. I have to get to The Excalibur right away."

"Fine, I'll drive you. We'll talk along the way."

"Cass, I don't have time to explain but I've got to take a taxi today."

He looked hurt, thinking I was avoiding a trip in his VW bug. "Sure," he said. "I understand."

"Look, you don't understand at all," I told him. "We'll talk this afternoon—and you can tell me your big news then."

I felt bad cutting him off, but I knew I was being watched. My instructions over the phone had been clear enough and I didn't want to do anything to make Nakamura nervous. The Centurion by the door gave a loud whistle and the first taxi in line drifted to the curb.

"The Excalibur," I said. As the driver pulled away from the hotel I had a final glimpse of Cass standing on the sidewalk, looking crestfallen. It didn't make me feel very good. I noticed the cab driver had not turned on his meter and that there was no hack license in the plastic holder on the visor. This did not make me feel any better. I wondered if he were a cop or robber, good guy or bad.

"Nice day," I said experimentally.

But the driver didn't answer as he took me speeding down The Strip to whatever it was that fate had in store.

chapter 39

The Excalibur Hotel stands at the southern edge of The Strip, a cartoon fairy tale castle with turrets and spires that somehow look as if they have been built out of cardboard. Whoever designed this place didn't go back to the old Arthurian stories for inspiration, only to Walt Disney. Somehow I expected to run into Dopey, Dumpy, and Grumpy in this castle, rather than Lancelot, Guinevere or Arthur. I had the taxi drop me off at the drawbridge where I took the moving walkway over the moat and passed through a stone passageway into the lobby. There were signs advertising the Canterbury Wedding Chapel on the second floor and King Arthur's Tournament—"Two Shows Knightly"—as well as an all-you-can-eat dinner for $4.99 at the Round Table Buffet and an Italian restaurant called Lance-a-lotta Pasta. Inside the lobby, I was confronted by—surprise—acres of slot machines, though here they were cunningly called "Medieval Slot Fantasy Machines."

There were lots of people milling about. The

Excalibur is the newest hotel on The Strip and really draws a crowd, though not the usual wraith-like figures you find in Vegas casinos. The cartoon design of the hotel seems to take the sting out of gambling and lures a more all-American clientele. I watched clean-cut families passing among the Medieval Slot Fantasy Machines.

I passed through the thick crowds. The last time I had met Johnny Nakamura had been at a desolate vista point after midnight at Hoover Dam—now we would be surrounded by a cast of thousands, which seemed a clever move on his part. There was safety in numbers. Presumably there were undercover police discretely on my tail, but they could easily lose me in such a crowd. I prayed they would not.

I made my way through a casino the size of a football field, passing down an aisle of slot machines into the Blackjack tables and roulette wheels where the gamblers looked more serious. People here were winning and losing without a trace of emotion—no joy, no sorrow. Above us on the ceiling I noticed the omnipresent "eye in the sky"—video cameras scanning the dealers and gamblers alike, making sure everyone stayed honest. I asked a cocktail waitress to direct me toward the Baccarat tables and was pointed to a far end of the casino.

Baccarat is the glamor game of any casino. People in the know pronounce it "bah-cah-rah," but if you want to appear a *real* Jet Setter you can always call it Chemin De Fer, which is the name it goes by in the casinos of Europe. At the Excalibur, a red velvet rope and two security guards separated the baccarat tables from the more plebeian games. Now that I was here, I wasn't certain what to do next. I had been instructed to sit down, play a few hands

302

and wait for someone to contact me—unfortunately, I didn't know the first thing about the game. In fact, the only Baccarat with whom I'm acquainted is Burt.

"Does the gentleman wish to have a seat at the table?" asked a security guard by the velvet rope.

"Yeah, I suppose so," I sighed. I glanced over my shoulder to see if Johnny might appear and rescue me from this, but there was no sign of the man. The security guard opened the threshold wide enough for me to pass through, and I was escorted to a green velvet table shaped like a large kidney bean. There were no less than three dealers present, each dressed in black tie and dinner jacket and looking very decorous. A waitress came by to see if I might like a complimentary beverage; I asked for a glass of orange juice. All this attention made me feel like a pig on the way to slaughter. Somehow I figured these nice people wanted something from me—my money, for instance.

The game was in progress as I sat down. There were four other gamblers at the table—a busty older woman with an enormous diamond ring on one finger; a bald man wearing sunglasses and a dark suit; a bearded Arab, also wearing sunglasses, in traditional white headdress and robe; and a young man in a white linen suit with a cigarette dangling from the corner of his mouth. I sat down in an empty spot between the Arab and the lady with the diamond ring.

All eyes turned my way as I joined the table.

No one smiled. Winning and losing money in Vegas was a tediously serious business. "Do not destroy my concentration, *pliz*," said the man with bald head. He had a German accent; I realized I had fallen in with a very international crowd. I settled back in my chair trying to look as much like James Bond as possible.

"So what happens next? Do we roll dice or pick letters out of a bag?"

"You place a bet," said a silvery feminine voice at my side. I looked up and saw a strikingly beautiful young Japanese woman standing next to my seat. She was wearing the tightest dress I had ever seen, with a slit up one side to reveal a long shapely leg. Either she had put that dress on two years earlier and grown into it, or someone must have helped her put it on this evening. Perhaps some lucky stiff would later have to help her take it off, too. Her small feet were in stiletto heels, her skin was pearly white, her lips fire-truck red, her hair long and black, her almond-shaped eyes dark and inscrutable.

"You must buy some chips, Mr. Allen. Give me a thousand dollars and I'll get you started."

"A *thousand* . . ."

"A credit card will do."

"Look, I don't want to appear cheap, but maybe we should move over to the slots."

"Mr. Allen, trust me," said my personal Mata Hari. "Sometimes you must risk a little to reap great rewards."

"You should be writing fortune cookies," I muttered—but I gave her one of my credit cards. The young woman passed it to a young man in a tuxedo who appeared like magic, and in a moment a small pile of multi-colored chips likewise appeared in front of my place.

"Baccarat is really terribly simple," said the lovely young woman. "The point is to get a total of nine with two cards—or an additional third card, if necessary. Now the way you number the cards is like this: two through nine count as their face value, aces are one and the ten and all face cards count as zero. Can you follow me?"

"To the ends of the earth," I said. It got nothing.

"Now the dealer will deal two cards, face down, to the player with the largest bet on the table, and then two cards to himself—the banker. You can bet on either the player or the banker, but if you win with the banker, you must pay the casino a five percent commission. This is the safest bet you can make at baccarat, because even with the commission the house edge is only one point six percent."

"I see . . . five percent commission, one point six percent edge," I repeated dutifully, trying to memorize. I found myself wishing we could play Scrabble instead.

"Now if the player's cards add up to an eight or nine, he automatically wins—that's called a *natural*. However if the banker's total ties the player's total, then the hand is played over. You got that? The other thing you need to know is that if your two cards add up to zero through five, you must draw a third card. However, if you have a six or a seven, you have to stand. Is that all clear?"

"No, but it's fun to watch your lips move."

"Why don't you watch me play a few shoes," said the girl. "I'm sure you'll catch on very quickly, Mr. Allen. You seem like a fast learner."

To my surprise, she winked at me. A chair was brought up for her, and she took a seat to my left, with the Arab gentleman to my right. She moved a small mountain of my chips forward on the table and the game began. Despite her brief description of the rules, I was lost. Maybe I hadn't been paying complete attention, wondering as I was when Johnny Nakamura was going to make an appearance. The first hand went quickly—or the first *shoe* as they call it in baccarat—and one of the dealers pushed a few mountains of colored chips back in my direction.

"We won?"

"Of course. Approximately four thousand dollars."

"Four thousand dollars! Maybe we should quit while we're ahead."

The girl flashed a brief smile and seemed to consider me a tremendous joker. She pushed my entire mountain of chips forward on the table. "Let's live dangerously," she said.

"I already am," I assured her. And then I heard a familiar voice in my right ear.

"All right, what do you want to see me about?" said the voice. It was Johnny Nakamura, but for the life of me I couldn't figure out where his voice was coming from.

"Well?" said the voice once again. I turned cautiously to the Arab gentleman on my right, who was semi-concealed behind his beard, dark glasses and flowing robes.

"Johnny?" I asked uncertainly.

"It ain't Lawrence of Arabia," said the Arab sourly. "Don't look at me—just keep playing and tell me what you want. I have a gun under these bed sheets, so don't try anything funny."

I didn't like the idea of the gun. Actually I had nothing whatever to discuss with Johnny since the police were supposed to appear at just that moment and end our all-too-brief encounter. But the fuzz was nowhere in sight. Meanwhile the game went on.

"Card for the player," intoned the dealer. "Card for banker," he continued, tucking a card beneath the wooden *shoe*.

"It's about Elliot Block," I improvised, talking out of the side of my mouth. "He had a set of your blackmail photographs in his room—I was wondering how he got hold of them."

"How should I know?"

"You didn't give them to him?"

"Absolutely not. I gave one set to Bobby, and that was it."

While we were talking, I noticed I had apparently just won another hand, for stacks and stacks of chips were pushed in my direction.

"How much this time?" I asked the lovely girl on my left.

"We're up almost twelve thousand dollars," she said. And then to my dismay she pushed my entire stack of winnings forward to bet.

"Let the young lady worry about the game, Mr. Allen," said my Arab friend. "What else did you want to see me about?"

"Well, why don't you tell me more about you and Michelle," I asked, stalling for time. *Where the hell was W.B. Walker?*

"What's there to tell? Michelle's a very unbalanced young lady, almost as crazy as her brother, if you want my opinion. We went out for a while when she was in Vegas eight, nine months ago—she broke it off when she started seeing this college kid, Ken, and frankly I wasn't all that disappointed."

My brain did a small somersault. I wasn't sure I understood him right. "Wait a minute—you're saying Michelle met Ken eight or nine *months* ago?"

"That's right. She started seeing him last winter."

"You're sure?"

"Of course I'm sure. I had my reasons for keeping a close watch on the girl."

I felt a jolt of excitement. Michelle, of course, claimed to have met Ken in the VIP spa on the morning her mother was murdered; Ken was her alibi! If she had met him long before, all kinds of new possibilities came to mind.

Michelle and Ken!

"Let's be certain we're speaking about the same Ken," I insisted. "Tall, blond, good-looking, a student at the University, wants to be a diplomat?"

"That's him. He's into health food—likes to hang out at a place called The Carrot and The Schtick."

I didn't like this, and I knew Jayne wasn't going to like it either. As I pondered Johnny's information, I noticed something else I didn't like—all my pretty multi-colored chips were being swept up by the dealer and taken away.

"Why is he taking all my chips?" I asked the girl.

"Because we lost, Mr. Allen—everything, I'm afraid."

"Everything!"

"Forget the money," said the Arab. "Is this all you wanted to see me about? Michelle and some college kid, and Elliot Block having a few dirty pictures?"

"These are significant details," I assured him. However, the Arab stared at me a long hard moment, and I could see a suspicion of the truth dawn in his eyes.

"Damn you! This is a trap!" he said suddenly with a sharp intake of breath. He started to pull out his gun from inside his robe, but before he could raise it in my direction several inexplicable things began to happen. Hands reached out from behind us, grabbing at Johnny and trying to get at the gun. I heard someone shout in my ear: "Duck! Get down, everyone!" It seemed like a good idea, only Johnny still had his pistol and was only inches away from me. Without pausing to think, I grabbed his wrist and tried to wrestle the gun out of his hand. A shot was fired toward the ceiling and I heard a few people scream. Then a bulky figure in a wrinkled brown suit was on top of Johnny and pulling him down onto the floor. In a moment, there were police everywhere with their own guns drawn, driving back the curious spectators and holding onto Nakamura. Lieutenant Walker lifted the Arab costume from his head while another cop snapped handcuffs around his wrists. The gangster lay on his back glaring up at me.

"You betrayed me, Mr. Allen," he said sadly.

I turned away, unable to meet his eyes. "So what the hell took you so long?" I asked W.B., who was just standing up from the floor.

"We had to be careful, for chrissake. There are a lot of people in this casino—we didn't want any of 'em to get hurt."

"But what if *I* got hurt?" I asked bitterly.

W.B. smiled. "Well, hell—you're a real tough guy, Mr. Allen. I thought you could take care of yourself. So what have you and Johnny been chatting about, if I may ask?"

I was about to tell him, but changed my mind. Frankly I was feeling annoyed at Walker and thought I wouldn't throw him Michelle quite yet.

Anyway, I wanted to give the girl a chance to explain herself first. This was serious business. If Johnny was right, Michelle had just become my number one suspect.

chapter 40

Somehow an assortment of TV cameras and journalists appeared, seemingly from nowhere. Understandably they placed great emphasis on the fact that a shot had been fired inside The Excalibur and that Johnny Nakamura had at last been apprehended in connection with the murders of Christie Hamilton and Debbie Dobson. As far as the media was concerned, the case was over except for a few days of headlines and hype.

Lieutenant Walker seemed to feel the same way. "Congratulations," he said, coming over after Nakamura had been led away. "I have to admit, there were times I worried about you. Times I wondered what the hell side you were on—but you really came through, Mr. Allen, and I want to apologize for all the bad things I've ever thought about you and tell you how much I've appreciated your help."

It wasn't the most whole-hearted testimonial I've ever received. Still, Lieutenant Walker and I shook hands, and there were a dozen cameras to record our big moment and the sense of a job well done.

"What about Nakamura's grandmother?" I whispered, as we smiled towards the cameras.

"Forget her," the lieutenant said.

"So when you fix your car, and at the end of the job you have an extra part left over—you just throw it away?"

"Why not?" asked W.B. "If the car runs okay without it, maybe the part wasn't necessary in the first place."

W.B. had a uniformed man drive me back to The Coliseum. Despite the atmosphere of self-congratulations, I felt vaguely uneasy. To tell the truth, I wasn't at all happy about betraying Johnny. He was a crook, but he had trusted me. More importantly, I still wasn't convinced he was guilty of the two murders. I also was feeling unhappy about Michelle. Jayne had practically adopted the girl, as she adopts all strays—cats, dogs, and lost souls. She would definitely be upset that Michelle had lied to her about Ken—*if* indeed the girl had lied, and the story wasn't a ploy on Johnny's part to cast suspicion away from himself. I decided I would check it out before telling Jayne.

The first person I saw back at the hotel was Cass, who was waiting for me downstairs in the lobby.

"Hey, Steve, I got to talk with you," said Cass, "Like I told you before, I found us a piece of news."

"Okay. You found out Elliot was dating Debbie Dobson?"

"No, that's not it," Cass said.

"You found the old woman who pretended to be Johnny Nakamura's grandmother?"

Cass shook his head, smiling. "Nope, I found Mike Corvino," he said. "Bobby's movie double."

It took a moment for the importance of this to sink in. Corvino was one of the loose ends I had fairly given up on. If Cass was right, and if Mike was willing to tell the truth, we could go back to the heart of this crime and learn who had done what, and to whom, and for what reason.

chapter 41

Cass was proud of himself, and I had to let him go on a bit about what a wonderful investigator he was. Eventually he even told me how he had managed to find Mike Corvino. Unfortunately, by the time he finished his tale my own excitement had faded somewhat. This was beginning to sound like a vintage Cass caper, with the emphasis on wishful thinking rather than hard fact.

Cass had started with a semi-brilliant idea, as he often will: He decided a very active guy like Corvino, a movie double and stuntman, would end up finding feminine companionship in Vegas. From there, he got hold of a photograph of Mike from a casting agent he knew in Hollywood, and then went around to all the casinos asking every cocktail waitress he met if she had any knowledge of the person in the photograph. His cover story was that Mike had inherited a fortune from a distant relative and Cass had been hired by the estate to try to locate the missing heir. But Cass can start with a good idea, and then get carried away. In this case, he went on foolishly to offer a reward for information. I was skeptical what this would accomplish in a town where there were lots of people who might be willing to lie for a few bucks.

I listened to Cass's story without a word of criticism, since I could see it meant a lot to him—it was a way of regaining his self-respect after the debacle of losing his limo by gambling. He proudly informed me that after two days of going around town, casino to casino, he had managed to locate an attractive young cocktail waitress at the Desert Inn who claimed she and Mike had been spending time together. Cass told her he wanted to surprise Mike himself with the good news about his inheritance and swore her to secrecy. Then he got her address, and she said she'd make sure Mike was there after eleven o'clock that night, and that there'd be a couple of bottles of champagne hidden in the refrigerator—it would be a surprise party celebrating Mike's good fortune.

A detail that worried me was that Cass hadn't seen Mike with his own eyes. In fact, the whole proposition seemed fairly iffy. Still, I agreed to accompany him after the show to the address the waitress had given him, though I wasn't all that optimistic about what we'd find. It could turn out to be just a cocktail waitress hoping for a reward.

Leaving Cass in the lobby I went upstairs to my suite, eager to pursue some detecting of my own. I was glad Jayne was out—there was a message she was having tea with a friend she had met at the brunch that morning. I wanted to check what Nakamura had told me about Michelle.

I began by calling the hotel manager and saying I wished to send a small thank-you gift to a young man named Ken, who worked in the VIP spa—unfortunately I did not know his last name. The manager put me on hold, and in a moment he was able to give me this information: The young man's full name was Kenneth Christopher Obrecht. This was a good start, but alas, the manager would not divulge Obrecht's home address; to give out such information is against the rules of the hotel. He suggested I leave my "small gift" with him at the main desk downstairs. I told him I would most likely do that.

Next I opened the Las Vegas telephone directory to the white pages, and I quickly found what I wanted. There were seven Obrechts in the directory, but only one K.C. Obrecht. I dialed the number. After three rings, a male voice answered.

"Ken? This is Steve Allen."

"Oh, hello, Mr. Allen—I know all about you, of course, but Ken's not here right now. I'm his roommate, Carl."

I used my gift ploy once again. I claimed I had a small present I wanted to give Ken to celebrate his anniversary with Michelle, but I wasn't certain if this was the nine-month anniversary coming up, or only the eight-month anniversary. With true love like theirs, I certainly didn't want to make such a major mistake.

There was a pause on the other end. "Well, Mr. Allen—maybe you should talk to Ken about this. I guess you know they're pretending they just met a few days ago because of Michelle being married at the time she was here last winter."

"Oh, I know all about that, Carl," I assured him. "Michelle and my wife Jayne are buddies; they tell each other everything."

"Well, if you know already, I guess there's no

harm. . . . I think it's coming up nine months since they first met at that crazy discotheque downtown. But Ken didn't tell me anything about celebrating an anniversary."

"It's a surprise," I told him. "Maybe you shouldn't mention I called."

I hung up the phone with a heavy heart. I had become a bit fond of Michelle myself. It was a pity she had lied to us.

I spent some time trying to locate her to hear what she'd have to say for herself, but Michelle was not in the hotel. I left some messages for her to call me when she came in, and then took a short nap and a shower to get ready for the evening's performance. With all this running around, I couldn't neglect the main reason I was in Vegas.

Fortunately the show came off better than ever. The combination of the reviews, Bobby's current notoriety, and word of mouth had carried our production to a certain critical mass where none of us could do any wrong. I left the stage with the applause still ringing in my ears and found Cass waiting for me in my dressing room. Michelle had not responded to any of my messages, but now it was time to see if Cass had in fact managed to find Mike Corvino.

He was keyed up. "Boy, we're really going to get to the bottom of this case! Maybe after this is over, Steve, we should quit show business altogether and set up a detective agency in some nice office in Beverly Hills. I can just see the sign on the door— JAMES CASSIDY & STEVE ALLEN, PRIVATE INVESTIGATIONS."

I ignored the billing and told him not to get too carried away. Even if we found Corvino, he might not talk. Or if he did, he might only repeat Wade Hamilton's final story, that Wade had hired Mike in order to implicate his father. There were lots of things that could go wrong, and I tried to prepare Cass for the fact that we might not get to the bottom of anything tonight.

After I changed into comfortable street clothes, Cass and I walked out of my dressing room almost straight into the arms of Bobby Hamilton and Elliot Block, who were coming down the hall.

"Listen, you tell Mike when you see him he's *never* working for Bobby again," said Elliot angrily.

"I beg your pardon?"

Elliot glanced at Cass. "Your driver here told me you were seeing Mike tonight—am I wrong?"

"Well, it's hard to say," I admitted, glaring at Cass.

"Don't listen to Elliot," said Bobby. "If you find Mike, just tell him to come to me—okay? Tell him I'm not angry about his trying to frame me, only hurt. If he needed money, all he had to do was ask."

"Sure, I'll tell him," I agreed. "*If* we find him."

Bobby slapped me playfully on the arm, and he and Elliot continued on down the corridor.

"*Well?*" I said to Cass, wanting to strangle him.

"Look, I'm sorry, Steve, but you gotta visualize how this happened. Before the show began, that Elliot guy saw me parking the VW Bug and he made a nasty joke about it, you see. So I bragged a little about how we found Mike Corvino and were about to bust this case wide open. I know I was acting like a big mouth, but I just couldn't help myself."

"Big mouth?" I asked mildly. "You've made certain *everyone* knows what we're up to tonight—

maybe you should give Lieutenant Walker a call just so he doesn't feel left out."

"You think I should?"

"I was being sarcastic, Cass."

"Oh," he said meekly.

His hurt look made me feel guilty. I tried to smile as I squeezed myself into the front seat of the Bug.

"I'm getting kinda fond of this crate."

"Well, I'm not," Cass said.

Neither of us knew it, but that would be our last trip in this particular Volkswagen. Ever. And that would be the good news tonight.

chapter 42

We took a left turn on Sahara Avenue, headed west under the freeway and kept going until we came to a part of Las Vegas I had never seen before. We drove past shopping malls, fast food restaurants and car lots that had optimistic banners and balloons flying overhead, advertising fabulous savings that could not be beat anywhere. The four-lane road, straight as a ruler, seemed to go on forever, mile after tedious mile.

Cass pulled into a brightly lit parking lot next to a McDonalds to consult his map.

"I hope you're not lost," I said.

"Of course not," he replied testily.

I avoided comment. Cass seemed to find what he was looking for on the map, grunted, turned off the overhead light and continued on his course. Two shopping malls further down the highway, Cass came to a red light, drifting a few feet into the crosswalk before coming to a complete stop.

"Strange," he said.

"What's that?"

"I could almost swear the brakes are going out."

"What's so strange about that? This old car's nearly a quarter century old—I'm surprised it runs at all."

"Steve, I checked the brakes yesterday. I took off the tires and had a good look at all the pads and drums—what kind of chauffeur do you think I am? I wanted to make sure old Bertha was safe enough to drive you and Jayne around."

"Bertha?" I asked cautiously.

"Bertha the Bug," said Cass, blushing a bit. "Cars have names too, Steve—just like people."

"Well, let's find a garage," I told him. "We can leave Bertha overnight and take a cab back to the hotel."

"Hey, it's not that bad," Cass said. "There's enough brakes left to stop as long as I'm careful—with a standard transmission, I can down-shift and let the engine do most of the work. Anyway, look around. This is the flattest goddamn landscape I've ever seen. We hardly even *need* brakes."

"I don't know," I said cautiously. "Maybe we should call it a night."

"Trust me," said Cass with his most winning smile. "Old Bertha could probably go another five hundred miles before the brakes go out all the way."

I gave in, against my better judgment. "Just go slow," I urged.

"That's all Bertha can do."

I sighed a little as the ancient VW Bug labored forward into the outskirts of the city. We passed a field of newly finished townhouses, all identical. "Quail Harbour," was the name of this particular real estate developer's dream, though I saw neither quail nor a harbour. Unfortunately, at the end of

Quail Harbour, the road began to climb upward toward a dusty mesa top.

"Cass, I don't know about this—what goes up, must come down."

"Steve, don't be such a worry-wart! The brakes are good enough."

As we climbed, I was struck by a ridiculous notion: Cass had managed to tell pretty much everyone what we were doing tonight; was it possible that the murderer had fiddled with our brakes in an attempt to put a permanent end to the investigating team of Cassidy & Allen? This was such a paranoid notion I had to smile. After all, despite Cass's assurances that he had checked the brakes, a vintage old crate like Bertha might be expected to have anything go wrong at any time, without recourse to murderers draining the brake fluid or cutting the lines.

"Glad to see you smiling, Steve," said Cass. "You've been kinda serious lately."

The road kept rising up to the top of the mesa; as far as I knew, this may have been the one and only hill in all of Clark County. At the apex of the hill we passed Lou's Gun and Ammo Shoppe, closed for the night, and then the road began to descend steeply toward a dry creek bed below. The Volkswagen gathered speed.

"Oh-oh," said Cass.

"What's the matter?" I asked.

"Pumping the brake peddle to the floor," said Cass. "They're gone with the wind, man. Ain't nothing there but wishful thinking."

We were in third gear and the tiny engine was revved up to a high-pitched whine.

"Can't you down-shift?"

"Sure," he said. Cass pressed down on the clutch, and as soon as we were out of gear, we really began to gather more speed. I heard a terrible screech of grinding gears and then only the sound of the engine racing in neutral and the wind whistling past the windows.

"Damn!" cried Cass. "The gears are screwed up somehow! I can't get it into second!"

"Put it back into third," I suggested, trying to keep the panic from my voice.

"No good!" said Cass.

We were now racing downhill past a darkened elementary school and a residential block of older houses. At the bottom of the hill there was an intersection; from there the road began to climb again. I was glad not to see another car in sight.

"If that intersection stays clear, we can just ride up the next hill to a stop," I said hopefully.

Cass didn't answer. He was clutching the wheel with a terrified expression. Down below at the intersection, a stop light turned yellow and then red. A station wagon came from a side street and made a left turn into our path.

"Oh-ooooohhhhh!" I said.

"Hold ooonnnnnnnn!" cried Cass.

Bertha barreled down toward the intersection, missed the station wagon by inches, and then continued across the dry creek bed and upward into the next hill. At last the old car began to slow, halted by the force of gravity on its upward climb. Unfortunately, this hill was not a long one and I was uncertain if we would come to a stop, or just sail merrily over the other side into the canyon beyond.

"Steve, if we die, or anything—I hope you forgive me," said Cass.

"Sure," I told him. "What the hell?"

"I mean, how many people get one last big roller coaster ride out of life?"

"That's the spirit, Cass. Look on the positive side."

The VW slowed toward the top of the hill and I began to feel we were actually going to stop before heading off down the other side. I was flooded with a sense of relief until a new possibility occurred to me: Without brakes, we would slow to a momentary halt, and then the VW would start falling *backward*, pulled like a pendulum back to the dry creek bed behind us. Cass seemed to realize this at the same time.

"Listen, man, I think it's about time to abandon ship."

"Right," I said. "We'll wait until the last possible moment."

The Bug came to within five feet of the top of the hill where its forward momentum finally gave out. For a brief moment Bertha stood in arrested motion; Cass and I simply opened our doors and stepped outside onto the gloriously solid pavement. Then, as we watched, Bertha began to slip backward, slowly at first but quickly gathering speed. Without someone inside to steer, the old Bug crossed the center divider and continued backward in the wrong lane until smashing through a guardrail at the bottom of the hill, sailing off the road into the dry creek bed, and landing upside down with a mighty crash. Cass and I stood near the top of the hill, watching the tires spinning emptily towards the sky. We heard a few creaks and moans that sounded like the final death throes.

To my surprise, Cass was moist-eyed. "She

wasn't much of a car," he said, "but she was all I had left."

"Hey, cheer up—you'll be driving a stretch limousine again," I told him.

"No, I won't, Steve," he told me softly. "I'm a loser. Screw up everything I touch. I couldn't make it as a cowboy, and then I couldn't make it as an actor, and now I don't even have any wheels left to make a living as a chauffeur."

"But you're one hell of a detective," I said encouragingly.

"Naw," he told me. "I'm lousy at that too."

"What are you talking about? You found Mike Corvino's girlfriend, didn't you? How far is it to her house?"

"It's close," he said gloomily. "It should be just at the top of this hill—but hell, the bitch was probably lying to me. Maybe she doesn't know Mike at all. She likely thought I was some kind of idiot, and she could get the reward money without putting out."

"Well, we won't know that until we see her."

Cass reluctantly tore his eyes away from Bertha lying upside down in the creek bed and turned to look at me. "You mean you still want to go through with this?"

"Why not?" I said brightly. "After all, Cassidy and Allen are not the sort of private eyes to be stopped by a little bit of car trouble!"

"I guess you're right," said Cass thoughtfully. He is not the sort of guy to stay down for long, and he was coming back fast.

At this point, I wasn't expecting to find very much at the girl's house, but I figured it was close, and what the hell—after nearly dying in a brakeless Bug, what else could happen to us?

chapter 43

We were looking for 131 Monte Carlo Circle, which turned out to be in a small community of stylish homes at the top of the very hill from which Bertha had slipped to her demise. After that near disaster, I was glad to be on foot. Out of doors, it was a beautiful night. One of the loveliest sights available to earthlings is that of the blackness of outer space as seen through clear desert air. In most major cities, on a moonless night, you're lucky if you can count forty stars. There are, of course, billions out there—some that even our most sensitive telescopes have not as yet been able to detect, but I'll never forget the beautiful shock of looking up into the black velvet void one night outside Phoenix, Arizona, where I was attending high school, back in the early 1940s. I could scarcely believe what was apparent, not the usual sprinkling of stars but untold hundreds and hundreds of them. I literally stood, like a creature that had just landed on a new planet, and stared in open-mouthed wonder at the splendor of it all, a recollection that now came flashing back to me as Cass and I walked along in a companionable silence, our footsteps making a soft crunching sound on the asphalt road.

Monte Carlo Circle went off to the left from the main road. We walked past sprawling single-story ranchettes on half-acre lots, pretentious Colonials with fake colonnades, and strange modern dwellings of glass and stone. Most of the homes seemed to have swimming pools and from their hilltop vantage point, they had an unobstructed view of the casinos and brightly lit hotels of Vegas, which rose up in the distance like some fabulous city of Oz. The house we were looking for turned out to be a Spanish-style mansion with a red tile roof and an ornate, heavy wooden front door. There were a number of tall cacti growing in a rock garden by the driveway, and I could smell bougainvillea nearby.

"I can't imagine a cocktail waitress living in a fancy place like this," I whispered.

"Me neither, but this is the address she gave me."

The darkened house showed no signs of life. Cass and I stood near a large cactus sizing up the place.

"Maybe she's an heiress," suggested Cass. "Maybe she's working as a waitress just for kicks."

I didn't reply. It seemed more likely that we were being set up for something—though for what and by whom was still a mystery.

"Well, what now, Steve? The place sure looks deserted."

"I can't believe we were brought here for nothing," I said. "Let's try the front door."

Cass and I walked up the tile steps and stood beneath the arched portico of the front door. I pressed the doorbell and from deep inside the house heard a faint two-note chime. There was no answer. In a moment I tried again, with the same result. Cass and I looked at each other. He shrugged. Out of general curiosity I tried to open the front door, but found it was locked tightly as a tomb.

"Well," said Cass slowly. "I guess we've been played for suckers."

"But why? Even if your waitress never met Mike Corvino in her life, there has to be a reason she sent us here. Let's walk around back—maybe we'll find something."

"Probably a big guard dog," said Cass.

I didn't like that thought. I hadn't considered a dog, but as soon as Cass mentioned the possibility, he appeared in my imagination, large and mean, a snarling monster with enormous teeth. "We'll be brave," I urged. "Anyway, if there were a dog, he'd be barking by now."

"Unless he's the silent, sneaky type," suggested Cass.

I was tempted to call this off, but forced myself to screw up my courage. "Follow me," I said. We passed around the side of the house toward the garage, and immediately saw something that made me stop in my tracks. Sitting inside the garage with the door open was a powder blue Rolls Royce convertible.

"Well, maybe cocktail waitresses at the Desert Inn get great tips," said Cass.

"I've seen this car before, Cass."

"Whose is it?"

"It was almost mine," I told him, leading the way through a gate into the backyard. If I had been briefly tempted to leave this house unexplored, I had changed my mind. With Cass on my heels, I marched past a swimming pool and came to a back door. I couldn't see a doorbell so I rapped loudly on the wood with my knuckles.

"Hello!" I called. "Anyone there?"

We got the same response as in the front—no answer. When I tried the latch, however, the door opened easily. I walked cautiously inside a darkened kitchen.

"Steve, you think this is a good idea?" asked Cass nervously.

"Absolutely," I assured him. "We've got to get to the bottom of this."

I tried the light switch by the kitchen door, but it clicked back and forth without any lights coming on.

"Anybody home?" I called loudly. "I know *somebody's* here!"

There was no answer. My voice reverberated in the darkened house.

"You know, man, it's kind of spooky in here."

"Cass, if you want to wait outside for me, go ahead."

"I didn't say that. You think I'm the sort of person to be afraid of a big dark house, for chrissake? I was only thinking of you."

"Do you have a match?"

Fortunately, Cass had been collecting match books at the different casinos. He struck a match and led the way forward from the kitchen into a large old-fashioned dining room that had a heavy chandelier and a long wooden table. In the flare of the single match, I had a brief glimpse of several dark paintings on the walls which seemed to show someone's ancestors, probably long dead. The room had a nightmarish quality. I tried a light switch on the wall but to no avail. Apparently the electricity was out everywhere in the house.

The match in Cass's hand went out, and we were left momentarily in total darkness. From somewhere above, I heard a creaking sound that might have been a footstep. Or an animal. I could hear my own breathing.

"Anybody here?" I called again, not quite so bravely as before. "Elliot, is that you up there?"

When Cass lit another match I can't remember ever being so glad for a meager light. I noticed his hand was trembling slightly as he held the match aloft.

"I hope this damned place ain't haunted," he said. "Maybe we should get the hell out of here."

"Not until we find out what this is all about. Come on, let's check out the rest of the place."

Cass handed me a pack of matches so we could both have light, and we walked with our small flares held out in front of us, passing into a large living room that had a high ceiling and big wooden beams overhead. The light from our two matches sent flickering shadows high into the vaulted ceiling. At the far end of the room I noticed several framed photographs on the mantle above the fireplace—I began to walk across the floor to investigate, but stopped in darkness when my match began to singe my fingers and I had to blow it out.

"Come here a second, Steve," Cass called from somewhere behind me—and then his match died, too, and the darkness in the living room was suddenly thick.

"I'll be right there, Cass. I just want to take a look at these photographs. Maybe they'll give us an idea of who lives here."

330

I lit a fresh match, and in the phosphorescent flare I walked quickly to the fireplace and held the match up to the frames. I was so startled by what I saw that I dropped my match and had to fumble for a new one. Across the room, Cass said something I couldn't quite make out. I was so interested in my discovery I didn't pay any attention.

On the mantlepiece there were two photographs which made my heart pound. The first showed Christie Hamilton, and had probably been taken shortly before her death. In the picture, Christie was wearing a bathing suit, leaning against the rail of the yacht on Lake Mead; she was smiling warmly toward the camera and death seemed to be a long, long way from her thoughts. The second photograph, standing side-by-side with the first, was of a pretty young woman I had never met in life but whose face was increasingly familiar to me now—Debbie Dobson, the hostess from the VIP spa. Debbie's picture was a staged professional portrait with a vague background of blurred flowers, the kind of thing she might have sent to elderly relatives for Christmas. Like Christie, she was smiling toward the camera. Either photograph alone would not have spooked me nearly so much as seeing the two dead women together—Christie and Debbie, smiling their ghostly smiles in the glare of my match as if someone were displaying trophies of his kill. My match burned my fingers, but I hardly noticed the pain; the light flickered out, and I was once again left in the velvety darkness.

There was a metallic taste of fear in my mouth. I turned around but couldn't see any sign of Cass or his match.

"Cass! Where are you?"

There was no answer.

I am not the sort to be afraid of imaginary phantoms, but the portraits of the two murder victims on the mantlepiece got to me. I felt there was something dreadful in this old house. I lit a fresh match as quickly as I could and held it aloft with a trembling hand.

"Cass!" I called again. "Cass, damn it, stop trying to scare me!"

But the silence which greeted me was as thick as the darkness into which I was once again cast the moment my feeble flare flickered and died. Unfortunately, I had a new worry—my supply of matches was going fast, and I didn't cherish the possibility of being trapped in this dark chamber without any light at all.

I tried not to panic. To show how brave I felt, I began to whistle "Take The A Train," but my mouth was too dry. I took a deep breath. Finally I lit one of my few remaining matches, and I watched the light chase back the darkness of the living room, reaching into the deep shadows. I took advantage of the moment by walking swiftly across the room towards where I had last seen Cass, but unfortunately I moved so quickly that the match blew out. I lit a new one, and this time cupped it in my hand to protect it from the breeze.

"*Cass?* Where are you, buddy?"

But there was no answer. Two more matches took me to the far end of the living room, where I found a door which led into another room, perhaps a den or office. Only two matches were left. I debated using them to find my way to the kitchen and out of this hellish house, but I didn't want to leave Cass behind.

I tried the first match, but my hands were shaking and I struck too hard—most of the phosphorous broke off from the tip and a stillborn flame sputtered for an instant before it died. This was a serious loss. Forcing myself to be more careful, I struck my final match, cupped it in my hand, and poked my head inside the next room.

I saw what seemed to be a large den with a TV set at one end. Then I saw a desk, and near it a long leather couch. On the couch, a familiar short wiry figure was lying face down, one hand trailing down to the floor.

"Cass!"

I heard a noise behind me. Something reached out and grabbed me hard, and I felt a wet handkerchief pressed over my nose and mouth with overwhelming force. I was aware that I had dropped my match onto the floor where it flickered and died.

The wet handkerchief had an overpowering smell that rushed me, in an instant, back to a hospital on the south side of Chicago. I was six years old and had just been brought in, semi-conscious, my face and chest covered with blood, which stained the imitation-fur collar of the new coat I had been given, modeled after Charles Lindburgh's pilots' jacket. My mother and I had been in the back seat of a Yellow cab which had crashed into a light fixture on the lake-front drive. Oddly enough, my clearest memory of the incident was that of something being pressed over my face, something with a horrible smell that choked and gagged me. I felt the same childlike helplessness now, tried to resist or call for help, but my consciousness flickered, as had my final match, and soon the blackness was complete. I slipped away into the long, dark night of unconsciousness.

chapter 44

"Hey, Steve," said a voice from a great distance. "Steve . . . wake up."

But I didn't want to wake up. I was quite happy with my eyes shut against the world, trying to make up for all the sleep I had missed since coming to Nevada.

"Go away," I told the nagging voice. My body was stiff and full of unfamiliar aches, my mouth dry as cotton. I wished fervently to return to the pleasures of dreamland.

"Steve! Come on, buddy."

I groaned, moaned but in the end opened my eyes, and was immediately sorry I had. The first thing I discovered was the reason my body was so uncomfortable: I was tied to a straight-back wooden chair with my hands bound tightly behind me. Cass was facing me in a chair of his own, apparently in the same predicament. We seemed to be in an old tool shed and though there were no windows, shafts of morning light were creeping in through a hole in a

334

roof. I wouldn't want to be in such a shed during a rain storm.

I had a crazy feeling of *deja vu* finding the two of us tied up like this. It took me a moment to figure out why.

"History repeats itself," I said to Cass.

"Did you knock your head or something?"

"My head is fine. It's my wrists that hurt. Anyway, at least we know how to get out of this situation."

"We do?"

"Sure. Wiggle around in your chair until you back up against something you can rub your ropes against. When you cut your way free, you can untie me."

Cass set to work. Fortunately, the shack in which we were imprisoned had plenty of rough edges to rub a rope against; Cass managed to back himself against an exposed two-by-four which held up part of the wall, and he began sawing up and down against the coarse edge. All this reminded me, of course, of Bobby and Wade going through exactly similar rope-untying activities—if indeed they had—only a few days earlier in a house in North Las Vegas. From Bobby and Wade, my thoughts drifted to Tako and Ahi, the two Japanese thugs with the *sushi* bar names who Wade had supposedly hired to do the fake kidnapping, with or without the help of Mike Corvino, Bobby's movie double. I had to wonder if Tako and Ahi were responsible for our present predicament. The M.O. certainly was similar.

Tako and Ahi . . . it was the damndest thing, but I felt that somewhere in my investigations someone had said something important that would make everything crystal clear, and that it had to do with

Tako and Ahi. Unfortunately, I was still groggy, not yet completely recovered from whatever anesthesia had rendered me unconscious, and the faulty computer that was my brain refused to make the proper connections.

"Did you get a glimpse of who knocked us out?" I asked Cass.

"No. I heard a noise, I went to investigate, and some sneaky bastard got me from behind. Before I knew it, it was lights out."

"Same thing happened to me," I admitted. "Let's hope we get loose before they come back."

Cass began to saw faster. As I watched him work, I kept imagining Bobby and Wade in the same position and kept thinking of Tako and Ahi . . . but the connection would not come.

Cass got out of his ropes in record time. He may not be the most predictable chauffeur in the world, but I can recommend his services if you are ever in a similar situation. His bony cowboy wrists were a big help. The sawing motion loosened his ropes after a few moments, and he was able simply to slip his hands out. Quickly, he untied his feet and came over to untie me. I stood up carefully, rubbing the numbness out of my hands and legs. Cass began to open the door to the outside, which creaked on its rusty hinges and nearly fell apart in his hands.

"Be careful they don't see you from the house," I warned.

"What house?" said Cass, stepping outside.

I had imagined that we were in some shed behind the mysterious Spanish mansion on Monte Carlo Circle, where our collective lights had gone out—but when I followed Cass outside I saw what he meant. There was no house, Spanish or otherwise.

We had been transported to some place in the desert. There was no sign of human habitation as far as the eye could see in any direction, not a telephone pole, not an electric wire—nothing but barren brown earth, an assortment of scruffy cacti, and some low dusty hills to break up the monotony of the land.

"This may be an old prospector's cabin—probably some old geezer lived out here looking for gold," said Cass, gazing mournfully at the broken-down shed. Then he looked up at the morning sun with a practiced eye. "I'd say it's about eight o'clock. It's cool now, but I bet it gets hot as hell out here when the sun gets higher."

"Swell. Let's hope whoever brought us out here left a jug of water at least."

My mouth was still dry as cotton from my drug-induced sleep and water held a big interest for me. Cass and I made a careful survey around the old shed hoping to discover some miraculous cold jug of sparkling liquid. Or a well. Or a gurgling brook. But there was nothing to suggest water had ever come to this barren place in any form; the land was dry, dry, dry. I caught sight of a lanky jackrabbit gazing at me from the shade of a sagebrush. The animal had a surprised look, as though he had never seen a human before. This was not a good sign.

In our survey of the shack and its surrounding land, Cass and I made only one discovery which gave us any cause for optimism: We found a road. It wasn't much of a road; in fact, it was hardly more than two vaguely discernible ruts side-by-side through the desert, but tire tracks were clearly visible near the shed, almost certainly from the vehicle which had brought us here.

"All we have to do is follow the road back to the main highway," I said with relief.

"Yeah, as long as the highway's not a hundred miles away," said Cass. "Without water we're not going to last too long out here."

"Then we'd better get going before the sun gets hot."

Without further ado, we started off walking along the dirt road. And then we walked, and we walked . . . and walked some more. For an hour or two it was almost pleasant. The early morning sun shone on our faces with just the right amount of warmth and the fantastic, brooding shapes of the Mojave desert had a grim beauty that was interesting to behold. I tried to pretend that this was fun—a scenic hike through the glories of nature. Good exercise, too.

After an hour, the sun began to turn cruelly hot, and it was no longer possible to act as if we were Eagle Scouts on an exciting adventure. I was wearing the wrong kind of shoes for such terrain—brown leather loafers which were beginning to rub against my heels and pinch my toes. As we walked up a long, gradual hill I kept imagining that when we got to the top, we would see a paved highway somewhere beneath us—perhaps even a small town. But when we reached the crest and looked down, all we could see was more arid, uninhabited earth stretching forever. I began to lose hope. The cotton-like dryness of my mouth had become agony; the sun was scorching us—I began to fear we might not make it out of this desert alive.

Cass seemed to sense the shift in my mood, and now *he* tried to be the optimistic one. "As long as we keep following this old dirt road, we gotta come out *someplace*," he said.

"Let's hope so," I sighed. I was beginning to fear that whoever had kidnapped us might easily have driven a number of hours from the paved highway, which could prove an impossible distance to travel on foot without water. Soon we came to a new and unexpected problem—the tire tracks we had been following had long since disappeared, with the ground either too hard in some places or too soft in others to retain an impression. Somehow we managed to make a wrong turn, mistaking a dry wash for our dirt road. It was an easy mistake to make, given the vague and aimless quality of the road, which seemed to disappear at times and then start again a few hundred yards further along. Cass and I discovered our mistake only when the dry wash upon which we were walking came to an unceremonious end by a jumble of rocks. Neither one of us could tell how long we had been traveling in the wrong direction.

We debated whether we should try to retrace our steps back to the road, but without knowing how far we had traveled in the wrong direction, this was a disheartening thought. Cass pointed to a high mesa top across the desert a few miles away and suggested we climb to the top of it; surely from such a vista point we would see some sign of human activity—a highway, a town, a telephone, a gas station.

I agreed this seemed a better plan than going back, and so Cass and I took off again across the trackless desert. The sun moved directly overhead and poured down its dry heat upon our heads. The journey was turning into sheer agony—now to add to the discomfort of thirst and heat and aching feet was the demoralizing fear that we were utterly lost. Neither Cass nor I voiced the fear aloud. We pretended to each other that as soon as we got to the top of the distant mesa, we would probably see—oh, a big hotel and golf course stretched out at our feet. We even began to imagine what it would feel like to amble down into the hotel bar and order a drink. Cass said he would begin with an ice cold bottle of Mexican beer, maybe a Corona, and then move on to champagne. Personally, I visualized a Perrier in a 10-foot tall glass with lots of ice and a twist of fresh lime.

We reached the mesa top about an hour and a half later. By this time we had taken off our shirts and draped the material over our heads to protect ourselves from the burning sun. I was beginning to feel like a misplaced extra from *Lawrence of Arabia*. The view from the mesa top was discouraging; we found ourselves looking out upon a vista of great and total desolation.

There was no golf course, no hotel bar, no Mexican beer, no champagne, and no Perrier. Just flat arid desert and dusty mountains as far as the eye could see. Cass and I didn't dare look at one another.

We rested for a while on the mesa top and then set out again. I felt curiously lightheaded; I could hardly feel my feet as they moved step after step across the desert. Cass and I walked in silence for a long time. Once we looked up to the sky and saw the white vapor trail of a jet plane streaking high above us. I briefly imagined the hermetically sealed world of jet travel—perhaps the passengers were eating dinner, or watching a movie. Perhaps the stewardesses were at this very moment moving up the aisles serving cool, delicious and oh-so-liquid drinks!

"And what would you like, Mr. Allen? Coffee? Tea? A tall, cool soft drink?"

"Water!" I cried aloud to the vapor trail high in the sky. "Just a lovely glass of water!"

As I traipsed through the desert, I found myself saying the names of the possible person, or persons, who had led us here to our deaths: "Elliot, Michelle, Ken, Johnny, Bobby, Tako and Ahi." I tried saying it in a different order, hoping this might cause a sudden revelation. I even added Wade to the list, though he was dead, as well as Mike Corvino who had disappeared. "Bobby, Michelle, Wade, Mike, Ken, Johnny, Elliot, Tako and Ahi." It was a little marching tune, the naming of the names, and for some reason I always ended with Tako and Ahi. They were the comic element of this drama, two guys with names straight out of a *sushi* bar. Octopus and Tuna. And then towards the afternoon, my light-headedness seemed to reach out and pull some information out of the dark realm of my unconscious—my brain made all the right connections. I suddenly saw the inconsistency of information I had been given from two different people. One was a lie, the other the truth. I pondered this for another mile or two, trying to fathom the meaning of the lie, and then the answer hit me. I stopped in my tracks and began to chuckle. In a moment, the chuckle turned into a laugh. Cass stopped long enough to give me a worried look.

"You all right, Steve? You gotta hang in there, buddy—you can't give way to hallucinations."

"Oh, I'm *fine!*" I told him, smirking. Actually, I had just figured out who had killed Christie Hamilton and Debbie Dobson—the very how and the why of it. And I laughed because the answer was so sim-

341

ple; it had been there all along. I laughed because I had been so stupid, and now it was too late—for I had a feeling Cass and I would soon be joining Christie and Debbie.

It was sometime later that Cass stopped and pointed a shaky finger at the desert ahead. My eyes followed to where he pointed, and I was stunned to see the turquoise waters of a gorgeous swimming pool shimmering ahead in the near distance.

"My God! A swimming pool!" cried Cass, as he began to hurry forward.

"Cass, hold on. It's just a mirage. . . ."

"It's heaven!" he cried. "Don't you see . . . we're dead, Steve—but Lord, if I only knew death was like *this*, I would have slit my wrists years ago!"

There was no stopping him. I shook my head sadly as he lurched forward, running crazily across the desert toward the strange and deceptive mirage. I figured he would discover the truth for himself soon enough—meanwhile, what harm could there be in a brief final fantasy of heavenly bliss?

The lovely mirage, at least, kept Cass from looking up into the sky where our real fate awaited. I had seen them for nearly an hour now, following us patiently, circling overhead—first there was just one enormous black bird, and then another one came, and then another still.

The vultures circled overhead, waiting for their dinner.

chapter 45

At nearly eight-thirty that same night, Jayne sat by herself at a large table with nine place settings that had been specially reserved for her near the stage in the Gladiator Arena. The people nearby finishing their dinners before the show must have thought it a strange sight—a woman by herself at such a large table, particularly if they recognized her.

Jayne's table was covered with pink linen, laid with good silver, and the eight empty places had pink linen napkins standing up neatly in place, folded like little hats. Jayne sat by herself quite contentedly, finishing a plate of fresh swordfish which had been baked with only a squeeze of lemon—no butter or oil—as well as a few lightly steamed vegetables. This was decidely not the usual Las Vegas hotel cuisine, which leans towards the pseudo-French and the pretentious, and generally tries to justify its expense by packing each plate with as much cholesterol and rich sauce as possible. Jayne had managed to charm the waiters and the kitchen into cooking her a healthy meal. Nearby a *maitre d'* in his black and white attire waited to refill her wine glass; contrary to her usual custom, Jayne was celebrating tonight by accompanying her meal with a small split of very dry, very good French champagne.

Michelle appeared, coming down the aisle with Ken in tow. She was wearing a stunning crushed blue velvet cocktail dress. She kissed Jayne on both cheeks.

"I just got your message an hour ago," said Michelle. "Are we too late to eat?"

"Of course not—I have friends in the kitchen, my dear," Jayne assured her. "Why don't you sit next to me?"

Michelle gazed uncertainly at the eight empty places. "Goodness, who else is coming? What's this all about?"

"You'll see soon enough. People will be dropping by—I thought it would be fun for us all to get together and have a good chat after the show."

Michelle sat down to the left of Jayne, and Ken took a chair on Michelle's left, appearing to be exceedingly uncomfortable. He was wearing a dark suit that seemed a little too tight in the shoulders, and a half-inch too short in the legs. Most likely he didn't wear a suit very often, and the clothes looked as if they had been bought during a less muscular period of his life and then left to sit in his closet.

"I don't sit down to fancy dinners like this very often," said Ken, knocking over his water glass with one nervous sweep of his hand. "Gosh, I'm sorry, Mrs. Allen."

Two waiters and the *maitre d'* hurried forward to mop up the spilled water, just as Lieutenant W.B. Walker appeared at the table. Following close behind him—looking dapper in a maroon dinner jacket—was Johnny Nakamura.

"Evening, Ms. Allen," said W.B.

"Hello, Lieutenant . . . Oh, good evening, Mr. Nakamura. I hope you haven't already dined."

"Eating at the Las Vegas City Jail isn't exactly dining."

"Isn't this cozy?" said Lieutenant Walker, smiling to himself. The lieutenant had finally shed his usual brown attire.

W.B. was basking in Jayne's company when Elliot Block came hurrying over. He was agitated, red in the face and out of breath.

"Jayne, have you seen Steve? We're supposed to start in five minutes and he's not backstage yet. Bobby's beginning to worry!"

"Relax," said Jayne. "I'm sure Steve will show up any minute."

"He's never this late," worried Elliot, glancing at his watch.

"He's on his way," replied Jayne. There was something definite in her tone that made Elliot stare at her in a questioning way. "Sit down, Elliot," she told him gently. "We have a place set for you."

"Oh, I can't, Jayne. I gotta be backstage when the show starts."

"Mrs. Allen told you to sit down," said Lieutenant Walker. "I think you should do as she suggests, Mr. Block."

Elliot opened his mouth to object, but slipped warily into one of the empty chairs, his eyes darting about the table.

"I hope you don't mind—I've already ordered a light dinner for everyone, to save time," Jayne said. She gestured to the *maitre d'*, who came hurrying

345

over. "Mario, you can serve the swordfish now, and we'd like everyone to be served quickly before the show starts."

The food had, of course, already been prepared, and within moments a small army of waiters appeared with plates. Then the waiters and the *maitre d'* departed and the lights began to dim.

There was a drum roll. The orchestra began to play "This Could Be The Start of Something Big." A voice came over the PA system: "Ladies and gentlemen, The Coliseum Hotel is proud to present—Mr. Steve Allen!"

The light man in his booth hit the big spotlight and I stepped forth into the circle of light to a pleasant roar of applause. I felt like applauding myself, out of gratitude for the miracle of my presence.

chapter 46

"**G**ood evening, ladies and gentlemen," I said. "You know, for the last fifty years comedians have been walking out on stages, all over the world, and saying, 'A funny thing happened to me on the way to the theater tonight.' Well, to tell you the truth, nothing funny has ever happened to me on my way to the theater—until tonight."

Polite laughter from the audience, about a 25.

Perhaps I should explain that I have a personal numbering system that relates to the volume of laughter that individual jokes are likely to elicit. In an ideal situation, all the jokes in the world would score 100 on a 0-to-100 scale. But that's fantasy. To deal with reality, there's nothing wrong with doing certain lines that deserve only a 15 or a 25. Naturally you can't do a whole act on that level, but it works out fine as long as every so often there's a response in the 85 to 100 range.

"Anyway," I said, "what happened to my driver Jimmy Cassidy and me was that we were almost wiped out—and I don't mean at the crap tables. This will sound a little wild, but we were actually kidnapped. I mean, really! And we were taken out to the desert and left there—I guess to die.

"Well, like all other comedians in the business, I've died from time to time. In fact we're all used to that. So if you have to die, I would say that the best place is onstage. It's much more pleasant than dying of thirst out in the desert, I'll tell you that."

There were a few people in the audience who were laughing heartily at everything I said. Thank goodness there are always a few such cooperative souls. Almost every successful comedian has his personal pushovers, for whom he can do no wrong. But the majority of people looking up at me this night were tittering uncertainly and beginning to mutter amongst themselves. Obviously I wasn't doing conventional jokes.

"If I may," I said, "let me tell you something about the reason why, for the last thirty-five years or so, on my television shows, I've been screaming the cry of the wild bird—*Schmock! Schmock!* Imagine, a grown man, a man who writes serious books and performs with distinguished symphony orchestras, yelling *Schmock! Schmock!* like a real idiot. Well, I'll give you the background on that. The story concerns two very successful Jewish gentlemen—wealthy, sophisticated, urbane, highly intelligent. They've enjoyed all of life's pleasures to the extent that nothing much remains for them to try. Anyway, the two of them are talking about where they might go for their next vacation. And one of them says, 'You know, I think I'm going to go to Africa and organize a safari, with a couple of white hunters, about 300 native gun-bearers, a line of elephants—the whole works.'

" 'Schmuck,' his friend says. 'Of all the stupid things I've ever heard you say, that's the worst. What do you know about running a safari? If you actually ever did anything of that sort you'd be a real schmuck.'

" 'No,' his friend says, 'I'm serious about this. I'm really going to do it.'

" '*Schmuck*, will you listen to me?' his friend says. 'It'll be the biggest mistake of your life. Everyone in the world who hears about it will call you the schmuck of all time.'

"But of course the man won't listen to reason, so he goes through with his plan, goes to Africa, lays out thousands of dollars, hires some white hunters, some black gun-bearers, and, just as his friend had predicted, the experience turns out to be total disaster.

"The white hunters get drunk and wander off, the elephants stampede, the other people mutiny, and finally the poor guy is lost, alone in the jungle. He hasn't had food or water in a week and he is, in fact, breathing his last. Finally he reels around under the hot sun and falls down. And the last thing he sees, when he looks up in the sky, is a bunch of big black vultures and buzzards screaming '*Schmock! Schmock!*' "

It got at least a 97, and after the laughter and applause died down, I said, "Well, at least now you know why I've been making that funny noise for all these years. I've actually never told that story in public before because I usually work clean, but it happens to be relevant to what happened to Jimmy Cassidy and me this afternoon. At one time we both thought that the last thing we were going to see was some desert buzzards circling over our heads."

"Good God, has he flipped out?" Elliot asked my wife in a tense whisper across the dinner table. Jayne told me later that he had gone pale at the mention of the desert adventure.

"This humor must be very subtle," said Johnny Nakamura to everyone at the table. "I don't get it."

"What happened to Steve?" Michelle whispered to Jayne.

"Just wait, my dear; you'll see," said Jayne once again with a Mona Lisa smile.

"But look, Jayne—there are policemen standing at all the exits," said Michelle, with alarm.

"It's part of Steve's big surprise. Relax. I'm sure *you* can't have any reason to be worried."

But Michelle looked worried, anyway, and so did everyone else at the table, with the exception of Lieutenant Walker.

Since on this particular night there wasn't the tremendous emotional pressure that had prevailed at the time of the opening show, I finally felt that it would be suitable to do at least a quick, modified version of my questions-from-the-audience routine. The cards had already been collected and brought to me backstage, so I got right to work on them now.

"You know," I said, "during the last few days I've had the opportunity to meet some of you folks personally and as individuals you would appear to be the salt of the earth. But, to the extent that I can judge you on the basis of these questions you've sent up, you would seem, as a group, to be a little on the flaky side. In any event, I'll try to answer some of your questions now. The first one is from an Irene Stelmazek of Chicago, and she writes, 'What sign were you born under?' I'm not exactly sure, Irene, I think it was 'Furnished Rooms For Rent.' Am I correct in assuming, given your questions, that you believe in astrology?"

"Yes," a voice called from the far left side of the room.

"Well, I won't debate the issue with you," I said, "but if there is anything to astrology, Jayne and I are probably a well-matched pair, because she's a Virgo and I'm a Weird-o."

It got about a 57.

"The next question is just signed Barbara and Jim. I'm glad they're back together again. And in what I guess is Jim's handwriting, they ask, 'How do you and Jayne get it on?' "

With a question like that, of course, you pretend to be shocked and do a long, frowning take to the audience, waiting to speak until the laughter has subsided. I chose to take the dumbbell, or literal approach to the question. "Well," I said, "I pull it over my head, and Jayne steps into it."

It not only got about a 75 but a rimshot from the drummer.

The next question was one of those lucky ones that can't miss, because of the subject matter. Some-one named Josephine DeMarco, of Teaneck, New Jersey, wrote, 'I watched your TV show all during my last pregnancy and when the baby was born, he looked just like you.' A question that funny, needless to say, gets its own laugh. But since I was under the obligation to top it, I said, "You're lucky you weren't watching reruns of Lassie."

Anyway, I spent the next happy few minutes continuing with questions. Because the routine ran a little longer than I had planned, I cut one musical number, but since the audience hadn't expected two, there was no way they could be disappointed.

And then it was time to introduce Bobby Hamilton, to whom, as always, I gave a big build-up.

He entered to the usual thunderous applause. As we stood on stage together amongst all the cheering and shouting, Bobby leaned close to me and said into my ear: "What's going on, Steve? There are all kinds of cops backstage."

"I'll tell you later, Bob. We've made some important progress in the case."

Bobby flashed me a questioning look, but the applause was dying down and the audience was waiting for a song. I departed to the wings. My legs felt like Jell-O and I was exhausted; I had a production assistant bring me a chair so I could watch Bobby comfortably from the wings, and I also asked for a glass of water. When the water came, I drank it slowly, lovingly, letting it linger on my tongue like a fine wine. I couldn't imagine taking a simple glass of water for granted ever again.

Bobby was wonderful, as always, though frankly I was beginning to tire of his tragedy *schtick*. I know Bobby had been through a lot, but the sad, brave dignity with which he faced the audience was beginning to seem contrived. Naturally a performer will use whatever works, but Hamilton, through his tragedy, had turned himself into a kind of Edith Piaf of American song, his music a triumph through tears. When I first heard Bobby sing after Christie and Wade's death, I had been tremendously moved. But now watching him do the same routine night after night, I had to wonder how real it was. The audience, of course, didn't share my reservations—they screamed, clapped, stamped their feet and wept.

Bobby called me back on stage—we did our soft-shoe routine and our two numbers for voice and piano, and somewhere in the middle of a chorus, I realized I was going to miss all this when it was over. Performing with a singer as gifted as Bobby Hamilton was certainly a rare pleasure.

We did four encores. This too also had become part of the show, and now the audience expected it. But finally the evening ended. The curtain came down, and I met Bobby in the wings. He was wiping perspiration from his brow and trying to fend off one of the young chorus girls who seemed to want to throw herself at his feet.

"Hey, have you seen Elliot, Steve? The guy's been acting strange lately—now he's totally disappeared."

"Elliot's sitting with Jayne at a table outside," I said gently.

"What's he doing there? You know, something very peculiar seems to be happening—I wish somebody would tell me what the hell it is."

"I will, Bobby. Let's just wait a few moments for the theater to empty out, and then we'll join Jayne and her guests outside. What I have to say I think will best be said to all."

Bobby smiled slowly. "Oh-oh! Why do I have the feeling that Detective Allen is about to let the last slipper drop?"

chapter 47

The vast dinner theater was empty except for a few waiters and busboys cleaning up, a policeman at every exit, and a table of nine near the stage at which could be found: Jayne, Michelle, Ken, Elliot, Johnny, Bobby, Lieutenant Walker, Cass, who had also joined us at this final moment, and myself.

I stood up from my chair.

"Thank you for coming," I said. "I know this has been a difficult and confusing time for you all, and I thought everyone would like to be informed of the results of our investigation. The killer tried to make this case seem as confusing as possible in order to obscure the central facts, but we now know this person's identity, as well as how and why Christie Hamilton and Debbie Dobson were killed."

There was a stir among our guests. "You're saying it's someone at this table?" asked Elliot, peering about unhappily.

"No, I didn't say that," I replied cautiously. "It may *not* be someone at this table at all."

"Excuse me for interrupting, Steve," said Bobby hesitantly, "But I thought the guilt in this case had already been established. I mean there was . . . an arrest."

Bobby had named no one, but everyone at the table turned to look at Johnny Nakamura, who scowled back defiantly.

"Yes, let's start with Johnny," I suggested. "He certainly seems the most logical suspect—a gangster. A blackmailer. A pimp—living dishonestly off other people's labors."

"Now wait a minute!" objected Johnny, beginning to rise—but then he glanced over at Lieutenant Walker, sighed, and sank back into his place.

"Johnny is the sort of person who can make you believe the human race is moving back to the jungle—except even in the jungle, they don't have creatures as predatory as gangsters. I don't doubt that this man has committed murder in the past, but—did he commit these particular murders?"

"I'm innocent!" muttered Nakamura. "I was framed. And I don't know why everyone's picking on me!"

I ignored him, as did everyone else at the table. "Now we know Mr. Nakamura was having an affair with Christie Hamilton and that he was using this—along with Christie's drug problem—to try to blackmail Bobby into signing an agreement to appear at the hotel he was planning to buy. Bobby's guaranteed annual appearance, it seems, would have secured the financing for the deal, and so this matter was of prime importance to Johnny's dream of becoming a major player in Las Vegas. But, as sordid as this may be, we have to ask if there was any

355

reason for Johnny to murder Christie? And the answer, of course—is yes."

"That's a lie!"

"We'll see," I said. "You see, Christie may have been unfaithful to her husband, but she was not at all happy to find herself used as a pawn in a blackmail scheme to coerce Bobby into appearing at Johnny's hotel. So she took counter-measures of her own. She told Johnny that unless he quit his demands, she would give evidence to the Gaming Commission that he was skimming profits from his slot machine operation at the Lucky Horseshoe to avoid income tax. This, of course, is a serious allegation and might have resulted in Johnny losing his license to operate *any* hotel or casino in the state of Nevada altogether. I think we can safely assume that for a man of his character, this would be more than enough motivation for murder. If he killed Christie, the threat would be ended.

"Now ironically, Christie's murder resulted at first in Bobby's arrest, which was very much *not* in Johnny's interest. If Bobby had been convicted of this crime, he would not have been able to appear at Johnny's new hotel, *ergo* the financing would fall through, and Johnny's grand scheme to have a place on The Strip would not succeed. It is for this reason, if no other, that Mr. Nakamura claims he's innocent. He says he would never have killed Christie Hamilton—and for a while I was inclined to believe him. But clearly Johnny stood to lose a lot more than a new hotel if Christie were allowed to make her case to the Gaming Commission. He would have lost everything. And if this weren't enough to make us suspect Johnny of murder, we also have our really strong card—Wade Hamilton's final confession.

"We'll deal with Wade's part in all this in a moment. Right now I want to point out that his final confession made a *very* convincing case against Johnny Nakamura, and it was upon this confession, of course, that Bobby was released from jail and a warrant was issued for Johnny's arrest. According to Wade, we must remember, Johnny was the mastermind of the whole thing, and Wade was an accomplice. It's important to note that Wade was supposed to make it seem as though his sister Michelle had done the crime, but Wade rather cleverly exacted his revenge against everyone. He framed his own father instead of Michelle, by hiring Mike Corvino, Bobby's old movie double, to appear on the scene just long enough to claim he impersonated Bobby at a very crucial moment. Mike conveniently disappeared after making this wild claim, so it was impossible to cross-examine him, and of course, Wade finally confessed that Mike was in *his* employ. Wade's idea was not only to frame his father, but in so doing make it impossible for Johnny to get the financing for his new hotel—a double stroke."

"You know, this is *awfully* complicated," said Ken, shaking his head.

"As I said, it was supposed to *seem* complicated in order to obscure the very simplicity of the act. So let's get down to some simple motives for murder, shall we? Motives that might implicate some other potential suspects in this case—like you and Michelle, for instance."

"Me and Michelle?" cried Ken. "Why, that's outrageous!"

"Is it? You and Michelle had plenty of opportunity to commit the crime—in fact, we only have your word for it that you conveniently left the VIP Spa together, at the crucial moment, for a romantic tryst upstairs in Michelle's room. As for motive—well, Michelle is set to inherit millions of dollars from her mother's estate. Unfortunately, although Michelle comes from a wealthy family, she has no real money of her own—and, of course, you have no money either, Ken. With Michelle's inheritance, on the other hand, you two would be able to go happily-ever-aftering in the Greek Isles, or wherever else you chose."

"But Steve, this is absurd!" said Michelle. "Ken and I just met that very morning. I mean, it *was* love at first sight, but honestly—there wasn't enough time to plan a murder together."

I gazed at her sternly. "Michelle, my dear, you're lying. As it happens, you did *not* meet Ken for the first time that morning, but nearly nine months ago. Isn't that right? You've been keeping him a secret because you're involved in divorce proceedings against your most recent husband, the rock music fellow, and you don't want Ken's presence in the formula to spoil your chances for a big alimony check."

Michelle lowered her eyes to her plate.

"Michelle, is this true?" Jayne asked, frowning at me.

Michelle nodded. "It is, I'm afraid. I met Ken last winter when I came to Vegas with my husband. I was quite ashamed of myself, really—I thought it would be best to pretend Ken and I just met. But it wasn't so I'd get a bigger alimony check."

"Then what was it?" Jayne asked.

Michelle turned her big blue eyes toward her father. "It was for Dad. I've messed up so many things in my life, I didn't want him to know I messed

358

up one more marriage by having some dumb affair with a spa attendant."

"Honey, I would have understood," said Bobby. "You know nothing can shock me."

"Maybe that's the problem," said Michelle with a sigh.

"Anyway, that's Michelle and Ken's possible motive for murder—the fact that they've been lying certainly is a mark against them," I went on. "They had opportunity, motive, and even a secret they wanted to protect. But now let's pass on to the star of the show—the talented and amiable Bobby Hamilton, who by his own admission is shocked by nothing, and also may have had reason to murder his wife."

Elliot stood up from the table. "I resent this, Steve! My client was charged with this murder once already, and he was completely exonerated. I demand an apology!"

"Oh, shut up, Elliot," said Bobby wearily. "Steve's right—I probably had the best reason to kill Christie of anyone here. Jealousy. Believe me, no one likes to be cheated on. It doesn't matter if you're a superstar or a clerk in a 7-11."

"That's right, but you had another possible motive too, Bobby," I said. "Money."

Bobby shrugged and smiled. "I'd stick with the jealousy angle, man. Money's never been such a big thing with me."

"No? But we're talking *lots* of money, Bob—possibly half of everything you own. For as it happens, you and Christie got married in California, a state with progressive community property laws, and you never made Christie sign a prenuptial agreement limiting what she might receive in case of divorce. And now the worst was about to happen—Christie was threatening to divorce you. Your pride was hurt, you were jealous, and you were about to be taken to the cleaners as well."

Bobby responded to what I was saying only with a sad sigh and a shake of his head.

"So you had your motive, Bobby, and we mustn't forget that. But now let's pass on to a *very* good suspect indeed—Elliot Block."

Elliot snickered a little and poured himself another glass of chardonnay from an ice bucket near his chair, probably to show how little concern he felt for anything I might say.

"Like Michelle and Ken, Elliot admits to being at the place of the crime only moments before the murders occurred—he claims he suddenly remembered a rather convenient call that was coming in from Tokyo, and so he left the VIP spa to go to his room. Well, as it happens, the hotel switchboard has a record of this call just at the time Elliot claims he made it—however, can we be absolutely certain it was *Elliot* who was upstairs in his room on the telephone? Perhaps Elliot had an accomplice make the call for him. Perhaps the accomplice even pretended to *be* Elliot for the benefit of the voice overseas."

"This is too goddamn much! So who was my accomplice?"

"The missing Mike Corvino perhaps. Who knows? With Mike's disappearance, we might imagine anything is possible—maybe Mike worked for *you!* Any way you look at it, you certainly had the opportunity to murder Christie and Debbie—so we must ask ourselves if you had the motive as well."

"Well, did I?" asked Elliot.

"Possibly," I said. "After all, you're an agent

with *one* client, Elliot—your entire economic well-being rests with Bobby Hamilton, and perhaps you felt Christie was going to prove a detriment to Bobby's career. There are all kinds of ugly possibilities. Maybe you were cheating Bobby out of some of his money, playing with the books? Maybe Christie found out about that, and you had to get rid of her."

"Nonsense!" cried Elliot, who was getting very red in the face.

"Is it? Well, I wonder. . . . I wonder particularly why a Hollywood agent should carry a gun, and why you had Johnny's blackmail photographs hidden beneath your desk, and Debbie Dobson's phone number in your bedside table?"

"Bobby gave me the photos—he thought I should know what was going on, and I hid them so no one would stumble across them."

"And the gun?"

"I carry it to protect Bobby," snarled Elliot. "After what happened to John Lennon and that poor actress, any major celebrity's a damn fool if he doesn't take proper precautions."

"And what about Debbie's phone number in your bedside table?"

"That's . . . that's none of your business!" cried Elliot, who had lost his cool. "Anyway, what right did you have to break into my room, you bastard? You stand up there with your high and mighty tone accusing us all, and you're nothing but a common hotel thief! Maybe *you* killed Christie and Debbie!"

"Elliot," I said gently, "I was right here in the Gladiator Arena at the time of the murder, surrounded by about twenty-five chorus girls, a full orchestra and God knows how many crew."

"Maybe you bribed all of them to lie for you!" Elliot shouted in desperation.

I smiled. "Relax, Elliot. Actually, I'm sorry about the way I busted into your room—I may have gone a little overboard in my zeal to get to the bottom of all this. But now we have to move on to a very tragic character—Wade Hamilton."

Elliot opened his mouth to object, but closed it again, apparently curious to hear what I would have to say about Bobby's unfortunate son. I had begun this discussion by admitting the murderer might not necessarily be someone present at our table, and now I felt all eyes upon me.

"As we all know, Wade was a young man with serious psychological problems. He hated his stepmother, Christie. He longed for his father's love and respect. For kicks, he beat up prostitutes."

"Steve, can't we skip this?" asked Bobby with a painful expression. "Whatever Wade was, whatever he did—hell, he's paid for it now."

"I'm sorry, but we can't skip this—not quite yet. Unfortunately, Wade's part in this tragedy is central to the whole business. It's very interesting, I think, that Wade told us three completely different versions of the truth. This is a little like the old Japanese tale of *Rashomon*, except that all the stories came from the same man, and we might wonder exactly where reality lies. Let's think about this for a moment.

"At first, Wade agreed that he and his father had been kidnapped, at the exact time of the murder, by two men named Tako and Ahi, who supposedly had been sent by Johnny Nakamura. According to that version, Wade and Bobby were taken to a house in North Las Vegas where they were tied up. Eventually they got free, phoned me in the middle of the night, and I drove out to pick them up.

"So that's version number one. A day later, Wade informs Lieutenant Walker that that version was untrue, a lie he'd told to protect his father. In version number two, Wade claimed that the kidnapping was faked to give his father an alibi—he says his father's movie double, Mike Corvino, was the person who walked out in front of the hotel and carefully asked the doorman for the exact time before driving away in a white Lincoln Continental limousine—and that Bobby meanwhile was upstairs murdering his wife.

"This was a very damning version of the truth. But now—look at this—we have version number three, which Wade told me just before he jumped to his death. In that version, Wade claims that Johnny Nakamura was the mastermind of the whole fiendish business, and that Wade framed his father, with Mike Corvino's help, in order to avenge himself for all the years of neglect. We all were inclined to believe version number three because it was told to me in confidence, and *in extremis*—at a time Wade first planned to murder *me* by tossing me off the terrace, and then later, when he discovered I was wired with a microphone and transmitter, he jumped off the terrace himself.

"We believed version three for a simple reason. After all, we said to ourselves: *What could Wade have possibly hoped to gain at such a moment by not telling the truth?* This is the crux of the whole business, I'm afraid, and unfortunately we all came to the wrong conclusion. As it turns out, Wade had a lot to gain with his final lie—and he very nearly succeeded in his plan to mislead us all."

"Wait a minute!" objected Bobby. "This really is too painful. I know what you're about to say—that Wade did the whole damn thing himself, without Johnny or anybody else telling him what to do. You're trying to tell me that Wade's the murderer—but it doesn't matter anymore. My son paid his dues, and we should leave this whole hellish thing alone."

I turned to face my old friend Bobby Hamilton. I was not happy. "Yes, I'm sure you'd like me to leave it alone, Bobby. But your poor confused son didn't kill anyone. You did. *You're* the murderer, my terrible old friend. And you deserve to rot in hell for it."

chapter 48

Bobby didn't deny my accusation—he didn't say a word, in fact, but continued to stare at me with a small, ironic smile that told me I was right. In his own way, I suppose the man had class. He would not now stoop to lie to me; the look in his eyes seemed to accept with a certain equanimity that he had played hardball and lost, but the smile said: "Prove it."

I was ready to do just that.

"Bobby, don't even bother to answer this lunatic!" Elliot said angrily to his client. "I want you to know, *Mister* Allen, that I object to this entire line of questioning—and furthermore, we're going to sue you for slander and defamation of character—and one more thing, if you ever think you're going to work in *this* town again, boy are *you* mistaken!"

"Shut up, Elliot," said Bobby quietly.

"But, Bobby, this mentally deranged—"

"Elliot, you're fired."

"I'm—"

"Fired," said Bobby, as the agent paled and

sank back in his chair. "Now Steve, I think the rest of us are hoping to hear how you came to this brilliant deduction that I am the murderer."

I shrugged. "Bobby, you were the most logical suspect from the start. You planned on that, of course—after all, your wife was having an affair, she was about to divorce you and take half your money, and if she died from unnatural causes you could be certain the cops were going to come right to your doorstep. So your dilemma was how to murder your wife and get away with it. And you came up with a very clever idea."

"What was that, Steve?"

"Me," I said. "I was your clever idea. You knew of my past modest success at playing detective, and that's the reason you contacted my agent and invited me to join your Las Vegas show."

"But that doesn't make sense, Steve—if I was about to murder my wife, the last thing I'd want is a clever detective around."

I shook my head. "No, you see you knew you'd be arrested—in fact, you were counting on it. You had given yourself a very clumsy alibi for the time of the murder, one that was designed to fall apart. But I was your friend so you knew I'd try my damndest to save you—you were counting on me to prove your innocence."

"That sounds like pretty dangerous planning," said Bobby. "What if you weren't in the mood to play detective?"

"Oh, you knew I'd try to help you. Hell, you've always been my favorite singer. And just in case my interest flagged, you hired an old Japanese woman to pretend she was Johnny Nakamura's grandmother and strong-arm me a little—that was a nice theatrical touch. You had her drive me around the block a few times, put the pressure on and then leave a dead fish in Cass's car so we'd both be terrified. You also damn well knew a stunt like that would backfire and keep me on the case until I got to the bottom of the whole deal. What you didn't count on, unfortunately, was that I wouldn't settle for Johnny Nakamura as the fall guy, but I'd keep going with the investigation until I arrived all the way back to you."

Bobby continued to gaze at me good-naturedly. "Clever," he said—but I wasn't certain if he was referring to himself or to me.

"Oh, it *was* clever of you, Bob. You let yourself be arrested, but you left an important piece of evidence for me to find that you knew would clear you. Once you were arrested and cleared, you thought you'd never be accused again."

Bobby smiled serenely. "And what was this important piece of evidence?" he asked, like a teacher prompting a dull student in class.

"It wasn't a thing—it was a person. It was Wade, Bobby. You sacrificed your own son to get away with murder."

Bobby had the decency to briefly lower his eyes.

I continued: "You see, Wade was not the vengeful son that he pretended to be. Quite the opposite— he loved you without any reservations. He worshiped you and spent his entire life wanting only to be loved by you in return. His loyalty was pathetic, Bobby—And you just used him, like you've used everyone else."

I thought I detected some flicker of emotion in the man for the first time. "Do you really think I'd ask Wade to kill himself for me?"

"No, that was Wade's idea—a real surprise for you, I suppose," I said with a sigh. "Your son's suicide was an embellishment on the theme that you had worked out together. I'll never forget how shocked you were when I told you of his death at the police station—for a moment there, you were almost human, Bobby. He finally impressed you—he finally got to your emotions. Maybe that's what Wade intended all along."

"Wait a minute! I don't understand any of this!" cried Michelle. "What did Wade actually do?"

"He did everything, Michelle. You see how cunning this was—Wade's three different versions of the truth were carefully choreographed to help Bobby get away with murder. In the first version, you'll remember, Wade reluctantly went along with the kidnapping story, but was careful to give Lieutenant Walker and me the impression that he was lying. Then we have version two in which Wade pretends he can't keep quiet another moment longer and must confess the terrible truth about how his father killed his stepmother—ironically, this version *was* the truth. And now comes the fancy twist to this case. Some weeks ago, Wade deliberately roughed up one of Johnny Nakamura's girls and let Johnny get a hold over him, knowing we'd discover that connection sooner or later. This was all concocted so we'd believe version three, the fake confession in which we think that Bobby is innocent—that Johnny is the real killer, and Wade was forced to be a more-or-less unwilling accomplice. My guess is that this was the extent of what Wade was supposed to do. The fake confession would set his father free, Johnny would go to prison for the crime, and a well-paid lawyer would get Wade off with some court-ordered psychotherapy, and perhaps—at worst—a brief prison sentence."

"Wade was willing to go to prison—for Dad?" Michelle asked in disbelief.

"The boy was very loyal in his own way, Michelle. Remember how he jumped in the water to save you that afternoon on Lake Mead? Your half-brother was a tormented and misguided human being, but he had plenty of guts. Wade figured his suicide would be the clincher—it would give a lot more credibility to version three of the kidnapping story, the one we were all supposed to believe. And so—in his confusion—he jumped to his death to get Bobby off the hook. I'll never forget his last words: 'Tell my father to think about me sometimes.' Maybe he thought you'd love him then, Bobby, but of course he was wrong. You've never loved anyone but yourself."

Everyone at the table was very quiet. Bobby sat looking off across the empty stage, deep in his own thoughts: I wasn't certain he was altogether listening to me.

"I just can't believe it!" said Michelle. "Dad, tell Steve this isn't true."

Bobby slowly turned his eyes toward his daughter, as if seeing her for the first time, and then he turned to me. "This is all a very interesting theory, Steve, but I don't think you're able to prove any of it."

"You're wrong, Bob. I'll admit some of what I'm saying is guesswork, but I can prove the main elements."

"Be my guest," Bobby said.

"You know what tipped me off? You made a careless mistake with something you said about

369

Tako and Ahi, the two supposed kidnappers. When I came to see you in jail, you claimed you had met Tako and Ahi only once before the day of the murder—you said they accompanied Johnny when he came to your suite to show you the videotapes he had made of Christie."

"So?"

"So the next day I had a little midnight chat with Johnny at Hoover Dam, and Johnny said he had never heard of Tako and Ahi. One of you had to be lying."

"And you believed Johnny? Steverino, I'm insulted—I've known you nearly thirty years and you take the word of a cheap gangster over mine!"

"Johnny's story made more sense than yours. Frankly, he was able to convince me that if he had chosen to kill Christie, he would have made it look like an accidental death. Once I believed him on that, I couldn't imagine why he should be lying about Tako and Ahi. Of course, I wasn't completely sure about this until the police located Tako and Ahi in Los Angeles—imagine my dismay when I discovered they weren't hoodlums at all, but out-of-work actors!"

"How did you find them?" asked Bobby—and I thought I noticed a worried look on his face for the first time.

"Oh, *I* didn't. It was W.B."

"Quite simple, really," said Walker modestly. "As it happens, Johnny's been bending over backwards to be helpful—trying to help himself, of course, to a lighter prison sentence. There's a small, tight-knit Japanese community in Vegas, and some of Johnny's people were able to locate the motel on The Strip where Tako and Ahi had stayed. From there it was simple. Tako—whose real name is Teddy Yashimoto, by the way—was dumb enough to give his true address in L.A. on his registration card."

"Actually, even without those two clowns, we would have had you," I added. "You see, W.B. finally figured out who Debbie Dobson's secret boyfriend was—it was you, Bobby. W.B. is a very persistent guy—he didn't like the fact that the piece of paper I found with Debbie's phone number in Elliot's room was *not* written in Elliot's handwriting. He became curious to see if he could match the handwriting to that of anyone else involved in this case, and he found it belonged to you. Maybe you wrote down the number for Elliot so he'd be able to find you."

"It was so I could cancel a date they had one night when Bobby couldn't get free," said Elliot sullenly, not so loyal to his sole client now that he'd been fired.

"Well, there you have it," I said. "The sad and sordid truth."

Bobby smiled vaguely. "You've been busy, man."

"Lieutenant Walker's the one who was busy, Bobby. I was tied up, you may remember. You managed to hire a girl at the Desert Inn to lure Cass and me out to a house you had rented on the edge of town—and you knocked us out with ether and had us dropped off into the middle of the desert to die. You were unhappy I was still investigating the case, and you were afraid if I kept digging I might stumble on the truth. The Spanish-style mansion, by the way, had been rented for you by Elliot—it was where you got together with Debbie. After all, you wanted to impress the girl, since she was vital for your plans. She helped set up the murder in the sauna, tipping you off when Christie was there and the time was right—the poor girl thought you'd marry her afterwards, but you got rid of her."

Bobby shook his head. "I don't know. This is pretty farfetched, man. You're saying I ambushed you and Cass out in that house last night, and then I drove you off into the desert? What would you say if I told you I spent last night with a very pretty young dancer from our chorus line whom I'm certain will be more than happy to vouch for my whereabouts?"

"I didn't say you were at that house *personally* last night, Bobby—it was your accomplice, of course, your very good buddy who's been working for you all along—your movie double, Mike Corvino."

Bobby laughed. "That's really good! But if Mike was here now, I'm sure he'd give me a clean bill of health all the way around. You see, Mike would do anything for me, Steve. I learned a long time ago that it pays to have friends."

"I'll bet you did, Bob. It's a pity you never learned to be a good friend in return. Oh, you gave everyone lots of money and gifts but that was pretty easy for you. You never gave of yourself."

"Hey, I'm a star," said Bobby with a mock-comic shrug.

"Sure you are," I agreed. "Unfortunately for you, Mike turned out to be not so loyal as Wade. In fact, Corvino's been talking like crazy ever since the police picked him up at the San Francisco airport about to fly to Tahiti with the two hundred grand you gave him to get lost. Mike's admitted everything—how he switched places with you on the day

372

of the murder and took your spot in the limousine and how he hauled Cass and me out to the desert last night on his way to Reno. You told Mike to shoot us and bury us somewhere in the middle of nowhere, but he couldn't quite force himself to do that. Anyway, he figured leaving us tied up in an old prospector's shack, with no water, fifty miles from the main road would achieve the same results."

Bobby looked wan and drawn. He smiled thinly; the smile of a chess player who knows he is losing but isn't quite ready to admit defeat. "Bull," he said finally. "I think you're bluffing, Pops. I don't think you've found Mike at all."

I glanced at W.B., who took out a small walkie-talkie from his coat pocket, giving an order into the mouthpiece. A moment later, a spotlight lit up the stage, and Mike Corvino was led into the beam by two uniformed policemen. It was amazing what a close physical resemblance he bore to Bobby Hamilton—only his face was more coarse somehow, less appealing. I had a crazy feeling I was seeing a distorted mirror image, a dark alter ego—maybe what the real Bobby looked like divested of money, talent, his famous smile and charm.

Mike peered out unhappily at the man he had imitated for so many years. He shrugged apologetically.

"Sorry, Bobby," said the double. "I sure as hell wish I'd made it to Tahiti."

chapter 49

Michelle, Lieutenant Walker, Jayne and I sat in our penthouse living room looking out over the bright and deceptive lights of Las Vegas at night. I told the operator downstairs to hold all calls—for the time being our living room felt like a small island of calm in the center of the media blitz that was gathering around us in the wake of Bobby Hamilton's second arrest for murder.

Michelle still had a lot of questions. Some were quite specific, concerning various facets of the case: She wanted to know, for instance, if her father had ordered Mike to fiddle with the brakes of Bertha the Bug, or whether those brakes had failed on their own. I told her we were still uncertain about this, but a police mechanic's initial inspection of the wreckage seemed to indicate that Bertha was simply the victim of old age, and that her brakes had gone out without any outside help. Strange accidents like this sometimes supplant the best laid plans; Mike was nearly saved from the need to murder us.

Michelle was also curious as to how the police

had managed to find Mike Corvino at the San Francisco airport, and W.B. explained how the powder blue Rolls convertible had been found up north in the parking lot of the Reno airport, where Mike had driven after dumping us off in the desert. By checking with the airport reservation counters, the police were quickly able to track him to San Francisco and learn of his travel plans to Tahiti.

Eventually Michelle arrived at some questions that were not so easy to answer. She wanted to know how a man we all regarded so highly—her father, one of the most talented singers in the history of American song—could turn out to be a cold-blooded killer.

"Michelle," I said. "This one is difficult, but I'll give it a shot. First of all, life isn't very much like the movies."

"What do you mean?"

"I mean that in pictures, evil people look evil. Nice people look nice. Unfortunately, in real life it often doesn't work out that way. Once, on a tour of California prisons, I sat in on a group-therapy session with five men who looked like perfectly respectable citizens. They could have been high school teachers, football coaches, bank executives. Everyone of them was a sexual psychopath. And I've known more than a few rough-looking customers who were really the salt of the earth. Now, as regards your father—what he had was a million dollars worth of charm. That famous smile of his—that warm, friendly look in his eyes. Even if he didn't have that great voice, he could have sold used cars to anybody in town. What I think is important for you to realize is that, despite your problems—and you've been frank enough about them—you're really a better human being than your father is. At least you know right from wrong. He never did. There were occasional tipoffs to his problems. He had a violent temper, but most of the time he kept it under wraps. And even when there were rumors about rough stuff—hell, he had enough charm to make people forget about it. He knew how to use that charm, too, because he's a glutton for affection. If he didn't get it right away, he'd try to buy it. You know how famous he is for his gifts—cash, jewelry, cars, whatever it took to buy respect. In that regard he was like the Mafia guys."

"It's all so sad," Michelle said, shaking her head and looking at the floor.

"It sure is," I agreed. "Did you ever see the movie or play *Amadeus?*"

"No. Why?"

"Well," I said, "It's about this guy who's quite a decent human being. He's a composer, too. Unfortunately his music is third-rate. His chief rival is a schmuck kid who is not a good person at all, but he happens to be named Mozart, and he's one of the greatest composers of all time. A true genius. The point is that talent and virtue have no necessary connection at all. There are people in our business who are both talented and decent. Unfortunately there's also a pretty long list of people who are brilliantly talented but otherwise scum of the earth."

"I guess you're right," she said, "but it's funny how people love my Dad. I did, too."

"Of course you did," Jayne said, taking Michelle's hand. "Your father is lovable. Unfortunately, for people like him, that love—from friends, from the public—becomes like an addictive drug. They can never get enough of it. They can't get enough money, they can't get enough fame, enough sex."

"That used to drive me crazy when I was a kid," Michelle said. "Women hanging around, flirting with him. I always knew he was cheating on my mother."

"Then," Jayne said, "you won't be shocked when I tell you that he once propositioned me."

"Really?"

"Yes. It happened years ago—before you were born, in fact. Steve and I went through a very difficult period, and your father heard about it. One night at a party at Irving Lazar's house he came over to me, held my hand as if he were just being friendly and helpful, and said that if I ever got especially lonely, he'd be glad to spend some time with me. It was very clear that he wasn't talking just about friendship."

"Michelle," I said. "This must be very painful for you. But no matter what your father's done, you don't have to stop loving him. Or loving yourself."

Michelle was very still. "You know, I've lost my half-brother and my mother, but somehow losing Dad almost hurts the worst. I don't know what the hell I'm going to do—I've told Ken I need to be alone for a few weeks to think about things. Maybe there've been too many men in my life, from Dad on down. And by the way, I feel *awfully* embarrassed about lying to everyone about meeting Ken last winter—I know I must seem like a flake, but I just didn't want my Dad to know about it. Funny, isn't it? I cared so much what Dad thought, but he didn't care at all about me—who I was, or what *I* might be needing."

"Well, Michelle, there are some of us who are blessed with great parents, and some who almost have to pretend we're orphans—we have to create ourselves from scratch. It's hard, but maybe the orphans of this world have something going for them—at least they can be almost anything they choose."

Michelle slowly nodded. "Thank you. I'm going to remember that, Steve. But I'm glad I'm not a complete orphan—I'll always have the memory of my mother. And you know what I'm going to do? I'm going to start that center for homeless children in East Los Angeles—I'm going to make my mother's dream come true."

"Good idea," said W.B. "And I'd like to be the first to give you a small donation of one hundred dollars. Mr. Allen, I trust you have your wallet handy."

With only a very small sigh, I reached into my wallet and pulled out five twenty dollar bills and gave them to Michelle. At least I had the satisfaction of knowing my gambling debt was going to a very good cause.

"Steve, what's this all about?" asked Jayne.

"The other day I bet W.B. a hundred bucks that Elliot was the murderer."

"But you don't believe in betting," said my wife.

"You bet I don't," I told her. "Gambling's a terrible thing—particularly when you lose."

Speaking of people who have lost at gambling, Cass joined us from downstairs and there was a happy grin on his face.

"Well, how is she?" I asked

"Perfect!" said Cass. "She doesn't even smell of tuna anymore!"

We were talking about Cass's burgundy-colored Cadillac limo. I had given him a check to take to the used car lot where he'd sold the car to raise money for his gambling spree. Fortunately, the dealer had not passed the limo on to anyone else, and we had been able to buy it back—for fifteen hundred dollars more than Cass had received for it, but it seemed worth it under the circumstances. I trusted I would never have to squeeze myself into an ancient VW again.

"Well, I guess we've wrapped this up," I said to my wife and friends. "I don't know about the rest of you, but I'm ready for bed—I could sleep for about a month!"

"Not so fast," said Jayne.

"I beg your pardon?"

"There's still one thing you haven't explained yet, dear," said Jayne, giving me a particularly thoughtful look. "In fact, it seems to me, you've been avoiding it."

"And what is that, dear?"

"How did you and Cass ever get yourselves out of the Mojave desert, where you were about to die of thirst?"

"Didn't I tell you about that?"

"No. The last thing you told me, you and Cass had vultures circling overhead, and you had just seen a mirage—a swimming pool, I think you said. You promised to tell me the rest of the story when you had more time."

"Well," I began, with some misgivings, "nine times out of ten, a mirage turns out to be imaginary—but this time it didn't. It turned out to be, well—real. And there was this pool, with pretty girls in—"

"Are you honestly trying to tell me you stumbled across a swimming pool and a bevy of beautiful girls miles from nowhere in the desert?"

"Exactly. It was kind of a dude ranch. Isn't that right, Cass?"

"Absolutely," said Cass. "Sort of a combination dude ranch-fat farm for pretty young girls. But I swear to you, Jayne—it *wasn't* a bordello."

"A bordello!"

"It's a place called Stallion's Corral," I admitted. "You see, in Nevada these places are legal, but they tend to be out of sight—way off in the desert. Cass and I were lucky to stumble onto it."

"I should say so," said Jayne. "And how long did you two stallions linger, may I ask?"

"Oh, only long enough to make a few phone calls," I assured her.

"And take a quick dip, of course," added Cass. "In the pool, that is."

The girls had feted us with Perrier and champagne, let us use their telephone, and finally two of them had driven us eighty miles to the police station in Las Vegas. And that's how Cass and I managed to be saved by representatives of the world's oldest profession.

Prepare Yourself for

PATRICIA WALLACE

LULLABYE   (2917, $3.95/$4.95)
Eight-year-old Bronwyn knew she wasn't like other girls. She didn't
have a mother. At least, not a real one. Her mother had been in a
coma at the hospital for as long as Bronwyn could remember. She
couldn't feel any pain, her father said. But when Bronwyn sat with
her mother, she knew her mother was angry—angry at the nurses and
doctors, and her own helplessness. Soon, she would show them all the
true meaning of suffering . . .

MONDAY'S CHILD   (2760, $3.95/$4.95)
Jill Baker was such a pretty little girl, with long, honey-blond hair
and haunting gray-green eyes. Just one look at her angelic features
could dispel all the nasty rumors that had been spreading around
town. There were all those terrible accidents that had begun to plague
the community, too. But the fact that each accident occurred after
little Jill had been angered had to be coincidence . . .

SEE NO EVIL   (2429, $3.95/$4.95)
For young Caryn Dearborn, the cornea operation enabled her to see
more than light and shadow for the first time. For Todd Reynolds, it
was his chance to run and play like other little boys. For these two
children, the sudden death of another child had been the miracle they
had been waiting for. But with their eyesight came another kind of
vision—of evil, horror, destruction. They could see into other
people's minds, their worst fears and deepest terrors. And they could
see the gruesome deaths that awaited the unwary . . .

THRILL   (3142, $4.50/$5.50)
It was an amusement park like no other in the world. A tri-level mar-
vel of modern technology enhanced by the special effects wizardry of
holograms, lasers, and advanced robotics. Nothing could go wrong—
until it did. As the crowds swarmed through the gates on Opening
Day, they were unprepared for the disaster about to strike. Rich and
poor, young and old would be taken for the ride of their lives, trapped
in a game of epic proportions where only the winners survived . . .

*Available wherever paperbacks are sold, or order direct from the
Publisher. Send cover price plus 50¢ per copy for mailing and
handling to Zebra Books, Dept. 3844, 475 Park Avenue South,
New York, N.Y. 10016. Residents of New York and Tennessee
must include sales tax. DO NOT SEND CASH. For a free Zebra/
Pinnacle catalog please write to the above address.*